I0596607

Open & Shut
A southwestern legal thriller

By Edward Donovan

www.OpenAndShut.net
www.facebook.com/openandshutthebook

This is a work of fiction. Names, characters and incidents are fictitious. Any resemblance to actual persons, living or dead, business establishments or events is entirely coincidental.

ISBN: 978-0-0077355-0-5

Published by Blackdog Press
PO Box 451
Russellville, KY 42276

www.Blackdog-Press.com

For information, please email us at *info@Blackdog-Press.com*
Your comments and reviews are welcomed at *info@OpenAndShut.net*

Cover design and book design by Kate Meyer, Cape Fear Publishers
Editing and page layout by John Meyer, Cape Fear Publishers

OPEN & SHUT

BY EDWARD DONOVAN

A SOUTHWESTERN LEGAL THRILLER

DEDICATION
AND ACKNOWLEDGEMENTS

This book is dedicated to the many people who have helped me survive and grow over the years I was writing this; then forgetting it, re-writing and forgetting, editing and finally finishing this project. It has been an interesting road with many side trips, sprinkled with the wonderful people I've met along the way. In particular, I'd like to dedicate this to the women who've loved me and who have allowed me the privilege of loving them as I've wandered along this road; and to the search for my own Erin and the hope that the thought of her has brought to me along the way. They have inspired the two major female characters and perhaps the continued hopes that many of us have of an exciting and wondrous romantic tale. But most particularly this book is dedicated to the most influential of the women in my life, my mother, of course. Like Mama Begay, she has tried to guide me through troubles, to teach me the wisdom of patience, demonstrate that simple acts of kindness are truly important and shown me the true unconditional love good mothers are known to do. I could not have been more blessed to have her.

There are far too many friends and family who have helped me during the course of writing this to acknowledge individually. From my aunt and cousin who let me hang out in their trailer on the desert plains of Moriarity, New Mexico and write the first draft twenty years ago; to professional colleagues and friends who inspired the characters; to the friend who finally convinced me to finish this; to the editor who patiently helped fix it and to the "creative department" who helped make it pretty; it has been a great journey with you all. So to all of you, and you know who you are, I sincerely thank you for your patience and support over lo these many years.

Ed Donovan
September 2016

Open & Shut

Edward Donovan

PROLOGUE

The knock had been anticipated and the lone occupant glanced casually at his watch as he slowly crossed the room. Peering through the peephole, he found the usual emissary stroking his bushy mustache between forefinger and thumb, lurking apprehensively at porch-lights' edge. He swung the door open and invited his guest in from the cool spring air with a wave of his thin tan hand. "That's what I've always liked about you guys, so damn prompt," he said with a stiff South American accent. The messenger seemed slightly removed this evening, a distant look on his face, his hands thrust deep into his jacket pockets; perhaps preoccupied with other matters, he thought. With no response forthcoming, he turned, shook his head and re-crossed the room, his visitor following in close tow. From the small telephone table drawer in the corner he retrieved a manila envelope. He turned, addressing the visitor again: "Here's the package to take back to our friend. It's the proof he wants." He paused a moment before extending the envelope toward him. "And I believe you have something for me in exchange." He smiled. The visitor nodded, pulling his hand from his right pocket, returning the smile coldly, and reaching deep inside his jacket.

In a flash, a whispered whoosh bounced through the room and the resident's brown-skinned body staggered back against the wall with a thud, the envelope clenched in his hand. His eyes glazed over and drifted slowly down his chest, toward a rapidly expanding crimson splotch. Life began its quick retreat as his knees buckled and he slowly crumpled. A red streak followed his downward creep along the wall until his body settled limply on the floor in a pooled position, the envelope resting silently at his side. A sardonic smile grew strangely across his now sallow face. He slowly closed his eyes as the final vestiges of life left through the wall, the strange grin eternally etched on his face.

The visitor calmly walked across the room, replacing the 9mm into its modified shoulder holster inside his jacket, again rubbing his bushy mustache in contemplation gazing back at the lifeless body and its grin. Death always intrigued him. He leaned close to the wall and coolly pulled the curtain back with the edge of a finger for a view of the suburban street. Assured of the quietness of his actions he gazed around, taking stock of the home. With unwasted motion, he pulled latex gloves from inside his jacket and onto his hands. He strode slowly back across the room to the corner table dropping to one knee and carefully removing the table's drawer and quickly setting it on the floor. From an outer pocket he pulled a second envelope and placed it in the back of the drawer among the other papers before replacing it and rising back to his feet. With a powerful thrust of his hand, he toppled the small table from its usual spot, spilling magazines and the telephone to the floor in the general direction of their former owner.

He casually, yet hurriedly, roamed through the small house, rearranging the décor, but searching methodically through drawers and closets, tapping the floor with his feet in corners, looking for any hiding place. As he went he displaced pictures, throwing any valuables into a sack he'd brought for the occasion with minimal noise. His search of the master bedroom was completed as he eyed the metal frame computer desk in the spare bedroom he'd been in before with the now dead man. He crossed quickly, glancing at his watch for a time check. Finding 2 thumb-drives, some paperwork but little else, he threw them into the sack before pulling the CPU tower from its place and setting them in the hallway. In a closet he found a small file cabinet hidden behind a bunch of clothes strewn across it. Throwing the clothes onto the room floor he pulled open the drawers, searching the files and pulling anything related to his briefing. In the second drawer he found the file he was looking for and put all the materials out into the sack. He'd found what he'd been told to get.

He looked through the remaining closets and bathrooms before returning to the front room, examining the ceilings and walls before quietly overturning the coffee table and looking under the rug. Pulling a knife from his pocket, he sliced the cushions from the sofa and chair, discarding them on the floor. He looked around, taking final stock of the home before returning to his former associate. Avoiding the pooling blood, he knelt next to him again, pulling the envelope from the now chilling grip; replacing it with the handset from the toppled phone. He patted his pockets for a phone before picking up the envelope and stood motionless for a moment, noting the dead man's grin again, before he grabbed the tower and sack, quietly leaving as he had come. His task was completed, as instructed.

* * *

The secure line flashed in the darkened, dungeon-like room. A smallish, shadowy figure lifted the receiver, answering without a sound.

"He's gone to bed."

"Do you have the package?" the figure growled.

"Yes. I'll update you on my return; it will take me a day or so to assure that the rest of the matter is handled as you directed."

"Good. I take it you have alerted the others, then?"

"I will be handling that as you wished over the next few hours."

"Very good. Take care of the other details and my man will meet you upon your arrival to retrieve the merchandise. Remain available for the next week and then you can take an extended vacation on the company."

"That will be fine. You know how to reach me."

The connection clicked off and the sinister, diminutive presence slunk into the darkness of an oversized chair. A scornful laugh echoed softly through the vault-like room.

DAY ONE

The Trek Homeward

Michael Kincaid, the newest of admittees to the Federal Bar, quietly made his way to a seat in the middle of the majestic courtroom's first row. He leaned a tattered satchel against the glossy mahogany railing, looking past the counsel tables to the ornate bench, unoccupied for the moment. He tried to push down the dry lump in his throat, but with minimal luck.

Michael glanced nervously around, noting the finely tailored suits that were quickly packing the large room. He felt oddly out of place in the off-the-rack threads his parents had bought him for graduation. He noted the obvious age difference between him and most of his newly found colleagues. Gazing down at his scuffed, five-year old cowboy boots, he felt out of place. The lump grew thicker. He fought the notion that the Federal court was no field for rookies, yet despite his near six-foot frame, Michael felt suddenly small. He looked around for water, wondering if he had time for a quick drink from the fountain he'd noticed in the hallway. He quickly decided he couldn't take a chance. It was already 8:28.

He tried to collect himself by thinking of the job at hand. Leaning forward in his chair, he pulled the case file from the satchel, his mind racing through the major points of his oral argument. He opened the file and scanned quickly through the short written brief. He felt a growing sense of confidence and liked again how well the motion flowed, melding law with fact. This eased the dryness in his mouth a bit. He was well prepared; he'd get through this just fine despite his friends' warnings of possible disaster. After all, it was just a simple request for a continuance; he couldn't get in too much trouble. He'd managed much more complicated motions already in his short career, in state court. Everything would go smoothly. What could possibly happen?

He'd quickly reviewed the court's posted calendar, which revealed a fairly typical day, twenty or so motions. He'd gotten lucky and his matter was third. For the newly admitted federal practitioner it seemed a pleasant omen for his first day in this new world. Undaunted and unimpressed with his mind's reasoning, the dry lump kept its hold and Michael grumbled to himself about remembering to bring water the next time. First on calendar would be a motion for remittitur, followed by an order to show cause for non-appearance at a deposition and then his matter. With his request for a continuance unopposed it would only take a few minutes and he'd likely be back in the LA sun in fifteen minutes total, thirty tops. Nothing to this federal stuff; just like state court, he thought, calming himself. The dry spot, however, had other, persistent ideas and he swallowed hard trying to suppress it.

"All rise," a bailiff suddenly boomed at exactly 8:30. "The District Court of the United States of America, Central District of California, is now in session. The Honorable Daniel Deal, Chief Judge, presiding."

From a hidden door in the paneled wall behind the bench emerged a parade of law clerks, court clerks and bailiffs, followed by the black-robed Danny Deal. The Real Deal. The most powerful judge on the Los Angeles federal bench. It was an amazing sight, majestic and far different from anything Michael had ever seen in state court or on TV, or had even been warned about. In a few moments he would have his first appearance in federal court and before the Honorable Judge Deal, no less. Michael Kincaid was completely terrified and the relentless lump now made quick progress.

The bailiff bellowed the first matter, English v. Reed. With that, the opposing attorneys walked through the gate in the mahogany railing to their respective counsel tables. The courtroom quietly came to order.

"Anything to add to the moving papers, counsel?" Demanding urgently, the old man's voice resounded powerfully through the room.

"No, Your Honor," the older, graying defense attorney stated from the defense side of the courtroom.

"Aaaaa . . . yes, Your Honor, on behalf of the plaintiffs there is one other thing I'd like to add . . ." the second, much younger attorney attempted from the left.

The voice calling from the bench cut him off immediately. "Counsel, why is this not in your moving papers?"

"Well, Your Honor, I was . . ."

"Counsel, you do know the Local Rules, don't you?" The lawyer didn't quite answer fast enough and Judge Deal, now obviously annoyed, continued. "Well, counsel, you seem young and rather unfamiliar with our procedures here, so let me ask you," his eyes sternly focused on his quarry, "they still teach the Local Rules in law school, don't they? And you do know the Local Rules . . . don't . . . you . . . coun . . . sel?" His voice tapered off in obvious disdain.

"Uh, well, uh, yes. Your Honor."

"Then you know that everything must be contained in the moving papers unless extraordinary facts exist. Do you have extraordinary facts, coun . . . sel?"

"Uh, well, uh . . ."

"Fine. Motion denied. The judgment stands as entered. Take me up on appeal if you like. Next matter!"

Instantly the bailiff bellowed, "Krindle v. Morrison." The acid increased in Michael's stomach and the dryness edged out onto his tongue.

This time a single attorney stood and approached counsel table.

"Good morning, Your Honor."

"I suppose you might think so right now, Mr. Barrett, but tell me why your client can't show up to his deposition."

"Well, Your Honor, as I told you two weeks ago, he is not a party to the action, merely a witness. He simply does not have the time to do it right now. My client is a well-respected Beverly Hills orthopedic surgeon and therefore extremely busy with his patients. We're in the process of scheduling it for July. It is very difficult with his surgical schedule."

"July? Counsel, didn't I tell you I wanted that deposition to proceed within the month the last time you were in here? Now you come in here, waste more of the court's time and tell me that your client simply can't get to a deposition that I've ordered he attend going on three months now. All I can assume is that the good doctor doesn't feel my orders are as important as his! You, on the other hand, should have known better!" The Real Deal's voice was now very firm.

"Your Honor, I understand your concerns, but I don't have absolute control over my client, besides the . . ."

Michael distinctly heard what amounted to a collective gasp from the gallery. The old man sat up from his perch, his eyes narrowing on the man standing behind the counsel table.

"I warned you the last time you were in here not to try my patience any longer. Rule One of practice is, if you can't control your client, then you shouldn't be his lawyer. You know that, counsel. You and your client are playing discovery games on my time and I'm not going to tolerate it any longer. You, counsel, are in direct contempt of my order." A loud bang came from the gavel bouncing off the walls. "And I am sanctioning you $2,500 personally, forthwith, for your past violation of the Court's continuing discovery order. Further, I'm going to give you a little time to think this problem through in the hopes of coercing your future compliance. The court also summarily finds you in civil contempt for your continuing violation of the court's discovery orders. The court wishes to attempt to persuade you to comply with its order. Bailiff, escort Mr. Barrett to the lock-up. We'll try again tomorrow and see what arrangements have been made for compliance."

"Your Honor, that's outrageous."

"Outrageous would be $10,000, sixty days on the finding of criminal contempt and notification to the State Bar. Want to try me, coun . . . sel? Now get out of here and figure out how fast you can get your client to that deposition. You hold the keys to your confinement, counselor.

Or better yet, have the good doctor come down here and waste a little more of the court's time. I'll explain it to him personally and you can go home. Your choice, coun . . . sel. Either get your client to that deposition or get him in here and you'll be in compliance with my order and I'll rescind the civil contempt. Defendant is ordered back tomorrow morning. Perhaps, Mr. Barrett, you'll have figured out a way to comply by that time. The Marshal's Office will make a telephone available to you."

"But Your Honor . . ." the defeated barrister weakly interjected.

"That's enough, Mr. Barrett. There are twenty others behind you on calendar today and you're not going to waste the court's time . . . or theirs. Marshall Johnson, three phone calls and then to lock-up."

"Yes, Your Honor" and a United States Marshall appeared and motioned for the newest visitor to Club Fed. The sunken attorney glanced back through the gallery to the door before reluctantly shuffling toward the bailiff. Michael watched in horror as he finally disappeared through the door hidden in the paneled wall. He slumped against his chair back, stunned, growing even smaller, as the dry lump completely took over his mouth with the passing seconds.

"Next case!" the Real Deal bellowed.

"Mason v. Carrico, Inc." the bailiff called.

"Oh, shit" the young lawyer mumbled as he reluctantly rose.

"What was that, counsel? I have pretty good hearing for an old man, but I couldn't quite make that one out. Hurry up, I don't have all day. Or are you trying to waste my time too?" His stern eyes scanned the gallery.

"Ya, ya, yes, sir, Your Honor. I mean, uh, no, sir." He scrambled sideways down the row of lawyers, clumsily tripping over patent leather shoes as he went. Stumbling through the gate he announced, "Michael Kincaid on behalf of plaintiff" as his satchel hung up on the left side of the gate, stopping his progress with a jolt, spilling his paperwork to the floor.

"C'mon, counselor, let's get this show on the road," the Real Deal blasted from his perch. Michael turned full circle and made a quick kneel and swoop of the papers scattered on the floor, turning his case-file into a jumbled, crumbled mess in his hands, his satchel dangling from his pinky. He rose, noting faces pressed into hands, a few forced blank stares desperately suppressing grins on heads turned to opposite walls and the occasional jaw-dropped expressions of the gallery. The lump now had full control.

With papers sandwiched between his hands, he reversed direction and made his way to the counsel table, plopping his former file and the satchel onto the table. Mercifully, the paperwork only scattered, none finding route to the floor. Collating the paper like a deck of cards, the newest federal practitioner could feel the two imposing eyes descend upon him, now affixed squarely on their next victim. Michael tried desperately to swallow the lump and settle his quaking voice. When he finally looked up, the Real Deal was immediately on him.

"Anything to add to the moving papers, counsel?" he demanded.

"No!" Michael nearly shouted. An undercurrent of chuckles resonated through the gallery. The old man's gavel banged hard with a shout of "Order!" Oh God bounced off the inside of Michael's brain and through his mouth to the rustling room. "I mean, no, sir, . . .uh, Your Honor," he stammered. "Everything is contained in the moving papers."

"Fine. Now we're getting somewhere. Motion denied. We'll see you here for trial in thirty days, counsel. And coun . . . sel, make sure you're ready, no further continuances. Madam clerk, please set this matter for trial on . . . let's see . . ." The lump had now completely taken over and his knees felt oddly shaky. Michael steadied himself, leaning over his hands cemented squarely on the edge of counsel table. "Uh, I believe the twenty-second at nine is available, if that's workable on the clerk's calendar."

"Yes, Your Honor," a mousy voice squeaked from the desk at the base of the massive bench. "The twenty-second will be fine. No other matters on the trial calendar."

"How's that for your calendar, counsel" the voice boomed back at him.

Michael swallowed hard, somehow getting out "Um, uh, I guess that will be OK . . ."

"Counsel, you're speaking for your client and the firm. I assume you understand that. So I'll ask you once again, is the twenty-second good for you and your client?"

"Uh, yes, Your Honor, the twenty-second is perfect."

"Thank you, counsel. See how easy that was? Very well, the twenty-second. I presume that you are acquainted with the Local Rules, counsel, and have no extraordinary circumstances that would prevent you meeting the timelines." The Real Deal wasn't asking, he was telling.

"No, Your Honor, that will be fine. Thank you," Michael meekly added, and the novice barrister madly stuffed the paperwork into his satchel as he spoke.

"So ordered. We'll see you for trial on the twenty-second. Tell Mr. Shelton that I expect him to bring you back with him for trial . . .since you set the date" came the voice.

"Um, OK. Yes, sir, I'll tell him" and Michael turned abruptly, heading swiftly for the mahogany gate, the lump now out in front, leading him to safety. This time he lifted the satchel over the railing and made a much more graceful exit through the gallery. Through the courtroom door he made a quick left, heading straight for the sign marked "Men's Room."

* * *

A large smile broke across the driver's face as he recalled that first day, speeding down I-40 towards Needles at seventy-five. It had been an adventure that often brought him a wry chuckle. Now, nearly twenty years later, he could almost even laugh at it. Not so much when Judge Deal recounted the same events as an example of how not to make an appearance before him. The judge didn't tell the story every time he guest lectured in the classes Michael had taught in Federal Trial Advocacy at his alma mater, but most times. Over the years he'd taken some ribbing from his opponents and friends, but less so these days. He now had the reputation that came with nearly twenty years in the middle of the Los Angeles federal litigation wars.

Michael numbly listened to the radio blaring the details of the city he'd left many miles behind. The top of the hour led with the usual O.J. Simpson trial updates. There'd been another drive-by shooting in the Compton area, the announcer flatly reported. A four-year-old dead. No arrests yet. Believed to be a result of the feud for territory between the Crips and Bloods in the South Central area. The City of Angels was clearly not at peace. "Authorities continue their investigation into the death of a Van Nuys resident earlier this week now calling it a homicide" the newscaster droned. "Anonymous sources closely aligned with the ongoing investigation have revealed that the man may be linked to a possible smuggling operation, but have not ruled out the act as a simple home robbery gone bad. Police have no solid motive or suspects at this time. In other news, a fiery crash on the Ventura Freeway left one female dead and two others critically injured . . . ." The distant report raged on as Michael grimaced. He flicked the radio off, happy to finally be putting L.A. further behind with each passing mile.

He continued on silently for several miles until a smile crept slowly back over his face, his thoughts finally returning to that first day. He chuckled as he remembered the looks in the gallery that day, thinking of what a curious adventure his LA life had been, as the vehicle sped past the sign atop the Colorado River bridge simply stating, "Leaving California."

****

The shadowy figure leaned back into his oversized chair in the dimly lit room. His beady eyes pierced the darkness in subconscious sweeps of the room. The past few days had been a living hell. The operation, Code EZL, had been dangerously close to being compromised.

The many years of planning, preparation and now execution had nearly been frustrated due to the abysmal possibility that his own security may have been breached.

But dead men told no tales, nor would this dead man's effects. In a few more hours, his man would be delivering the materials to Anderson that would close the matter once and for all. In a day, the whole sordid affair would all be over. A nice, neat little package with no one the wiser, thanks to the help of his contacts at Justice. They should be securing the site now and he should have their preliminary report by mid-day.

The eyes closed slowly as he mumbled, "Blackmail me, will you?" He chortled to an uneasy rest.

* * *

It was a half hour before sunrise when Michael passed the idle helicopters of Grand Canyon Air and the unmanned National Park Service entrance gate. A left at rim's edge, a couple more miles, and in the distance he could see the waning lights of the El Tovar Hotel beckoning him to an awaiting dawn performance. To the east, the blackened curtain had opened, with the darkened horizon faintly giving way to a progression of midnight blue.

Michael parked and grabbed his coat, hurrying toward the hotel's balcony. He had just enough time to make it to his seat before the sun ever so slowly peeked above the mountains somewhere off in New Mexico. With its first rays splashing at the South Rim, the colors of the canyon began to awaken themselves. The green of the pine trees on the North Rim showed themselves first, the red sandstone mesas now glowing to the north as Michael closed his eyes, envisioning the light streaming down the Mokidugway Pass into Monument Valley. Opening his eyes, he noticed how the light had now slowly flickered down to the whites of the wind-whipped canyon top. Ever so slowly, the morning light began to lick its way farther down the South Rim's limestone crown, picking up speed as it reached the sheer canyon walls, hurtling its way toward the floor. Down and down it went, advancing its rays toward the mist-shrouded Colorado River below.

An exposé of reds, greens and browns, rivaled nowhere in the world, now lit up before him and Michael thanked his good timing. He knew that in the canyon no two sunrises or sunsets were ever the same. Once it was over, each one remained only as memory, never to repeat again. With each passing minute the colors changed shades, a beautiful woman trying to decide which coat to wear this day.

His thoughts drifted from the majestic beauty the canyon offered to the native Hopi and Navajo peoples who had inhabited these lands for centuries and to the surrounding area's largely unknown significance. He turned and gazed back to the jutting San Francisco Peaks where the Diné believed their gods summered, then back to the now fully lit chasm from where the Peoples believed their forefathers had emerged onto the earth through a reed from the underworld. His thoughts were now focusing to the friends he'd soon see. He grew anxious to press on in his drive toward Saturday dinner and the old stories his friend Joseph's grandfather would tell.

Michael returned to his vehicle and started down the slow Park Service road along the canyon rim toward Cameron. With each passing mile the view of the canyon changed. He bypassed the normal turnouts with locals selling their jewelry, instead picking up speed as he angled down the twisty road leading out of the park.

It was nearing noon when the Explorer finally reached Kayenta, twisting northward through the town towards Monument Valley. Miles in the distance to the southeast stood the first sentinel, Church Rock, guarding the entrance to the valley of carved monoliths. Ahead, with each passing minute, the Valley's magnificence grew. About five miles from the base of Fourth Mesa, Michael slowed considerably. To the caravans of tourists that passed this way, the rutted pathway jutting left was an inconsequential offshoot of the road that meandered through the giant monuments lacing the valley and ornamenting John Wayne films of old. He edged off the roadway heading south of the Three Sisters and Gouldings' Trading Post and instantly retreated a hundred years into the past.

The Explorer slowly bounced down the path, its navigator trying unsuccessfully to dodge the numerous potholes before curving away from the foot of Fourth Mesa and the Sisters. Ahead he could see the line of power poles making their way across the desert towards Gouldings. A lucky break for the Begays when Goulding agreed with his neighbor Hosteen Begay to allow them to tap into it many, many years ago in exchange for letting it cross his land. Just beyond the poles he could see smoke drifting aimlessly in the still afternoon air from Mama Begay's outdoor Navajo oven.

As he pulled to the front of the house, dogs came from every direction barking their welcome. Michael switched off the engine and sat patiently, knowing it would be a few minutes before Joseph's mom would appear and he could politely step out. Such momentary waits were demanded by the etiquette of this foreboding land, the Navajo Way as they called it. The Navajo would never have the effrontery to step on to the land of another without first being invited, unlike white European culture, which rudely and historically barged in wherever they wished.

Not for the first time, he noted the home's traditional simplicity. It had been built in the same manner as all Navajo hogans had been built since First Man and First Woman constructed their home near the place of their Emergence from the canyon. It had four main support pillars, each aligned with the cardinal directions, the front door oriented to the east to greet the rising sun. Along the north wall ran a weathered overhang. Beneath it, on a leveled dirt porch, sat the three rocking chairs he'd spent hours in with his friends Joseph and Kevin. Across, and to his right, sat the old, earthen sweat lodge, cracked and decayed over weathered time. Next to that sat the Navajo oven, wafting delicious aromas of piñon, juniper and sage. Michael rolled down the passenger side windows and caught a whiff of the baking fry bread. With each taste of the aroma, memories of his old friends raced through his mind.

His thoughts traveled to the likely goings-on inside. Mrs. Begay would be preparing the usual Saturday meal, as she had done for many years. It had become a tradition with their Corn Clan relatives over the years. Although Mama Begay had lived a hard life in this hostile land, Saturday dinners were always had.

Widowed by Vietnam at twenty-six, she had essentially raised and provided for her five children alone. Joseph's father had been killed in some far off rice paddy for a country that rarely counted him a son. Her Corn and Bear Clan relatives had helped, but mainly she had done it on her own, selling jewelry and sheep over the years, richly deserving the admiration most had for her. Despite meager earnings, she had always provided for the Clan's weekly meet for Saturday dinner. Sometimes there were many, sometimes sadly only herself, but there was always Saturday dinner and everyone was welcome. Michael, though unannounced, would be especially welcome, but then again, everyone was at the Begay home.

* * *

The buzz from the intercom caused the pursed eyes to open to an alert, active stare. A secretary's voice announced that Anderson waited. The pacing figure shadowed in near darkness stopped, seemingly pleased with the intrusion, and barked for the subordinate's admittance. "Perhaps this is finally over," he thought, slinking into his chair, flipping on a desk light. Anderson softly closed the door behind him. "Let me have that," he growled impatiently, his pudgy hand motioning with a quiver toward the envelope that Anderson held.

Anderson slid the envelope over the front of the desk, its momentum taking it towards the stubby hands that anxiously waited. "There's also a computer outside and these," the junior reported, setting the files, some disks and a few other items on the desk. Pulling the envelope closer to him, his stubby hands fumbled with the seal before finally ripping it open, yanking the papers from inside. He quickly flipped through the pages until stopping at the last one. His beady eyes narrowed as he stared into the memo for several moments. He abruptly grabbed the papers from the desk and slammed them into the desk's top drawer.

His voice airily cracked, "That will be all."

"Uh, yes, sir" Anderson replied, withdrawing quickly, happy to be away from the strange little man who'd been acting even stranger lately.

Left alone in the dim light, he bent forward and slid from the chair to his feet. He again began pacing back and forth, his hands clenched behind his back, moving with a jitter along the edge of the light released from the small desk lamp. With his every step followed a bent, squat shadow, his distant stare suggesting that something was still inexcusably wrong.

Over and over in his mind he pondered the plausible threat the memo contained on its last page, "Did you think I'd trust you? Unless you have all copies, you'll get yours soon!" Questions without answers pummeled his mind. Stung by the note, he fumbled for acceptable answers. His own insurance had turned against him. Had he acted too hastily or was this just the idle threat of a former associate gone greedy? His man had gone through everything, hadn't he? He searched through the files finding another copy, calming himself. Things will be fine, he assured himself. Besides, his friends would find any other copies. The stubby fingers twisted among themselves. He reasoned this didn't warrant alerting the Old Man, not just yet. He could handle this matter himself. He returned to his seat. He slunk back and uneasily settled into the oversized chair, throwing his squat legs over the corner of the desk, landing them with a thud. He needed to think. He'd gather a new plan and then brief the Old Man with a slightly bent version of their associate's untimely death. Hopefully he need never know the entire truth. But he needed to be told something; he'd called twice already.

* * *

From the half-opened door Mrs. Ellen Begay finally emerged. She was a short, portly Navajo woman of sixty-three. She wore a white linen dress, speckled with the turquoise and silver jewelry that traditionally adorned Navajo women. A brilliant smile rose across her face as she immediately recognized the driver and animatedly waved for him to come join her.

Michael stepped from the Explorer to the required sniffing and approval of the dogs. After a few seconds, their duty done and finding no treats, they departed in various directions and Michael walked over to the welcome of a warm hug from Mama Begay. The cheery, weather-worn woman invited him to the kitchen, the gathering place in the Begay home. Michael took a seat in a wooden chair at the dining table as she headed for the refrigerator offering something cold to drink, returning with an Orange Crush. With a polite smile she set it on the table then quickly resumed her cooking as though nothing had stopped her for even an instant. After a few moments, she quietly asked, "What brings you to Saturday dinner?"

The question was justifiably curious, yet politely reserved. A more direct query, like "What are you doing here?" though thoroughly acceptable in western culture, would be far too intrusive for the genteel manners of a traditional Navajo woman such as Ellen Begay.

She listened, splitting her time efficiently among the variety of dishes being prepared, while Michael recounted the years since last he'd seen her, though he was sure she had earlier been updated on most of it from Joseph. Regardless, she reacted to the stories as if it were the first time she had heard them, partly out of Navajo courtesy to the speaker and partly out of her joy at hearing them first hand. The Navajo reservation could be a desolate, lonely place and conversation could be sparse. Tradition would not allow her to ask too many questions, so she would simply glance back if something needed clarifying. Otherwise, she listened attentively while she worked.

Michael gave her the standard story. After graduation and a year with the firm, he had taken a risk and started his own, barely making ends meet for the first couple of years, mostly on simple state court matters. He recounted the firm's expansion on the heels of a couple of high-profile murder cases. He stumbled a bit and became fidgety after relating that he and Lori had carved out a nice little life together.

He paused for a few moments before saying that over the years he had saved some money and, what with Lori now gone, there wasn't much left for him in Los Angeles. He'd tried plenty of cases and didn't need any more right now. So he'd downsized his trial work, become "of counsel" to his own firm, packed his bags and headed for home-cooked meals at as many places as he could hit. He turned toward Mama Begay and a slight smile came back across his face. The Begay home just happened to be first on his list, he concluded, and his voice trailed off. He became noticeably distant.

The silence was mercifully broken with the crackling of gravel as an old green pickup pulled into the front yard. Two women sat motionless in the truck allowing the requisite couple of minutes to pass.

"That would be my Bear Clan cousin and her sister's daughter up from Shiprock. You picked the right day for Saturday dinner, Michael. Tonight are the Spring dances and sing. Many people will come and they've come up early to help with the preparations. It will be good to visit with the Bear Clan. They have not come for a very long time."

Michael remained at the table while Mama Begay went to greet her visitors, shortly returning with the two new guests. Michael rose and was introduced to Joyce Naggie and her niece Mary, now a sophomore in high school her aunt proudly announced to Mama Begay, seemingly embarrassing the young girl. The four took seats around the kitchen table and the two older women began relating the goings on of their respective clans.

Ellen Begay began with the general happenings around Keyenta and the Begay home. She spoke simply of how Joseph had eventually returned home after medical school and was now the chief medical officer at the tribal hospital in Window Rock. In true Navajo tradition, and without even a glimpse of boastfulness, she understated his friend's accomplishments.

She omitted that her son had graduated from college with a 3.8 and a double major in biology and chemistry. That from his junior year on, every major medical school in the country had pursued him. That he had turned down full rides to Harvard and Stanford to accept a similar offer in the surgery and public health programs at the University of Arizona. He'd completed his residency at the Mayo and by the time he was finished he had literally hundreds of offers for more money and status than most could ever dream of. In the end, and without a moment's hesitation, Dr. Joseph Begay chose to return and answer the needs of his own people, accepting a lower paying, entry-level position with the Indian Health Service. Over the years his skills had elevated him to what amounted to the head medical authority for both the Navajo and Hopi tribes.

Mama Begay continued by relating that daughters Janet and Scarlet Beth were both married, soon to bless her with grandchildren, she hoped. Jaxson still helped with the sheep and some of the silverwork for the jewelry that the family matriarch crafted. Mrs. Naggie smiled earnestly and proudly for her cousin. The young girl sat motionless, detachedly taking the room in, occasionally intently studying the faces around her, but not saying a word.

And of Hosteen Begay, she reported that all was well. He helped where he could, but spent most of his time with Jaxson and the sheep at his hogan and sweat lodge high up on Fourth Mesa. "Grandfather will be here in an hour," she exclaimed with urgency, and the three women unanimously withdrew from the table, immersing themselves in preparations as Joyce Naggie offered her account of the state of the Bear Clan. Her sister was still working with her husband selling jewelry over near Cameron so Mary had been staying with her for school and they began speaking about things in Shiprock.

Michael noticed that the young girl was glancing at him every so often as she prepared her dish. Somehow he felt as if she was wondering what this white guy was doing out in the middle of the reservation, which was perfectly understandable and he kind of laughed to himself. He glanced up to her and gave her a polite smile . She smiled back softly preparing the squash, the reserved and pleasant smile of a Navajo, the corners of her mouth upturned just slightly on her round brown face. Her eyes diverted down to the squash, the common shyness of the people evident, but Michael also sensed something else as her eyes rose a few moments later. Their strange sense of awareness not usually found in a teenager, particularly in a young Navajo girl. She seemed different in some way, perhaps a sense of something odd, but perhaps that was just the changing times.

The cousins were finishing their updates and Mama Begay returned to the table to offer Michael another soft drink. He politely accepted and excused himself to go find one of the old rocking chairs to the side of the hogan. He sat down and then looked northeasterly toward the redness of Fourth Mesa 10 miles in the distance and to its right, somewhere out there, Fifth Mesa and the Mokidugway. He rocked slowly, wondering to himself why she hadn't spoken of her youngest, Johnson Junior. He pondered the question for a moment, concluding that he would learn of his exploits later. He slowly drifted off to sleep; exhausted from the road, but glad to know that dinner, a sing and the sweat lodge would be the order of the evening.

* * *

The squat man had just finished reading the debriefing sent over from Justice. Based on the finding of drugs and a large sum of cash in a bedroom floor-safe, the case had been preliminarily ruled another senseless murder attributable to the LA drug turf-wars. The case really had no leads and investigators truly doubted they would ever solve the case, unless someone turned on the shooter. The consensus seemed to be that the city was just that much better off. One less drug dealer and no one really cared if the case was solved anyway. Just what he'd hoped for.

What wasn't there was what disturbed him. No paperwork of any significance had been found, despite thorough searches by both his man and the agency associates from Justice. But there had been outsiders involved at the scene and his man had said nothing about a safe. That had to be checked out first and then if necessary he could expand his own search. And he'd have to talk to the Old Man soon. He'd called again. He'd get this going and then get back to him.

* * *

The screams gathered his attention toward the mangled vehicles across the street. He darted toward the wreckage to see if he could help, greeted by the tortured steel that was her former car. He recognized it immediately. He called to her, but the only answer came from the plaintive wail of the sirens approaching in the distance.

Michael awoke with a tremor. He focused his eyes back toward Fourth Mesa, wondering if he would ever rest peacefully again. He glanced around, noting thankfully that he was alone. He purposely turned his thoughts toward a scan of the distant horizon, far across the San Juan into Utah. He searched out the small cliff that made out the Mokidugway and thought about its legendary beginnings.

Hosteen Begay had told him that long before the dawn of motorized vehicles, the Navajo and their Hopi neighbors had long shared a problem. The land was rich with beauty, but poor of water, game and trees. From their native lands they could easily see Fifth Mesa at the end of Monument Valley, the Colorado Plateau, with its pine trees looming two thousand feet straight up. Hundreds of years before the great explorers of Europe were even born, an ancient shaman was visited in the sweat lodge by the Yei gods. They told him of a pathway that led to the top of Fifth Mesa. In his vision, the shaman was told that he should follow this pathway and at its end he would find the game and wood to help his people survive. The shaman followed the spirit's words and when he returned days later, he told the people of the vast forests filled with deer, elk and rabbit.

For many, many years, the Navajo and their neighbors had used the path and respectfully hunted and logged the area at the top of the Mokidugway, taking only what they needed. In time they built a chute, which quite inventively allowed logs to be vaulted to the sand, over a third of a mile below. For centuries, the tribal peoples used the lands beyond the Mokidugway to tame their unforgiving homeland below.

Then, after centuries of struggling to survive in these inhospitable lands came the struggle not even the Yei could help them win. It started so innocently. First, a couple of pale-skinned men began hunting atop their sacred lands. These were eventually followed by the loggers who claimed the right to bring down wagonloads of timber from the plateau to build the towns of the expanding white culture. Over time, the Mokidugway was unceremoniously transformed from a sacred pathway to a wide, unpaved logging road rising among the cliffs between the Valley of the Gods and the Goosenecks of the San Juan River. Down the Mokidugway came truckloads of timber from clear-cutting operations. Soon, the deer and elk retreated deeper into the forests. The sacred gift from the Yei was forever changed. It was no longer theirs.

Despite the transformation, it remained a remarkable place, albeit a bit off the beaten path. Michael had first gone there with Joseph during college and still considered it one of the most breathtaking sights he'd ever seen. They had arrived at sunset and had the view almost to themselves. Only one lone tourist, busily studying a map and desperately trying to locate where in the hell he'd made that wrong turn, shared the view. From the perch, it seemed you could see forever in any direction but due north, that view kept secret by the remains of the dense pine forest. To the southwest he'd followed the course of the San Juan River until it met up with the Colorado, which then meandered for a hundred miles to the west before finally entering the canyon. Above the canyon, the San Francisco Peaks leapt skyward with majestic fury, standing as sentries to the summer residences of the Kachina and the Yei. To the southeast stretched the checkerboard lands shared by the Hopi and Navajo. A gigantic game board for the Kachina and Yei to play from their homes in the mountains.

Farther south, the White Mountains led west to the Salt River Gorge, eventually flowing to the open deserts of Phoenix and the saguaro-filled basins of south-central Arizona. Slightly further to the west, First, Second, and Third Mesa sprung up south of Kayenta, finally leading to Fourth Mesa, near Joseph's home, stepping toward them across central Arizona. As night came, Michael and Joseph had watched the blinking lights of descending airplanes on approach to what they guessed must be Gallup or Phoenix.

A slight movement along the foreground of Fourth Mesa drew Michael's daydreaming eyes away. His vision strained to make out the silhouette of a lone man approaching in the distance, a black dog walking at his side. He leaned back in the rocker, closed his eyes again and drifted back to the memories of the Mokidugway. Hosteen Begay would be arriving in about fifteen minutes.

* * *

Anderson closed the door behind him, his de-briefing with his superior complete. He hadn't liked what he'd finally heard. One operational man down, a temporary shutdown progressing and a potential security breach. What should have been a simple operation was turning into a serious mess. Over the last couple of weeks, the little man had kept him largely in the dark; this latest meeting seemed to be something of an exception. Something was wrong, but he didn't know exactly what. Strangely though, something also told him this might turn out to be his own salvation. He'd never truly liked this assignment. He was a professional, a military man, and he longed for his days with naval intelligence. Nevertheless, duty demanded that he do what could be done to assure that the operation would not be compromised. He'd better contact AZ, just in case, and reassure himself nothing was abnormal. He'd also better get a computer guy on this possible security breach ASAP.

* * *

Hosteen Begay seemed as he always had, perhaps just a little more bent with age. In his right hand he carried his walking stick, an intricately carved piece of cedar that had been given to him when he was a young man. Joseph had told him one time that it was the stick used by Chief Manuelito on The Long Walk, the Navajo version of the Trail of Tears. In 1864, after a series of uprisings on their traditional lands, including a daring attack by 1000 warriors led by Manuelito against Fort Defiance, Arizona, the Navajo were given a choice, either face the wrath of Phil Sheridan's troops or walk to Bosque Redondo, near Ft. Sumner, New Mexico, hundreds of miles away. With no real choice the diyin diné e, the Peoples, began The Long Walk. Thousands died along the way, the few that survived found themselves in a place having its own troubles adapting, after the Lincoln County War and Billy the Kid. As the story went, Manuelito spent his 4 years in Bosque Redondo praying to the Yei for a return to their homelands and carving on his walking stick. When they were finally allowed to return 4 years later, a young boy named Henry Chee Dodge accompanied that aging warrior back to eastern Arizona. Dodge would later become the first Tribal Chief and before Manuelito died, he had passed the walking stick to Dodge. Dodge would in turn mentor a young Hosteen Begay and eventually began to teach him in the old ways. In time the staff was passed from Dodge to his student, the old man approaching, or so the story went.

To his left bounced his ever-present friend and companion for more than a decade, barking his greeting in the decreasing distance. The bowed man was dressed in his usual white linen shirt, blue jeans and boots. His wizard-like appearance was accentuated by his frosty white hair, pulled back into a ponytail, befitting of the well-respected shaman he'd become to the People. The lines in his face told his weathered life's story of nearly ninety years, yet the alert eyes and wide smile still spoke of the young man inside.

"Greetings, my young friend. What brings you to Saturday dinner?" the old man politely inquired.

"To see you and the rest of the Corn Clan. To enjoy your food and sweat lodge," Michael replied.

"This is good. We shall have time later to talk, my friend . . . but first I must see if I can be of assistance and help to get the sweat lodge ready." He disappeared toward the kitchen to politely announce his arrival.

Down the road, and almost as if cued, Michael could see the telltale dust. Joseph was approaching. How he always showed up just after his grandfather's arrival was always a marvel to Michael. It was almost as if somehow elaborately planned. As the vehicle neared, Michael noticed that, instead of the accustomed pickup he expected came a brand-new crew cab diesel. Apparently life was good for the doctor. The big truck pulled to a stop next to the Explorer and Joseph stepped out. He started to speak, but Michael cut him off.

"I know, 'What brings me to Saturday dinner?'"

"I see you've been speaking with Mother and Grandfather."

"Of course. I did have to answer the required parental questions."

"I'm sure. So what's up?"

"Nothin', just passin' through. Got hungry around Flag."

"Right. Never could turn down a free meal, could you?"

"Nope. Where are Lisa and the kids?"

"Down in Window Rock. Scott's got a big tournament game today. I couldn't get down there because of patients, so I . . ." the conversation continued on in general chitchat for a few minutes before they finally meandered toward the kitchen.

Over the next couple of hours a more vehicles arrived, carrying the other members of the related clans who would celebrate with them in the Spring dances and sing. As the women prepared in the kitchen, the men prepared for the dances and the sing. Michael and Joseph, at the guidance of the Fire Man elder from the Bear Clan, began building the fire ring. It would become the focus of the first portion of the evening, the sing. The other men, with Hosteen Begay, began preparing the sweat lodge to the east of the fire ring.

In about two hours the men and women were finished with their various tasks and dinner was served. As usual, it was a feast. Mutton and corn were the main courses. Hosteen Begay gave thanks to the Bear Clan families gathered who had butchered the plump sheep, with the Corn Clan's Saturday dinner the benefactor. The aroma of fresh-baked round bread hung lightly above sage-spiced air. There was blue mush flavored with the roasted mutton, vegetables from a cousin's garden, and fry bread. And of course there was corn. Roasted ears, corn stew and kneel down bread, all made from the staple that had supported their daily life for centuries. No Saturday dinner would be complete without that which had brought them life and allowed them to continue.

When dinner had ended and clean-up was completed, the group re-assembled outside around the freshly lit fire. It was springtime, a time of rebirth, and a time to sing thanks to the Yei for bringing the People through another long winter just as Changing Woman had sung long ago. Michael took a seat on the sandy desert floor at the edge of the ring. A slow drumbeat grew around the ring as the sing began with Hosteen Begay. In the old tongue he began his first of four songs as two Bear Clan cousins danced round the circle at firelight's edge. His song was soothing and Michael gazed through the ring watching the embers and sparks fly high up into the deep blue night to join the stars as the dancers swayed on the other side. Though Michael could not understand the words, he was sure that his song acknowledged the Yei gifts of good fortune and good friends. After he'd finished his fourth song, the drum was passed to Joseph and a second singer began. In all there would be four different singers, four different drummers and four different rounds, as tradition demanded.

After nearly an hour, the chants and dancing around the circle ended. The old shaman left the circle and neared the fire, raising his arms high into the sky and speaking slowly in the ancient tongue. In a few minutes he had finished and the Sing was over. The men in the circle slowly made their way to the sweat lodge for their meeting, while the women retired to the kitchen to attend to matters of the home and the clans. With a polite grab of Michael's arm, Joseph led his friend toward the sweat lodge with him.

* * *

Anderson was relieved when he finally received the report. Nothing unusual. He leaned back in the chair in his small office. An uneasy feeling lay heavy on his mind. In the few months since appointment to the agency, he had never seen quite this much quick action. Truth be known, his assignment had been largely mundane. Morning reports of "All is well" were collated into a nice, neat little briefing, which he submitted to the uncomfortable presence of his superior every other day. There were the occasional trips to the Caribbean to deliver or pick up diplomatic pouches from a bank. It was nice duty on the rare occasion he got to stay more than a few hours. Mostly the job was administrative. Pretty boring, compared to what he would have believed covert ops to be. He was really nothing more than a glorified courier with rank.

Yet every ounce of his Annapolis training told him something wasn't quite right with this operation. He'd begun to sense it a couple of weeks ago. Tielson had seemed clearly on edge and was more irritating to Anderson than ever before. He'd never really cared for the hairy little man from the first moment he'd met him, but he hadn't truly detested him until recently. Lately there'd been a rash of calls from the Old Man. Questions that no one had real answers to. Requests that he more closely monitor an operation that he really knew nothing about other than reports that "All is well." But all wasn't "well" and he could feel it.

Maybe again, his rational side tried to tell him, he was just over-reacting. Maybe he was looking for some excitement that wasn't really there. He closed his eyes, reassessing his months on assignment with the operation. The only things he really knew about were general. "An interagency destabilization effort" was how it had originally been outlined to him. He wasn't really sure who or what they were destabilizing, but it was definitely interagency. He'd certainly been exposed to the different wings of the government.

In the end he could land only two concrete beliefs. First, he couldn't trust Tielson; he'd lie to him in a second—it was the agency way. Only the top man knew for sure which of the layers of fact among deception was bullshit. Therein lay the second thing he could count on: in the agency's eyes a junior man was sacrificial to the cause. Somewhere, the back recesses of his mind nagged at him to look into this one carefully on his own. Whatever this little man was up to might not likely be in his, or necessarily the nation's, best interests.

* * *

Michael stepped into the mudded hut, immediately noticing the contrast between the cool night's air and the humid, stale warmth inside. Memory and sensation touched his mind. His body was seized by the intensity of the heat emanating from the small pit at the center of the round space, a small fire in a ring adjacent to it. Hosteen Begay directed him to sit on the bench opposite the fire along the eastern wall, the long-ago-directed place for a guest. The old wooden bench creaked as it accepted his weight and Michael leaned carefully against the backrest assuring himself it would accept his weight. Joseph took his place next to Michael as fire-cast shadows danced magically on the curving walls.

Hosteen Begay directed the elders to the other three rickety pews, arranged at the cardinal points and surrounding the fire and pit as they entered, before moving across the room to a small table and bench at Michael's immediate right. The Fire Man elder from the Bear Clan knelt near the fire's edge, a bundle of sage switches in his hand and a bucket of water to his side. Using the sage bundle, he splashed water onto the heated black lava stones that he had pulled earlier from the blazing outside fire and placed in the earthen pit. Michael watched the smoke and steam rise from the pit and felt the heat intensify.

"For you, my friend." Michael turned to find the old shaman handing him a rolled smoke from a tray containing small cornhusks, roots and yoyviva, a mixture of wild tobacco, cedar, rain tobacco and perhaps a few other ingredients the federal government wished they wouldn't add. Odd, he thought, that a people's customs, passed on for millennia, were now questioned by a late-coming government that had also usurped their tribal lands. Hosteen Begay passed him a piece of root, which he took with his other hand, and then the tray was passed to his right to a Bear Clan cousin. Michael watched as he rolled a smallish cigar from the tray, using a dried cornhusk as a rolling paper. When he had finished, he took a root and passed the tray on to his right. And so it continued until finally it returned to Michael and the shaman. From the other side of the fire-ring, the Bear Clan elder rose, lifting a glowing stick from the ring and handing it to Hosteen Begay. He first lit his cigar before passing the stick to his right. In a few minutes it had made its way all around the room.

When each man had finished his cigar, Hosteen Begay placed the root in his mouth and began to slowly speak in English since one among them did not understand the ancient tongue of the People. To do otherwise, even during this sacred ceremony, might be insulting to their invited guest and not in keeping with the Navajo Way. He spoke of the thanks that should be given to the Yei fathers for the many gifts they had given them. The gifts of spring and of new life, as he tossed pine boughs on to the fire. The gifts of the friendship of the lodge and of the life bestowed upon each of them, now adding yucca leaves to the now crackling fire. Continuing with the advice that in this time it was good to re-visit their simple beginnings and be thankful for the Yei gift of the haneelneehee, the Emergence of First Man and First Woman.

They were created, the shaman began, when the Yei chiefs transformed them from two primordial ears of corn. Upon transformation, they were placed at the lowest level of four lower worlds, each one stacked directly on top of each other. In this lowest level, First Man and First Woman shared their world with Coyote and the insect people.

They attempted to live in the first world according to the rules and customs given them by the Yei, the Navajo Way. But First Man and First Woman, along with the others with them, were given to quarreling, adultery and strife. Despite repeated warnings by the Yei chiefs from the surrounding oceans that they were not living as they should, these peoples were unable to mend their ways. After repeated failings, the Yei chiefs released waters from the surrounding oceans and the first world was destroyed. Those that survived, including First Man and First Woman, were forced to flee upward to the next level.

In the next world new peoples of various identities, including birds and Pueblos, joined them. Again they settled in to this new world, again they repeated their same mistakes and again the waters were released and the second world was destroyed. The survivors fell into the same routine at the third level, where they were joined by Coyote, and were eventually chased from the Third World. Finally, First Man and First Woman, along with the diyin diné e, the survivors of the Third World, were forced to flee upwards through a reed that punctured the earth to the present-day level of earth. After traveling through the reed, they arrived on the surface at a place somewhere in the bottom of what is now the Grand Canyon. At that time though, the land we know today had not been created by the Yei and they found nothing but featureless dried mud. The Yei promised that if the People lived right in this, their final chance, that they would be rewarded with a land not only rich, but created in the People's own eyes.

With this in mind, First Man and First Woman built the first sweat lodge in which they, and the Diné, gave thanks to the Yei for their Emergence and planned what the world should be like. This time they lived as the Yei chiefs instructed and raised the child Changing Woman. She was the daughter of Long Life Boy and Happiness Girl, and they had brought her with them from one of the lower worlds when her parents were drowned by the waters. As they continued to live by the Navajo way, the Yei gave them the powers of creation, held in First Man's medicine bundle until the Yei instructed that it be used.

Over time, Changing Woman grew and matured. Eventually, the Yei instructed First Man to give her the medicine bundle containing the creation powers. The Yei had not allowed First Man to use these powers because they feared that he might use them unwisely. They then rewarded the Diné for living well, creating the Navajo world as it exists today and as planned by the People in their sweat lodge. The Yei then showed the created land to Changing Woman. Their homeland was to be bounded by Four Sacred Mountains, symbolizing the four worlds of the People. They were directed by the Yei, through Changing Woman, that they should never leave their homeland. She was shown that the land contained the Four Great Rivers and from their bounty, the People would be assured continued life.

But First Man and First Woman would never share the homeland given to the Diné. The Yei gods told them that they must leave the earth as they had come, through the reed, as their punishment for their repeated failings in the lower worlds. They were returned through the reed and made the chieftains of witchcraft and death.

Changing Woman was then told by the Yei to use the powers in First Man's medicine bundle to create the Navajo people and the land they would share. She did this by using her own skin and forming four couples, the ancestors of the first four Navajo clans. From these four clans grew other clans and from these four couples grew other couples. The People lived the Navajo Way as directed by the Yei and now many inhabited the land among the Four Sacred Mountains.

And each year, as they had done since the time of Changing Woman, the People gathered in their hogans and sweat lodges in springtime to feast, dance and sing thanks to the Yei for providing for them and granting them another year in the fourth world. Each year the men gathered in the sweat lodges to remember the gifts given them, to ask the Yei for another year in their homeland, and most important, to show them the future as it may come.

Hosteen Begay paused for a few moments as the Fire Man exited the sweat lodge, returning in a few moments with nine more black lava rocks for the pit. Placing them in the pit, he paused for a moment and picked up his sage bundle and splashed water onto the rocks. The heat made Michael feel lightheaded and he closed his eyes and began chewing on the root. He listened as a drum took up a steady beat in the recesses of the lodge, a low voice began singing. With each passing moment he drifted further toward a state of total relaxation, the same state he'd experienced many years before in Hosteen Begay's sweat lodge. His breathing and pulse slowed as his senses took on a being of their own. He could taste the different types of wood emanating from the fire outside. Pinion, juniper and the ever-present sage again hung heavily in the humid air. His skin sensed minute fluctuations in temperature as sweat seeped from his pores. He listened intently as the crackle of the fire just outside was replaced by soft singing from across the room. Into his soul flowed the music, hypnotizing his mind.

Whether from the effects of the root, heat or the entrancing drum marking time, a handful of playful images began emerging from the shadows of Michael's subconscious thoughts. Slowly they began taking shape, strangely lit by a fire pit around which they began to gather inside his eyelids. A rainbow-colored figure, bent forward from a deformed and hunched back, pulled what originally seemed like a clarinet from behind his shoulder. His spindly hands pulled the instrument to his mouth and he began to play. Oddly, the music that emanated was flute-like and reverberated gleefully from the ground, a consequence of the soloist's misshapen body. Michael listened, delighted, to the sweet

music wafting through his ears, noticing the shape of a coyote apprehensively approaching, sniffing, slowly stalking at the outer edge of the
light.

As if called by the music, a woman emerged from the shadows,
her face distorted by the flickering light growing in the pit, yet her gait
soothingly familiar. She paused hesitantly by the fire, eyeing Coyote as
he nervously pranced back and forth at shadows' edge. Michael watched
as three more figures now emerged from the piñon-junipers to his right.
A featureless figure of a man was led blindly by two others toward the
opposite side of the fire from the lute player and woman. As they moved
further into the light he could see the man was covered by a plain white
woven blanket; the other two were dressed elaborately, their mid-sec-
tions elongated, one carrying a bow with squiggly lightning-bolt arrows
extending from his quiver, the other carrying a spear in his hand. Michael's mind immediately flashed back to the many petroglyphs he'd
seen of the Yei Gods in the Mesa Verde-Escalante areas and Chaco Canyon over the years. The two Yei positioned the man near the fire before
they began to dance slowly around the fire, slowly expanding their circle, keeping Coyote away in the shadows as the lute player and woman
retreated north and away from the fire towards vague sand dunes in the
distance.

Michael noticed that above the dance now flew Big Fly, whom
he recognized immediately from the shaman's old tales. This was the
Yei's guardian of the Diné, darting occasionally toward Coyote, who
still lurked nervously. Finally tiring of Big Fly's continued pestering,
Coyote dodged his way toward the shadowy sand dunes in the northern
distance now following the lutist. The mystical dance around the man
continued. From the stars above shot brilliant light, encompassing the
fire and the dance.

Big Fly returned, swooping down, landing lightly upon the man's
shoulder as the music softly distanced. The guardian nodded his head
to the man, drawing his attention away from the dance toward a small-

er figure coming forward, wearing a plain brown Hopi Ku?itu mask, shrouded from the shoulders in a reddish, woven blanket, pausing, perhaps reluctantly, at shadow's edge. The masked figure slowly edged slightly toward the light as three others now emerged in tow from the shadows. The smaller figure was unadorned, far different from the other three and their more elaborate but dim detail. Michael's mind drifted back to images of the old carved Hopi Kachina dolls he'd seen since he was a kid. The two Yei dancers slowed to a near stop, dancing in place, fronting the man, but also welcoming and creating an entrance for the three Kachinas and their plain masked friend to join them. One of the Kachina moved slowly forward, the others sheepishly keeping some distance, moving to shield the mysterious figure behind them just at light's edge.

Big Fly leapt from the man's shoulder heading straight toward the distant sand dunes, Michael's attention following. He could faintly see the woman from before now following the lute player up over a large dune. Coyote approach cautiously before taking a seat on the dune's shoulder, watching the pair carefully, occasionally sniffing the air, until Big Fly swooped down, chasing him to a jump, skip and a dart over the dune. The lute playing continued, growing dimmer, more distant, with each passing moment.

Near the fire now both Yei and the three Kachinas appeared immersed in serious discussion, occasionally glancing toward the featureless man, then to the dune, and finally back to the still mysterious figure at shadow's edge. Suddenly there was a loud thump and for the first time Michael noticed one of the Kachinas had a drum, which he was now thumping on. A hard beat was followed by three softer beats, as he led the five out of conversation into an animated dance among themselves.

Michael's mind homed in on the drummer, sensing familiarity, carefully observing his mud mask, its round snout for a mouth, big square ears with a rectangular Mohawk tuft of mud for his hair. He wore a simple brown scarf tied around his neck, a brown kilt around his waist, a red and green stripe circling around its lower third. Michael's mind dug hard, the electricity of the search pulsing through millions of neurons, until finally recalling the figure he'd seen in the display cases of Kachinas in the Fort Lewis College library. Mudhead, a little voice sparked, a humorous sort, known to the Hopi as Koyemsi. He'd passed him hundreds of times during his studies and Mudhead seemed to be in every Hopi dance he'd seen. A clown, a jester, always interacting with the peoples and playing games. The other two were a puzzle, though; no memories came forth. The one with the drum had seemingly led the discussion between the Yei, Mudhead and the other Kachina; while the third seemed more a companion of Mudhead's as the dancers comingled.

The faint sound of the lute player began to grow in his left ear, keeping time with Mudhead's drumbeat. Big Fly now descended, taking an approving hover above the fire and ongoings. The music grew louder as the lute player emerged alone from behind the distant dune, his earlier slow song now replaced with a more upbeat jig. With this the dancers' activity increased. The mysterious masked figure at shadows edge, invited by the others, now advanced into the dance, with a slow and apprehensive gait. The five dancers all lifted their hands and playfully grabbed at the Ku?itu mask as the figure advanced directly toward the man, growing closer, leaning in to him and reaching to touch the man's shoulder.

The light nudge brought Michael's eyes open slowly and begrudgingly, as the creaking of the bench and movement from Joseph getting up drew his attention. When he closed them again, the dance was over and, sadly, the dream was gone. Reality had been restored. The flutist had stopped playing and the fourth round of rocks had made their entrance into the sweat lodge. Reluctantly Michael adjusted in his seat and focused his eyes to see Joseph and the Fire Man splashing the last of the water onto the superheated rocks as Hosteen Begay slowly neared him, leaning his walking stick against the table.

"I can see from your face, my friend, that the Yei have shown you your way," the old shaman said calmly, placing a warm hand on Michael's shoulder and taking a seat. "I know that much troubles you, but you must follow this path the Yei have shown you. Tell me of what you have seen."

Michael recounted in detail the dance of the Kachina and Yei; of Big Fly and Coyote; of the man, the woman and the mysterious masked figure. "What other dreams?" inquired his listener, so he reluctantly, but only generally, told him of the other, more terrifying, nightmares he'd had for the last few months. He held back his perceived sin in not being there for her. The shaman listened attentively, occasionally smiling and nodding, similarly to the priest-penitent confession moments of Michael's Catholic upbringing. By the time he had finished, the last of the steam had dissipated and Michael was washed out, drenched in sweat, tears and his own guilt, chin cupped in his hands, his mind oscillating between confusion and despair.

The shaman told him to sit back and enjoy his sweat lodge's warmth. That they would talk of this again later after he spoke with the other elders and perhaps…before his voice trailed off, as if thinking better of what he was about to say, noting the confused and distant look in his eyes. Michael nodded reflexively, but was too exhausted to talk further. He just leaned heavily into the backrest, now unconcerned with its steadiness. The old man again placed a reassuring hand on his shoulder as he rose and grabbed his walking stick, moving slowly back toward the opposite side of the lodge and the others. Michael closed his eyes, hoping, praying this would someday all go away. His mind wandered into dizziness as the old shaman spoke softly of the dreams with the others near the fire's edge, glancing back occasionally toward Michael.

Edward Donovan

DAY TWO

Old Friends, New Acquaintances

When he opened his eyes, it was morning. Everything and everyone, including the fire, the dancers and Big Fly, were gone. Michael rose, stretching the kinks from a night's sleep on a wooden bench, rubbing his eyes before stumbling forward and pushing open the flap that was the door. The onslaught of the brilliant eastern sun dazzled him for a moment while his eyes painfully adjusted. After a few moments, and with his equilibrium somewhat restored, he gingerly stepped from the lodge and rounded toward the house. There he found Joseph sitting in a rocker on the front porch.

"Good Morning. Sleep well?" came the call.

"Don't even remember my head hitting the bench," he laughed.

"You left us pretty quickly. Must've been a tough drive. Grandfather said we should not disturb you."

"Yeah, I guess it really took it out of me."

"So, what are your plans?"

"On my way back east to see Mom. You knew she went back to live by her sister after Dad died, right?"

Joseph nodded.

"Of course you did. Anyway, I'm going to stop up and see Kevin first. Stay at the motel for a couple of days. Just gonna take a little vacation and end up where I end up, ya know?"

"Yeah, you've been at it a long time. It'll be good for you."

"Well, you're the doctor, but that's kinda what I was thinkin'."

After a moment's silence, Joseph asked, "Have you talked to Kevin recently?"

"Talked to him before I left LA. Told him I'd be in this afternoon. Said if I saw you guys to tell you to quit being strangers and come on up. He wants to see his godson."

"Yeah, Lisa and I haven't had the chance to get up there in a long time, but I keep close tabs on the boy. I always have my sources."

"Funny, that's what he said. Said some of the college students you're working with were staying at the motel."

"He works out a pretty good deal for them," Joseph said. "The tribe pays for the room, and Kevin keeps an eye out for them. Their mothers know they're in a good place and that makes them happy. With friends. You know."

"Sure do."

They reminisced a while longer, but it was time to get going. "'Miles to go before I sleep,'" Michael quipped. He noticed again that everyone had gone, including Hosteen Begay, which was a great disappointment. Michael was curious if his dream had any meaning and believed only a shaman could truly interpret it. Joseph reassured him, telling him that he knew his grandfather had spoken with the elders and dreamwalker about it last night and had told Joseph he'd speak to Michael about this soon, but for now it needed to wait for another day.

"When will we see you again?" Mama Begay called, emerging from the front door at the moment Michael was headed in to say goodbye.

"Soon. Very soon," Michael reassured her.

"Hopefully you'll stay a little longer next time." Mama Begay smiled, disappearing back into the hogan to continue whatever duties she was involved in.

"Hopefully," he said inaudibly to himself.

"Will you come to Window Rock?" Joseph asked. "Lisa and the kids would love to see you."

"Of course. As soon as I get back from Mom's and the return trip. I'll drag Kev with me."

"That would be great."

With a wave he hopped into the Explorer and was heading back down the dusty road. A right onto 163, back through Monument Valley, then finally to Kayenta.

On instinct he almost turned west on 160, back towards Los Angeles. With a shake of his head, he made a wide left and circled east. Ahead in the distance, the massive crossed arms of the Sleeping Ute called him in the proper direction.

* * *

Tielson squirmed in his seat, the likelihood of compromise banging at his front door. He was now thoroughly unnerved. He stood and began pacing across the back of the office, his eerie bent shadow cascading against the wall, occasionally hurtling obscenities to the chair.

A knock at the door gathered his attention and he returned to his chair, barking admittance.

The junior man came through the door. "You wanted to see me, sir?"

"Yes. Anderson. I'll need two independent operatives immediately for a West Coast matter. I need something found. Quickly and discreetly. This is very special and I want somebody reliable on this. I'll brief them personally. You'll need to take another trip south to satisfy the financial needs."

"I'll get on it right away. I do know of a team the company has used in the past. They're based in town and I can try and talk with them this afternoon. I've heard they are extremely discreet."

"Used them before and discreet, huh? Who are they?" The beady eyes narrowed onto Anderson.

"I don't think you'd know them; ex-special ops. A couple of guys I knew of from Naval Intelligence. Supposedly they've been used a couple of times on small coverts. They've always been quite good in the past. Never a problem."

"Pros at surveillance?"

"That's their reputation."

"What about interrogation?"

"I'm sure they're familiar with the techniques, but I can inquire."

"Good. Find out if they're available and assure their versatility. There may be additional duties other than strict surveillance. Set a briefing for me with them tonight outside the agency."

"Yes, sir." Anderson left the room immediately, heading purposefully toward his own office. A security breach was one thing, but a security breach and independents for interrogation was another. Tielson was looking for a leak and Anderson knew full well what his instructions confirmed: something was unusually wrong and he had no answers.

* * *

It was just after one when Michael broke the southwestern crest of the San Juan Range, just past Hesperus. From that perch he could see the glacial valley that formed the natural boundaries of his home. Durango, Colorado was a sleepy little mountain town with all the accouterments, and a few extras thrown in. The valley in which it lay was sheltered by mountains on all four sides, fourteeners to the north and west. Powering its way through the middle of the valley, *El Rio de las Animas de Perdidas en Purgatorio*, the Animas River, formed a formidable obstacle to anyone crossing from one side to the other. Spanish for The River of Lost Souls in Purgatory, it had earned its name from an unfortunate party of Spanish Conquistadors. Under the command of the seventeenth-century explorer Escalante, they had attempted to cross the swollen stream during spring run-off. Their efforts proved deadly and it received its name. While it still claimed the occasional life, it had been all but tamed by the hordes of river rats who visited its banks each year.

Along the Animas led the tracks that ran to Durango's past. While the area had the requisite Colorado ski area and the usual summer fare of fishing, camping, hiking, biking and boating, it also had something else that set it apart from other such Colorado towns. It had a train. Not just any old train, but a real live gold and silver train, to which the city owed both its birth and its continued life. Up until the 1880s the region had remained largely uninhabited, save by the large tribe of Mountain

Utes who'd lived in the area for centuries, and the occasional trapper. All that changed when veins of rich ore were discovered in the mountains up north. With that discovery came the miners. With the miners came the soldiers to protect them and the eventual establishment of the US Cavalry Post at Fort Lewis. There was plenty of gold in them thar hills, but two minor little problems existed. First, how do you get a rather large object, a train, filled with tons of ore forty-five miles south through several eleven- and twelve-thousand foot passes, narrow gorges and along cliffs hundreds of feet above the river? And once you figure that out, how do you get the native Utes to let you do it right through the middle of their traditional hunting grounds?

In response to the first part of the problem came American Ingenuity in the form of The Denver and Rio Grande Western Railway. After carefully surveying the route, they put the problem to the drawing board and the solution became rather evident. If the canyon was narrow, why not the train, too? The designers of the 1880s must have just loved that deduction. Through this type of necessity, a mother's child was born and in 1882 the narrow-gauge railroad was created. With the ability to move the stores of riches from Silverton, the other problem would just have to be solved by the military.

Troops under the command of General Phillip Sheridan were given the task. After a few minor skirmishes between local Utes and miners came the command that the country was to be civilized, if necessary at the barrel of the Winchester. Sheridan was fully prepared to follow the same ruthless tactics he'd become infamous for, until he met Chief Ouray. Ouray was a wise old Ute warrior and was well traveled by standards of the day. He'd been to Santa Fe and Denver and seen the endless trail of white settlers who'd mostly bypassed his lands—until now. He'd learned the white tongue and knew of Sheridan's exploits during the Civil War and his continuing victories in the Indian campaigns. He also knew that if his people were to survive they would have to learn to live with the whites who were arriving in Ute lands in greater numbers every day.

In the end, Ouray proved a rather shrewd negotiator, under the circumstances. Sheridan, on the other hand, seemed to have had his fill of agreement by force. The two great chiefs met and agreed that the Utes would "share" their sacred hunting lands in the San Juans with the white miners and settlers. They would agree to reside permanently on their two southern wintering grounds near the Sleeping Ute and on the mesas to the south of the new white town near the Army's fort. Sheridan agreed that the Utes could still use their hunting grounds so long as they did so peacefully alongside the others who would settle in the area. Ouray then asked for something Sheridan hadn't quite anticipated. The chief told him that the future was clear to him. In time his small group would be greatly outnumbered and he realized that his people would someday need the tools to live within the white culture. In exchange for this sharing arrangement, Ouray asked that the government share its culture with his people and teach them the white men's ways. Sheridan agreed that the government would found a free Indian School at Fort Lewis to teach the people, now confined to their reservation. Over time and by further treaty, the school joined the state system and become a junior college. By the time the three friends attended, it had become a well-respected small college, keeping its name and, uncharacteristically, its promises to Ouray.

While "The Fort" still educated the locals and tribal members, the train no longer carried miner's riches. Today, along the upper Animas, it carried tourist gold, the community's new lifeblood. As the train eked its way through some of the most spectacular alpine scenery America has to offer, tourists retreated a hundred years in time. The summer tourist industry kept the restaurants, bars and motels alive, and allowed locals such as Kevin Daniels to make a reasonable living in the small town. After the real estate market temporarily collapsed, Kevin picked up a great deal on a broken-down motel. He had to restore, refurbish and remodel, but he didn't mind. He was in paradise. Besides, some rich fool from Texas or California would someday pay him ten times what it was worth.

Michael's Explorer edged up Main Street to the north, finally pulling in to the Silver Spruce Motel. As soon as Michael parked, Kevin emerged from the house next door.

"What took you so long? I expected you last night."

"Saturday dinner at the Begays.'"

Kevin just smiled, nodded, and walked over to shake his old friend's hand.

"You haven't changed a bit, Kev."

"A few pounds here and there, a few more gray hairs, but that's the good life for you."

They walked into the house, a small two-bedroom with a converted attic. The living room was comfortably furnished with a big cushy sofa and some chairs. Michael slid onto the couch.

"How about a beer?"

"Thought you'd never ask." Kevin opened the refrigerator door.

He came back across the room, slid into a chair himself and the two old friends talked away the afternoon.

* * *

Tielson pulled up in his silver standard-issue Ford and found a parking spot near the monument. A lucky stroke, considering the mass of humanity that visited every day. He hurriedly shuffled the approximate quarter mile to where he found the path under the trees that led to the bench he'd been to so many times before. The cherry blossoms were alive with the freshness of spring. Their pink and white blooms reflected off the placid water before him at the pathway's edge, completely unconcerned with the affairs of men. Behind him scurried the many tourists, flocking to see the great monument to the brilliant author and architect. From beneath the dome of the circular white marble building, Thomas Jefferson gazed through the columns, past Tielson and the Tidal Basin. Taking no notice, down the path the stubby legs shuffled toward the stately, older man seated on the wooden bench, hidden down the hill and below a stand of bushes. Benignly he tossed peanuts to a group of ducks that had gathered ten feet away, acknowledging Tielson with only cold eyes, before tossing the remaining duck feed three feet to the left of the seat the little man was certain to take. The happy beneficiaries quickly waddled over.

"Good afternoon, sir" he said in a gravelly voice, taking his seat on the bench beside which the ducks were feverishly attacking their spoils.

"To some, Tielson." Disdain for the man was clearly evident in his refined voice. Oh, how he wanted to distance himself from this . . . this . . . thing. Soon enough, he reasoned, but first he had to find out what the pig had gotten him into. "I spoke with our associates who are not having such a good day. They've had to implement a shutdown and are rather concerned with their loss. They're wondering how their liaison could have been compromised." He paused. "I'm wondering, too."

"There is great concern, but I do have some preliminary answers you can pass on to them. It seems their man had a side business and he was looking to expand. And not necessarily in a direction beneficial to us. Apparently, these other associates were not pleased with his services. He managed to phone in an alert, but by the time we got someone there, he was already dead. We did what we could on short notice to deflect attention."

The older man listened without response to Tielson's report and seemed to settle a bit.

Tielson continued. "There seems to be nothing to be concerned with at this time. Justice reports a search of the residence uncovered some rather incriminating evidence leading toward his other associations and far removed from our operations. From what we can tell, our operation has not been jeopardized by these unfortunate events. However, we may wish to continue with this short shut-down, just in case."

"Perhaps that's wise. I'll discuss this further with them, but we need to correct the situation as soon as possible. Our friends are not happy with this interruption. I strongly suggest you work with them to implement a transition in short order. Our associates can shut down for a week, ten days at the most, without affecting operations. A new man must be in place by that time. Get in touch with them on the selection and make sure any problems are rectified well within that period. Perhaps we should think about putting in a couple of independents to look around for any potential problems and confirm whom he was associating with. For our own knowledge."

"I'm already looking into it, sir. I'll see who's available and I'll get to the bottom of it."

The older man didn't seem buoyed by the assurance, but continued, "Do what is necessary and use the resources you deem appropriate."

"Yes, sir. I'll get right on it."

"I need not remind you what is at stake here. I have to go now. Keep me informed."

The older man rose and turned without further addressing the squat man. He disappeared down the opposite path, through a stand of trees rounding the basin and toward the Federal Bureau of Engraving building. Tielson slid forward and rose to his normal bent gait, staring blankly at an old mallard that was blindly searching for a scrap of food the younger ducks might have missed. He leered at it for a moment before landing a swift soccer kick that sent the feeble duck tumbling. Turning from its squawks with a hideous smile he headed back out towards the monument.

* * *

After a few hours and several beers, Kevin finally moved the conversation to what he knew his friend probably needed.

"How about a room? I'm sure you're whipped from the drive."

"Best in the house?"

"But of course. Nothing but the best for the counselor from Los Angeles."

"Hey, only lived and practiced there."

"Well, considering how much you practiced, you should have started becoming good at it, right?"

"Yeah, yeah, yeah. Heard 'em all. Let's go."

They walked over to the office, through the front door, amid Kevin's call that it's "just me." Kevin rounded the front desk and slid the dividing curtain to the side, stepping into the living quarters to find Luigi Morrealli, the Spruce's long-time live-in manager. Luigi sat in his La-Z-Boy recliner along the wall separating the living quarters from the front office. The television set was tuned to the Special Orders session from Congress on C-SPAN, but Luigi clearly had not been giving it the attention he usually did.

"Sorry to wake you, Luigi. I thought you'd be up."

"Just an after dinner cat-nap." His voice crackled a bit as the recliner folded back into a seat.

"Luigi, you remember Michael Kincaid?"

"Of course." He slowly stood, taking a few short steps towards his visitors. "It's been a few years, Michael, but how are you?" He leaned out, extending a large paw towards his visitor.

Michael grasped his hand, saying, "Good, Luigi, good."

"Is Room Two open?" Kevin queried his manager.

"Yep, no takers," he said with a warm, wide smile. "Coffee's on in the mornings early. And sometimes, when the boss does his job, there's even donuts."

"Well, don't worry about me. I'll be up at the crack of ten."

Both Kevin and Luigi chuckled. Kevin retrieved the key from the desk in front, and with a wave, they were out the door with Michael's promise of a return for coffee in the morning. Kevin walked Michael to the room and let him in, handing him the key.

"I'm sure you're tired, so I'll let you get some rest. I've got some errands to run in the morning, but hang out; I'll be back around noon. I'm sure you and Luigi can burn at least a couple hours talking politics."

"At least," he agreed. "See ya in the morning."

Kevin pulled the door closed before sauntering off, enjoying the beautiful early spring evening.

* * *

Anderson dropped Tielson off at the front door of the posh Georgetown eatery and watched as the squat man shuffled toward the door being opened before him. He looked away with a mild grimace of disgust before pulling from the curb in the standard GSA sedan in search of a parking spot and a cup of coffee.

Tielson gruffly informed the maitre d' that he was late for his party. He curtly demanded he be directed to the Donner party, with his normal sardonic grin. The black-suited man looked oddly at him before leading him to a table in the rear of the dining room. He greeted the two individuals seated at the table with a terse, "I take it the reservations were sufficient?"

"Yes, quite sufficient. Some pasta, Mr. Tingley?" said the man to his left. "The angel hair is quite good tonight."

Tielson waddled to the unoccupied seat to his left, inwardly enjoying the stealthiness of this assurance that he had the right men. Perfectly innocent conversation, unlike the movies and their "Rain in Spain falls mainly on Jane's damn brain" bullshit. Where'd they get that crap from, anyway? He thought to himself. It was really unnecessary. After all, who could possibly know of both the reservation and the pseudonym he'd given himself but the right men? Just the same, he'd always liked the idea of spy games anyway.

"I've only got a few minutes before I have to get back," he said in the tone of self-importance he'd always bestowed upon himself. He slid a satchel toward the man on his left. "Everything is in there that you will need. Review the instructions carefully tonight. There are specifics that I need. These must come first. There are two contact numbers in the briefing materials that you are to use solely for contact on this operation.

The first number for general updates through my subordinate, the second is a secure line. Use the second number to report directly and only to me for anything out of the ordinary. If you take the assignment, your reservation out is for tomorrow afternoon, 1:35 at Dulles. My man will meet you one hour before your flight to deliver your operating capital. Final payment will be available upon your return. Any questions?"

"No, I'm sure it's covered in your briefing. We'll be in touch in the morning."

"As I've said, it's all outlined in the package, photographs included. This is a national security surveillance operation, so pay attention to the details and the manner in which I want you to proceed."

"I take it we're dealing with a security breach here, sir?"

"Yes, we are. That is why this is delicate. We thought we had the leak secured, but subsequent information seems to indicate otherwise. We believe sensitive documents are on the verge of being traded with unfriendlies. We must find these documents and then plug the leak. We have a trail developing, however things are volatile and ever-changing. You'll have to be flexible while handling the matter, possibly with extreme prejudice and certainly with expediency."

"Understood. Anything other than surveillance at this time?"

"Not at this time, but things change, and I suppose you can handle anything I put to you?"

"We can handle it."

"That's good to know. This leak must be closed, but for the time being, just stick to the outlined plan and find out what I want to know."

The two men nodded.

Tielson left abruptly, shuffling hurriedly across the room. As he reached the maitre d' station he paused on his stubby legs and glanced over his shoulder. The two men talked quietly at their table. Anderson had better be right about these two.

DAY THREE

Pleasant Homecomings

The fire crackled brightly under the dark starry sky. Embers billowed into the night past the juniper trees at the edge of the clearing where Coyote prowled through the brush. From between two piñon trees emerged the rainbow-colored lute player, Kokopelli, his instrument grasped tightly in his spindly right hand. The Kachinas, Mudhead and the other two followed. Kokopelli placed his lips to the whistle-shaped mouthpiece and began to play a merry tune. Mudhead began a drumbeat, singing an announcement of the good fortune that would soon be brought, as the other two Kachinas began to sway with the music. The lyrics concluded but the flutist played on. The three now danced slowly in a circle around the fire pit, their figures aglow in the firelight.

From the darkness to his right emerged the Yei chiefs again, this time carrying yucca strips and pine boughs in their hands, flanking the featureless man. They positioned him at fire's edge; his face hidden and fixed squarely on the ground, before joining the others in the circular dance around the fire and the man. Darting in and out of the stars above came Big Fly, the guardian and protector, enjoying the show. Kokopelli's music stopped abruptly as the Yei chiefs tossed the yucca strips and pine boughs into the fire, a brilliant light exploding as red embers from their offering flickered into the sky.

Slowly and softly, Kokopelli began to play again as the mysterious Ku?itu masked figure materialized from the shadows of the junipers and stepped into the brilliant light, her silhouette finally revealed. Again shrouded in the reddish blanket, she was quickly joined by two of the Kachinas rushing to her escort. Big Fly came lower in his hover, an obvious smile of approval lighting his face. The others darted back from the fire to encircle the mysterious figure and the man in dance, each one grasping at the Ku?itu mask, now trying desperately to pull it from her face. The figure whirled wildly; her hair splashing from behind the mask, but none could ever get hold.

* * *

Michael slowly opened his eyes. He felt strangely peaceful. At least it wasn't one of his usual mornings. He despised the mornings. That's when he missed her most. Maybe today would be different. Maybe today he wouldn't miss the smell of her hair, the softness of her skin as he caressed her awake; or that blank, beautiful stare she held on her face as she sipped her morning coffee. Maybe today his memories would give him a break. Today he was back in Colorado among old friends and it felt good. His morning hadn't been so bad.

He swung out of bed, but fell right back in, his head dizzied as the blood was slow to reach equilibrium at this altitude. His mind may have felt good, but his head settled to a deep, dull throb. He'd been at sea level to long. He stood slowly this time, rubbing his face and gaining balance. When his eyes finally focused, they cast his subconscious attention toward the table that held his briefcase.

He staggered over, the effects of the last two days evident throughout his body, and he popped the latches and lifted the lid. Instinctively he thrust his hand into the corner of the leather case, extracting an aspirin bottle. He popped one into his mouth before sliding to the cabinet above the kitchenette's sink and retrieved a glass. He half-filled the glass from the tap and downed the aspirin with a quick swig. The icy cold made his teeth tingle a bit with the frigid refreshing taste he'd missed.

In his travels he had found this, too, was something unique to the western slope of Colorado. Not only was the water crystal clear, possessing a sweet taste, but it was also perfectly cold to the taste straight out of the tap. In LA, the water was warm and tasted chemical. To get a similar drink was a minor chore. You had to either have it delivered and rent a cooler, or go to the store, buy the water and then refrigerate it. Between the cost of the product, refrigeration and gas or delivery charges, it had always seemed to Michael to be an unfair financial undertaking just to get a simple glass of cold water. It had always been a pet peeve of his against life in LA. In Durango he need only to turn on the tap. He finished the glass, feeling good to be home again.

* * *

Anderson disembarked from the corporate Lear, notifying the captain that he would return within the hour and leaving instructions to be refueled and ready to return at that time. He grabbed the aluminum briefcase and hurried down the ramp.

He bypassed the multi-colored horde of tourists patiently queued for their passage through Customs. He darted toward the empty aisle designated for diplomatic traffic. Anderson flashed his credentials to the same old customs official, who simply nodded as he hurried through unchecked.

The early morning sun blazed hot already and the air lay humid on his face when he emerged from the terminal. He eyed the black sedan with consular plates awaiting him and hopped in.

"Take me to the bank, Jim."

"Yeah, mon."

The car jolted forward from the curb and headed out of the airport along the palm-lined boulevard. It took only a few minutes to arrive at the city center. Jim stopped directly in front of the bank. Anderson, with his briefcase, jumped from the car. The driver pulled away to begin a continuous circle around the block, knowing he wouldn't be long. He never was.

After about seven turns around the block, Anderson was waiting with his briefcase where he'd been left. The car halted for a few seconds to retrieve its passenger before turning toward the airport. In ten minutes the American would be gone again. Then Jim would be free to fish the white sand beaches near his home until the next one came.

But this mon, this Anderson mon, was different from the others he picked up. Nice enough, but different. Never stayed more than a few hours, at most. Never no time for da fishin'. No time for da beaches. No time to roam the streets or to look at the pretty ladies. But no mind to Jim, tho'. Anderson was a minor intrusion once, maybe twice a month, but the Americans paid Jim well and didn't really use him that often. Strange people, these Yanks, he thought as the car pulled up to the terminal entrance, paying him just to sit around.

"See you soon, Jim."

"Yeah, mon. Sometime you come back for the fishin'. mon. I'll take you."

"I'd like that, Jim. Maybe soon. Maybe very soon."

Jim smiled. He knew the type. This mon would never slow down enough for da fishin'.

* * *

The aspirin and a shower had done him good. Michael's thoughts now turned to hot coffee and he left the room towards the office. Rounding the southwest corner of the glass-enclosed office, he noticed Luigi talking to a young Navajo man. Michael walked in, his mind noting the bell triggered by the front door. As he entered, he eyed the coffee pot, mercifully half full, next to the door on a side table against the glass wall. He poured a Styrofoam cup full as the young Navajo, maybe about 21, smaller, with a round face, probably one of the college students Joseph had told him of, politely left with a "Thank you." But Michael sensed some tension and the young man clearly wasn't happy about something.

"Different sort of people," Luigi said, shaking his head.

"Yes, I suppose," came Michael's muttered response. "What's up with him."

"Oh it's the same old thing with these college kids, never enough money, always something, a daily occurrence around here. He's ok though. But hey, I snatched you a couple of donuts. Come on back," Luigi called, disappearing through the doorway behind the desk. Michael followed, stepping through the opened curtain into the living quarters.

"I've got better coffee in here, anyway. You like a good cup of coffee, I suppose!" he exclaimed, disappearing into the kitchen.

A donut box lay open on the veneer coffee table near the center of the room. Michael crossed the room and took a seat on the sofa next to the easy chair where his host had been apparently sitting. From the small kitchen at the sofa's far end, Luigi turned from the counter carrying two steaming cups of black coffee. He set them on the small end table between Michael and the chair before resuming his seat. Michael observed that he'd aged well over the years since he'd last seen him, but the passage of time was evident from his slow shuffle. He was dressed casually in baggy pants, an old dress shirt and slippers. The television was fixed to C-SPAN. It was time for the Senate's morning one-minute speeches.

Michael sipped his coffee as Senator Mark Buccola rose to take the lectern. The junior senator from Virginia was all the rage on the Hill. A few years back, after 25 years in private business and graying into his own, he'd thrown his hat in the ring for a vacant seat. He'd come from a long lineage of politicians, had the political machine to get elected, and after one term had risen to the top in relatively short time. The party line attributed it to good political instincts, but the insiders credited his meteoric rise to the more likely influence of his daddy, one of the residents who'd spent many a year on Capitol Hill. A regular chip off the old block, most said, but still many wondered under their breaths. Seedy rumors abounded about the other connections he had made over the years in labor and big business. There was talk of a possible presidential run in the fall, though, so he was for real. He was charismatic and polls of likely women voters adored him.

"You know Michael, I just get a kick out of these guys. They can't tell which story supports which lie," Luigi said with a chuckle.

"Have a high regard for politicians, do you, Luigi?"

"Other than the fact they're mostly just a Goddamned bunch of thieves and cheats, not really." He chuckled a bit before continuing, "There's a few good ones, but most of 'em would sell out their own mothers if it furthered their political ambitions. Like this guy." He pointed toward the speaker stepping down from the podium. Luigi lit up a Pall Mall straight, blowing a smoke ring from beneath his long flowing white beard. A vision of Gandalf, the Middle-Earth wizard, echoed somewhere in Michael's mind.

"Probably so," Michael benignly answered as Buccola withdrew and Senator Garth Shackelford of Kentucky was recognized for his one minute.

"It's been a few years since I've seen her, but how's your mom?"

"She's fine." Michael embarked on the thumbnail version as Senator Shackelford droned on about the ravages of crime and drugs.

* * *

With the possibilities of compromise and failure banging at his front door, Tielson was thoroughly unnerved. He'd gathered a few answers in the last hours that had pointed his search in a different direction. It would have to be checked immediately, and with discretion. He would personally brief the ops on how he wanted the situation handled. He paced anxiously across the back of the office, the eerie bent shadow again cascading against the wall, occasionally hurling obscenities to no one there. The heated argument he heard inside his head from one of these imagined companions was suddenly broken by the intercom's buzz.

"Yes, what is it!" he demanded.

The secretary's voice was meek. "I'm sorry to disturb you, sir, but I have Anderson on the line for you."

"Put him through." The secretary gratefully released the line with a reserved, "Yes, sir." Tielson waited the few seconds it took before the phone rang again and he punched the lit button.

"What have you learned since our discussion last night?"

"Well, sir, I've had some of our people look into what you asked about."

Tielson tried hard to listen past the whine of the engines emanating from behind Anderson's voice.

"They've just called me back and confirmed that there is a likelihood of corruption and that someone could have gained access to the files as suggested. We're trying to get exact details, but the tech guys worked backwards from the operational files and found an unsecured entrance through Langley, which apparently has been used recently, in the past few weeks. They're attempting to backtrack to the initiating source now. They tell me that if someone knew what they were looking for, they could find just about anything they wanted. Apparently the system is not as secure as the agency would like it to be. Needless to say, it was a previously unknown shortcut to the heart of the system. It has now been secured. I don't suppose you'd like to give me a hint as to what this is about?"

"It doesn't concern you, Anderson. Just do as you're told."

The little bastard's condescending voice infuriated the junior man and his resentment towards him increased. He stewed quietly on the other end.

"Damn it! This is just great!" Tielson yelled, causing Anderson to instinctively yank the earpiece away. He paused before continuing. "All right, all right. What about AZ?"

"Last check, day before yesterday, situation reported normal. Normal flow, with no disturbances. No other communications since. I'll follow up upon my return?"

"Yes, of course." Tielson paused pensively, but didn't continue.

Without further instructions forthcoming, Anderson tried to take the exit opportunity he'd been given. "Anything else, sir?"

"Are our people ready to leave at 1:35?"

"Yes, sir."

"I assume you will have no problem arriving back by that time."

"No, sir. We're less than an hour out. That should put us back before noon."

"Good. Then I'll meet you at Dulles at their gate at noon. I'll need to go over some additional details with them at that time. We'll discuss this matter further then."

"Yes, sir."

"I'll expect you at noon. Let's get this done properly. We can't afford another mistake."

Anderson heard him hang up without another word. He closed his eyes, quick thoughts filtering out the drone of the twin jet engines. "We can't afford another mistake" echoed through his mind. The reprehensible pig would blame him for whatever problems existed if he got half the chance. If in the end there would be slaughter, Anderson was now certain he'd be the lamb sent. He wasn't about to be the next Ollie North, and he lamented the day he'd fallen in with this thug.

* * *

Luigi returned with a fresh cup of coffee as a voice bellowed from the television set. "The Chair recognizes the honorable senior senator from California."

Michael, like most Americans, knew immediately exactly who this was. He had actually met the good senator at a fund-raising event he had begrudgingly attended at the behest of an influential and high-paying client. As chairman of the Armed Services Committee, he was quite influential and a better bet than Buccola to be the next president. Even his apolitical secretary Trish, for some strange reason, had insisted that he go, saying it couldn't hurt to meet one of the most powerful men on the Hill.

"What do you think about this guy, Luigi?"

"I still can't figure him out after all these years." Luigi paused as

Senator Howard McRae adjusted the microphone and began his obligatory words of thanks and praise for his colleagues on both sides of the aisle.

Michael was a bit puzzled in the way he said it, asking, "What do you mean by that?"

"Well, . . . I knew the guy in World War II," Luigi gruffly continued. "Never really knew what to make of him. Good soldier, but too reckless."

"You know Senator McRae?" Michael's interest peeked out from behind the steaming coffee.

"Sure. For years. We fought together in the Palau Islands."

"Palau? Never heard of it."

"I'm not surprised. Most people haven't. I'll tell you a story about the guy if you want."

"Sure!" Inside knowledge always fascinated the attorney in Michael.

"Well, the battle for the Palaus" he began "the brass called it Operation Stalemate, was largely forgotten because of the Philippine campaign and McArthur returning. Really just a footnote in the Marianas Campaign in most history books, between the battles of Guam and the Battle of Leyte Gulf or Iwo Jima. A bunch of islands down there below Mindanao. Anyway, McArthur and Nimitz disagreed on whether the Philippines even needed to be taken. Nimitz wanted to take a couple of hopscotch islands and just go straight for Japan; McArthur wanted to liberate his friends the Filipinos first, using an airbase on Peleliu to protect his flank, and then move on to Japan.

"Nimitz seemed to want Peleliu too, for some strange reason, and upon that they finally agreed, although no one ever figured out why since that island didn't really seem important to either plan militarily. Scuttlebutt at the time was it was more about after the war with the US wanting control of the Dutch Indies oil fields, but who knows what Washington is ever truly up to?" His voice trailed off for second. "Anyway, Mack and I eventually ended up on Peleliu together through some rather odd circumstances." The old man chuckled under his flowing beard as he stroked it wish his hand, memories clearly coming over his face before he continued. "The place was nothin' more than a buncha sharp coral rock sticking up out of the ocean, but it was a short hop from all of Southeast Asia and the Philippines. Roosevelt flew to Pearl and after hearing both plans eventually decided to take the Philippines first, so MacArthur could make his triumphant return and they also agreed to take the Peleliu.

"They sent in the 1st Marine Division first—the Old Breed they called 'em—landing down on the southwest beaches and started to take the island. They said after it was pure unimagined hell on those beaches, a barrage of crossfire from the Japanese guns. Fire came from everywhere, but when they'd take the ground they'd find nobody. After about three days they finally took the airfield and found the maze of interconnected tunnels they were using for movement. For ten weeks after that it was almost hand-to-hand cave fighting, the first time in the war. The Nips fired from everywhere and nowhere, which led the Marines to get a different weapon, the flamethrower. After a week pushing the Japs to the north of that damned island and with seventy percent casualties at places like Bloody Nose Ridge, Dead Man's Corner and The Point, the Seabees were finally brought in to start re-building the airstrip and defenses we'd just blown up.

"As soon as it was level and could take planes, the brass started bringing in reinforcements and close-air-support Corsairs from Ulithi Atoll. McRae was one of the pilots. After that first week we got hit with a small typhoon, much smaller than the one that caused those major problems for Halsey and the fleet a month later. When the storm cleared, the Nips started their counteroffensive. They knew what we were up to and they sure as hell weren't going to let us use that strip without a serious fight. From that base they knew we could easily hit their oil supply routes or the Philippines I guess."

"We didn't know it at the time, but somehow they managed to slip a heavy cruiser, the *Chikuma*, past Halsey's defense forces during the storm. Somewhat quite the embarrassment to the admiral as I remember, so it never got much press. They eventually sailed the damn thing into the inlet on the west side of the island from us. The Nips were desperate by that time Michael, and it wasn't but a few weeks later that they started hitting ships in Leyte Gulf with those first Kamikaze flights. The decision to sacrifice had already been made when we hit Peleliu. At first light they started shelling the center of the island. That area was only about two miles wide so they were pretty well zeroed in and hit us hard. We of course had no idea where it was coming from, but after about ten minutes of shelling all of a sudden thirteen tanks roll out of the jungle from the west trying to slice the airfield right in half."

Michael sat back sipping his coffee, completely entranced, as Luigi continued.

"Anyway, that was the day that crazy fool won his Navy Cross. He was seventeen, like me, lied on his enlistment papers but they didn't look real hard in those days." He smiled. "And he deserved it, too, that's for damn sure. Saved a lot of boys' asses that day, mine included."

"Navy Cross? What happened?" Michael, now hooked, interrupted.

"Well, when the Japs started hitting that runway with their eight-inch guns we all dove into the nearest foxhole trying to figure out what was going on. We finally saw the tanks coming as soon as they broke cover from the trees. Fortunately the Seabees had managed to get some of the anti-tank barriers in, ditches and mines, at least enough to hang them up for a few minutes. All of us took off and headed for the anti-tank guns, everyone but that crazy son of a bitch McRae who split off back towards the planes. He ran across that exploding runway, jumped in a Corsair and calmly started it. Shit was blowing up all around him, but he just turned the thing around, dodged a few bomb holes and took off just as tanks started busting through the barriers. Never saw anything like it."

"Wow."

"Yeah, obviously living a charmed life. Well, anyway, he gets airborne and I guess calls in some of his buddies. He must have known it would take 'em a few minutes, so what does he do?"

Michael shrugged.

"Damned if he doesn't circle around and starts strafing the tanks giving some of the boys time to get to their guns and drive them back. During all this I guess he finally spots that cruiser, which by this time was closing in on Orange Beach Two and direct sight of the airfield. Craziest thing, I tell you. He pulls that bird out of a run at the tanks and heads straight for the cruiser. He didn't have any bombs on that Corsair, but he started up so much shit with them with his guns that they forgot about shelling the island and started firing on him instead." Michael sipped his coffee intensely.

"Damn stupid of them, though, with him only having his fifty cals. They'll do some damage, but they ain't gonna sink no damn heavy cruiser. Anyway, he kept 'em busy until two of his buddies showed up from over at Koror and what with the hell that was breaking loose, they broke off the attack and sailed off to open waters while our Corsairs doubled back to cover the airfield. She wouldn't last much longer though, we'd sink the *Chikuma* a month later in the Battle off Samar in the Leyte Gulf. That day was really the only major counteroffensive the Nips ever took on Peleliu. They stayed in their caves mostly waiting for us to weed them out, other than nighttime sniper attacks. There was a lot of hard fighting over those next few weeks. Once we had a good hold, the Navy turned its attention to the Philippines and a few weeks later we had Leyte and they started to take those islands back too. From there, well, you probably know the rest of the story. I'll tell you this, though, a bunch of us boys would have never come home if it hadn't been for Mack."

"Unbelievable." Michael leaned back, reflecting on the tale. "Do you ever talk to him anymore?"

"Matter of fact, spoke to him the other day. Talked to him about a couple of things I thought were important, but he didn't seem as though he could be bothered. Didn't mind chit-chatting about what I'd been up to lately, shit like that. But ask him to check into something for me and it's 'Give me your number and I'll get back to you.' Doubt if he'll even look into it."

"Well, you never know. He might do something. Sounds like a fairly honorable guy, maybe our next president if the pundits are right. They say he controls all the strings." Michael gave Luigi a closer look. "I didn't know you were a career military man."

"Wasn't, really. Just during the war. Mainly served as a civil service man."

"What did you do for the government?"

Luigi grinned. "Started as a radio man, eventually special forces and finally a safecracker."

"A safecracker!? Get out of here. What the hell does the government need a safecracker for?"

"C'mon, Michael, you're not that naive. Lots of things. I started in military intelligence breaking the Jap safes open. My father was a locksmith, as was his father. That's what I was doing on Peleliu. I was young but I had a skill the military needed at the time, and I'd been learning it since I was a boy. Lot of fun, but you had to watch out for the booby-traps."

"They had them booby-trapped?"

"Of course. A lot of secret stuff in there, codes and all. Had to be careful or the entire thing might blow up in your face."

"How long did you do that for?"

"About forty years. Semi-retired back in '88. Could pretty much open anything. Had my own business out there in Los Angeles after I left the government. Kept it going even when I moved out here. Once I left, my partner handled most of it. I'd just fly in for contract jobs when they needed me. Still do occasionally."

"What was it mainly, people forgetting their combinations?"

"Some of that, but generally I could get the combination from the factory if that happened. No, mainly middle-of-the-night jobs for the feds. DEA, IRS, ATF, those guys. They'd get a safe that needed opening and they'd call us in."

"You did that stuff, huh?" Michael knew something about that line of work from his days in LA. He'd heard the defense bar horror stories of the feds swooping in and picking up a search warrant from the local DA's pro-law enforcement magistrate. Seemed the feds were always on the trail of some drug kingpin. Boilerplate warrants would, of course, cover any safe they might run across. Unfortunately for the feds, rarely would it hold anything incriminating. Still, they just had to check. They'd pay thousands of dollars to get into it and generally find nothing, so the stories went. Sometimes it would pay off, but not usually. The people they were after were wise guys and not likely to make that kind of mistake. "That's amazing. What's the wildest thing you ever ran across?

"Really, it was mostly routine. Typically the DEA would call me in on short notice. I'd get there, drill the safe open and they'd have a look inside. Like I said, pretty routine."

"Still, I don't know that I could handle working with a bunch of feds."

"I didn't like it much myself, but it's what I did. Besides, I managed to put some distance between them and me anyway. I couldn't stand most of 'em either."

"How'd you do that?"

"Part of the routine. I'd just ask if they knew whether it was booby-trapped or not. That would generally get 'em off my heels. They'd just wait in another room, just in case."

"Were some really booby-trapped?"

"Never. No crook with any sense would ever put anything incriminating in a safe, so there was never a need to bother. But it let me do my work in peace and that's what I wanted. Besides, they might not pay me so much if they realized just how easy it was to get into most of 'em," he concluded with a chuckle. "Plus, once I had her opened up, I could look inside to satisfy my own curiosities. I guess safes and curiosity are leftovers from my military work. You can learn some interesting stuff that way."

"I'd imagine so. And you still doing this?"

"Nah. Not much anymore. Just a trip every now and again."

"Fascinating . . ."

* * *

Anderson met Tielson at noon near the gate posted for the 1:35 flight to Los Angeles. He handed him the briefcase and told the senior man that everything had gone according to plan. He assured him that he had confirmed that the men had the qualifications he wished for and handed him two airline tickets for Los Angeles. Tielson nodded, taking them and sliding them into his jacket's inside breast pocket. They took seats, Tielson fidgeting with his stubby fingers as they waited for the other two parties to arrive. Anderson searched his mind for a way to find out what was going on, but his boss suddenly slid from his seat with the briefcase, ordering his junior man to wait there while he met with their people.

Anderson watched as the man seemingly slithered over to the two independents who'd now taken seats on the opposite side of the small waiting area, near the check-in desk, as instructed. Tielson spoke with them for several minutes, leaning close for a few moments before they nodded their apparent approval. He straightened, pulling tickets from his right outside coat pocket, passing them and the briefcase to the shorter of the two men, who responded again with a simple nod. Anderson took a mental note, something's odd. They spoke for several more minutes before Tielson withdrew a manila envelope from his left pocket. He nervously tapped the envelope on his right hand as he spoke with the two men before finally handing it over. After several more minutes, their business apparently concluded, Tielson turned from the men who promptly rose and rounded out of the waiting area away from the LA flight and headed down the concourse. Anderson watched as the two men disappeared into the crowd. Tielson returned to his subordinate without a word, with a curt motion for him to follow as he passed him by.

* * *

They'd talked for another hour or so about politics and world events. Michael's ears were running low and he was glad to see Kevin coming across the parking lot towards the living quarters, momentarily appearing through the unlocked side door.

"I figured I'd still find you in here, the way you lawyers like to talk."

"He hasn't had a chance," said Luigi, who flashed a bright grin.

"That figures from you too, Luigi." C'mon, Michael, places to go, people to see."

"I'll see you tomorrow, Luigi. Thanks for the coffee."

"Sure. Stop on by when you get back or in the morning and I'll bend your ear a little more."

"It'll be a pleasure," he called as he left, closing the side door behind him.

Michael stopped by the room to pick up a few things, then met Kevin by his Jeep. They spent the rest of the afternoon dropping in on friends, finally stopping by their old stomping grounds at Farquahrts for a pizza and several beers later in the evening. At about nine, they headed back to the motel. Michael excused himself, mumbling something about passing out two nights in a row, feeling the mixture of altitude and alcohol. It took a lot less to get you bombed at 6,800 feet than at sea level when you weren't used to the thin air.

Kevin, quite a bit less affected, just laughed as he watched his old friend stagger to the door of Room 2, fumble with the key, drop it twice, and finally fall through the door with a thud. Kevin just shook his head as his barrister buddy comically climbed up the couch and onto his feet, shutting the door with a wayward push. After a couple of crashes, and a few chuckles from Kevin, a light came on in the window. Kevin knew Squire Kincaid was in for the night.

He stopped by the office for a couple minutes to say goodnight to Luigi, who of course was still watching C-SPAN. He walked back outside. All quite as usual on a Durango evening. He headed for a peaceful sleep. It would be his last for a good many days.

Edward Donovan

DAY FOUR

Something Amiss

Lori was kneeling, carving something into the sand with a stick. Her beautiful blonde hair cascaded over her shoulders. By the time he got near her she was finished and he looked at her work with a smile: "L ❤s M." She looked back at him, her eyes wide and glistening, her moist lips slightly parted, anticipating a kiss. He tried to reach her, but the sand began rising around his ankles, slowing his final steps. She smiled lovingly at him and started to speak, but no words came. From behind Michael's left ear came the loud, deafening crash of metal on metal. He twisted in the sand, which was now rising toward his knees, greeted by a low howl from Coyote, seated on the shoulder of a dune in the distance. The plaintive wail merged together with the high-pitched scream of sirens quickly approaching from behind. Bright light poured down from the gray sky. He instinctively shielded his eyes with the width of his hand and twisted back toward Lori as the sand swallowed him to his waist, but she was gone. In her place now stood Big Fly, as three figures emerged from the shadows. The sirens encompassed him; he threw his hands to his ears until the sounds fell silent.

Michael's eyes shot wide open and he stared at the white ceiling above him. He knew the rest of the dream and didn't ever again need to see the ambulance or mangled car images in his mind, didn't ever again need to feel the sand swallowing him whole. It had awoken him often over the last few months, wracking him with guilt. She should never have been there in the first place, if it hadn't been for him. He moved his hands up to rub his forehead, rolling over on the pillow, trying to fall back to sleep.

He lay there for a while before saying out loud to the bedroom walls "I'm fricking sick; maybe I really do need a shrink." He rose to his feet, continuing to mumble to himself and hating the mornings ever so much more. He was really beginning to wonder if he'd ever shake the terror of her death, to have a morning where this miserable past was indeed the past, headed for the shower.

After dressing, an ice-cold rinse of toothpaste from his mouth reminded him of the cavity he had long neglected. He cringed from the sharp pain the cold, clear water caused in the exposed root and he instantly hated the iciness. His hand shot up to soothe the pain with a rub to his jaw, complaining aloud to his mirrored image, "Well, isn't this just a special morning anyway. Probably no damned coffee or donuts, either!" His stomach growling, he knew he needed something fast.

He combed his hair and headed out, thrusting the door open, instantly thinking sunglasses as he slammed his eyes shut, the bright morning sunlight of a Colorado day etching white dots on his eyelids. Again he cursed the morning, and for good measure, his tooth, the water and anything else he could think of. He slowly let in bits of sunlight through his lids, his eyes still refusing to adjust. Clearly his head wasn't the only thing with a hangover.

He managed to finally open his eyes fully and started to take a step to the left when he stopped dead in his tracks. Cop cars were everywhere. An ambulance, with its lights still flashing, blocked the Main Street entrance to the motel. Across the parking lot, near his house, Kevin was talking to a guy in a dark suit and tie. A detective, obviously. They always seemed to look the same.

Michael moved toward them wondering what could be going on. The commotion seemed to be focused around the front of the motel. He looked around and spotted a squad car with what clearly appeared to be an arrestee in the back seat. Michael took a few steps toward the car, trying to get a better look. The obviously younger man had his shoulders pulled back in an awkward manner, his hands clearly forced and restrained behind him, but he sat strangely calm and motionless. His focus fixed straight ahead, almost as if spellbound. Michael couldn't see his face completely, it lay hidden behind his long scruffy hair, but he thought he recognized him as the young Navajo he'd seen in the office in conversation with Luigi the day before. His attention was finally drawn to the glass office, noticing several people emerging from the private quarters and heading toward the office's front door. "Oh, no! Luigi, shit, Luigi . . ." and he detoured in the direction of the side door to the living quarters, only to be met by a gurney wheeling out. What the hell is going on, his mind raced. He detoured again, glancing again at the kid bypassing with purpose to where Kevin stood motionless and now alone. His friend took notice and came towards him, shock in his eyes.

"Kev, what's going on?"

"Luigi's dead" he said with disbelief in his voice.

"What?" Michael turned the astonishing news over in his mind for a moment, without any result. "How? What happened?"

"Someone shot him. They think one of the Navajo students here, Benjamin Yazzie, did it, he's over in the car there" with a motion toward the young man and squad car. They think Luigi must have found him robbing the register. Some money's missing. They say he was about to run when they found him hiding upstairs in his room. A hundred forty-seven dollars. That's all there was."

"What makes them think it's this kid?"

"I saw him coming out of Luigi's back door early this morning, on my way over to do some things in the shed. It was strange, so I went over to check on Luigi and that's when I found him on the sofa. I called the police and when they got here I told them, and that's when they went and found him up there hiding, the bastard."

"Oh, Kevin. Man, this is terrible." Michael rubbed his forehead.

The detective now approached them, asking Kevin for a few more details, his notepad and pen in hand. Michael couldn't believe what was happening. Was he back in Los Angeles? This was Durango, Colorado, small town USA. Murders weren't commonplace. Let alone one like this. And he must have slept right through the entire thing only two doors down. What the hell was going on? He'd seen Luigi only the day before, for the first time in years, and now he was dead, and by a Navajo's hand at that. It was unbelievable.

Michael watched as the ambulance slowly pulled from the parking lot. Sadly, Luigi Morrealli was in no hurry. No more war stories, no more letters to politicians, no more nothing. Death was a final event and all too soon was revisiting Michael.

An officer got into the occupied squad car and pulled away equally slowly, certainly en route to the La Plata County lock-up. From the living quarters appeared the photographer and the medical examiner with their bags of forensic tools. Their job done, they left to pursue their clues, professional detachment on their blank faces.

"Michael, this is Detective Snow. He's handling the investigation" as the plain-clothed policeman turned his attention to Michael.

"Nice to meet you," Michael mumbled, extending his hand.

Snow greeted him with a firm handshake. A level, unsmiling gaze instinctively sizing up the person he was meeting, a hazard of the occupation that Michael knew came with the territory. As their hands parted he assumed an erect posture, crossing his arms and with a detached professional demeanor he began with "I regret the unfortunate circumstances, but I'd like to ask you a couple of questions, if that's OK."

"Sure, I understand, but I don't think I can be of much help."

"I just need to cover some minor details. You and Mr. Daniels arrived home last night around nine p.m., right?"

"Right."

"What did you do after that?"

"Oh, I fumbled around a little. Watched some TV and went to bed," he said and for some strange reason hoping he looked innocent. He wasn't, however, about to volunteer that he'd walked in, sort of, turned on the light and fell face-first into the bed and quickly passed out. Unless, of course, it became necessary. Some things were better left unsaid he thought.

"Did you hear anything out of the ordinary last night or this morning?"

"No, I didn't. I slept pretty soundly, though. The sirens must have woken me up, but I don't recall hearing anything other than that."

"No gunshot?"

"No, no gunshot. Definitely not. I gotta believe I'd have heard something like that."

"Maybe, maybe not, Mr. Kincaid. But it is strange. Apparently no one heard anything."

Spoken with the inherent suspicion of a detective, Michael thought. He replied, "Yes, detective, that is strange, very strange indeed. No one heard a shot?" And Michael turned the tables a bit to see what information he could get.

"No. No one we've interviewed as of yet. I suppose it's really not that odd though, the walls would have kept the sound in and what with the effect of Main Street traffic noise, well . . . but, of course, the investigation is continuing."

Strange indeed, Michael thought. "So robbery's the suspected motive, then?" the attorney in him inquired.

"From everything we've looked at, it seems like robbery-homicide. Pretty simple, actually. Looks like it's open and shut."

Open & Shut. The words echoed in Michael's mind. He found himself instantly defensive for no apparent reason. He hated that trite little saying, having learned long ago that nothing was ever that clear-cut. No matter what the situation or case, nothing ever seemed to work out that simply. Something always seemed to be strange; something was always out of place. Open & Shut, indeed.

"You seem pretty sure detective."

"Well, if you look at the evidence we've already got, it seems the logical conclusion. We found a bloody thumbprint on the handle of the side door. Since Mr. Daniels saw the suspect coming out that door, I'll bet Yazzie's prints match. We also found some blood in the suspect's room. We'll type it, but I'd bet it'll match the decedent's."

Kevin winced noticeably.

"I'm sorry, Mr. Daniels," Snow meekly offered, to a kind nod from Kevin, before turning back to Michael. "Besides, faced with the mounting physical evidence, I have a feeling this one will confess. That would make it open and shut."

"Maybe so . . . but" holding on to the end of the statement. Could things really be that simple? A friend, killed by a Navajo student, in a town where the last murder was over a decade ago. And no one heard a thing?

The detective looked at him queerly when he didn't receive the response he'd expected. He nodded his head, removing himself from the conversation with a polite "Thank you both for your assistance. I'll be back in touch, if necessary. Call me at this number if you remember anything else." He passed Kevin a card as he left. He had more important things to do than listen to some drivel that might create additional work. He'd have a signed confession before the end of the day and he was sure of it. He quickly took his leave of the scene, headed for his unmarked detective's car.

"Maybe so. Open & Shut," Michael mumbled to himself. The instincts of a defense attorney opening the door to doubt, whether real or imagined.

"I gotta go, Michael," his old friend told him in a defeated tone. "I've got too many things to do right now. Calls and arrangements have to be made. I'm going to have to call his son and tell him." Tears welled up in Kevin's eyes and began a slow trickle down his cheek. The reality of the last couple of hours finally took hold. Michael placed a reassuring hand on Kevin's shoulder.

"I'll take care of Luigi's place if you want."

"That would be a big help Michael. I'm not sure I've got the stomach to go back in there right now." With these words, a great burden seemed to lift from his friend's shoulders. Michael knew that having to deal with the site of the homicide would be too much. Besides, the attorney in him needed to satisfy some now nagging professional curiosities anyway. Kevin nodded and, stunned from the events of the still early morning, pulled away aimlessly carrying his grief.

Michael returned to his room, Open & Shut continuing to echo through his brain. He might not like the saying, but an arrest that quickly at the murder scene usually meant one thing, guilt. He sat quietly, staring at the room's blank television, wondering why such crazy things happened. After a few more moments of pondering, he decided that if nothing else, he needed to at least call Joseph. The defense attorney in him knew the young Navajo man would need someone to help him and Joseph might know whom to contact. Michael dialed the doctor's answering service from memory, knowing it would be the easiest way to reach him, they always knew where he was. He told the girl at the other end that it was an emergency and asked that Joseph telephone him immediately.

Within a few minutes his flip phone rang and Joseph was on the other end. Michael told him what he knew and Joseph said he would get in touch with Benjamin's mother. Joseph said he just couldn't believe the young student could commit such a heinous act. He'd known him for years and had been mentoring him with his schooling, as he wanted to be a doctor like his cousin. He had shared the sweat lodge with him many times and his grandfather had also been teaching him the old shaman ways. He said Benjamin was truly following in the traditional Blessing Way, the *hozhooji*, awakened to the natural order, making constructive choices and healing from intentions and decisions that become destructive. He was doing well in pre-med, Joseph really couldn't accept the way the police had it; surely there was another explanation? Stranger things had happened Michael replied. But in any event, the police would get to the bottom of it Joseph concluded. Wouldn't they?

Michael sat on the sofa trying to make sense of it all, but he simply couldn't. Murder generally didn't. It might have a motive and a reason, but the taking of another's life could never make sense, at least not for Michael for he too was taught of the Blessing Way by Joseph's grandfather. But it wasn't his affair, was it? He needed no more cases or causes, only time to heal. Luigi's killer had been caught red-handed. Hopefully he'd just confess and it would be all over.

His thoughts turned to the previous day and his conversation with Luigi. He could see his flowing gray hair and the smoke rings springing from his beard. Michael hadn't known him well, just in passing over the years. But he knew him well enough to know him as a kind, gentle man who didn't deserve to die this way. He vowed to see Benjamin, or whoever did this, punished.

He stood knowing he had a miserable task before him that he just wanted to finish in the living quarters. Delaying the inevitable, he went to the phone book, looked up the number and dialed.

"Durango Police Department, non-emergency. May I help you?"

"Detective Snow, please."

"One moment, please."

In a few seconds, another voice answered. "Snow"

"Detective Snow, Michael Kincaid here. We met this morning."

"Of course, Mr. Kincaid. I certainly hadn't expected to hear from you so quickly. What can I do for you?"

"Well, I was wondering if you're done with the crime scene. Police tape tends to have a negative impact on a business, not to mention blood. I'd like to clean up a little, if that's OK with you."

"Fine with me; we're all done. We have photos and video of everything and the crime techs are finished."

"Thanks. By the way, can I drop in and see you?"

"If you wish."

"Probably tomorrow. I'm sure you have your hands full today."

"Definitely, quite full. You seemed a little puzzled this morning. Feel free to come in and ask any questions you may have. I just want justice for Mr. Morrealli."

"Thanks. I guess it's the lawyer in me."

"That's OK, Mr. Kincaid, I won't hold it against you."

"Please, detective, call me Michael. And I appreciate that."

"See you tomorrow, then."

"Thanks again."

Michael hung up the phone and went out toward the office. After a few steps, long strands of yellow crime scene tape intercepted his path. An ominous sign that something very wrong had occurred at this place. He pulled down the closest end and gathered the tape up into a bunch as he made his way toward the front office door.

Walking through the entrance, his eyes instinctively searched for anything out of place. Quite a task, since he'd only been in the quarters twice, once tipsy and once hung-over. Everything seemed to be as he remembered it, but he was still a little foggy and desperately needed some coffee for the task that waited.

He turned to the coffee pot in the reception area and found the filters and coffee inside a side table's cabinet door. Quickly he had a new batch loaded. He grabbed the pot and was headed for Luigi's kitchen when he noticed a water cooler in the corner, slid in next to the tourist brochures. He shook his head with a slight chuckle for a second, went over and filled the pot with gratitude for the more easily accessible water. He returned to pour it into the coffee maker. Immediate caffeine would be required to restart his senses this morning and he watched patiently for an indication that the old machine was working. With the first gurgles, he knew help was on the way. He'd wait out the brewing time with a look around the office before tackling the living room.

He made a quick survey of the front room, but again, at first glance, nothing seemed out of place. But something was always out of place and Michael knew it. You just had to learn to recognize it. In his years with the coroner, the DA's office and in the practice of law, there was one constant in every crime scene: something was always out of place. No one could truly commit the perfect crime. Generally it was just a small clue, not necessarily the big obvious ones that television would have one believe would break down a case. Sometimes it wasn't even physical. But where?

Posters for local tourist attractions lined the walls. A small ice machine sat on the Main Street side, the three outer walls being knee-high panel jobs with big windows extending the rest of the way up to the ceiling. The floor was lined with several small plants and low stands, haphazardly arranged, leaving a wide-open view of Main Street and the parking lot.

He pulled a Styrofoam cup from the stack on the edge of the cabinet and the pot from its hotplate and poured the cup full. Gazing around the room he still found nothing. He really hadn't expected to though. Nobody with any sense would hold somebody at gunpoint in a three-quarters-glass enclosure right on Main Street. He paused. That is, unless of course it was robbery gone wrong, as Snow had suggested. But for Michael, that just didn't add up for some reason. He thought back to the morning before. Neither Yazzie nor Luigi had seemed really at odds at the time. No loud or harsh words between the two and Luigi had never mentioned Yazzie during their conversation.

He stood in back of the front desk, where he'd seen Luigi standing the morning before, talking to his now alleged Navajo slayer. For the first time, Michael noticed the overturned wooden cash drawer. It had obviously been knocked from its place on the middle shelf, where the proper sized space now sat empty. Only in Durango would someone leave cash just sitting out, and a man who dealt with safes at that.

Assuming Snow's version of the facts, with robbery as the motive, the perpetrator would have had to either enter through the living quarters' side door or have forced Luigi from the front to the rear. Either was possible, given Luigi's propensity for leaving his door unlocked. Other than the money taken from the overturned cash drawer, nothing associated with the body of the crime seemed to have occurred in the front room. Since no blood trail led from the front, both the killer and victim would have been back in the living quarters at the time of the actual act. He felt relatively sure of that.

His coffee in hand, Michael stepped through the door, pushing the curtain aside, into the living room. To his immediate left was an old brown office desk, strewn with papers spilling onto the floor. Another grey metal cash box, containing only change, sat open among the papers. A telephone, fax machine and message pad sat on a corner of the desk, against the wall. A skim through the messages didn't yield much. Only one message had been left for Benjamin Yazzie within the last month, and that was two days ago, but Michael couldn't make out the scribbled name and "home". Maybe the kid had problems with money at home; that might make sense. Nothing much else seemed interesting or related. In the corner of the desk under the lamp he found a gold pocket watch. He examined it carefully before returning it to its spot.

He turned and glanced back across the room and his eyes fixed squarely on the sofa where he'd sat the day before as they talked. It was apparently where Luigi sat during the last seconds of his life. A crimson stain curved out and down the sofa's corner, gathering into a small pool on the corner of the cushion. He took the couple of steps over and carefully slid the cushion out, expecting—but not finding—a larger pool.

He looked carefully at the top of the bloodstain and the hole marking the bullet's flight. Michael snatched a pen from the desk and stuck it gingerly into the hole, watching it protrude at about a forty-five degree angle from the floor aiming straight toward the side door. The assailant would have had to be standing above and in front of a seated Luigi when he stole his life. He noted that the sofa had been moved slightly away from the wall. Stepping over and leaning in, he found a gouged-out hole in the wall. The criminalist obviously had been unconcerned with having to patch the hole from where he had dug out the slug for ballistics. Michael pulled back from the couch and adjusted his angle of the shot. On the coffee table, he noticed, the donuts still sat from the day before. An empty cereal bowl sat next to the box. In front of Luigi's chair lay his house slippers, never to be used again.

In general, the room seemed a bit messy. Not a ransacked mess, but the controlled mess of having been lived in. A dining table sat on an imaginary dividing line between Luigi's living room and the kitchen-dining area against the Main Street wall. On the table sat a computer. Michael was immediately drawn to it.

Upon inspection, he found it wasn't a computer at all but rather a simple old Brother word processor. What he didn't find troubled him. No disks anywhere. That was definitely out of place, but probably easily explainable, what with the police having already been through here. Still.

"Michael, you're sick man, I tell you, sick," he spoke to himself again. "Here you are looking for some mysterious clues when they probably already have a signed confession." He paused momentarily before issuing further advice to himself. "You've got to get out of this business. It's beginning to affect you." Ignoring his own advice, his instincts pressed on with the duty at hand.

He moved around the table into the kitchen side of the room. Dishes were stacked high in double sink. The faucet dripped steadily. On the window above the sink, the yellowed curtains were pulled back. Although the window was big enough to crawl through, the screen was still on and the glass wasn't broken. So that was unlikely to have been used as an entrance or exit. Through the open window he saw a walk-through area and a large wooden fence that separated the motel from the KFC next door.

He pulled open the refrigerator, against the wall adjacent to the bedroom. Here, he discovered a cache of leftovers in various stages of decay. Once again, messy, but nothing out of place.

He next went to the bedroom. It was furnished with a double bed, unmade; a nightstand with a light; and a chest of drawers. Clothes were scattered throughout the room in piles. Luigi, it appeared, had been getting ready to do laundry. He opened the drawers of the chest, which revealed only a couple of pieces of clothing in each of the various sections. Luigi must not have overly enjoyed doing laundry, though, based upon the piles on the floor and the almost empty drawers. The many unused hangers in the mostly empty closet seemed to confirm this idea.

Michael thought of the chore to be reckoned with. Laundering and boxing this mess was going to take hours. He headed from the bedroom and once again caught sight of the sofa.

"That's got to go first."

He made his way outside through the side exit and down to his own room's door, noting it to be a total of nine steps. He had either been very drunk or very sleepy not to have heard a gunshot, especially with an open window and a fence to carry the sound right to his room. That drinking-at-elevation BS really must be true, he thought.

He noticed Kevin's Jeep was still parked outside and walked on over to the house. The front door was open and Kevin was sitting on the couch, a beer in one hand, a cigarette in the other, staring distantly off toward another place.

"Hey."

Kevin nearly jumped off the sofa, tension easing to recognition as he took note of his visitor.

"Sorry, Kev. Didn't mean to startle you."

"I'm just a little unnerved right now. It's OK, Mikey boy. Come on in."

Mikey?? Nobody called him Mikey.

"Kevin, you OK?"

"I guess. I found him, you know."

"Yeah, that's what you said."

"The blood was everywhere. I went over to see if he was breathing. I touched him, but he was already gone." Kevin looked up sadly. "I've never seen a dead body before. I mean, like that."

"I know, Kev, it's pretty shocking the first time. Especially with a friend."

"I just can't believe that Benjamin could shoot him."

"Its hard for me to believe also."

"Luigi never hurt a fly. Stayed in there and watched the tube or wrote his letters. Never bothered anybody. Did you know he was with me from the beginning, Michael? Couldn't pay him what he was worth, but he didn't care. 'I'm retired,' he'd always say."

Kevin took a drag and a drink.

"Kevin, is there anything I can do?"

"No, not really. I called his son earlier. He's going to make some arrangements and call me back. I gave him Detective Snow's name and number to call if he wanted to. Not much else to do. I'm just going to sit here and hoist a few to him and wait for Frank to call back. Care to join me?"

"Maybe later. I thought maybe I'd start taking care of cleaning up the living quarters, if you want me to."

"Yeah, sure. I'll get up and help you."

"No, Kevin, I'll do it. You've had enough for today. Sit here and get shit-faced if you want. I'll handle this. Have you got a dolly and a couple of boxes?"

"Yeah, out in the shed," and he was handing him a key from his pocket. "Why?" and his tone changed, slightly.

"I'm going to move a few things in there."

"I appreciate it, Michael, but it's not your problem. I know you were planning on heading to your Mom's tomorrow. I can handle it."

"Plans change. I don't have to be anywhere tomorrow or the next day. I can stick around for another couple of days and give you a hand. You can probably use the help, Kev. Believe me, Mom'll understand."

"Thanks, bud. Everything's in the shed. I'll come over a little later."

"No need. Why don't you just stay here awhile and then I'll come back over for a brew when I finish."

"Sure . . ."

Michael withdrew as Kevin took another sip from his solace. He knew the many complications associated with anyone's death. Let alone a good friend. And he knew that people reacted differently to death. He'd learned that with the passing of his own father and then, too recently, with Lori. But dealing with death was innate to the human spirit and each person had his or her own method by which to cope. Kevin would have to find his way on his own.

He'd go and clean up the living quarters himself. It would be easier for him than for his friend. But Michael also had an agenda. Aside from sparing his friend more grief and the fact that it needed doing, Michael wanted to know why several things he'd seen didn't make sense. Nothing major really, but worth a closer look. Besides, he really didn't have any place to be any more.

* * *

The intercom buzzed at Tielson's desk and he quickly reached his stumpy hand for the receiver, answering with a grunt.

"Sir. Good news. Our people reported in while you were gone. I asked them why they hadn't phoned earlier, but they said they have been unable to establish a secure line and thus the delay in reporting. I suggested that they buy a drop phone and use that to report in. You should be hearing from them within the hour."

"Very good thinking. Were they successful?"

"They didn't say, sir. As I said, they were not calling from a secure line and were reluctant to discuss matters with me."

"That's good. It sounds as if they're at least trying to act according to protocol. I think things are working out. I knew these two could be counted on. Direct their call to me as soon as it comes in. That'll be all." He hung up.

Tielson leaned back in his chair, a crooked smile developing upon his pocked face for the first time in days. He'd chosen wisely and his people were following instructions. The thought comforted him. He was sure that they'd find it. Perhaps, in a few hours, he could finally report positive news to the Old Man.

* * *

Before going back to the office, Michael stopped by his room and telephoned his mom to tell her he was going to stick around Durango for a few days. After speaking with her for several minutes, he hung up and noticed the light on the phone, alerting him to a new message on the in-room voicemail system. It took him a few minutes to figure out how to retrieve the message, but quickly returned the call from Joseph. He had asked that Michael call him at his mother's house. Joseph answered on the second ring.

"Hello."

"Joseph. Michael."

"Hey. Thanks for calling back so quick. Grandfather happened down from Fourth Mesa. He said he felt something was wrong. I told him about what happened there and he wishes to speak to you. Let me get him."

There was a momentary pause before Michael heard the phone being picked up.

"Hello, my young friend," the voice announced.

"Hello," Michael answered.

"This sad news of my friend brings me great heartache, very hard for me to understand . . ." and the old man's voice trailed off sadly.

"Yes, murder is very hard for anyone to understand." Michael was a bit puzzled.

"I know the young man they have accused, along with his family. He is a student of mine in the Navajo ways. I spoke to him only the other day. They are good people and he has been raised right in the Navajo and Blessing Ways. I spoke with them and told them I would look into this thing, but I am only an old man in need of help. You are skilled in these matters, my friend. I would ask you for a favor. To look into this for me and tell me what I should tell our Bear Clan cousins. They are very concerned at this news. If you find that Benjamin did this thing, then I will accept that. If you do not, I would ask for your help."

"I do not know if there is anything I can do. The police believe they have their man and they seem to have the evidence, but I will give it a look as you wish."

"Thank you. I will return to my lodge today to begin the prayers, but I would ask that you come speak of this thing with me and our Bear Clan cousins as soon as you can."

"I will try to talk to the detective and to Benjamin; then I will come to see you."

"Thank you again, my friend. I do not believe this young man could so easily violate the spirit of another man's life."

"Maybe, maybe not. We'll have to see."

"Yes, we will."

Michael hung up, thinking great, just what I didn't want, a case. But for Hosteen Begay, and Luigi, he would look into it.

Soon Michael had been to the shed and returned with three boxes and a large appliance dolly. He tossed the boxes into Luigi's former bedroom. He removed the cushions from the sofa and lifted it up on end, placing the dolly under the armrest. He moved the sofa and dolly, leaving them standing near the door. He quickly compared the door and sofa, pleased that it would easily pass through.

He returned to where the sofa had sat, looking closely at the mess now exposed on the floor. It hadn't been moved in quite a while based upon the amount of accumulated dust. Michael knelt down to more carefully examine the vacated space. The bullet hole was the obvious object out of place. Below the hole, on the carpeting, Michael found paint, drywall and wood chippings, remnants of the wall that had earlier held the slug.

He continued his search finding the usual lint balls, coins, paper clips and scraps of paper. He'd missed it at first and had actually walked away before he sensed something that didn't belong. His instincts were still a little dulled, but returning, at least. He looked back, scanning the area, finally eyeing and focusing on what only his subconscious had initially seen. He walked over and knelt down to observe. It was a small piece of silvery, pliable metal. He looked very carefully at it before scooping it up with a small piece of paper. His hand trembled. The combination of an empty stomach and caffeine had created an impossible situation for an adequate examination.

He took it to the desk and set it down, going to the kitchen to retrieve a Baggie before returning to the scrap. He turned on the desk light for a better view. Just what he thought, and probably not where it should have been. He slid it into the Baggie, remembering the silver wrapping that his father had routinely pulled off his insulin bottle before his daily injections.

He played with it gingerly through the outside of the bag, careful not to break it, but assuring himself of what he'd found. He studied it for an extended time, running the possibilities. He looked back at the sofa again and eventually came to the same conclusion he'd reached when he first saw it. He shoved the Baggie into his pocket. He suspected he'd be needing it for Benjamin Yazzie's trial.

* * *

Anderson answered the secure line on the second ring with a simple "Yes?"

"This is Tompkins."

"It's about time you called back. Are you on a secure line?"

"It's secure."

"Good. What do you have to report?"

"I'm required to report direct only," he stated without emotion.

Anderson was a little taken aback with Tompkins attitude. And what could be so hush-hush in a simple surveillance op that he would be required to report the information direct? And where were these guys anyway? Something was fishy here and he felt the hair stand up on his back, wondering what the little man was really up to and capable of. "I'll put you through."

He punched the "hold" button and connected to Tielson. "I have

Tompkins on the line. Shall I patch him through?"

"Yes, damn it!!" came a grunt, without hint of civility.

Anderson didn't liking the brusque tones of the two men or about being kept in the dark by both when his butt was right in the middle. Fortunately for him, and his expanding concern for self-protection and curiosity, transferring the call on the antiquated, federally issued system allowed him to stay on the line without anyone knowing. He listened silently and heard Tielson pick up on the other end.

"Do you have it?"

"Not yet, but we believe we know where it is."

"Then why don't you have it?" the little man insisted.

"We weren't able to put our hands on it, but . . ."

"Wait a minute." The squat figure sat up in his chair. "Did everything go according to plan?" Tielson asked.

"Not exactly as you had outlined."

"What do you mean?" he demanded, his voice lowering to a growl as he started to rise from the chair.

"We found your man as instructed. He said our information was wrong and he didn't know what we were talking about. Of course, we did not believe him, so we spoke with him at length and were very persuasive. He never admitted to having it, but I certainly believe he does."

"I wouldn't expect he would lightly admit to it. I assume you are continuing with the interrogation?"

"Well, sir, not exactly. We had a slight problem as we were concluding the interview."

"What problem?"

"There must have been an interaction with the drug. He apparently had a heart attack."

"What?"

"Yes, sir. And then we were interrupted."

"Interrupted? You left a witness?"

"We don't believe so, but we may be forced to secure our presence with prejudice."

Anderson's mouth fell wide open. He had to swallow a gasp, lodging as a lump somewhere in his throat.

"Wait. You're telling me someone may have seen you? Oh, that's just perfect. I told you to be discreet and you leave a witness. Wonderful. Just how do you propose to solve this problem?"

"Rest assured, we don't believe anyone saw us, and it's pretty much solving itself. Just not in the way you had anticipated. We might need a little nudge in the right direction from other associates, but I'm sure we can make it all go away with some attention."

"What about the package?"

"We were unable to complete a full search, but we believe there's a good chance it's there. We'll know within twenty-four hours. There are a few other details you need to know to advise us how you want to further proceed."

"And what does that mean?"

"It means we may need some help. I'm not sure at this point exactly what; I'll need some further details first. This was really out of our control, but it looks like everything will work out just as you wanted."

"Everything except you didn't complete the job?"

"No, but we'll have another opportunity. We've already gathered the information we need. As I said, we just happened to be interrupted before we completed our task."

"And just how do you expect to get another opportunity."

"I have ways. Leave it to me. Give me a few hours to flesh out some additional details. Let me assure you, we have always managed to complete our assignments in the past. This is no different. It'll just require some additional efforts and some mild assistance from your end." The man's voice grew cool and this comforted the little man in a strange way.

"All right. Do what you think best. It seems I have no other choice at this time. I need these loose ends tied up immediately. Do you understand?"

"I do. I'll have a memo faxed to you according to protocol in the next couple of hours. Then you can decide how you want to continue. We'll clean up the other details from here."

Anderson listened as both lines went dead. At least now he knew the problem was being caused by something very tangible, and apparently worth killing for. As he lightly hung up the phone, he wondered what the little bastard had gotten him into.

* * *

Michael had been at it for hours and had gotten most of the mess cleaned up, but he still had other things to do. He certainly wasn't finished yet, but getting the sofa into the shed was a major step forward. He headed back to Luigi's, noting with relief that Kevin's Jeep was still there.

Back inside, he looked around the room with. What's next?

In the kitchen he grabbed the trashcan and made a cursory inspection of its contents, just to make sure nothing important had been foolishly discarded. Nothing had, as expected.

He moved on to the refrigerator, throwing out anything that was a leftover or remotely on its way to spoilage. The rest he put back in. Next, he tackled the dishes and kitchen, spending an hour or so meticulously cleaning the room. He wiped down the counters from fingerprint dust, and before stacking the dishes in the cupboards, he looked through them all. Mentally he'd taken an inventory on each one's contents and their arrangement, filing it away in his mind for later use, a technique he'd refined and mastered over the years.

Michael, not always the hardest-working student, had taught himself a great memory tool in law school for use when he needed it, which was often. Over time he'd developed the ability to take a photograph in his mind and later recall every detail. In turn he could use the information as needed. It had come in very handy when he'd have to cram for finals and, in future years, in his practice. He could now use it freely on demand. He could actually visualize a forty-page motion, in mid-argument, and extract the name and date of any case cited, as needed. Quite helpful, really. Since he didn't know what he was looking for, he had hopes that something later would trigger a recollection of something he'd see now. But what?

The cupboards contained the usual fare. A couple had spots for food, spices and other supplies. Three more held pots, pans and dishes. One was full of assorted souvenirs, pictures and memorabilia. Michael neatly packed away anything personal, using some of the clothes strewn on the living room floor as packing material. He'd then place the box in a corner, out of the way, labeled it and registered it in his mind, then went on to another. Methodically, following this system, he cleaned the home and inspected the clothes pile, noting they smelled fresh, not used.

Under the sink were cleaning supplies. A row of four drawers to the right of the sink yielded nothing. The first and second drawers were half the depth of the third and fourth. The first contained silverware, the second, utensils. The third was a bit difficult to pull open, probably warped over the years, and stuffed with miscellaneous dishtowels and washrags. Kevin would need to plane it down for the next tenant and he made a mental note to mention it someday when the time was right. The fourth had nothing but more utensils, but was at least a little easier to pull open. Nothing unusual.

The bedroom yielded even less. He stripped the bed and then made it up with some clean sheets he'd found in the motel's maids' storeroom. Next, he packed up and inspected the remaining clothes from the living room, bedroom and closet, leaving one dark suit alone in the closet. Luigi would have need for it one last time, on his final journey home.

He packed up the scant few other belongings in the closet: shoes, ties and belts, and packed each item away, careful to be sure nothing was secreted inside a pocket or anything obvious like that. Then he wiped off the nightstand and lamp, noting the heavy dust accumulation on the bottom of the wet rag.

Before he did the finishing cleaning and inspection, he'd take the rest of the night off and sleep on it. Perhaps after a night of rest and reflection, his subconscious would point something out. He left the murder scene and walked over to check on Kevin. The door was still slightly ajar and Kevin was asleep on the couch, surrounded by several empty beer cans. Michael scavenged for a blanket, and laid it over his friend. He shut off the lights and left the music playing softly. He locked the door and pulled it closed behind him.

He stood on the porch for a few minutes while his eyes adjusted to the reduced light, then found the big cushy chair he'd seen on his previous trips and sat down. It was a cool, pleasant night and the traffic on Main was slow. A near full moon lit the Needles to the northeast. The last vestiges of winter snow caused the mountains almost to glow.

Michael shut his eyes for a moment and began to run things over in his mind, the cushy chair absorbing him. The scrap he'd found, the bullet angle, lack of blood on the sofa, the dust and disorganization. He mumbled to himself, "Where is it?" before drifting off.

* * *

Tielson leaned back in his chair, the faxed debriefing still clutched in his hand. He rested uncomfortably in his chair hoping the plan would finally put this to rest before it got further out of hand. They would be monitoring the situation and completing their task by night's end. There would likely be a few loose ends to clean up on his end, but Tielson was well prepared to handle that. He shut his eyes again, waiting for the hours to pass until morning.

* * *

He could see her in the distance. She sat picturesquely astride the horse atop a sandy dune, her hair flowing around her and blending into the palomino's mane. He yelled for her to wait and immediately started running across the sand toward her. His legs labored and muscles throbbed with each step through the deep sand, desperately trying to reach her. Stumbling now, he watched as Coyote crept low and slow to her side, his tail tucked between his legs. In another moment Kokopelli joined from behind the sandy hill, lifting his instrument and beginning to play a slow mournful tune. Lori waved and the palomino turned to follow the hump-backed flutist's song back over the dune as Coyote skipped with glee, his tail finally wagging, following well to the rear.

Michael screamed for her to wait and pressed harder, but again the sand weighed him down and he lost ground. He finally collapsed to his hands and knees, his heart pounding, sweat dripping down his body as Lori disappeared slowly over the dune with the instrumentalist and the still-dancing trickster. Michael's head bowed and tears began to flow, the music growing fainter, now well beyond the dune.

Something startled him. Touching his shoulder. Turning his head he saw Big Fly perched there with a smile. Tears continued to stream down Michael's face. Suddenly Big Fly jumped into the air and darted into a hover above the piñon and juniper forest at light's edge. Beyond him grew a faint light, increasing in intensity with every passing moment. In the distance Kokopelli played louder and quicker from behind the hill, as Coyote returned hesitantly, lurking, his tail again tucked, an evil look in his eye and clearly up to no good again.

* * *

Michael slowly opened his eyes. He was drenched in sweat and held his hands to his face trying to ground himself back to reality, shaking off another bizarre dream of her, his mind wondering why Coyote was becoming more involved. He rubbed his arms and legs to generate heat and feeling against a touch of cold in the air. His left leg protested, still asleep, not wishing to join the rest of his now semi-awakened body.

He looked around, wondering what time it was and how long he'd been asleep. There were no cars on Main and everything was pleasantly quiet. A virtual "no creature was stirring" kind of eve. His attention was drawn to a noise from the motel.

He still couldn't move his napping leg so he was stuck to his vantage point. He watched, rubbing his leg as it began to tingle toward alertness. The man partially emerging from the shadows near the motel office seemed out of place, particularly when he hesitated for a couple of seconds to look around. He was white, about six feet, dressed all in black and difficult to see.

Michael couldn't quite make out the face, but even in the dim light the man looked like what his sleepy brain remembered of Detective Snow. He wanted to get up and go talk with him, but the leg wouldn't cooperate and he was forced to plunk back into the seat. Snow walked the length of the dimly lit motel toward a car near the end of the parking lot by the alley. He went to the driver's side, looking around before sliding into the standard Government Issue, the requisite multiple antennae protruding from the trunk. It was similar to the one he'd seen him driving yesterday. Michael leaned forward in his chair as the car backed from the parking spot.

After a few moments of reflection, Michael wondered what Snow was doing here this late at night. Or was it late at night? How long had he been asleep? He rose again, his leg now somewhat cooperative, and limped toward the end of the porch. The detective's car pulled quietly out of the motel's rear exit-way, pausing momentarily at the edge of the alley. A second individual appeared from the shadows and got in the passenger side. The unmarked car turned left and then disappeared into the alley behind the motel's large maintenance shed.

Michael slowly made his way back to his room and was surprised to find the clock on the kitchenette's wall reading 5:07. Snow must be an early riser, he thought. Or maybe some doubt was creeping into the detective's open and shut case. He'd have had time to question the suspect by now; maybe Yazzie said something Snow didn't like. Something had made Snow check Luigi's place; wonder what? No worries, he could ask him later. But from somewhere, the little voice was back, echoing Lewis Carroll's Alice, saying "Curiouser and Curiouser." He climbed into bed for a couple more hours of sleep, thinking that today might prove an interesting day. He had no idea just how right he would be.

DAY FIVE

A Trail Develops

Michael was abruptly awakened by the knock at the room's door. He was initially thankful for the lack of morning nightmare, but his relief quickly changed to "Who the hell's banging on my door at 6:33" anger when his eyes finally focused on the clock. His muscles were sore from his sleep in the chair and he tried to stretch out some of the kinks. A second series of persistent knocks had him grumbling and slowly moving from the bedroom toward the door, not pleased. He swung the door open with force, ready to lash out on some poor unsuspecting maid, instead finding Kevin.

"You always answer the door like that?" he asked, a quizzical look on his eyes, handing him a cup of coffee. Michael realized without embarrassment that he was standing in the doorway clad only in his underwear. He muttered, "Funny . . . ya jerk . . . come back in a coupla hours." He slammed the door shut in his startled visitor's face and staggered back toward the bedroom. Undaunted, Kevin let himself in with his passkey, calling cheerfully, octaves above his normal vocal range and carrying steaming coffee cups. "Housekeeping!"

"Go play in the street, why don't you?" came a return from the bedroom.

Kevin just laughed, remembering their days as roommates. Michael was never very good in the mornings, least of all before eight, and anybody that knew him knew that. Over the two years they'd been roommates in college, it had almost became sport waking him up.

"I've . . . got . . . coffee," came a singing call.

"What the hell do you want so early?" Michael snapped, returning a few moments later, now wearing faded jeans.

"Well, I guess I just wanted to say thanks for helping yesterday and apologize if I was kinda short. Anyway . . ." and his voice trailed off quietly, the steam wafting into the air.

Michael nodded sleepily. He made his way to the sink and filled a glass with water, slamming a big drink into his mouth. The cold liquid instantly found his neglected cavity again and pain shot through his jaw. Grimacing and growling slightly to himself, hating mornings again, he swallowed hard. After a couple of seconds of further unawakened reflection he turned, an incredulous stare fixing squarely on his friend. "Wait a minute, let me get this right," his voice grew mockingly ripe. "You woke me up at six-freakin'-thirty in the morning just to thank me and to apologize for nothing? Unbelievable. You're welcome and you're forgiven." He paused and set the glass on the counter. "Now then . . . if you don't mind, would you please leave me so I can ponder your penitence." He shuffled his feet toward the bedroom mumbling to himself before glancing back and adding, "Surely you don't plan on making a habit of this? Let me suggest you talk to a priest. He can grant you the true salvation you really need. I'm going back to bed." He circled towards the bedroom.

"Still the same old lovable guy in the morning, I see."

Michael completed a shuffling circle and reluctantly returned, not amused. "Don't you have some little old lady to overcharge or something? Why are you bothering me? Leave me alone; I want to go back to bed!!!" Again he turned for the room.

"No, you're not. We've got things to do."

"Like what?" he retorted, finishing yet another leaning circle and again returning to the unwanted conversation. Exasperated with his friend, he finally conceded to the far too early nightmare and plopped down on the couch, casting a dull stare toward the coffee still steaming in Kevin's hands.

"Like finding out who killed Luigi," Kevin said. "I just can't believe he'd kill Luigi, he sure as hell didn't need to kill him for money. If Benjamin needed something all he had to do was ask, Luigi was always lending those kids money here and there. Mostly from my till I'm might add" a slight tick of a smile developing for a moment, before he continued.

"You've been watching too much Law and Order or something? I'm a bit more skeptical, but what brought you to this enlightened conclusion so damn early in the morning?"

"I've been thinking about it all night, I couldn't sleep. First of all, he's Navajo. They're not that barbaric" Kevin announced.

"What, you never heard of war parties and scalping?"

"Sure, that's what you gotta do to get Bronco tickets."

Michael looked at him, un-amused.

"Seriously, Michael, you of all people know how they are. Sanctity of life, the Blessing Way, the stuff we learned in Southwest Studies and all that. There's very few murders on the reservation and those that are usually are about domestic violence, not robbery." Kevin paused, looking over to Michael.

Michael had no argument with this. It was what had made him wonder in the first place, too, especially after Hosteen Begay going to bat for the kid. He'd thought along the same lines in the last 24 hours, even if it was way too early for such thought. Still, reassurance by numbers and at least Michael wouldn't be the only one looking like a lunatic if this case went somewhere.

"So are you just going to stand there and hold that or what" finally relenting to the realization that he wasn't going to get any further sleep. Kevin reached over and set the coffee on the small table in front of the sofa, taking a seat at its other end.

"Well . . . I suppose you could be right, Kev," he said numbly, sipping his coffee and setting it back on the table. "Something else sure seems to be going on here. I'll admit I've got one of those funny feelings about this. But the evidence is really against the kid despite all that. I saw them kind of arguing, you saw him coming out of there this morning, the cops found blood and he certainly didn't look like he was protesting his innocence sitting in that car staring ahead." He paused and his mouth grew open wide with a yawn. He stretched the kinks from his back and shoulders. After a few moments he picked up his coffee again. "But I agree that there are a few things that just don't make much sense."

"Like what?"

"Well, let me ask you a couple of questions first. OK?" Michael was somewhat awakened, with a couple of more stretches and the caffeine now slowly entering his bloodstream.

"Sure."

"Was Luigi a diabetic or something?"

"No, or at least not that I knew, and I think I would have known that. Why?"

"Well, did he go to the doctor a lot, inject insulin or drugs of any type, stuff like that?"

"No, not that I'm aware of. I mean, he was an old man, Michael. Sure, he went to the doctor, but I know for a fact he didn't inject any type of drugs. What are you implying?" Kevin's voice carried a tinge of concern.

"Nothing, really, and I didn't think so anyway. What about friends or visitors? Ever see any?"

"Sure. Lots of people would drop by and see him. Mainly people who'd stayed here before as monthlies. A few others."

"Anybody out of the ordinary?"

"No, not anybody that I can really remember."

"Think about it for a while, Kevin, it might be important. Ask his friends if they saw anyone 'odd' around here the last couple of weeks."

"Shit, Michael, this is a motel. We get 'odd' people in here all the time," he said with a chuckle. "I'd be out of business if it wasn't for strangers and oddballs."

"Yeah, probably so. It's a needle in a haystack, that's for sure, but I'd still like to know if somebody out of his past or an old customer or someone popped up in the last couple of weeks."

"Well . . . he did go somewhere last week. Got back a day or two before you got here."

"Well, that's a start. Any idea where he went and for what?"

"Jeez, Michael, I have no idea. With all this mess, I barely remember my name. He was gone early last week or the week before. Said something about he had to go to LA to visit his partner. That wasn't that odd, really, he went out there every so often. This last trip maybe came up a little sudden, but he was generally pretty mum about things he was working on. He didn't really say much when he got back. I remember thinking that he wasn't his usual talkative self, but I just assumed he was tired from the trip. Think it's important?"

"Probably nothing, maybe something. If Benjamin didn't do it, then it might be. Right now, everything is important, at least until we can eliminate a few things. Think about it and try to remember anything he might have said or exactly when he was gone. Anything else?"

"Well, now that you mention it. He did borrow my Jeep to go over to the rez after he got back. Said he was going to go straighten out a few things with the tribe and their payments. Somewhere over around Chinle and then Kayenta, I think he said. He loved that area anyway and I figured he was just making an excuse to get over there. He always liked going and visiting the Mokidugway, Monument Valley & Moab over there. He knew some people over there too, certainly through the students. He had a great affinity for the folks over there. You, of all people, can understand that."

"Yes I do, certainly one of my favorite spots too. But that's a lot of ground from Chinle to the Mokidugway to Moab. Can you pin it down a little?"

"Not off the top of my head, but I'll think about that one too. You know, it's a little odd that he would say something like that, though. The tribe's pretty good on payments and he did seem distant in some respects. As if he had something on his mind. But as I said, maybe he just wanted to get out of here too."

"Possibly, but certainly sounds like that's something out of place," Michael said, almost to himself. "Kevin, do you know of anywhere Luigi stashed valuable stuff? You know, like money, jewelry, important papers, computer disks; things like that? A safe, maybe."

"Hell, Michael, Luigi didn't really have anything of value."

"Actually, Kevin, I'm thinking perhaps Luigi did have something of great value and if Benjamin didn't do it, maybe that's what got him killed."

"Come on, Michael. This isn't James Bond here."

"Maybe, maybe not. But one of two things is certain: either Benjamin killed him for money or someone else did for some very specific reason. I just can't see a hundred and forty-some dollars being that reason, as you said the kid didn't need the money. So we need to look at the why. If Benjamin did it, maybe he was drunk or maybe it was the money, but then why didn't anyone hear a gunshot? How couldn't you, nor I, nor anyone else for that matter, have heard a gunshot? I wasn't any further than forty feet away and it was a big bullet! It doesn't make sense. So if Benjamin didn't do it, then someone else did and covered it up. To do that they must have had a reason, and a good one. When we find the reason, we'll know who murdered him, either way. Just some odd tidbits, but added up, it makes you wonder."

They sat, pondering their own thoughts for a few moments until Michael, rubbing his forehead with his hand, muttered softly, "Where, oh where is it?"

"Where's what?" his friend answered, perplexed.

"Where's what's been bugging me all night. Luigi's hiding place, his safe. If he had something important enough to be killed over, he'd know it and he wouldn't make it easy to find. He worked military intelligence, after all. So if he was killed for something he knew or had, I gotta believe he'd have stashed it. Not necessarily in a metal safe, per se, but some place safe where he could hide things and make it hard to find. Think about it. It's critical."

"I can't think of any place, Michael. I don't even think he had a safe-deposit box. His computer disks were . . ."

Michael slapped the heel of his hand against his forehead. "I am sooooo stupid. I overlooked the obvious."

"What did I say this time?"

"Just the obvious," he said, a tinge of sarcasm in his voice. "I just wasted a bunch of time last night looking for some mysterious hiding place. I didn't even think of a safe-deposit box, I must be tired." He was rushing into the bedroom before he'd finished the sentence. "We've got to find a bank statement or something that'll help. Give me a sec to get dressed," he called from the bedroom.

* * *

Tielson was bone tired. He hadn't really slept in days and last night had been no exception. He hadn't stopped plotting since he'd read the debriefing. He'd spoken with Tompkins three times in the last several hours to coordinate operations and to receive updates. Figuring out what to do from here had kept him up all night, but in the end Tompkins was right. It took little effort to nudge things into the right direction. The evening's thoughts had prompted a rash of early morning calls to pull in a favor or two from his connections over at Justice and the other departments, but now everything was in place and proceeding in an orderly manner. He hoped that the few details left hanging and out of his immediate control would be cleared up in the next day or so and this entire affair would be finally put to bed without further complication.

* * *

Kevin was waiting at the door as Michael emerged from the bedroom pulling a shirt over his head. "Come on, I know just where he kept that kind of stuff." Michael was awake and in hot pursuit. By the time he reached the office door, he saw Kevin starting to pull open the bottom drawer of the desk.

"Wait, Kevin," he cautioned. His friend immediately halted and looked up.

"Don't just go diving in there," Michael warned. "You need to inspect everything you touch in here. Look, man, if someone other than Benjamin did this, they were probably professional, so we need to be very careful. We might get lucky if they've left something out of place or out of order. Look around generally for the odd thing, not the normal thing. A turned paper in the wrong file or a misfiled file could really help to figure this out. That sort of thing. Go cautiously and carefully, recalling where you and Luigi put things. Understand?"

"Sure." Kevin grabbed a handful of files and pulled them out, holding them in Michael's general direction.

"Don't you listen?" Michael said, breathless and exasperated.

"Sorry, man, I just want to know what's going on. I'll check out the desk. I'll go slowly, I promise. The one thing we did do is keep up with these motel records. These are the banking files."

Michael nodded and took the files, taking a seat on the armrest of Luigi's chair. He scanned them generally, but also looking for specific things. Kevin's accounts, both business and personal, were held at the Second National Bank. The only evidence of Luigi's personal finances was a single deposit slip to an account at Second. He found several business statements but nothing showed a debit or action connected to a safe-deposit box. Not unusual, really. There could be a hundred simple explanations for the lack of Luigi's records. He might have filed his sensitive personal financial records elsewhere or not even saved them at all. A box might simply be provided free with an account. Or . . . the murderer could have taken the records, covering the trail Michael was now on.

The records themselves weren't really the issue. If Michael took up the cause of The People of the State of Colorado v. Yazzie, he could easily file a discovery motion for the bank records or serve them directly with a subpoena duces tecum. He could easily get the records for cause. All he really wanted to know right now was simply whether Luigi might have a place to stash something.

Michael's attention was now drawn to his friend's grumblings. "What's wrong?"

"These things are all mixed up," Kevin said. "I can't find anything. They're backwards. Either Luigi just went through this or someone else did. I didn't leave these files like this."

"Hold on, Kevin!" Michael's voice tensed. "Are you sure?"

"Very sure. He was pretty conscientious about keeping the records in order so I didn't have to do much for end-of-the-month reports because I hated doing it and he knew it."

"It certainly doesn't surprise me. I'm starting to think someone meticulously searched this place."

"Really?"

"Yeah, there's just a deposit slip in here of Luigi's. Assuming he kept his bank records in here?"

"As far as I know he did. What makes you think someone searched the place?"

"Just a feeling, really, but some circumstances are adding up and it's not making good sense." Michael paused before continuing. "Take these records, for example. I think someone carefully went through this file looking for something. But what?"

"I don't understand."

"Neither do I. Something just doesn't feel right about all this. Then again, we may just be nuts, too." Michael took Kevin through his search of the place the night before. His voice came alive with a case for the first time in a long time. "For argument's sake, Kev, let's say Benjamin Yazzie did kill Luigi; then robbery would be the logical motive, right?"

Not waiting for a nod he continued, "But I've got some severe problems with that right now. Benjamin had a long stare on his face in the back of that police car yesterday. Not exactly the look of someone who'd just whacked someone he knew, and in cold blood at that, possibly a bit in shock. Not the look of someone who'd stolen money, then taken the time to calmly go to his room and start packing before he ran. It didn't seem like the look of a cold-blooded killer. It was more like the look of a confused kid who'd just seen his first dead body. Kind of like you were last night."

"Which leads me to the second problem I've got. As you correctly pointed out, there's the issue of Navajo culture and the sanctity of life. You know that no Navajo would ever take a life without a good and specific reason. Food possibly, revenge maybe, but money? I don't think so. As you said, there's no unsolved murders on the reservation. Sure, maybe domestic violence or one drunk kills another, but that's the exception, not the rule. He didn't seem drunk and I can't imagine he had a personal grudge against Luigi. As far as money as a motive, the tribe paid his room expenses and then probably gave him a living stipend to boot. Tuition and fees were free from The Fort. Why risk all of that, probably at least a thousand a month, all for a hundred and forty-seven dollars? Doesn't make any sense, unless trouble at home and Joseph doesn't think that."

"I agree, but he couldn't have known what was all that was there."

"True, and no offense, Kevin, but this ain't exactly the Ritz-Carlton" as he rose from the armrest. "There's no way someone's going to even remotely think you've got a couple of grand in cash in the till. Not for a moment. Especially someone living here who could watch the business."

"I suppose I should be insulted, but I see what you're driving at."

"The point being, the only logical motive Benjamin could have for killing him would be robbery, but . . . there'd have to be enough to risk the thousands he was already getting. That's not the case here. Sudden rage? Unlikely. So why would he do it, especially in light of it violating every tradition in Navajo culture" turning and walking to the center of the room and lifting his hand to his chin and mouth, rubbing it as if in deep thought.

"OK, it doesn't make sense." Kevin nodded his agreement so far.

He crossed back toward Kevin, pausing and then with the last rub of his chin he continued with "so how about a second possible explanation? Let's take out the Navajo cultural issues and say a junkie, or somebody, randomly picked this place to rob. Get whatever he could. Not very likely, either, do you think?"

"Why not?"

"First of all, Luigi died on the couch. No signs of a struggle. The bullet hole in the back of the couch indicates he was sitting. Doesn't make any sense. I suppose they could have surprised him, made him sit on the couch and then shot him, but I don't think so. I doubt, what with that baseball bat I found in the corner up front and his military training, that he'd just let someone take him at gunpoint, sit him down on the couch and then just let them shoot him. Then there's the question as to why no one heard a gunshot? Why are personal banking records missing? And why is that file out of sorts."

Michael had begun pacing slowly as he brought his closing argument back around to the jury of one, liking the logic so far. Turning to Kevin, gaining eye contact. "So, working with the only thing we know for a fact, Luigi was seated on the couch when he was shot. How'd he get to that position? And why not a lot of spatter or pooling? There are only two reasonable options to explain what happened. First, whoever shot him came in through the back door and surprised him, probably the most likely. Or two, they came through the front door, got the drop on him and then moved him back to the living quarters. Right?"

"But why is the side door more likely?" Kevin asked, sizing up the argument.

"Well, let's say a normal robber, if there is such a thing, comes through the front door. Why go past the money, which is what he's after, then sit Luigi on the couch, shoot him from the other side of the coffee table, rifle through the desk, walk back to the front, grab the money and run?"

"So it doesn't make sense, I agree, but I suppose it's not impossible, though."

"Sure, but not very probable either."

"OK . . . So . . . ?"

"So . . . especially in light of this," and Michael stepped to the desk, reached over to the corner of the desk, turning and raising his hand with a gold pocket-watch, displaying it to Kevin proudly.

Kevin took it from his hand and looked at it. He knew the watch. Luigi's father had given it to him when he was a boy. Passed down through the generations of the Morrealli family. Luigi had told him it was to be given to his son after he died. It was his most prized possession. It was 14-karat gold with intricate designs on the cover and back. The timepiece itself was equally awesome. Swiss workings and an ivory watch face with the words "Geneva 1802" inked on it. Michael assumed it to be worth thousands.

"I suppose a robber or burglar could have missed it."

"No way. And, by the way, it's 'they,' Kevin, 'they.'"

Kevin looked up from the watch with a questioning look. "They?"

"Yes, they. Give me a second and I'll bet you'll come to the same conclusion." He shrugged off the question until the right time and continued with his hypothesis, taking a couple of paces before continuing "They wouldn't have missed it. It's just not what they were after. If robbery was the motive and somebody took the time to search that desk, don't you think they'd have found this on top? Just like I did?"

"If they saw it," Kevin replied, already accepting the plural.

"Oh, they saw it, and that's where they made a mistake. They tried to make it look like a robbery, but only after the fact. They ended up leaving the watch in their hurried cover-up, thereby betraying their actual motives. A robber who had just killed someone and taken the additional time wouldn't have missed it, I'll assure you of that. No, more likely something different happened, which brings us to what I think really happened." Michael paused for both a breath and dramatic effect. Kevin, the juror, sat wondering.

"No, sir, something more sinister was afoot here," he crossed back toward the coffee table grabbing a file as he went. "You, yourself, provided the final, confirming clue" he turned lifting the files high in the air with his hand looking direct now at Kevin.

"I did? What?"

"The files are backwards" as he began to pace in front of him. "You said it yourself!" gesturing toward him "Not merely mixed up."

"All right, I'll bite. So what?"

He leaned his backside against the desk and began "well, here's what I think happened. I thing Luigi was watching C-SPAN as usual. Someone surprised him through the back door. It wouldn't have taken long for someone watching the place to see that people just walked into Luigi's quarters unannounced. A much more discreet entrance, anyway."

"So why couldn't someone have come through the front and moved him back?"

"Well, it's just a hunch, but mainly because of his slippers."

"Huh?"

"I'll bet he didn't just go out to greet a potential customer in his bare feet?"

"No, he always put on his slippers. I don't think he thought of his feet as a selling point."

"OK, then, that's a habit. I found his slippers under the coffee table, roughly about where he'd have taken them off if he were watching TV. I also found a cereal bowl on the table."

"All right, so Luigi never cleaned up regularly. That doesn't mean much."

"I noticed that, believe you me, but that's why I went through this place yesterday with a fine-toothed comb. When I washed the bowl, the leftover milk was kinda gelled. It was still slightly liquid and a couple of drops of milk came out when I tipped it up, so it hadn't been there but a few hours. My guess is he had a late-night snack."

"Sounds right. Luigi liked to eat cereal at night. Jeez, Michael. You must've been bored yesterday."

"No, just skeptical. I told you I went through the place with a fine-toothed comb, no stone unturned." It sounded almost boastful. "Everywhere except inside the desk, which I left for you, hoping you'd be better positioned to find something out of place than I was. You, of course, completely cooperated by discovering the backward files." Michael smiled, patting his friend on the back, then returned to seriousness. "Anyway, I think they got in that way." He pointed to the back door.

"You keep saying 'they.' Why?"

"Well, let me tell you" leaning against the desk. "Somebody obviously went through this place" motioning with his hand around the room "and with precision at that. They must have started with the desktop, a logical place to start a search for what they were looking for. Probably a photograph, maybe a document or something tangible, since they bothered to go through the desk, and specifically the files. Something physical, at least. That's how the watch got forgotten. It also explains two other things. First, where are the computer disks?"

"I have no idea," his friend answered, watching has Michael turned, driving his finger into the air.

"Ah . . . but realize that Luigi's computer really isn't a computer. It's a word processor."

"So what's the difference?" Kevin asked.

"Well, this word processor doesn't have an extensive hard drive or memory. It's an extremely old machine. I doubt you could even buy one if you had to. Therefore, the only way to save his work or letters would be on a disk and there's not a single one to be found anywhere in this place. Odd, don't you think, in light of Luigi's propensity to write letters?"

"Definitely odd. Come to think of it, I do remember seeing some disks around here. None anywhere?"

"Nowhere. That's what led me on that wild goose chase to find a safe or a safe hiding place. But maybe you've solved that with the safe-deposit box suggestion. I looked for hours for a good hiding place or a safe."

"Well, hopefully that's over. Go on."

"OK. The effort wasn't a complete waste, though. His cupboards had been gone through, too."

"How could you tell?"

"The dust. It was under some of the various boxes and glasses, and dust doesn't usually collect under things. I could see imprints where things had been too. The dust just didn't seem to be where it was supposed to be. Plus, the clothes in the bedroom. They'd been gone through, too."

"How could you tell that?"

"Actually it wasn't anything real brilliant. I just kinda fell into it, literally. I had cleaned out the closet and was moving a box when I tripped over a pile of clothes and came up close and personal with a second pile. While I was picking myself up, I noticed creases. I took a whiff from a polo shirt and it had that fresh, just-washed smell. Never known a chain smoker's clothes smelling fresh after a day's use."

"True."

"Definitely. All this, coupled with an almost empty chest of drawers and it all points to the same thing. A methodical, unhurried search. Which is why there had to be more than one."

Michael paused, as if waiting for his Watson to acknowledge his skill. When that praise never came, he continued by answering the question on Kevin's face.

"There had to be at least two. One guy wouldn't be able to hold a gun on him and at the same time do a thorough search. I kinda doubt that if you had just shot someone you'd stick around and search the place completely, especially if someone could just walk in and catch you. And you certainly wouldn't leave your potential victim unattended.

You'd necessarily be in a hurry, splitting time watching your victim, and certainly not very careful. I think that's why your files were backwards, not merely mixed up, and why I suggest Mr. Yazzie is innocent of the crimes alleged."

"Go on. I feel like an idiot, but I don't follow you."

"Elementary, really," he said in his best Holmes accent taking back his perch leaning against the edge of the desk and pointing. "Someone went through these files by taking them all out together. They probably placed them on the desk and individually went through them, placing them on the desk in a pile as he finished each one. Clearly looking for something specific. Then they put them all back in, only backwards. One person couldn't have been that precise in the search without taking his eyes—or her eyes—off Luigi. They wouldn't have been able to search the bedroom thoroughly, either, without losing sight of Luigi. Therefore, I submit someone else had to be watching him while the other searched. Plus, if someone was searching the place, Luigi would have had to know he was in trouble. Look at his background. I don't think he'd have just sat there if the chance came for him to hightail it out of here when his lone assailant turned his back. And with that, gentleman of the jury, the defense rests."

"Seems reasonable, Michael. You've got my vote."

"Thank you. It's a winning defense strategy, but it doesn't answer the ultimate question. You and I have to answer that. If Benjamin didn't do it, then who did and why? Those answers, hopefully, are at the bank. Now, let's go."

Both men hurried out the door, each saying he needed a couple of minutes to get ready. Michael was waiting when Kevin met him at the Jeep.

"What took you so long?"

"Joseph called. He sounded stressed."

"I wondered how long that would take."

"What, now you can predict the future too?"

"No, not at all. But this ain't my first rodeo either."

* * *

The grey-haired man used a secured private line instead of his normal government line, listening as the phone rang a couple of times before it was answered with a simple "Si?"

"Buenos Dias."

"Buenos Dias, my friend."

"How is it there today?"

"Just fine. Bright blue and warm."

"Wish I was there."

"That is the price you pay to serve."

"I suppose. I've checked into the matter we discussed and I am told that any problems associated with this are under control. I believe you should be able to resume financial operations very soon. As I understand it, our people are working together right now for the appointment of a new liaison."

"Yes, we are working on that now, but we are trying to cope with this great loss."

"Yes, I understand. Regarding that, it appears to me that some other interests may have been being served here. If that is the case, it may not be such a great loss."

"Yes, that is an unfortunate possibility and I am looking into that personally. But, as you well know, things aren't always as they appear."

"Yes, that can be true, also. Let me assure you, we are equally displeased with these events. I hope this is merely a coincidence that is outside either of our control, but I will have more information on that in a few days. For the time being, I suggest we work together and concentrate on getting operations back on line. We can look into this matter from both ends and discuss it further."

"Yes, Señor, I believe that will best serve our respective interests. I thank you for the call. I knew you would be able to look into the matter, as you've always done."

"Well, thank you, but it is really the entire Party that does what it can for its friends."

"Yes, and our thanks to the Party will be forthcoming."

"Well of course don't feel obligated. We'll talk again soon. Enjoy your evening."

The man hung up the phone and sipped his frozen drink. "Politicos Americanos. Mi madre." He closed his eyes to the bright late afternoon sun as the waves crashed loudly in the distance.

* * *

In the few minutes it took to drive the mile to the bank, Michael began to take control of his case. He'd been down this road before. He knew that trying to get records out of banks and businesses wasn't always the easiest thing. He could always get a subpoena later, but he really needed to find out what was in there now. He just knew, based on his experience in LA, that this wasn't going to be easy.

"OK, Kevin. We have to handle this intelligently. We've got to get into this box, if it exists. I'll handle it; just back me up. These tellers are so intimidated by lawyers they'll give you anything, including access to a safe-deposit box, if you do it right."

"Michael, I think there's an easier way to handle this."

"Listen, Kevin, leave it to me," he insisted, his voice a little louder, his plan now settling into place.

"But . . ."

"Look, I know how to handle this."

Kevin rolled his eyes and shook his head a bit. "OK," he responded with a smirk. "Whatever you say. You're the lawyer".

Kevin turned right from Main onto Ninth Street. They rolled past the old turn-of-the-century buildings housing the various art galleries that had sprung up in Durango over the past few years. The Jeep bounced over the double track running parallel to Narrow Gauge Alley and Kevin made a quick left into the bank parking lot. They leapt from the vehicle and pushed through the doors, Michael calmly asking for the person responsible for safe-deposit boxes. He confidently strode over to the woman they'd been directed to.

"Good morning," Michael called to the woman across the counter, bent into a file cabinet, before diverting his eyes toward the vault to the left. Its open door seemed to be calling a clue to him. He could almost feel it.

"Good morning. May I help you?" she answered, before twirling, papers in hand, a polite, helpful smile coming to her face.

"My name is Michael Kincaid. I'm an attorney from LA. . ." he stated, his eyes still drawn to the target.

"I know that, Michael. You don't recognize me! Has it been that long?"

Michael's brain kicked in immediately and his eyes followed, closely in tow. "Oh, of course I do," he instinctively nodded, scanning the desk and eyeing the previously unnoticed nameplate. "Mrs. Edgemont!" He smiled, and fixed his eyes on the now familiar face. "I didn't know you worked here."

"For the past five years," came the response.

"How's Brad, Mrs. Edgemont?" and they made quick family small talk about his former classmate and swimming teammate. This might be easier than he'd anticipated, he thought, still not noticing the wry smile on his friend's face at his side. It took a few minutes of updates before he could finally steer her back onto the trail.

"Mrs. Edgemont?"

"Dori, Michael. You're not a child anymore."

"OK, Dori. I'm working on the Morrealli murder."

"Oh, that nice man Luigi. He told the funniest stories. What an imagination. I remember one time he was telling me . . ."

"Dori," Michael quietly interrupted. "I don't mean to be rude, but we're really busy with this. I hope you can understand. I was wondering if Luigi might have had a safe-deposit box here."

"Well, of course he did, Michael. Everyone with an account like Mr. Morrealli's has access to a free box. We have over 400 boxes in there." She motioned toward the target.

"Great, Mrs. Edgemont." Michael was pleased that they were finally making progress. "Well . . . as I said, we're investigating his murder and I was wondering if I might be able to get a peek inside?"

"Well, Michael, I can't just let you look in it. There are bank procedures I must follow, starting with a signature and . . ." Mrs. Edgemont began reciting the standard bank procedure for admission to a safe-deposit box ad nauseam. Michael looked back to Kevin, finally noting his quirky smile.

"Mrs. Edgemont?" Kevin interjected.

"Oh, yes, Mr. Daniels. Can I help you?"

"Mrs. Edgemont, Mr. Morrealli was very close to me."

"Yes, I know. He would always talk about you. Thought of you just like a son."

Kevin smiled, a warm, peaceful feeling coming over him for the first time in a while. "Well, since you are aware of our relationship, I was wondering if you might let me look."

"Of course, you should have said so in the first place. You'd obviously be allowed to. You're the named beneficiary in the event of death."

"Finally, we're getting somewhere," Michael gasped under his breath, without acknowledging his own bungling attempt.

"Where do I sign, Mrs. Edgemont?"

"On this ledger," she responded. "But it won't do you much good."

"Why not?" Michael interrupted.

"Well, because I suppose there's nothing in there anymore."

"What do you mean?"

"Well, some IRS agents showed up this morning and seized the contents. They had a court order to confiscate the contents of the box. Mr. Steele signed off on it personally."

"They what?" Michael gasped.

"Well," she started to explain again, this time in detail, motioning for the boys to follow her toward the vault. Michael and Kevin listened intently as she recounted the unexplainable events of the morning. Showing them a counter to stand at, she disappeared into the vault, re-emerging with the box. She sat the box on the counter. Upon inspection, it proved to be indeed quite empty.

"It was very strange, Michael," she concluded. "In my five years at the bank, I've never seen that before."

"Yes, Mrs. Edgemont, there are some very strange things going on in this case," Michael said. "We've got to go, but we certainly appreciate your help. Tell Brad I'm staying at Kevin's, if you talk to him. Tell him to call me."

"I will and I hope you find what you're looking for."

"Thank you, Mrs. Edgemont," Kevin called before Michael grabbed his elbow and steered him toward the door.

They were barely outside before Michael spoke, waving a finger in his friend's face.

"That's pretty odd, man. I've got a really bad feeling about this one. We've got a mountain of shit here and we may end up swimming in it before it's all said and done."

"I'm getting the same feeling. Got any idea what it means?"

"Not really, but I can tell you this: the IRS doesn't just routinely seize safe-deposit boxes at death. They especially don't do it within twenty-four hours under a court order. It just doesn't work that way. There are procedures that have to be followed or it's illegal and they lose the contents to some hotshot tax or estates lawyer. Somebody, and I mean somebody with pull, wanted to see what was in there. I don't know who Luigi pissed off but my guess is he pissed off somebody really important. We've got to talk to Snow. There's a couple of questions I'd like to ask him."

They hopped into the Jeep and headed back up Ninth, across the tracks and Main and up to 2nd Avenue, looking for a parking spot near the cop shop.

* * *

Tielson placed the phone down and closed his eyes, leaning back into his oversized chair. Everything was working just as he'd planned it. The loose ends were tying up nicely and his operation would soon be secured again. He'd deleted the records on his computer and burned the copies he'd finally gotten back. The only copy left would be the one he'd keep hidden for his own protection. No one would blackmail him again. And he certainly wouldn't trust his most prized secret to those computer idiots who'd assured him his system could never be compromised. These computers were not secure and he'd never trusted them in the first place. His mouth crinkled upward as his thoughts savored the way it was tying up into a nice, neat little bundle. He faded slowly into a much-deserved nap.

* * *

Kevin decided he would just stay in the car, he really didn't feel like talking to the detective any more and Michael agreed. The lawyer climbed out and walked up the sidewalk to and through the double glass doors to the young police officer sitting at the watch desk. Michael asking politely for Detective Snow. After a few minutes of waiting a uniformed officer beckoned him through the secured door, down a hallway and into a conference room. In another few minutes Detective Snow stepped in.

"Good morning. What can I do for you?"

"Just a couple of things I'd like to ask you," Michael replied. "I was wondering if I could get a copy of any reports you might have."

"I figured that would be your first question. Lawyers are just as predictable as you guys think cops are. Here are copies of the preliminaries." Snow passed them to him with a little grin on his face.

"I guess we are predictable, so you'll know the next question."

"Has Benjamin Yazzie confessed yet?"

Michael nodded.

"No, to the contrary. He says he didn't do it."

"Do you believe him?"

"Let's just say the circumstantial evidence is stacking up against him pretty heavily. We found his prints on a glass of water on the victim's coffee table."

"Well that's not good, although there could be many reasons for that. But do you believe him?"

"My investigation is continuing, we'll see."

"Ah, so you're not 100% positive. Don't worry, won't quote you, all I want is the murderer too. There's some problems with this, certainly doesn't make a lot of sense."

"Let's just say I have my curiosities, but I gather you do too, so ask away."

Michael appreciated the detective's frankness. "Did you take any computers or drives or maybe disks from Luigi's place into evidence?"

"No, we didn't find any, but I'd suggest you ask BIA, not me," Snow said, a noticeable air of displeasure in his voice.

"BIA?? . . ." Michael exclaimed, obviously perplexed. This turn had completely confused him. His face wrinkled quizzically before asking, "what does the BIA have to do with this?"

"Damned if I know. Last time I looked, Durango wasn't on the reservation. All I can really tell you is that some federal guys showed up here earlier and said they would handle the investigation. Not the local boys either," he said with evident disdain. "Said Mr. Yazzie was wanted by tribal and federal law first and they'd be taking over jurisdiction."

"Find that a little odd, Detective?"

"Indeed I do. Don't like it much, either."

"Got any idea what's going on?"

"Damned if I know. They came in and took over the investigation, that's all I was told. My chief says I'm off the case, so I guess I'm off the case."

"Don't suppose that kinda upsets you that the feds start coming in to your town and telling you what to do?"

"Yes, as a matter of fact it does."

"So when's the last time you saw a federal investigation supersede a local murder charge?"

"Never."

"Never seen it either. What if I told you that I have some doubts as to Yazzie's involvement and could maybe you why?"

"Well, then I'd be rather interested in listening, strictly from an un-interested third-party kinda curiosity standpoint since I'm off the case, if you know what I mean."

"Sure do, but before I confuse things, first tell me what has happened on the case from your end."

"Well, they were here very early this morning. Before I arrived, in fact. Two special agents out of Denver. Apparently told the chief the Bureau of Indian Affairs would be co-handling the investigation with the FBI and that we were to lay off. The line was that the Bureau believed it could involve interests of national security, due to some prior relationship Mr. Morrealli had to intelligence. Since Mr. Yazzie is Navajo, BIA has initial federal jurisdiction and we should forget the incident ever even happened until they were done with him. They wanted the prisoner, but the jailer wouldn't let him loose without a federal transfer order. I'm sure the chief tipped him off, he wasn't very happy about it from what I heard. That stopped them, but they said they'd be back for him with an order tomorrow." He paused a moment before adding, "I'm sure you get the idea, right?"

Michael nodded, patting down his pockets in search of the cell phone he knew he'd left in his car. "Got a phone?"

"Yeah, you can use that one there," he answered, pointing to the corner.

"Long distance, is that OK?"

"Sure, as long as you promise to explain what you think is going on. Maybe you have some better idea because it doesn't make sense to me."

"I don't know that I'd go that far, but give me just a second. I need to make this call first."

Michael dialed quickly and the familiar voice answered.

"Mr. Kincaid's office."

"Hi, Trish. Nice to know the office is open."

"Hi, Michael. How's the fishing?"

"Not too good. Haven't even gone; but I'll explain later. Got a little job for you. Call Leonardo in Denver. Tell him I said he owes me one and the time to collect has come. Tell him to find out who the transfer magistrate is up there and check to see if there is a Benjamin Yazzie, that's Y-A-Z-Z-I-E, on the afternoon calendar. Oh, and if so, who's requesting the transfer. Got it?"

"Of course."

"It's kind of important."

"Isn't it always. I'll handle it, but this doesn't sound like fishing."

"Actually, maybe it is. Just see if he can get the information. Call me back on my cell or at Kevin's after you talk to him. Got his number?"

"Sure do."

"Thanks, Trish."

Michael paused for a second to re-gather himself. Every synapse in his body was now firing. His mind was alive again and in its territory.

"My apologies, Detective. Something I needed to have done quickly. In answer to your question, I have pretty much assured myself that Luigi's place was thoroughly searched and robbery wasn't the reason. Luigi had a word processor that needed disks for use; Kevin told me he used disks for his letters. If you didn't take them, why would Benjamin Yazzie? Doesn't make sense if he was stealing money. No value to him. Anyway, it's a bunch of little things like that, coupled with some major problems I've both got with the whole affair. First off, I can't understand why I didn't hear a shot. I was only a few feet away. Looking at it, it just doesn't add up to me. Do you have any direct evidence that shows that Yazzie did it?"

"To be honest, not really. It's all pretty much circumstantial." The detective reached over and pulled the police report back to himself, flipping through the pages to the narrative section. "Let's go over what I've got so far. We've got a deceased male from a gunshot wound to the thorax. A 9mm slug recovered from the wall. Mr. Daniels, reported seeing the suspect, Yazzie, leave the office premises at approximately 0630 hours and subsequently discovered the body at 0635 hours. He then contacted our office, whereupon I was assigned to the homicide investigation. Other officers were on the scene and had affected the arrest of suspect Yazzie, who was in custody when I arrived. Yazzie denied any responsibility for the crime to the responding officers. I observed the crime scene first before directing the criminalist on what I wanted. I was escorted by Officer English, the first arriving officer, to the suspect's room where he pointed out what appeared to be blood. Samples were taken by forensics. The deceased was transported to the Coroner's Office at Mercy for autopsy. In subsequent interviews with the suspect, Yazzie has continued to deny any involvement in the crime and asked for a lawyer. His request was turned over to the Public Defender's Office and interrogation was discontinued. That's pretty much all we have."

"You're right, not much but circumstantial stuff."

Snow shook his head, adding, "Not as open and shut as I'd originally thought, especially in light of this morning's peculiar happenings. Something stinks here!"

"Things aren't as they appear, I'll grant you that. I don't suppose your people checked the bullet to see if it was fired from a muzzled weapon."

"You think a silencer?"

"Maybe, would explain why nobody heard anything and a good lab can tell from the bullet's markings."

"Well, uh, no. We never really got that far and we really don't have that type of forensics here. I know our guys downstairs looked at the bullet striations but beyond basic ballistics we'd send it out. A silencer, really?"

"Well, I'd say if no one heard a shot, it might be worth the question. If the shot was fired from a muzzled weapon, then I'd say Benjamin Yazzie is out as a real suspect, unless of course someone found a gun with one or believes he somehow stashed it."

"Nope, we haven't even recovered the gun yet. I think I can have someone check into that. The evidence in the case hasn't been turned over yet from property and you know how things can get lost in there for a few days, especially a bullet."

"Yeah, but rarely does it work to my benefit so early," Michael chuckled. "Perhaps they'll be very happy if you did find it missing. I'd stay away from sending it to the FBI lab, though."

"Well we wouldn't want to upset them" Snow chuckled. "I've got a friend with the Colorado Bureau of Investigation up in Denver. He'll know what to do with it."

"Now, here's the big question: why do they want this investigation? You're perfectly able to convict Mr. Yazzie and get life. Why are they so interested?"

"Beats me, but as you said, doesn't make a whole lot of sense."

"Well, it would be nice if you guys could keep Benjamin here until I can get some answers to that question."

"I don't know what I can do about that. If they show up with a transfer order there's not much we can do."

"Maybe not, but at least maybe you can stand in their way a little and cost them some time while I pull a few tricks myself."

"Pardon me for saying this Mr. Kincaid, but this seems absolutely absurd. You want me to help you keep a murderer in custody here, against my chief's wishes and the fed's orders. Come on, get serious."

"An alleged murderer, Detective. Ah, c'mon. Get some excitement in your life! You really want to just sit around and wait for your pension to vest?" He paused for a second hoping for a grin or something, but when it didn't come he continued. "That's exactly what I want you to do, and let me tell you why. Because if he didn't do it, then you've got a murderer running around loose in Durango and he's going to get away with it. If we work together, we'll get this figured out. But I really could use your help."

"Well, let's play it by ear and I'll see what I can do. No promises, though."

The conversation continued with Michael telling Snow what he and Kevin had learned so far. It was almost one when he finally left, plan in hand, until he neared the Jeep and suddenly stopped.

"Damn it! Just a sec, Kev" he called to his friend in the driver's seat. "I forgot to ask him something. I'll be right back."

He reappeared a couple of minutes later, looking perplexed as he got into the vehicle. Kevin turned toward him, asking what was going on.

"Snow hasn't been back to the motel."

"What are you talking about?"

"I saw someone come out of the office early this morning and get into one of those standard undercover cars cops always drive around in. I just assumed it was Snow. Maybe it was the fed boys getting a look, but then maybe not. Something else Snow told me, Kevin. Luigi's body was apparently picked up late this morning by some army personnel from the coroner's office. Snow just got an irate call from Dr. Bustee, the pathologist."

"Dave's dad? Yeah, so what does that mean?"

"It means we got something very strange going on here, buddy. Far too many federal people running around here for a local murder. Even if it does involve an Indian."

"Kevin, did Luigi hang out anywhere in particular in town other than at the motel?"

"Really, other than occasionally to the Elks or the VFW I don't know of anywhere."

"Might be worth a stop by there to see if anyone happened to hear anything about Luigi, if anyone knows anything they'd know it at the Elks."

"Yea, probably would, but I can't go now as I need to take care of a couple things for about an hour."

"That works out. Why don't you go run your errands Kevin and I'll take a walk down to the Elks, its only 2 blocks from here. Grab me when you're headed back?"

"That'll work, how about I meet you back here about 1" Kevin replied and with a wave Michael turned south down 2nd Avenue in route.

Michael crossed the street and walked past City Hall past the pink flowering blossoms on the trees coming to life after a long winter. He reached the front entryway to the Elks, climbing the rock stairway, through the outer door and in to the foyer. He pushed a button, a voice said yes and Michael answered with "visiting Elk," a buzz gaining him access to a place he'd been intimately familiar with twenty years before. Nothing had changed in the intervening period. Not even the bartender. "Michael Kincaid." A bit of an Irish brogue cried out from across the bar as Michael rounded the corner into the bar area.

"Hello, Stubby." Stubby O'Brannon was an institution in Durango. He'd been a fixture around town for as long as anyone could remember, and that was quite a few years. He'd come from the old country near Cork with his wife in their early twenties. Long before the food chains had come to town, Stubby's "Poor Boy" drive-in and the local A&W had been the only places the high school kids could hang out. He'd sold the place in the'80s with the entrance of fast food and had been the bartender at the Elks ever since. Michael's father and Stubby had been good friends and when Michael turned twenty-one, Stubby helped him get a job bartending at the Elks so he could make extra money while he was in college. Stubby had taken the time to teach him to be a proper Irish pub-tender and Michael had always been grateful.

And then there was Erin O'Brannon. They had met when they were 12, bumming into each other while getting silverware in the cafeteria. She said something funny and invited him to join her and by the end of lunch a boyhood crush was born. They had always been good friends, and at times, perhaps even a little more.

Michael's mind jetted back to the summer before their junior year. They'd spent one particularly wonderful summer together. Days at the pool while Michael was lifeguarding and Erin working the concessions stand; nights going to the drive-in and 'dragging Main' with the rest of the kids. It had always remained pretty innocent though, high school puppy love. Midway through the summer, Michael ended up in the hospital for a battery of tests after suffering some severe migraines. He could still remember as if it were yesterday when Erin came by with a card and her infectious smile to comfort him. She was wearing the shortest pair of cut-offs he'd ever seen and a skimpy white tee shirt, likewise cut off at precisely the right spot. They'd almost needed to treat him for a heart attack when she climbed up on the bed next to him, placed her arms around him and pulled him close. They'd have tried him for murder had he been able to get out of bed when the nurse kicked her out moments later.

They were an item by the time they'd started their junior year. They dated for the entire year but drifted apart over the following summer. Erin was traveling with her family to the old sod of Ireland and Michael seemed to be at a swim meet every weekend. By the start of their senior year there had been a misunderstanding or two, one in particular, and from there they started to drift, traveling in different circles, different classes, although they managed to catch an occasional movie together. Their friends had always assumed they'd get back together in time. There was always something good between them, buried slightly under the surface, whenever they were together. But the next year Erin left for CSU to pursue an engineering degree and Michael stayed to go to The Fort. They had remained somewhat in touch over the years, more so through family than directly with each other. Michael knew that she'd eventually married a guy she met at CSU and the last time they'd spoke was living happily in Denver with her husband. He made a mental note to give her a call someday soon and catch up.

"I heard you were back in town. How have you been?" Stubby asked.

"Great Stubby, great. And you?"

"Doin good, gettin older and fatter, though. How about a beer? My treat."

"If you're buying, I'm drinking" he smiled.

Stubby returned in a few moments carrying a foaming goblet of nutty brown ale, as he loved to call it.

"Erin was just asking about you the other day."

"She was?" he said nonchalantly, his heart strangely beating faster as it had so many years ago. "How, what . . . how's she doing?" he uncharacteristically stammered.

"OK, I guess. She's back in town, you know. Working down at Ernst Engineering."

"No, I didn't. I thought she was in Denver?"

"Her and Ricky couldn't work things out so they went their separate ways. She came back a few months ago. You should give her a call. I'm sure she'd love to hear from you."

Stubby had always liked Michael. He'd always thought him a good kid. Partly because of Michael's father and partly because he was a good kid. And Stubby had always particularly liked the fact that he was Irish Catholic. Secretly, he'd been a bit disappointed when Erin married outside the Irish - and worse a Presbyterian! For he was truly an Irishman at heart. Michael's father and Stubby had even conspired to get the two back together over drinks at the Elks on several occasions, for Michael's father had thought very highly of Erin, too. But ultimately their schemes went down the tubes as Michael ended up in LA and Erin in Denver.

"That's too bad," Michael said with feigned sorrow. "I'd enjoy seeing her again. Maybe I can give her a call while I'm here."

"I'm not sure if I have her new number on me, I'll check, but if you've got a number, I'll see her later and pass it on."

Michael nodded, telling Stubby he had a cell phone and was in Room 2 at Kevin's, hurriedly retrieving one of his cards from his billfold, his mind still drifting back to those thoughts of so long ago. They continued their conversation for another half hour before Stubby slid another frosty beer in front of him replacing his empty. Suddenly unconcerned with the pressing affairs he'd come with, Michael interjected what he thought were slyly phrased questions about Erin, trying to get the full story on what she was doing these days. The old bartender of course saw straight through it, but he was more than happy to relay the information, knowing full well his daughter would have been mortified had she been present. A father's sadness evident, he spoke of what he felt was the quashing of his daughter by what life had brought and the corresponding broken heart she couldn't seem to get over. It all clearly worried him.

In time, Michael related the years he'd spent in Los Angeles and his life with Lori, although he shied away from too many details about her death, a sad story that Stubby already knew and didn't need to ask about. After a pause and a sip off his beer he continued with his leaving LA, his coming to stay with Kevin at the motel, eventually moving around to the Luigi affair.

"Yeah, I'd heard about that, Michael. Did that Navajo kid really kill him?"

"Too early for me to tell, to be honest, a lot of things don't make sense right now. Did you know Luigi, Stubby?"

"Not really, other than in here. It's not like the old days when you really knew everyone who came in here. A lot of people have moved here in the last few years, bunch of mostly Californians wanting to show us how to live" a taste of bitterness in his voice "but he'd come in every once in a while. Maybe every other week or so, once a month kind of thing. Wouldn't say much, just sat in the corner and had his shot and a beer."

"Did he have any friends?"

"Not really that I knew of. Oh," he paused. "Him and Ol' Nick, maybe. I'm sure you remember him, would shoot the bull about old war stories whenever they were both in. In fact, now that I think about it, those two got pretty tanked up in here about a week or so ago. Must've really tied one on. Haven't seen Nick since. Went over to the VFW, I think, after I cut 'em off. Hell, they were so drunk they could hardly even walk" he laughed "but off they went across the street. Nick's probably still pissed off at me; probably drinking over at the V for a few days to punish me."

"Maybe. I'll take a walk over there and see if he's in. As I remember, Nick never goes more than a couple of days without a drink at one of the two places."

"That's for damn sure."

"Well Stubby, got to get to gettin'."

"I imagine so if you're defending that kid."

"Yep, definitely got a few irons in the fire. Thanks for the beers. I'll stop back by in a few days when things calm down a bit."

"Hope you do. And here Michael, I found Erin's number, give her a call" he insisted, sliding a folded piece of paper across the bar to Michael.

Michael took the paper and slid it into the front pocket of his jeans. "I will. See ya."

Stubby picked up the empty glass, walked straight to the telephone and started dialing the second Michael went out the door. "Hi, guess who I just ran into? . . . Michael Kincaid . . . yep, he's in town, gave me his card and asked if you would call him, I didn't have your new number handy so . . . ." as he continued, a smile growing across the father's face.

Michael walked across Second Avenue and stopped by the VFW to find Nick, but no luck. The bartender said he hadn't seen him since Monday. Nick had gotten falling-down drunk and said he was drinking to an old comrade, but the bartender wasn't sure who. The guys at the

V were all too often toasting an old comrade who'd gone on over. Nick had finally left at midnight when they kicked him out so they could lock up. They called him a cab but no sign of him since. The bartender knew Luigi and confirmed that he and Nick were known to tip a few back now and again. "Damn shame about Luigi," he concluded before turning back to wipe off bottles in his apparent mid-afternoon routine.

Michael slowly sipped his beer, thinking about Luigi, Nick and Benjamin for a few minutes before he slipped back to thinking of Erin. His mind was awash with memories of the girl from long ago.

It was the first time in many years that Michael Kincaid had thought about a woman other than Lori.

* * *

Anderson watched the eerie gait from across the room as his superior paced back and forth in the far shadows of the room. His bushy eyebrows occasionally lifting up, then down, amongst snorts from his nose rattling his long protruding nose hairs, now blending into a growing mustache. The plodding steps of the bent shadow traversing the wall betrayed its owner's anxiety. Anderson's subconscious analyzed the silhouette's movement, trying desperately to put a face on what it reminded him of. With each passing step, Anderson's disgust for this figure strangely increased. He wasn't sure exactly why he'd been summoned to the inner chamber; he just knew the shadow was waiting on something and wanted him there when it arrived. Since, in addition to his other talents, he happened to be a bit of a document and computer expert from his days at Annapolis, he supposed those skills had something to do with it. The shadow never involved anyone in anything without a specific reason, however convoluted that reason might be. Everything was on a need-to-know basis. If he were here to inspect a package, it must be to authenticate it and somehow link it back to the breach of the system. Anderson knew that Tielson was, in essence, clueless as to computers, which is probably what had gotten him in the mess they were now dealing with. Tielson was of the old guard and, like too many others around the agency in similar positions, had never bothered to catch the technology wave. He had underlings for that.

His mind wandered, thinking of what he'd learned over the last few hours and days and what he could speculate from there. In the past few hours, Tielson had been forced to confide many more details to his junior, but Anderson still didn't know what it was all about. He'd been taking some direct reports from the independent ops since Tielson had been strangely unavailable. From what he had gathered, someone had broken through the agency's firewall and extracted something from Tielson's private files, something very important to the little man, that much was clear. It also seemed logical, or at least he hoped, that the file was now on its way back with a courier whose arrival they were awaiting. With a little luck, maybe Anderson could find a way to exit this mess unscathed. Probably not, and his loathing increased as he watched the shadow continue its pace, like a sentry on its rounds.

He now knew there was clearly more to this operation than he'd been led to understand. This angered him. He'd been completely blown away when some of the puzzle pieces started coming together. Whatever Tielson and the Old Man were up to had larger implications than the clandestine operation he'd been told he was supporting. Efforts to destabilize an "unfriendly" foreign regime were common and acceptable practice within the agency. However, the death of an American citizen, no matter the circumstances, in the furtherance of that operation was not. It flew afoul of everything the former midshipman believed in and the oath he had taken. Tielson's sloppiness or ruthlessness in handling the situation supported Anderson's theory that he was in the middle of something he hadn't really bargained for. The fact that Tielson could have done something so stupid as to leave a paper trail was unnerving. Maybe it was operational insurance, maybe blackmail material, maybe something else. Regardless, one thing was certain: in the wrong hands, the package could undermine the operation and likely the entire group.

Tielson had seriously screwed up by even having the package. Now it had fallen on Anderson's doorstep to fix. Oh, how he loathed this thing parading in front of him.

His repugnance had seriously increased in the past few days, even more so within the past few hours, what with the half-truths Anderson was now certain he was hearing. Tielson had been going on earlier about how the independents had seriously screwed up, creating problems that should never have occurred and Anderson feared it might get worse. He also knew what the shadow wouldn't tell him. Now they'd apparently eliminated the only known link to the trail of the package. Without that source, could anyone really be sure that this was the only piece out there? Could anyone be sure that other evidence wasn't floating around, ready to be discovered, and thereby reigniting the entire mess again?

Of course not. Tielson's sloppiness had put them all in danger. An acrid taste grew in his mouth as he continued trying to put a face on the shadow, now slowing its pace. The lieutenant commander knew that if other bombs lay out there and they didn't find them before someone else did, it was all over and every one of them would hang. He sarcastically questioned himself: "Or would they?" Instinctively he knew he'd be the first sacrifice. He'd be branded with the leadership role of this "band of rogues" and those above him would just deny everything.

The craggy voice droned on about how no one had followed his instructions; how this should have never happened this way; how all this could have been avoided if his subordinates would have followed his instructions. Despite the ranting from the shadow now fixed upon the wall, Anderson knew they'd done exactly what they'd been told. They'd plugged the leak, as he'd requested. His eyes fixed squarely on the shadow, his subconscious finally and quietly placing the tag on the figure his conscious mind could not.

Mercifully the din was interrupted by a ring of the phone. The little man darted for the handset, picking it up before the second ring. "Send him in," came the grunt. In a short moment the two were joined by a clean-cut, business attired man carry a silver briefcase. "Let me have that," came a second grunt and the man passed the briefcase over to the fidgety hands. "Check into a hotel and stand by for further instructions. You'll probably be returning tomorrow." Without word, the man turned and exited with a mere nod.

Anderson felt a strange coldness permeate through the room as a hand shot to dial in codes for the locks. With the silvery case unlocked, he popped the latches and opened it. His thick hands pulled out what looked like a short memo, sheathed in a clear plastic cover. His head moved to within inches of the paper as his beady eyes took stock.

"Anderson, can you tell me if this is the original document taken from my files?" Tielson extended the package toward him.

He pulled the paper from the sheath, quickly scanning the first paragraph. He muttered "possibly," but Anderson knew he couldn't be sure. No one could. Authentication was a waste of time. Any printout of the information would look the same. Tielson must really be an idiot when it came to computers. What he really wanted to know was if this were the only copy, which of course he couldn't answer. Anderson continued scanning as the squat figure moved uncomfortably closer to him until he felt the labored breathing on his left arm.

He stepped to the oversized desk in an effort to distance himself, but Tielson edged back to his shoulder. He tried to ignore the presence, turning his attention back to the document's contents. He could instantly confirm what he expected to find. Indeed, it seemed to be an original printout of a scanned letter with hand written notes, likely what was hacked from Tielson's private files. The document, coupled with Tielson's concerns, alone seemed to confirm the computer boys' assumption that the system had been compromised. He was somewhat surprised by the detail in which the operation had been outlined. He finished scanning the first page and some of the notes, feeling Tielson draw even closer, knowing he wouldn't have much more time with the document. By the time Anderson had flipped to the second page, Tielson was demanding answers. Anderson kept scanning, comprehending what he could. It seemed that the operation described had some strange twists from how Operation EZL had been outlined to him.

A not-so-gentle nudge from a hairy arm pulled his attention from the document. When he looked up, Tielson's contorted face demanded answers.

"I believe I can say that this appears to have come directly from our system," Anderson told him, "if you can verify the contents."

"It's the original, then?" His voice was almost pleading.

"Well, sir, it seems to be an original printout," he replied.

Anderson could see what passed for glee roll across Tielson's face. The wheels were turning quickly before he brought them to a screeching halt. "But . . ."

"But what?" an angry face retorted.

"But: I cannot say if it is the lone original printout. It would be very easy to simply print a second or third or simply make a copy."

Frustration and disbelief now rolled across his face. "Is that possible?" he muttered almost to himself.

"Quite possible. It's unlikely we'll ever be able to be fully sure what's out there." He jabbed a finger in the air in the general direction of his senior, taking a slight measure of satisfaction, and turned his attention back to the document.

Tielson snatched the memo from Anderson's hands, much to his displeasure. He hadn't been able to take full stock of the document and hadn't even been able to look at the concluding page. Tielson circled the desk before the shadow took up its slow pace again.

"We need to continue close surveillance of the situation. Then I want to know exactly what those two did and why. I ask these morons to carry out a simple mission and they go off half-cocked. I want them to follow up for the next week and then they're out. You understand me, Anderson? They're out. Get rid of them. Rescind their contract. This wasn't part of their instructions. Get someone else in here that can carry out a simple covert surveillance." Tielson was pleased with his feigned anger and continued his sentry-like pace, memo clutched at his side.

"Yes, sir."

"The operation could be jeopardized by their actions!"

"We don't really know that to be the case, sir, but I've already got our other independent looking into the details for me. He should be getting back to me soon."

Tielson said nothing in response, just continued in his gait, staring out of cold dark eyes.

"Sir, it's all in their report." Anderson motioned to the several pages he'd earlier laid on the desk. "What do you want me to do from here?"

"Nothing more. Not a damned thing. You and your pros have done quite enough, thank you."

"Yes, sir." An overwhelming compulsion to choke the living shit out of this pig rose in Anderson's mind.

The shadow along the wall suddenly paused in what Anderson presumed to be thought, before the rough voice continued. "Keep them on the payroll for another week. They're already there and we need to keep an eye open anyway. Tell them to watch for someone who could have any copies. We need to know if there is anything else out there. Tell them to stay out of sight and observe. Understand? And let me know when our other guy gets in touch."

"Yes, sir. There is some good news, sir. AZ has phoned. There is still nothing unusual there."

"Report situation acknowledged to AZ, proceed as previously instructed, situation yellow. Now get out of here and get me some additional information, I need some time to sort out our next move."

"Yes, sir."

He turned and gratefully started for the door. God, how he hated this bastard. He now knew for sure that he was being played. What he'd read in the memo confirmed that. Simple surveillance indeed. He'd have to figure some way to distance himself from this mess if he had plans of surviving. He didn't trust the misshapen little freak and he hadn't joined up for this. He wondered just how much the Old Man truly knew.

He reached for the doorknob and glanced back to observe the shadow crossing the wall at the same slow, deliberate march. The shadow plodded, each step forcing itself in front of the next. Plodding. Stepping. The shadow's fat feet progressing with a thud at each step. He watched until the thudding finally struck an answer to the front of his mind. A troll, guarding its bridge.

* * *

Michael and Kevin met up on 2nd Ave at 1. To Kevin, Michael seemed miles away as he got in to the vehicle, mostly quiet during the ride back to the motel except for an occasional smile that would reflexively cross his face every so often. When they reached the parking lot Kevin finally asked "So what's up, find out anything interesting?" And Michael answered back with "a few things" before smiling at his friend and finally coming back to the now, flawlessly changing course to the present and suggesting a plan for the rest of the day. In the end they decided to split the work with Kevin calling Joseph back with some general questions about Benjamin and Michael calling Maas, the PD's office, and Trish. Upon arrival, they went their separate directions, each on their appointed missions.

Michael returned to his room, kicking off his shoes as he closed the door. As he made his way to the couch, he pulled out the money and other contents of his pockets laying them on the coffee table, his eyes fixing on the folded piece of paper with Erin's phone number on it. After a few moments of thought, he picked it up and unfolded it, staring at the number and thinking about calling her, feeling strangely guilty for the thought. He folded it back over, placing it back on the table, thinking maybe later before sitting on the couch. He thought about the situation for a while longer, what ifs bouncing through his mind, until finally forcing his himself to return to the necessary tasks at hand. He slid over to the room phone and entered lawyer mode.

He first called Judge Maas, who was happy to hear from him. The Honorable Allen Maas had been his father's personal attorney and an old friend of the family long before he had been the arbiter of justice in La Plata County. He'd written a letter of recommendation, which vitally helped Michael get into law school. Judge Maas, like Hosteen Begay, had been a counselor to the young man over the years. He had followed Michael's education and was always there to lend a helping hand when the Socratic method of law school became too much.

After some time, Michael broached the Yazzie matter. The judge was well aware and atop the situation, clearly quite displeased that the federal court was usurping his jurisdiction. He was willing to discuss the case, but the code of ethics had to be satisfied and the District Attorney's Office needed to be notified of this ex parte communication and invited to join in. Michael agreed. After a quick instruction to the Judge's clerk and a few more minutes of small talk, the judge was joined in his chambers by the district attorney. An arraignment for Benjamin Yazzie was set for that afternoon.

The district attorney, predictably, was about as happy as Snow and Judge Maas that the federal government had unilaterally decided to come in and take over a murder case in their town. When Michael gave him an easy way to acquire jurisdiction over the case, he was only too happy to climb on board. The whole thing took barely thirty minutes. Next, Michael quickly called Trish to get a Leonardo update and to give her some additional instructions. He also placed a call to the P.D.'s office with a request for Mr. Bontani to give him a call when he had an opportunity.

Michael paused for a second, leaning back into the couch and checking off things in his mind. By now, Trish would have begun preparing the pro haec vice motion for Judge Maas's signature without being asked. She knew him and knew he'd eventually want it. Judge Maas would have already put in a good word to the local Public Defender's Office and seemed sure they would be willing to allow him to act as co-counsel in the case if things went that way. Though not a licensed Colorado attorney, Michael could appear through the pro haec vice rules, where an attorney licensed in another state is allowed to come in on a one-case basis to another state, so long as he was a member in good standing in his own state, had a member of the local state's Bar with him as second chair, and the judge approved. Check, check, check.

As a result of Judge Maas's recommendation, the case would be turned over to the local PD's assistant deputy for major cases, Breton Bontani. Bontani had a strong reputation in town as an intelligent young lawyer, with a lot of fight in him. Just what Benjamin would need in defense counsel. He was only three years into practice, but he'd done quite well on minor felonies in those short few years, but it was unlikely he was truly ready for a full-blown murder case.

Bontani, for his part, knew of Michael Kincaid as it turned out, looking at the phone message on top of the stack of messages his secretary handed him when he returned from court. He'd first noticed Kincaid due to several appearances on the nightly cable news shows while defending a wannabe actress charged with the murder of her rich, movie-producing husband. The press had eaten the story up. To Michael it was just an impossible case with an equally impossible client. She was a real charmer, but it got him a lot of airtime.

The prosecution argued that she had killed him out of rage when she learned that his production company had canceled plans for a strangely conceived sitcom. It would have been set in a Hawaiian tourist submarine. Apparently the pilot episode, starring his client the talented Ms. Gates, had met with less than stellar reviews from advertisers. After viewing the show himself, Michael felt assured that the production company's management had done the viewing public a great favor. An additional $5 million life insurance policy motive didn't help matters. As his defense, Michael managed to shift the focus to the "true" motives on the production company's shady financing schemes and/or the possibilities stemming from the dead man's penchant for luring beautiful starry-eyed bimbos to the casting couch, only to toss them aside for the next hopeful starlet. Susan Gates' fate would have also likely ended up on the cutting room floor too, but for her own proclivity towards conception and the child she promptly began carrying.

In her defense, Michael showed that more than one of the dead producer's conquests had threatened to get even. He offered a host of witnesses who were well aware of Mr. Gates' antics. Not surprisingly, he'd had to fight with his client because she didn't exactly enjoy the company of the bimbos and gold-diggers this strategy inherently associated her with and, quite rightly, depicted her as. By the end of the case, the press was in a feeding frenzy. When Michael's instincts proved correct and he'd gotten the notorious—and undoubtedly guilty—bitch off, the media proclaimed him that year's courtroom genius.

Bontani had always appreciated Kincaid and the hide-the-ball defense he'd used so effectively. Now, within forty-five minutes of a nice chat with Judge Maas and a message from Kincaid, Bontani was heading to his office to ring him on the phone to discuss the case.

* * *

Michael walked out of his room door stretching his arms and legs, leaving the door open behind him to find Kevin coming across the motel's parking lot.

"What's Joseph got to say?" He diverted his friend's path toward the murder scene.

"Exactly what you thought. Benjamin couldn't do it. He knows him; he's Navajo and Bear clan. Everything you said, but with details. Apparently his mom knows of you and wants you to defend him if you think you can help. Joseph said he'd appreciate anything you can do, also. Says he's a good kid and no way he's done this thing. Respect for life and the Blessing Way, all that."

"Yep, what I expected and guess I may now be helping defend the man who supposedly killed our friend. There's irony for you. Pretty weird, Kev."

"This entire thing is getting pretty weird. What's next?"

"Well, I think we need to look through the office again, I really feel we're missing something."

"Like what?"

"I'm really not sure" and his voice fell off, wondering for a few minutes until the ringing of his flip phone interrupted his thoughts. He excused himself from Kevin with a "I need to take this" heading for Room 2, Kevin pointing and diverting toward the office, as his friend answered with a calm "Michael Kincaid".

"Mr. Kincaid, Bret Bontani. It's certainly a pleasure to meet you and perhaps have the opportunity to work with you."

"Likewise, Mr. Bontani, I've heard good things about you. And please, call me Michael. Mr. Kincaid was my father."

"OK, Michael it is. I suppose we've got a lot to do so, why don't we get started. Call me Bret."

"I like your attitude, Bret. Look, I don't want to give you orders or anything—and I hope you're ok with me possibly coming in as co-counsel on this—but I'm afraid we've got little time for manners if we want to save Mr. Yazzie and I really need your faith and trust for a day or so until I can figure this out. Is that OK?"

"Sure. I can hold off any wolves from second chair for a few days. Just fire away."

Michael was pleased. Al Maas had cut him a break.

Michael continued. "I've taken the liberty of having my secretary Trish begin typing up a motion which she can email or fax over to you. Its being worked over by me and a colleague in Denver, but it'll have your name on it. I hope I wasn't too presumptuous, but it's the only way I could do it. I'm not of record, pro haec vice, yet."

"No problem. I completely understand. What kind of motion?"

"Two of them really."

"Two? Not wasting any time, are you?"

"As said, there's no time to waste. You'll understand once you get the motions. Seems the feds have a very big interest in taking our client away. One motion is for bond, the other is in essence a motion to quash, sort of; it's a bit complicated, as you'll see. Hopefully it leads to an arraignment. Pleading him not guilty, of course."

"Of course, but Michael, wouldn't it be wise to hold over the arraignment for thirty days or so, so we can review the charges?"

"Under normal circumstances that would be good thinking, but not in this case. The feds are trying to take control of the case and we need the State of Colorado to exert immediate jurisdiction. If we don't, we'll lose him, and believe me, we don't want that to happen for a whole host of reasons."

"I agree, but why do the feds even care?"

"I don't know, but don't worry about that right now. Trust me, they want him and you'll know more about this than you want to in a day or so. Take this as fact: this is the most important arraignment you'll ever do."

"No offense, but I'm sure I'll do another murder arraignment."

"Maybe so, but it'll never be a ride like the one you're about to take. It's just a hunch, but I'll bet this'll be the strangest arraignment you'll ever see and strategy-wise it's a bad idea for me to be there for it. All I can tell you is this case is not what it seems, so expect the unexpected when you go into court. Here's what I know for sure. Maas has you calendared for 5:00 p.m. today. The DA has already agreed to arraign him at that time. Don't be late, whatever you do. Maas will, of course, grant the discovery motion and deny bond. Don't worry about that, it'll just happen. Your job is to make sure that no one stops that arraignment before you enter Yazzie's plea. Be prepared for anything, especially an assistant United States attorney who might stop by. I'm not sure exactly what they'll pull but I've got someone on the inside up in Denver working on this right now and we'll know before you appear and you'll have the right ammunition. Just don't buy in to any of their nonsense, demand your client's speedy trial rights, and you'll be fine. One of us will be in further touch before 4 as we know more."

"Sure, I understand. But I just don't get why an AUSA would show up on a simple state murder arraignment. Sounds like you think we're going to have some real trouble."

"I know we're in for trouble. I just don't know how much, when and exactly what. The Feds have already taken over the investigation from the Durango PD, and I'll bet there's an AUSA in town as we speak, but I've got confidence in you. I hear, you're pretty good at rolling with the punches."

"Thanks. I do all right."

"One other thing. My secretary Trish will send you a set of points and authorities on an obscure 1800s statute in about an hour or so. Read it, feel free to make changes if you feel necessary, but be ready to argue it at 5, because I'd bet my last dollar you're going to have to use it. If you can, call me after you've finished to talk about this mess. Right now I've got some other things I've got to do and I apologize ahead of time for not being there with you."

"I can handle anything some AUSA can throw at me."

"Well then . . . . Good Luck."

"Thanks. I'll call you when I can after this is done."

"Great, and thanks again for your help."

"No problem. Bye."

Michael hung up and called Trish again.

"Law offices of Michael Kincaid."

"Hi. Did you get my email with the first draft?"

"Hello to you, too."

"Sorry, Trish. I'm under the gun, literally."

"It's OK."

"You get the email?"

"Yeah, first draft is done and over with Leonardo. Said he'd have updates and edits with the hour after he gathered some further information. I'll get any edits done and get it sent over to you as soon as I can for final review and then send it out to everyone and the court before 5. Already got the emails and numbers."

"Don't worry about final review from me. If you think it looks good send it, not a lot of time. You're one in a million, you are. So, um, what are you doing for the next week or so?"

"Nothing's certain. Thought I might flip over to Greece and get me a hot lover after I get out of the office, but other than that, not much."

"Think you could put the Grecian god off for a little while?"

"I suppose. What did you have in mind? A week in the Caymans, maybe?"

"How about a ski vacation in Colorado?"

"It's April and eighty degrees in LA. You mean there's still snow there!?!"

"Snow, yes, but unfortunately the ski area is already closed, so really a no-ski vacay."

"Well, fortunately, I don't ski anyway. So I guess I can't pass up an offer like that, now can I? Too enticing. A Colorado ski vacation at a closed ski area. When do I leave and what should I pack?"

"First flight after you get the motions out; and bring that laptop of yours with an open mind."

"Sounds like we've got a case."

"Maybe, we'll see. Leave a message and let me know when to pick you up."

"You got it, boss."

* * *

Michael closed his eyes for a while to think, until a rap at the door stirred him. He looked through the peephole, saw it was Kevin, and opened the door.

"I've finished with the desk, so I thought I'd come over here before starting with anything else."

"Just finished with the public defender and Trish. How'd you make out?"

"Nothing, really. Gotta hand it to you, though, Michael. I'd never have gotten that mess cleaned up. Thanks."

"No prob."

"You've got a future, though, if you ever decide to quit law."

"Oh yeah? In what?"

"Housekeeping, of course."

"Gee, thanks."

"I gotta ask you a question, though." Kevin turned serious. "Why'd you clean up the front desk if you didn't want to touch the interior desk?"

"What? I didn't even touch the front desk. What are you talking about? Show me."

Kevin walked him over to the office and pointed to the second shelf, next to the cash drawer, saying no way Luigi had stacked those guest receipts like that, they were a mess the other day.

When Michael looked he realized immediately it was out of place with everything else he'd found. It had been the first place he'd checked and he'd forgotten about it. Nothing major, but another confirming circumstance of a sloppy search. The pile of guest registrations and the like next to the cash drawer was perfectly stacked. Nothing on its own, but in light of the place's overall messiness, one thing was clearly visible. Whoever had helped in the killing had gone through the shelves and then neatly stacked them back, at some point. But when, something didn't add up.

"Totally missed that and no thief would have stacked that up." His mind flicked back to the scene from before, not recalling the stack like that. "Strange. Wonder what else I missed?"

The second he said the words he knew the inevitable was coming. And if Snow hadn't been there last night as he said, then who was? The federal boys? Or possibly someone else. Somebody was looking for something, though, that was for sure. Something tangible that they hadn't found before. He moved quickly to the kitchen with Kevin, questioning and in tow. Rounding the corner he stopped dead in his tracks and his shoulders shrank. On the floor, in front of him, lay the sticky third and fourth drawers from the sink cabinet, washcloths and towels spilled on the floor. Overturned, one drawer exposed a false bottom. No wonder it hadn't seemed to fit.

They'd most likely finally found Luigi's safe, just a little too late. Michael cursed his ineptitude. He looked at the broken wood that only a few hours before held utensils, towels and probably the answer to Luigi's murder. He shook his head slowly muttering to himself "real brilliant, Mr. Holmes".

They spent the rest of the day cleaning up the place after having been ransacked again. After a couple of hours they'd had enough and Kevin went back to his house and Michael to his room. He turned on the television and lay down on the couch thinking of everything he'd seen and learned over the past days, from a beautiful Canyon sunrise to sitting in this room. What was next, he thought, as he drifted off into the background of the television until startled by his cell phone ringing, instinctively answering with "Michael Kincaid" blinking his eyes and trying to bring the room into focus.

"Oh Mr. Kincaid, so formal" came a gentle, toying voice from the phone.

His eyes brightened, his breathing skipped as his subconscious quickly connected the dots, remembering the sweet, entrancing voice, and glancing back at the caller ID and recalling the piece of paper before he replying sweetly. "Hi Erin, how are you?" His normally steady voice a little too quaky for his liking.

"Very good Michael, I'm impressed. I'm great, how are you and why haven't you called me yet?"

"I could never forget it and I'm getting better all the time" a smile now encompassing his full face, continuing "and I was really just about to call you" not coming up with anything better to say.

"Sure you were, but I know you'd have eventually gotten around to me. You know its funny you are here now, I had the strangest dream about you the other night. Thought about you a couple of times last Saturday and now you are here. Pretty odd, isn't it."

"Yeah, I suppose so."

She laughed a little before asking what brought him to town and the two begin talking with the naturalness of two good friends who hadn't talked in a while. They remembered old times, the time they'd spent together since kids, their summers at the pool and about where life had taken them. They talked about his trip from LA and going to visit his mom with a few stops in between. Erin in turn caught him up on what she had been doing in Durango. Both politely avoiding the negative things from their pasts they both knew each other knew. After some time Erin reluctantly said she needed to go do some work she needed to complete before tomorrow, as she was hoping to get out of the office for a few days. Michael admitted he needed to make a couple of calls too, but he really didn't want to hang up. She told him she hoped they could talk again soon since he might only be in town for a short period before saying good-bye, a pleasant smile coming to her face as she hung up the phone.

Erin slipped back into her chair thinking about Michael. It was so good to talk to him and she'd missed his stories and tales much more than she'd remembered. She could still remember him, as others probably did not know him. The young shy boy she'd met so very long ago. She reached over and turned the desk light out, closing her eyes and remembering the first time she saw him. The new kid in town, getting on the bus for the first time and tripping up the stairs as he got on. All the other kids moved towards the edges of their seats, but Erin slide over to the window allowing him a place to sit. She thought he was cute, for a boy, and a wide smile grew across her face as she settled comfortably in her chair thinking through the many days they'd later share until her thoughts focused on how it somehow all went awry.

In the darkness she thought carefully back to their high school days, looking inwardly toward herself and how her life had turned out. In truth, in high school they were both a little full of themselves, she thought with soft giggle and an upturn of her lips. But there really were times with him that had always left her a little noncommittal because he seemed somewhat indifferent. She knew she liked him and he liked her, but their relationship never seemed to develop the something more she had always wanted in a man she'd want to stay with forever. Then again, the one she'd chosen hadn't worked out either so maybe she just wasn't a good judge of men she thought.

Still, Michael had his moments. The first guy that ever brought her flowers. The first guy she'd ever danced with, although they were only 10. The first guy for many things. She had thought she loved him, but she became unsure as it became more real. But they were both young and new to these type of relationships. Perhaps had they stayed together they would have matured together, or perhaps too they would have ended in divorce rather than Eden.

She'd enjoyed seeing him again, a few years back at their reunion. He'd changed quite a lot by that time, out of law school he'd seemed more mature, rounding well into a good man. But she was with her husband, and although she still harbored some feelings for him, she wasn't about to open herself to any of those possibilities with all the problems she was having in her marriage. She opened her eyes, staring out into the darkness and loneliness of her home, as she seemed to do every night now. She pulled her self up from the chair making her way in to bed, now thinking back to the summer before her senior year and the young boy that had captivated her heart as she drifted asleep.

A couple miles away in the motel room Michael lay quietly in his bed also thinking about Erin… and Lori… and Benjamin Yazzie. So many thoughts raced through his mind; from his joy at talking with Erin, to his guilt of it being too soon after Lori was gone, to Benjamin sitting in a jail, likely scared to death. His mind drifting, drifting . . . drifting, into a deep sleep.

DAY SIX

Evil Always Raises an Ugly Head

By six Michael was wide-awake. Unusual for him, but now he stared blindly at the motel ceiling, gazing down to the part in the curtains through which the morning darkness dissipated outside. Pale yellow light crept in from the east.

Thankfully, his morning nightmare had been replaced by the less ghastly version, but with a twist. Kokopelli was there again, gleefully playing his instrument atop the dune. So too was the Hopi jester Mudhead, pounding out his steady beat as the other two Kachinas swayed with the music. As before, the Yei chiefs flanked their man, walking him to fire's edge, before joining the others in the circular dance around the fire and the man. Big Fly, the protector, hovered in the stars above as the mysterious Ku?itu masked woman again emerged from the shadows, stepping slowly into the light. Big Fly swooped down to the man's shoulder, sending a smile of approval toward him as the mysterious masked figure drew closer. The other two Kachinas dodged playfully between the man and approaching figure, and in so doing, Michael's mind could finally observe them.

A pointed yellow snout protruded from the mask of the one that had interacted with the Yei chiefs. A dividing line of red crossed above his slit eyes of his Ku?itu mask at center brow, separating the top third of red from the mostly blue face. His left eye was yellow, his right blue. On one side of the mask, a small squash protruded from his ear; on the other, two erect eagle features pointed up to the stars. His upper body was pinkish brown, a red sash was painted diagonally across his torso, wide aqua colored rings tinted his biceps, and two strands of turquoise beads hung around his neck. He wore a simple white kilt with black triangles for side bordering, complimenting red and blue raincloud designs, and his squat legs emerged from beneath the black hem above red moccasins.

The other Kachina was painted much differently. Black and white rings ran around this body like an old prison jumpsuit. From the top of his mask jetted two conical tubes, black and white stripes leading up to the point and strands of brown straw extruding from the tips. His mask was mostly white, save for the black slits for eyes and the pronounced black grin etched widely across his face. Around his waist hung a blue sash, leading down to a white kilt and red moccasins like the other.

Together they all danced around the figure as it advanced toward the man, playfully grabbing at the mask.

Suddenly, from out of the dark Coyote leapt toward the group, the trickster snatching the Ku?itu in his jaws mid-flight, bounding and running from the group toward the distant dune. The figure whirled wildly, the reddish blanket cast off, falling helplessly into the featureless man, catching her as she fell.

Atop the dune, coyote pranced with glee, slinging his head high in the air several times before releasing the mask with a forceful upward thrust of his head, its momentum carrying it high into the stars before it exploded into a brilliant flash. Michael's attention drew back to the woman, her hair spilling to the ground and Michael gazed deeply toward her eyes, searching for her.

And when he calmly woke from his restful sleep, his search was continuing. It was a strange dream for sure, but in some ways oddly comforting to him. He felt refreshed, lying there thinking about its significance, as he had so many days ago in Hosteen Begay's sweat lodge. He chuckled to himself, stirring a bit and thinking perhaps he'd have to become an earlier riser if these were his new morning dreams, peaceful but weird. Eventually he allowed his thoughts to flow back from these amusing and pleasant dreams to the actual nightmare that had been unfolding the last forty-eight hours.

L.A. seemed an eternity away. Early morning searches, federal seizures of Luigi's body and few assets, assistant US attorneys running all over the place, and the only tangible piece of evidence that might explain it all: gone. Yesterday afternoon's events hadn't disappointed his expectations, they fit perfectly into the ever-increasing pattern of bizarreness that had worked its way through his entire week. He groaned, rolling over on his side, staring at the wall a couple of feet from his nose.

And in the middle of all this, there was Erin. Lovely, wonderful Erin. His childhood love. He rolled back to his back, staring again upward, a wide smile now embracing him. He wondered what she looked like now, how the world and time had changed her. He vowed he should definitely she her. He wondered if she still was the same girl at heart he knew so long ago; or had life's trials transformed her as her father had alluded to. Had life really beaten her down like it had him, surely not he hoped. Erin always had an irrepressible character. She was always upbeat and optimistic and seemed so on the phone last night. He hoped the world had not changed her but also made his thoughts turn to how much it had changed him. He was no longer the shy young boy or the young high-schooler he had been so many years before when he knew her well. He knew the legal practice had changed him, and not necessarily in good ways. He had become calloused in many ways, less trusting, always taking any story with a grain of salt. He'd become a doubter of human nature, in general, what with the many cases he'd dealt with over the years. And with Lori's death, he'd began doubting the good in life even more. He'd begun to feel as if there really was no good in the world, and particularly no good for him. He was surely no good for Lori, he hadn't been there for her when she needed him most, paying attention to clients more so than to her, leaving her alone that day to go up PCH to meet some client with a sad story. And then she was gone, taken away so quickly. He'd never be any good to anyone any more. Would he?

He rolled over again thinking at least he could feel good in his work and about their one small victory of the day. Benjamin remained in the county lock-up, provided the feds hadn't pulled some kind of midnight coup. They wanted him bad, though. But why? He was still somewhat surprised by their show of force yesterday afternoon. Before he'd gone to bed he'd talked to both Bret Bontani and Leonardo. From what he'd pieced together from both conversations it turned out that indeed a couple of hotshot AUSAs and their clerk had made the trek down from Denver to visit Judge Maas. Apparently just one lawyer wouldn't do to get the message across. After they'd gotten rebuffed by the jailer a couple of times and couldn't get help from the DA for some strange reason, they simply turned to one of their other many colleagues in the Denver office and had a signed transfer order by 1 from some "ready to sign anything" federal magistrate. With plenty of governmental money to make it happen, the 2 AUSAs, along with their clerk and a federal Marshal just for good measure, took the 20 min drive to Centennial airport, caught a private one hour hop down to Durango to hand-carry the signed order in plenty of time for all five to be in Judge Maas's court filing their paperwork by 3 and demanding the clerk place them at highest priority on the court's late afternoon calendar call. They'd been efficient, if nothing else, but they didn't know Mr. Yazzie was already on the calendar.

Law was certainly a business of who you knew, the money you had and the power you could wield in the courtroom; and the most powerful and well-heeled litigant in the world was the US government. The armies of attorneys, investigators and clerks from a single agency would dwarf any Wall Street firm. If they wanted you, they'd get you. One way or the other. If Justice couldn't get the job done, then Customs, Revenue or a whole host of others would. Just ask Capone. And they sure seemed to want Benjamin.

But this didn't just feel like DC run amuck. To Michael the whole thing seemed . . . well . . . rather personal. He rolled to his back, shifting his stare on a cobweb in the far corner. Getting Benjamin wouldn't be that tough for someone with influence and a stake in the matter, he thought studying the cobweb; a simple favor from Justice would likely do the trick. A call from Washington to the local US Attorney would get the ball rolling nicely. Then a quick conversation with the magistrate's clerk regarding the urgency and national interest in the transfer of Benjamin Yazzie to federal custody, coupled with the appropriate paperwork, would advance the matter immediately to the top of the calendar or the judge's chambers. Any magistrate, with eyes toward a federal judgeship, would be more than happy to be helpful. After all, an endorsement from the US Attorney for the district couldn't hurt their future consideration and might even move the magistrate to the top of the nominees' list over time and plenty of cooperation. With no opposition and some nice supporting affidavits to make it all nice and legal, a transfer order was issued for one Benjamin Yazzie, student and enemy of the Federal Government, sending him to an uncertain future as a guest of the Bureau of Prisons.

It must have seemed so well set up to the team of federal prosecutors when they were finally placed on the court's calendar for 5. Michael had roared with laughter last night when Bontani recounted what transpired in the courtroom. The feds didn't even know what hit them. Judge Maas was so stirred up by the time the assistant US attorneys appeared before him, what with a federal court trying to usurp jurisdiction in a local murder trial, that he made them wait until around 5 when everything else was finished. And then the judge had shut down the lead AUSA with the first words out of his mouth.

Leonardo's info on the case had been deadly accurate and the feds walked into the ambush without expecting a thing. Leonardo had somehow, and Michael didn't ask how, gotten into the Yazzie federal case file in Denver before the court clerk had sealed it under a protective order. That information had tipped Michael off to the peculiar and antiquated federal statute that formed the basis of their order to transfer. Public Defender Bontani simply sat quietly as Assistant United States Attorney Charles Thompson stepped to the lectern to make the case for the People of the United States of America, followed closely by AUSA Atkins and their clerk, who took up positions at counsel table, the Marshal walking over to chat with the Sheriff's deputy assigned to the court.

Judge Maas had barely given Thompson the time to announce his appearance before he began demanding an explanation as to why the federal government wanted his murder suspect and why it needed 2 lawyers, a clerk and a US Marshall to acquire him. Thompson conceded that the State of Colorado might hold concurrent jurisdiction, but argued there existed a federal question, which took primary jurisdiction over any claims. Holding a brief in his right hand and arrogantly waving it in the air, he stepped from behind the lectern and started around the counsel table, stating, "It's all contained in the moving papers and the signed magistrate's order." As he passed behind his chair, AUSA Atkins stepped over and unceremoniously flipped a copy onto the table near Bontani, returning to his seat without word. As AUSA Thompson rounded the front corner of the counsel table, Judge Maas's large bailiff stepped right into his path and away from the Marshal.

"Don't step in my well, counselor," Judge Maas stated, mildly, without looking up.

The bailiff took the document from AUSA Thompson's hand, remaining until he turned and began his retreat to the lectern. Bontani quickly leafed through his copy, finding exactly what he'd been tipped to by Leonardo. Michael gave it credit as a somewhat ingenious jurisdictional argument, relying on an obscure statute that the feds had excavated from over a century before. Somebody must have had that one in their back pocket from God only knew when. They'd probably gotten some great brownie points for their cleverness. And clever it was.

And it probably would have worked on most judges in the state, but not a thirty-year sitting judge with concerns about Big Brother in his courtroom and a spot on Opposition supplied by Leonardo and his staff; which Bontani nonchalantly forwarded to the Court, through the bailiff, before rising and stating "Your Honor, Mr. Yazzie hereby submits his Opposition to the motion and demands the Court retain jurisdiction and set an immediate arraignment and jury trial in this Court so that he may clear his name of these heinous charges of which he is not guilty" before flipping a copy on to the prosecution's table to the astonished looks of the 2 AUSAs and their clerk.

A quick review of the briefs Leonardo had emailed Michael and the annotations to the statute in the US Code they were relying on showed its original Nineteenth-Century intended use was for US Marshals to arrest and transfer outlaws hiding out in the Indian Territories of Oklahoma, bringing them to answer before the nearest federal court. Apparently, in the 1870s, the federal judge in Fort Smith, Arkansas—one Judge Isaac Charles Parker—got fed up with the lawlessness and the outlaws' ability to avoid punishment by hiding out in the Indian Nations. After much complaint, Congress obliged with a statute, and soon Judge Parker was "extraditing" the infamous bandits and desperado Injuns of the Old West to justice in Fort Smith. Over time, the annotations showed, he judicially expanded his statutory power to place original jurisdiction in his federal court when a crime victim was a present or former federal deputy or member of the military. The judge had cited the need to control the process of the Court and the authorities vested with power to enforce its orders. No one had ever really challenged the old judge on the expansion of his powers. Then again, it seemed no one with any sense generally ever questioned Judge Parker. The territorial governments in his day were just glad to be rid of the notorious criminals, who never seemed to stick around long enough for appeals.

Using this statute, Judge Parker had become very effective. In time he'd hanged sixty-eight men for various crimes, doing more to clean up the Wild West than Wyatt Earp. This finally earned him his nickname, The Hanging Judge. Long before Judge Roy Bean was The Law West of the Pecos, Judge Parker was the law west of the Mississippi.

The annotations showed two other interesting tidbits. In 1883, Judge Parker had used the extradition law to convict and sentence Belle Starr to nine months in the Correctional House for stealing her neighbor's horse. Second, this statute hadn't been cited since well before 1900, by which time Colorado had been a state for a couple of decades. That second point became the first point in the defendant's opposition brief.

The simple five-page Opposition was quietly handed to the judge by the bailiff, but Bontani had probably not even needed it. Judge Maas studied both briefs for the required period of time before addressing the attorneys. In the end he'd only needed a few seconds and the first point to hold the antiquated statute unconstitutional as a violation of the US Constitution's 10th Amendment, reserving the state's right to try its own criminal defendants. Judge Maas also ruled the order invalid since it applied the federal statute to a state, as opposed to a US territory, as the law had been designed and intended from his reading of the legislative comments in the annotations. Maas slammed his gavel and stated matter of factly "the US government's motion is denied, Mr. Yazzie will remain in local custody pending further orders of this court."

AUSA Thompson was livid at the ruling and told Maas so in no uncertain terms. He couldn't believe that a local judge would have the nerve to reject a federal magistrate's order and declare a federal statute unconstitutional.

"This court has unmitigated gall," he'd said as he stepped around the counsel table, furiously waving the order in his hand. He approached that small area called "the well" where attorneys were traditionally forbidden. The burly bailiff again stepped into his path, his bulky arms folded across his chest, a scowl planted squarely on his face.

"Mr. Thompson!" Judge Maas, his ire now raised, looking up from his bench his eyes squarely fixed on Thompson before sternly stating "I suggest you take your opinions, briefcase and butt out of my courtroom before you end up in the cell next to Mr. Yazzie counselor. You're on the verge of criminal contempt in my courtroom Mr. Thompson. If you don't like my order, I'm sure you know where the Appeals Court building is located up there in Denver."

Straining, trying to get a line of sight toward the judge around the massive bailiff, Thompson finally huffed, "I am well versed in the location of the appeals courts, Your Honor, and you can be sure I'll be visiting them. I'll be back in a couple of days!" He finally reversed; stomping back toward counsel table like a child just told he couldn't play with his favorite toy, retrieving his briefcase and associates as he passed.

"Come on back any time, Mr. Thompson. We're always open for law and order in La Plata County," the judge called as the bailiff stalked closely behind the departing feds catching what he thought was a slight laugh from his colleague from the Marshal's office. As Thompson stepped through the door, Maas gave him one final shot: "But don't come near my well again!"

Five minutes later, now joined by the DA, defendant Benjamin Yazzie was personally brought before the Court whereupon he was arraigned, a plea of not guilty was entered on his behalf, bond was denied, a jury trial was set and Michael's pro haec vice motion approved. They would live to fight another day with the feds.

But despite this temporary victory, Michael's thoughts were still troubled. Why did they want his new client so badly? The state court was perfectly equipped to try and convict Benjamin. This wasn't some oddball issue of federal civil rights justice for a fallen war veteran, as unconvincingly argued by the government's motion. No, it was something else. The one logical conclusion was that someone very high up had something to hide and that a prolonged trial might just dig that up. And therein lay further implications.

Something in this unfolding story was way out of sorts. Each recent turn had increased the likelihood that Luigi had been killed for a very specific reason. These developments had increased the odds that he had known something he shouldn't have, and this knowledge was apparently immensely disturbing to someone. But it wasn't some average Joe. No, this was someone with the power and influence to ensure it wasn't brought out into the open. Therein lay the inherent consequence that had been troubling Michael's thoughts. In order to save his client and find Luigi's killer, Michael Kincaid would also have to learn this deadly secret.

It wasn't really troubling for himself. Michael was never the kind of guy who frightened easily and he'd learned long ago to be cautious. But this time, for a couple of reasons, he just simply didn't care about his fate anymore. He rolled uneasily onto his side, his eyes moving downward to the corner where carpet met trim. He'd become lost at the instant of her death. The truth was that his heart was still broken, his will to go on still wavering . . . his future still uncertain, as it was with others who'd similarly felt the pain of such a sudden loss of a loved one. But he was also furious with this ongoing subterfuge and didn't really care who he pissed off. He wasn't afraid of the consequences. He'd been in some nasty spots before. And besides, killing the attorney on a case was way too messy for most criminals. His only true worry was for his friends. They, whoever they were, would have to assume anyone associated with Michael's defense might know something too, and would necessarily be in danger right along with him. That clearly meant Kevin, Trish, Bontani and anyone else who might become involved. Michael had to limit their exposure as much as he could.

The more Michael thought about the federal lawyers' pompous, stop-at-nothing attitude, the more he tossed in the bed. It was as if they believed no one could touch them. Perhaps they were right, but not even The Mob was that arrogant. In trying to get Yazzie into federal custody, AUSA Thompson had spoken of a country defending an old comrade in his death. This from the same people who had ordered the same old war veteran's body taken from his family, under the auspices of a formal military burial in Arlington.

Military burial my ass, Michael thought. Whoever was involved didn't give a shit about Luigi Morrealli. They cared only about themselves and their own agenda. He was going to find and hang the ones responsible, just as lethally as Judge Parker would have.

He'd thought enough about it for now and rolled to a seated position, deciding to get a shower and some morning coffee. The back door to the office remained unlocked, why bother when everybody was coming and going anyway. Once in the front-glass enclosure, he loaded the coffee and poured some water from the water cooler into the machine, shaking his head in amusement. He watched as the traffic passed by on Main and after a few minutes of brewing-coffee sounds, armed with two fresh steamy cups, he was off to repay Kevin for his wake-up call the day before. Daylight was burning and he was on a case.

Michael pounded for at least five full minutes before the door swung open, this time the tables turned. Michael handed him a cup of coffee. Kevin didn't say anything, just grunted and stumbled to the sofa.

"You need to get a shower; we've got a full day ahead of us." Kevin nodded with half-opened eyes.

"You talk to Joseph again?" Same nod. "You get everything set up?" Same nod. "For tomorrow?" Same nod. "Are you a moron?" Same nod. "All right, get your shower and come on over, we've got to talk." Same nod.

* * *

Anderson was already seated in front of the desk when the troll arrived. He'd been debriefed and ridiculed by the troll early that morning, learning the latest "facts" as Tielson would have him believe. He watched loathingly as the smallish legs shuffled toward the desk. Tielson started grumbling again before he reached his seat. "I trust you have some better intel for me as to why this man killed our contact."

"I have additional information, sir. Over the last couple of hours I've been in touch with several of our people, but it is an evolving situation."

"Have they found anything else?" he asked, sliding into the over-sized chair.

"Not yet, sir. They've reported no activity."

The troll just grunted in his direction. "Anybody know of the agency's interest in this matter?"

"Nobody appears to be. But Sir, I'm not sure it's all good, though."

"Like what?" He wheeled toward the junior man.

"Well, I'm not sure what it really means, but Tompkins reports the motel owner and an attorney are nosing around out there."

"Nosing around what?"

"The situation. Tompkins reports that this lawyer may be working with the public defender."

"So what? Just another scumbag lawyer sniffing around for a fee. That's one of the things that makes this country great, Anderson. Everyone is entitled to a spirited defense." The little man chortled as he slid back into his oversized chair. "Besides, any involvement on the part of the lawyers should be short-lived."

"Well, sir, I'm not so sure about that. They were apparently successful in thwarting Justice's attempts at taking jurisdiction."

"What!" The little man shot from his chair, beginning his familiar slow, steady march.

Anderson gazed disgustedly toward the shadow pacing along the wall. Refocusing, he reluctantly added, "Yes sir, but that's not what makes me worry most. The second attorney's not a public defender or even a local from what our people can tell. It seems he was just staying at the motel. We're not sure what interest he might have."

"I see. This could be concerning to us," he said coolly, but Anderson sensed Tielson was truly troubled by this entire conversation. The shadow stopped and turned slightly. "Does this lawyer know anything? Who is he?"

"We really don't know, a guy named Michael Kincaid. All we know is that things aren't proceeding as smoothly as you'd have liked and he's just appeared for the defendant. We're monitoring the situation, but we can't even be sure of his true connection right now."

"Michael Kincaid huh? We'll need to deal with this the right way this time. Up front." He placed his stubby fingers across his lips and rubbed, thinking. After a few moments his beady eyes visited themselves intensely upon the junior man. Through his fingers he said, "Perhaps he needs something else to think about," he mumbled.

"Sir?"

"I said, I think I need to speak to Tompkins. Get him for me. Right now! And get this info over to the Old Man, those were his guys that messed this up."

Anderson looked toward the wretched figure across the desk, nausea rising in his gut. He slowly rose from his chair with a reserved, "Yes, sir." Apparently the troll had intentions of doing more than merely guarding his bridge. The implication of his comments were that he intended on going on the offensive— and that Anderson was now, reluctantly, stuck squarely in the middle.

* * *

Michael left, not sure if Kevin even knew he had been there.

He stopped back by the office, grabbed another coffee and called Trish at the office. No answer. It was a bit early, but where the hell was she? Damn. In Durango.

He picked up the motel phone and called the Stratler Hotel. She'd be there. It was the nicest and most expensive in town.

"Stratler Hotel. How may I direct your call?"

"Patricia Cochrine's room."

"One moment; I'll connect you."

A pause, a ring and . . .

"Forget something, Michael?"

"Hi, Trish. Sorry. I fell asleep."

"Sure. No problem. It's just going to cost you, that's all."

"I don't like the sound of this. What's this costing me?"

"At least a limo ride from the airport and a suite at the best hotel in Durango."

"I didn't know Durango even had a limo. Figures you'd find one."

"A girl's gotta do what a girl's gotta do."

"Take the morning off, with my apologies for forgetting you. I'll meet you at the Diamond Belle there in the Stratler at one. Have yourself a good breakfast in the room. Check out downtown, the train, the galleries, and I'll call you if I need you."

"Sounds great. Think I'll take a check around and look for some art. That should cost you a little more. You can afford it, though."

"Trish, just remember, we don't have a paying client right now. Take it easy on me."

"I know. Spoilsport."

"You're incredible. Thanks. Gotta go. Bye." He hung up.

* * *

Kevin was headed across the parking lot towards Room Two as Michael peeked out the window. With a shout, Michael diverted him towards the office. When Kevin was in talking distance, Michael started in on him.

"Man, you look like hell."

"Thanks. Good morning to you, too. I didn't sleep all night."

"Yeah, this entire sordid mess can give you nightmares."

"I talked to Luigi's son again last night and he said someone from the military had finally returned his call about the services. They said that the arrangements were in the works, but that's all he could tell me."

"I'm not surprised."

"Why?"

"They probably have to buy some time and hide their mistakes. Whoever we're dealing with here probably never intended on having Luigi found at all. Even if he was found, it wouldn't have been for a long time. He'd have just simply disappeared. These guys weren't playing games, Kevin. They were searching pretty intensely. They must have been scared off by something, probably Benjamin, but it doesn't really matter. Remember, they came back to finish the job night before last."

"For what, though?"

"For whatever Luigi had on them, I suspect. Like I told you, these guys were looking for something and it was something specific, I'll guarantee it. They would have interrogated him as to what he knew and what he had. These guys were pros, assuming some hunches are right. My guess is they used some kind of a little helper to get their information. But it would have had to have been something exotic; toxicology screens are routinely done these days during autopsies. A routine tox screen probably wouldn't have revealed the presence of a truth serum or something, but who knows what happens if someone started digging. That's why they involved the VA. No body, no tox screen. It's that simple."

"That's a bit far-fetched, don't you think?"

"That's probably not even the half of it, Kevin. You yourself said Luigi didn't take insulin or other drugs, right?"

Kevin nodded.

"Well, one of the things I found after moving the couch was a small piece of rounded aluminum or some kind of foil. Not foil really, but you know the stuff they seal IV drugs or aspirin bottles with?"

Kevin nodded again.

"Well, I found a piece. By itself it doesn't mean much, but what with the facts being stranger than the fiction in this case, it makes me wonder if they injected him to find out what he knew. A needle mark or tox screen might alert a pathologist. If not, why take the body? Nothing to cover up. Then again, I might be nuts and the kid's guilty."

"No, you've been right so far. I don't like the implications, though."

"Kevin, if you want to take a step back from this, I'd understand. It's probably going to get even hairier and it won't take long."

"No, Michael. This is more my fight than yours. If anyone's going to take a step back, it should be you, not me. Since I know you won't any more than I would, I think we're both in to the end."

"Yeah, let's just try not to be ended."

"Sounds good, but what are we going to do about Luigi? It's just not right. He deserves better."

"Tell Frank that I spoke to the army and that they will be shipping the remains to wherever he likes, Arlington if that suits him, and they will be in contact with him in the next few days to make the final military burial arrangements. Send my condolences."

"Will that happen?"

"It should. The heat's got to turned up a little bit on them yesterday and somebody's butt is going to get roasted. They'll send him home eventually, too many eyes on it now."

"But you said . . . I mean, what about the tox screen?"

"No sense them creating a federal incident over the body. Cremation would be an easy solution to the problem. Someone in defense will make a big issue to the family about their mistake to the family. They'll explain and apologize all over themselves. They'll supply an honor guard and a trumpeter and the family will forget about the mix-up. They're burying their loss, not suspecting foul play."

"Why not just bury him and say they didn't think he had a family? Sweep it under the rug."

"Probably that's exactly what they'd hoped would happen, unknown homeless vet found based on tattoos, but I think we've put a stop to that thinking, though."

"How?"

"Well, Frank's contact with Veterans Affairs most certainly raised a red flag. No matter what we're dealing with here, not everyone in the government could be involved and they can't cover every base. Questions will be asked and answers will have to be provided. Plus, I have this friend up in Denver, a guy named Leonardo. He's going in with a writ of mandamus against the Defense Department today."

"A writ of what?"

"Mandamus. It's what you use to make a governmental agency act in a certain manner. The court mandates that they do what you're asking for. In this case, it's kinda like a literal habeas corpus motion, which means "return the body" in Latin. We're asking the court to order the Defense Department to turn over Luigi's body."

"Will it work?"

"It'll do its job. What do you think Defense can do, oppose it? No, they'll tell the judge they're looking into it and if they've got the body, by mistake, of course, they'll return it to the family. Eventually they'll come up with something stupid as an excuse, something like their records showed no family to claim the body or something. Just trying to help a veteran and made an administrative error. The judge will order his return and it'll be put into motion. A little callous-sounding, but that's the way the system works. Somebody'll take some heat, though, and I'm sure they won't think too much of us poking our noses in all over the place. In this case, I think the heat will roll downhill right on top of us."

"On us? Sounds like they'll be upset with you more than me."

"Probably, but it doesn't much matter. You're the one I'm working with so they won't care too much for you, either."

"But it's worth it, Michael. He was a good man and he deserved better than this. If nothing else, he at least deserves a proper burial by his family."

"Yeah, he does, and he'll get it."

"So what's next?"

"Well, I've got to go to the coroner's first and see if they left any tracks. Then it's down to the jail to interview Benjamin. Something's been bugging me that I read in Snow's report."

"What's that?"

"According to those reports Snow gave me, Benjamin said Luigi wasn't dead when he got to him. Like I said, maybe Benjamin scared off the real killers. According to Benjamin, he reached down to see if Luigi was breathing, which must have been how he got the blood on his hand. More importantly, according to the report, Luigi said something to Benjamin before he died. Snow told me he originally assumed Benjamin was lying, but I'm not so sure."

"What did he say?"

"That's what I want to know. Snow's report said it was 'Hello, Cody' and then something about someone named 'Zell.' Know anybody by that name?"

"No, I don't, but I'll ask around."

"Do. While you're at it, see if you can find any more of Luigi's buddies, particularly Nick. He had to have other friends. See what you can do. I'm meeting Trish at one at the Belle. Meet me there and I'll introduce you, then I've got a couple of other things to deal with in the afternoon."

"Fine, but who's Trish?"

"My secret weapon. See ya."

Michael reappeared from Room Two a few minutes later, now dressed in a coat and tie. He jumped into his Explorer and zoomed away in an instant.

He drove over to the Sisters of Mercy Medical Center, heading into her bowels. After a bit he reached the office of Dr. Daniel Bustee, the hospital's pathologist and the part-time county coroner. One of Dr. Bustee's sons had been in high school with Michael and he was hoping he'd remember him. He knocked on the door and after being asked in, he found the balding man looking up.

"Michael Kincaid!" he smiled. "It's been a long time since I've seen you. I wondered how long it would take for you to come down to the dregs of Mercy. How are you?"

"Fine, Dr. Bustee," he replied, a bit of a question in his smile.

"You must be here on the Morrealli case. I saw in the Herald this morning where they were speculating through sources that you were added to the defense. Big news stuff for this little town."

"Really?" Michael said, with sincere surprise. "News always traveled fast around here, but that's quick even by Durango standards."

"Murder's rare around here and any news is big news for a small-town newspaper. What can I do for you? I'm sure you're very busy right now preparing the defense."

"Well, the news I heard was that you didn't get to finish your work."

Dr. Bustee shook his head negatively.

"Well, I was wondering what you did get to do and if you found anything unusual."

"Other than that hole in his chest and the military boys showing up?" He paused, exhaling sharply. "Well. I only had an hour with the body and couldn't do much other than an external. I had finished the overall and had just cut open the chest cavity when they were in here demanding the body for a federal investigation." Dr. Bustee turned slightly and shook his head again. "Didn't buy it for a second, but not much I could do." He paused again, and in a lowered voice continued. "Really kinda upset me the way they handled it, all high and mightily, and demanding everything associated with the case. Now that I think about it, Michael, I guess I might have forgotten to tell them about the blood and fluid samples I pulled."

"You have blood?"

"Of course. Unlike some others, I pull them first as a routine."

"How about a defense split?"

"I've had one waiting for you. All packed in ice, ready to go. Come on over here." Dr. Bustee reached into a cooler and extracted a small Styrofoam container that contained a vial of blood, handing it to Michael.

"Thanks, Dr. Bustee. I'm quite amazed."

"Don't be. This didn't make sense the way it happened. It bothered me, so when I saw the paper today I packed it up for you since I know there are no labs in the area."

"Well, I'm glad it did bother you. I don't suppose there was anything else?"

"I only had a few moments in the chest cavity, but I'd bet I would have found evidence of a heart attack from the quick look I had. The gunshot may have been post-mortem."

"Really?"

"It's nothing more than a gut feeling, but . . ." and his voice trailed off.

"So the gunshot may not have killed him?"

"Maybe not, hard to tell under the circumstances, but I might get some indications through some blood work that I'm doing myself. Should be finished tomorrow, but I think there's a possibility that he was actually dead before the bullet even hit him based on the blood coagulation I saw. There was some obvious evidence of a massive coronary just on the quick look I got."

Michael thought back to the surprisingly small blood pool he'd found. "Could I call you and find out what you learn?"

"Certainly." Dr. Bustee retrieved a card from him desk, returning to hand it to Michael. "There was one other thing I happened to notice. He had some type of a prick on his skin, located on his neck. I didn't really get the chance to inspect it, but there was definitely a mark there. Could have been a number of things, if that helps."

"It helps."

"You don't sound too surprised, Michael."

"I'm not. Something strange is going on, particularly if you think there's a possibility Luigi died of a heart attack."

"Well, as I've said, the way this was handled certainly seemed odd to me. You know it really irritated me, their taking the body in the middle of my work. Didn't seem right, sort of suspicious, so out of my own curiosity, I didn't see any reason to cancel the lab requests. Now I think I'm going to ask for a full organic, stat, so we'll see. Like I said, should be finished in the next day or so. I'll let you know the results when you call."

"That would be great. I think I'm going to The Fort and see if a friend of mine from my chemistry days can look for some exotics on a mass spec."

"Might be a good idea. We don't really have that kind of technology here at Mercy, but the Fort Lewis lab's got the right equipment for that. I agree that something's definitely odd here."

"Something's not right, for sure. Thanks, Doc. You've been a great help already."

Michael walked out into the hospital parking lot. Confirmation of the injection site confirmed in his mind what Dr. Bustee was hinting at and what Michael himself had feared. Luigi had definitely been killed for a specific reason and by professional people. Confirming the presence of a drug that shouldn't have been there would make for a good reasonable doubt case for Benjamin. But it wouldn't answer the ultimate question.

He got in the car and took off for the jail, not noticing the silver Ford four-door as it circled out of the parking lot and slithered into traffic behind him.

* * *

Michael Kincaid, attorney at law, entered the station, finding sergeant, Jesse Hunter manning the desk. Sgt. Jess, like many others in town, had been a friend of his father's and was a longtime veteran of the force. He was surprised he hadn't retired. That was the advantage and disadvantage of a small town. Everyone knew everyone, and each had just a little dirt on the other.

Jess had busted Michael and some friends drinking beers down by the Animas River right after the start of their senior year. Michael, Brad Edgemont and Steve Himple had ditched school one afternoon to take Brad's new raft out for a test ride and they had gotten some beer for the trip. When the got to the put-in, they pulled down into a rutted offshoot between some shrub oak and down to the river's edge. Michael and Brad were talking about Brad's new prize and the ride down the river, when Steve shouted from the back:

"Cops, man, cops."

Michael and Brad ignored the proverbial boy who cried wolf. It was his same old game, but Steve persisted.

"No, really, man. Cops!"

Having seen this show too many times before, Michael started to turn, ready to tell Steve to shut up, when he noticed the cruiser angling down the exit behind some scrub oak out of the corner of his right eye.

Michael quickly grabbed the beer and frantically started tossing cans lightly out the window, trying to bounce them down the small slope leading to the river, hoping they would quietly find the cover of water. For the most part he was a good shot, unfortunately not all the evidence would cooperate. Michael could only look hopelessly as 2 cans came to rest in the grass, inches from shelter, 3 more easily visible in the shallow water, as the police cruiser pulled up to them.

All hopes of secreting the evidence were dashed as Sgt. Jess and his partner, the newly promoted dogcatcher, emerged from their car. The teenagers were motioned toward the cruiser.

Michael, gladly distancing himself from his icy-cold former friends, got out and walked toward the car, trying to keep any line of sight blocked with his torso, Brad and Steve out their doors. The rookie walked toward the boys, anticipating the biggest bust of his short career. His disposition clearly showed that ditching seniors and beer were a disgrace to the town and wouldn't be tolerated on his watch. Michael went straight to the higher-ranking officer.

"Sgt. Jess." Michael sheepishly smiled.

"Michael…what are you boys doing?" Jess said in that questioning police voice no one ever wants to hear.

"Oh, just thought we'd take advantage of the nice day and go for a ride on the river."

"Yeah. Sure. Bet you thought it might be a nice afternoon for a beer, too," the rookie officer chimed in. "I'll also bet if I look around here, I'd find some, too." All three friends immediately shook their collective heads, wishing the guy was back pursuing ferocious felines.

"I'll handle this. You're still in training," Sgt. Jess said, taking control of the situation. A subdued wave of relief came across Michael until the sergeant continued. "Aren't you boys supposed to be in school?"

Terror forced Michael's mind into scramble mode.

Brad stood there trembling, his face turning various shades of red and purple. Michael quickly noted he would get no help there. Momentarily, Steve started to say something, but Michael cut him off, fearing what might come out of his mouth after a couple of beers.

"Well, . . . we were in school earlier," the explanation began. Michael desperately hoped his instincts would continue what his brain could not. After he paused a little too long, the senior officer continued. "I think it's wonderful you were in school earlier, but I'm concerned about now."

"Well, you see, it's like this . . ." Michael stalled, trying to come up with a story. "We were in school."

"You said that," the veteran retorted impatiently.

"Well we were in school, but we were . . . well . . . you see . . . we were . . . ah . . . excused." The story was begging to take focus and so instinct, or more likely fear, took over. "You see, Sgt. Jess, we're all three in this honors class for the last two periods of the day. We've got this group semester project and the teacher let us go, the whole class go, in groups to figure out what we were going to do." Not very good, but it was a start.

"The teacher let you go?" Sgt. Jess exclaimed, sounding shockingly amazed.

"Yeah, that's right. It's Mr. Webb; he's real liberal like that. He gives us a lot of freedom get our projects done, we're often excused from the classroom." Michael's voice picked up steam.

"That right, boys?" the Sarge turned to address Steve and Brad, both already nodding and not really knowing what else to do.

"Well, I know Darren Webb and I've heard that about his classes," he said, the quarry now clearly dead in his sights. "I'll have to tell him how nice it is of him to be so liberal and that you boys thanked him."

A collective sigh came out of all three. Could he really be buying this line?

"Rafting, huh?" The sergeant questioned them as he headed directly for their nemesis, lying in plain sight at river's edge. He stopped just short of the beer, only three feet away, looking into the vehicle. The under-aged youths waited anxiously for the impending, "What's this?" Restless moments passed before Sgt. Jess mercifully turned around and walked back without speaking until he was squarely in front of the three friends.

"I'll tell your dad I saw you, Michael, next time I'm in the Elks and that you were having a fun day. You boys have a good day, too. Hope this doesn't get to be a habit for Webb. Hate to see you boys miss a good education. Then again, I suppose a day of rafting is good for your education, too. See ya, boys. Don't be getting in any trouble."

"No, sir," came unanimous voices.

Both officers got back in their car and disappeared as quickly as they had approached. None of the three could figure out how he'd missed the beer. They didn't care. They'd gotten away with it. When no one brought it up over the next several days, they knew they were in the clear. The counselor had seemingly won his first case.

A few years later Michael's father, over a few drinks at the Elks, had related the story back to him, he and Stubby O'Brannon laughing the entire time. His father had taught him a little about humility that day and what Jess really knew. Now here he was again. Face to face with the old family friend, but this time on a professional footing, yet Michael was strangely uncomfortable. He silently slipped a card on the desk, roughly near where Sgt. Jess was reading the newspaper. Now grayed and aging, he looked up with a big smile. "Michael?"

"Hi, Sergeant Jess. How are you?"

"Great, Michael. I heard you were back in town. Defending that Yazzie kid, I hear."

"Yeah. Gotta do something for a living."

"Oh, you lawyers. Law school teaches you polite excuses for what you do." They both chuckled slightly. "Suppose you'd like to see your client. Come on back."

Michael opened the door when it buzzed and met Jess in the hallway, off to the side.

"Seems you've done well for yourself, Michael. Saw your mug in the papers a couple of times over the years. Guess you finally gave up ditching school."

"Yeah, well, uh." Michael couldn't believe he was actually stammering again, but he was.

Sgt. Jess led him back to a conference room before giving him a wry smile and retreating to get Yazzie.

The La Plata County Jail was a far cry from the Men's Central Jail in downtown LA that Michael was used to. At LA County, the attorney-client room was just a big open area with rows of tables. Attorneys on one side, prisoners on the other. Guards stationed all around. This was a small palace by comparison. An interview table occupied most of the center of the room. Four matching chairs surrounded it. A telephone sat on a corner table at the far edge of the room. It was a smaller copy of the room he and Snow had been in the day before. As he waited patiently, his thoughts drifted back to that day in high school. Unfortunately, there was more to the story. As it turned out, they never got the new raft out that day and didn't go down the river. Instead hightailing it back to school, leaving the beer where it lay, before they got in any more trouble. They eventually got their river trip though, making a plan and going the next weekend over to Moab and Professor Valley, camping and floating down the Colorado with the new play toy.

But that would come with a cost. Michael and Erin were supposed to be going out that same Saturday to a new movie she'd been waiting for and really wanted to see. He'd promised her for weeks he'd take her even though he really didn't want to go. The problem for Michael was it was a mushy chick-flick and rafting with his buddies sounded like a lot more fun to a 17 year old. Erin and he could go to a movie anytime, but rafting season was ending. It eventually created a small spat between the two, as often happens with young lovers when one wants to do one thing and the other another, ill-equipped in the art of compromise. It escalated over the next several days until Michael said something stupid and Erin responded with "well maybe I'll just go with someone else if you're not interested." Michael retorted with "I don't care" or something equally stupid. Neither truly meaning what they'd said. But genies don't go back in bottles and lines were starting to set. When she happened into a boy from drama class that Saturday and he happened to ask innocently if she wanted to go see the movie with him and some other classmates, she said yes with Michael off with his friends.

Of course the innocence of it all didn't quite make it back to Michael from his football buddies, who'd been roped into the movie by their own girlfriends. They watched in shock as Erin and some skinny drama nerd came in, joined later by another couple. His buddies made it sound much worse than it was and Michael was hurt, even though she told him about going the very next time they talked and that he really was just a classmate. His misunderstanding had hit a nerve though and it just made things worse. Over the years he'd thought about the whole affair occasionally, concluding rightly it was the biggest mistake he'd ever made and that he'd overreacted and blown things out of proportion, attributing it to a combination of youth, Irish temper, raging testosterone and absolute stupidity. And when the memory would occasionally wash over him, it had always made him feel guilty about both of the women he was lucky enough to have had grace his life, especially now with Lori gone.

As Fall led into Winter, they'd see each other here and there between classes, maybe catch a movie and they even got back together over the holidays, going skiing several times and hanging in the lodge for après ski. In January she unexpectedly told him she'd gotten a full scholarship to CSU and was thinking about going directly there, instead of starting at the Fort and transferring for upper division engineering classes her junior year, as she and Michael had always talked about both doing. By that time, he felt he shouldn't stand in her way, but sadly not knowing how to simply say "I wish you'd stay." He'd regretted not saying it, instead foolishly turning away from her in a huff in response to the news. When Prom rolled around, they both went with someone else, neither equipped enough in relationships to know how to pull themselves back together. When she finally left for Fort Collins in August her parents had a nice going away party. Michael of course went and they talked quite a while. He offered to take her up there, but she said her Dad was going to take her. They promised they'd stay in touch and occasionally during their freshman year they did talk, until he met someone and so did she, and then of course the conversations all but ended. They'd reconnect at their 10-year reunion and spoke occasionally in the years that followed, but nothing of any regularity. They were two ships who'd long passed in the night.

His thoughts were interrupted as the door creaked open and Benjamin Yazzie was led in moments later by Sgt. Jess, his hands cuffed, his feet shackled, looking very lost and confused. He did indeed look young; the report had said 21, but he seemed much younger. 5'6", slender and wiry, his feet making a scratchy sound on the floor as he shuffled in. The thought of the scrawny coyotes that wandered the southwest quickly came to mind. Hardly the type that could easily overpower a man, he thought, but then again Luigi was an old man. But he looked more frightened than murderer and Michael watched him carefully, studying him as Jess sat him on the seat opposite Michael. "Could you take his cuffs off Jess?"

"I suppose. There'll be someone just outside to take him back when you're finished. Good to see you again. I'll be at the Elks later. Come on over and buy me a beer. You owe me a couple from the ones I left you down by the river."

Nailed again raced through Michael's mind.

Jess chuckled as he shut the door, winking and taking note of the attorney's reddening face. Michael closed his eyes for a few moments before turning back to address his client.

"Hello, Mr. Yazzie, I'm Michael Kincaid."

He looked directly at Michael, his large brown eyes maintaining contact with Michael; his thin face a bit pockmarked red with his youth as he pulled his scraggly hair over his ears. Michael watched him carefully, examining him, thinking he seemed a bit nervous a first, but to be expected he knew. "Yes, they let me call Joseph and he told me about you. He said you would come. He and the shaman have spoken highly of you in the past."

"That's nice to know."

"I'm in a lot of trouble, aren't I, Mr. Kincaid?"

"Yes, I'm afraid you are, but please call me Michael."

"What am I going to do? I swear to you, I didn't kill Luigi. He was my friend, I would never hurt him." He blurted out.

"If that is the truth, then the truth will win out. I think you'll be OK. But you'll just have to ride this out for a few more days and then I think we may be able to get you out of here. You're going to have to have some faith and let me and Mr. Bontani do what we can do."

"Yes, he came to see me too and I believe you. Thank you, Mr. Kincaid."

"I need to ask you a few questions, is that ok?" The young man nodded. "What were you and Luigi talking about when I saw you the other morning?"

"He was angry with me."

"What about?"

"He said I wasn't studying enough, you know, that type thing. Said he was going to have to call Joseph if I didn't start working harder. He was worse then my mother! He was always on my case, all of us there, making sure we were getting our homework done, eating right, you know. He cared about us, he cared about me, better than my own father did, I would never hurt him."

Michael continued sizing him up as he spoke, he didn't fidget and held his hands together, fingers interlocked. There seemed no hint of falsehood, he appeared to genuinely care about Luigi and clearly saddened by his death. But then again, Michael pondered, perhaps he was just a good actor, others had been and only time and good investigation would tell. He'd make a believable witness on the stand though, if it ever came to that. Still, there was something quite different in this kid but Michael couldn't put his finger on it. There's was a calmness and a presence to this young man, something Michael hadn't felt before. Something unique. He'd sensed the strange calmness while watching him sit in the police car the day of the murder but had really attributed it to shock. But now that he was in his presence he sensed something different. Eventually his mind would figure it out, but for now there were more pressing issues and he just needed to know some things.

"Benjamin, something else, something very important. Did Luigi say something to you before he died?"

He spoke quickly and firmly. "He did. He said, 'Yeh Tay Cody Zell.'"

"That's exactly it?"

"Yes, sir."

"Anything else?"

"Not really." He paused for a moment, thinking, subconsciously pulling his hair behind his ears. "Well, he did also ask for water, tó he asked, but by the time I had returned with the glass he had started his journey. I did not know what to do so I went back to my room to get my prayer sticks. To help him with his journey. Before I could get back to him the police were at my door. I know it was wrong to leave him like that, but I did not know what else to do."

"Its OK, Benjamin. I understand."

There were other questions and other answers before he left, but Michael felt like he had what he wanted by the time he left. He wasn't sure of his innocence by the time he left, but it sure seemed less likely he was guilty of murder. He arranged with Jess to allow Benjamin to call home again and assure his mother that he was OK. He also got Jess to agree to give him back his prayer sticks, which Michael knew would help comfort him and were booked into property when he was arrested. Finally and most importantly, with some prodding, Jess said he'd talk to the Jailor and they'd keep an eye on the kid. He admitted he really didn't look like he belonged in there and he'd be damned if the Feds were going to take him without a serious fight. He thanked Jess profusely; promising to buy him that beer he allegedly owed him some day soon.

By the time he'd exited the facility, he had figured out that Snow had loosely translated part of what Benjamin had said. Snow had presumably translated yeh tay, which Michael thought might be a shortened version of yeh tay hey, the traditional Navajo greeting roughly meaning hello. And then there was the new part, tó, asking for a last drink of water that would never arrive in time. Luigi's last moments made a little more sense now on some levels, and a little less on others. He'd have to figure out who the hell this Cody person was and hope he might have some idea why Luigi's last words would be to tell him hello before asking for water. It didn't make a lot of sense.

It was just before 1:00 p.m. as he left the jail. He made a couple of phone calls before heading for the Belle. Trish and Kevin were seated near the rinky-tink piano player, enjoying conversation and a drink.

"Well, I see you found each other."

"It was easy. All I had to do was look for the prettiest girl in the place."

"I see you've been working your wiles, Trish."

Trish glanced up with a "Who, me?" look and a shrug of her shoulders. She returned to her drink with a giggly laugh. Clearly these two would be of no help today.

"Wanna beer, Michael? I'll get it."

Michael nodded and Kevin headed for the bar.

"Don't go breaking his heart, you vixen."

"Wouldn't dream of it. I like this little town. Might want to stay a while. Your friend available?"

"Yeah, he's available, but you've got work to do. Don't forget."

"I always have work to do. How about a vacation day first? Kevin wants to show me around."

"I'm sure he does and you're in luck. I've already given up on you two for the day. I need to check some things out anyway."

"Good. Now that we have that resolved, I was wondering, boss, I found this great painting I've just got to have. Think you could advance me some money?"

"Depends."

"Well, it's only $1,250, it's a Youngblood original and it's got all those beautiful Southwestern colors I so love."

"$1,250! You've got to be kidding."

"It's an original."

"I'll think about it. Let's see if we can get this case resolved first."

Kevin returned and Michael had a sip off the cold beer. They talked for about a half hour, mainly about finding Nick and what he'd learned from Benjamin. Kevin had tried calling Nick at home, but got no answer. Before he'd come down to the Stratler, he'd taken the short ride up the mountain to Nick's but there was no sign of him. With a "please, see if you can find him. And ask around about this Cody Zell guy" Michael rose telling his friend he needed to get going. He would enjoy hanging out, but he'd leave them to enjoy the warm spring day while he finished up some things. He suggested Trish let Kevin show her around town and then tomorrow they'd likely head over to Kayenta.

"Where are you going" Kevin asked, not really overly caring about the answer.

"There's something I need to handle, but don't you two venture off too far" he smiled wryly. "I need to go see someone up at Fort Lewis, Les Sommers."

"Les from chem labs?"

His friend nodded. "He's a professor in the chemistry department up there now and he's expecting me so I'd better going."

Kevin and Trish nodded and Michael was out the swinging barroom doors, back on to Main slowly meandering towards his vehicle as his phone rang. "Michael Kincaid" he answered.

"You really need a better greeting" she chuckled.

"Hi Erin, and what's wrong with my greeting" he smiled as he continued happily on his way.

"Too formal, but we can talk about that another time. I was wondering if you were doing anything tonight?" she asked, a dry spot in her own throat this time.

"No plans, really" came the reply thankfully.

"Well, . . . I was wondering if you'd like to have a drink and maybe some dinner with an old girlfriend maybe?"

"Is my old girlfriend asking me out on a date or something " he answered trying to sound coy "I think I might like that very much. Where and when?"

"Maybe I am, maybe I'm not. I might just be hungry too. How about around 7, I need to go home first after I finish at work, maybe meet me at the Muldoon?"

"That sounds great, I'll be there."

"Well, then, I'll see you there."

Michael hung up, his gait now buoyant and easy, as he walked up the hill to his vehicle.

* * *

His secretary had alerted him over the intercom that Tompkins was on hold. He punched the line, demanding, "What is the status of our little complication?"

"Nothing really to report. They appear to be several steps behind our end."

"That's good to know, but I'm not sure that's the case. I want you to add a little heat to those we discussed if the opportunity arises. Nothing too excessive. Take your surveillance to the next level, also. Do you understand?"

"I believe so, sir. We'll see what we can do."

"Let me know." He unceremoniously clicked off the line.

* * *

After cleaning up and dressing for over an hour, the result of some unexplainable and ridiculous youthful first date type jitters, Michael finally made it downtown at 6:55. He luckily managed to find a parking spot in the alley behind the Stratler making his way in quick-step the block-and-a-half up to Main and down toward the train depot. The lightness in his steps still evident and he smiled pleasantly to the tourists as they passed. When he'd left LA, it was this feeling, the feeling of being back home amongst old friends, that he had been chasing. He had many good friends in LA, but it wasn't the same as those you actually grew up with, especially in a small town. Those friendships grounded you. The last few days had kept him from the feeling that had begun its emergence at the Canyon a mere few days ago. Had it truly only been six days since then? So much had transpired, it really seemed much longer.

He hurried his pace, nervously glancing at his watch crossing 6th Street as the "Don't Walk" signal demanded some urgency. He slowed to an easy walk passing the General Palmer House, and then came to a stop as he approached the large bay windows of the Solid Muldoon. He glanced through the glass, past the patrons seated at the window table, and into the bar. His eyes searched amongst the Victorian settees, and the customers occupying them, for a quick glimpse of her. In the southern corner, seated on a curved Victorian ruby red felt settee, he saw her. She was more beautiful than he'd even remembered. The years had been a friend to her and time had only added to her loveliness. He stood motionless for a few moments before noting the awkward look from the women seated just inside the window. Michael smiled noncommittally at her and took the couple of steps toward the open door, turning his attention back toward Erin and spotting her again as he stepped through the foyer.

Her emerald eyes burst open, a warm enchanting smile settling on her pretty face as she caught her first glimpse of Michael. He hadn't changed a bit, still possessing those boyish good looks that had caught her eye so many years ago. She watched as he confidently strode across the bar toward her, harkening back to the summer when they'd first gotten together. She'd loved that summer poolside and flushed at the memory of some of the other fun they'd had together. It was her first taste of love, innocent and so captivating. Rafting trips down the Animas, hiking in the mountains foraging for wild raspberries and chanterelle mushrooms, skiing during that following winter and cuddling next to each other aside the roaring fire at the Lodge at Purgatory. She wondered momentarily what had gone wrong for their fun to have come to an such inconclusive end and then her mind flashed through the turbulent, unsatisfying years she'd spent in the interim. But here he was again, not as young and perhaps a little weathered by his own experiences, yet her heart palpitated as it always had whenever he drew near. She felt as a blush had overcome her and her mouth dried a bit. She felt slightly silly.

"Hello, Erin," he said softly

"Hello, Michael." She stood, revealing a handsome, curvaceous figure. She was dressed in a teal silk blouse, a short black skirt with tasteful black pumps that accentuated her firm and shapely legs. Michael stood again motionless for a few moments before reaching toward her as he accepted her hug, lasting a moment too long with her squeezing him a bit too tight to be merely "old friend" politeness. She buried her head onto his shoulder and neck as Michael reflexively stroked her mid-length blonde hair and the back of her neck, both treasuring the moment. In time, she lifted her head to plant a light kiss on his cheek, whispering breathlessly in his ear "it's been too long".

"It has" and he pulled her to a tighter hug, gladly returning her kiss on the cheek before reluctantly releasing her with a step back. "You look amazing, Erin. You've haven't changed a bit; you've gotten even more beautiful, it that is possible. I've missed you."

"Ah, Michael," she smiled demurely, another slight blush reddening her face. "Still have that silvery Irish tongue, don't you? I've missed talking to you." Michael smiled back to her as she took his hand and pulled him toward a seat on the old style loveseat.

"What have you been doing with yourself, Erin?"

"Not a whole lot. Just working. No social life to speak of" she said crossing her legs and draping her wrists over her knees.

"That must be your choice. I can't imagine there aren't a hundred guys in Durango that wouldn't love a date with you."

"Well, thanks, Michael, but to be honest with you, I haven't really been interested in anyone lately, I guess I've become jaded with all that has happened." And Michael could now understand the hurt that Stubby had eluded too, and in that pain he felt his own. "Of course you know that Ricky and I got divorced and since then, well, you know, not much interest" and for a mere second her mind raced back to those trying times until she was snapped back to the present as Michael snickered sarcastically "Yep. Cried about that for two straight weeks when I heard" with an exaggerated wink. "He was never good enough for you Erin," he added.

"Thank you for saying that Michael, I'm not so sure about that, we all have our issues, but you're so sweet, though maybe a bit influenced" smiling pleasantly back at him, grabbing her glass of wine and taking a sip before continuing. "Anyway . . . as you probably know, we lived up in Cherry Creek for the last fifteen years, but we always seemed to have troubles. A couple of years ago, Ricky got caught up in some tax evasion and money-laundering accusations with his business and it really was the last straw for me. We were divorced about a year ago. Ricky's still up there; we haven't really spoken much lately. I think he'll stay in

Denver, or at least I hope so, but I think he's finally working through his issues, I hope." Michael caught a tinge of annoyance in her voice and watched as she clearly withdrew a little.

"I'm sorry to hear that."

"Don't be. It's probably for the best but I cared for him a lot" she said matter-of-factly in a voice Michael had heard from injured women many times in his practice. "We really hadn't had much fun together for years. The first five were ok, but the last ten were hell."

"Did you have any children?"

"No . . . we never . . . I mean, I always wanted a child, but Ricky kept wanting to wait until we were more financially stable. By the time we'd finally gotten stable I'd lost interest in having a child with him, so it never happened" and her voice trailed off again as she reached for another drink of her wine.

Her pain was evident and as the waitress thankfully neared during the awkward silence that followed he motioned for two more glasses, before changing the subject. "So how long have you been back and what have you been doing?"

"About eight months now" she responded, pulling back from her memories. She regained her smile, saying, "I've got a house up on Riverview now, kind of up by where you lived. I've been working for Frank down at Angst Engineering for the past six months or so. It's not what I was used to doing in Denver, but it's a living and in Durango that's not the easiest thing."

"That's for sure." Michael nodded.

"But enough about me. What about you, Mr. Big-Time LA lawyer?"

"Just trying to keep my clients out of jail. Unfortunately, most of them deserve it, but they pay me well and it's what I do. I just try to give them the best defense I can."

"Dad says you're going to defend the Navajo kid in that killing here. Is that right?"

"Kind of looking that way."

"Doesn't he deserve to go to jail?"

"I don't really know to be honest with you. The more I learn the more I think he was just in the wrong place at the wrong time. I'm going down to Kayenta and Monument Valley tomorrow to see his folks and hopefully clear up some of the defense."

"Monument Valley?" She paused, a big smile drifting across her face and eyes. "I haven't been there in years. I think the last time I was out there was when you and I went there in high school. Do you remember?"

Of course he did. How could he possibly forget? "Our picnic on the edge of the Mokidugway, I can remember you being scared to death looking off the edge" and they both broke into laughter. "I'm looking forward to going out there again" he smiled, remembering back to their adventure. "Its short notice, but you're welcome to join me if you like" he said half-jokingly. "It should only take me a couple of hours to do what I need to do. We could have the rest of the time to ourselves for a picnic; could be back that night. I'd probably throw in a surprise or two. Any interest?"

"I don't know about that Michael, but maybe, I'd have to think about it and check with Frank to see what's going on" knowing full well work was pretty slow and she was thinking of taking a day or two off anyway. Still, it would have to take some thought. "It would be great to go out there again" she paused, thinking. "And I suppose even Frank would agree that I could use a little fun in my life. I'll think about it."

"Its short notice, but it would be nice to have some company on the drive."

Her sweet face wrinkled to a smile, she really did need some fun in her life. She was flushed though; too many things were bouncing around in her mind. "Why don't you order us an appetizer or something while I use the Ladies' room. I'll be right back."

"But of course." He watched as she walked toward the restrooms down the hallway in the rear, heads turning as she passed. As she disappeared down the narrow hall he hoped she would. The both could use someone to talk to, the troubles they were both going through. With Erin he could be open he thought, they'd shared enough together early in life that the conversation wouldn't be totally awkward. She could understand his pain through her own pain. But somewhere off in the recesses of his mind, the thought persistently cautioned "too soon, too soon."

By the time she rejoined him on the settee, the waitress was bringing some cheese and crackers to enjoy with their wine. They talked and laughed of happier times for the better part of an hour before Michael suggested dinner as they finished their drinks. Fortunately, he'd thought ahead. Another mutual high school friend of theirs, Sean, was now the chef at the Palace Restaurant and he'd called ahead to say he might be bringing Erin in for dinner around 8.

Michael pushed open the Muldoon's front door for her, as they turned right en route toward the railroad depot. Upon arriving at the Palace, they were guided to a candlelit corner table in the front room, looking out at the 1880s depot and the train. Sean met them after they'd been seated. He had completely understood when Michael had called to book a reservation and told him he was bringing Erin. It was a small town, with a small high school and Sean was happy to have the opportunity to see old friends.

Tonight, the chef proudly explained, in honor of his two guests—his friends—he'd prepared a pheasant with wild rice and assorted vegetables that was simply exquisite. Erin and Michael applauded their friend as the waitress arrived with a Napa Valley Merlot, compliments of the house, naturally, displaying it to Michael. He politely nodded and took the tasting honors as she poured a little before rounding the bottle and pulling it back as she stood awaiting his approval. Swirling the smooth liquid in his mouth, his inner checks delighted in the fruity, peppery taste, a hint of blackberry in its silky flavor. He nodded with a "very nice" and the waitress made the rounds pouring Erin, then Sean, a glass before returning to Michael and setting the bottle in the middle, disappearing quietly toward the back of the house. Sean enjoyed a quick glass with them before politely withdrawing, saying he had to check on the kitchen. They sipped on their wine, continuing to talk, an easy playfulness filing the air. In a few moments the waitress appeared with a plate of melt-in-the-mouth medallions of mozzarella fresca, buffeted by a ring of fresh raspberries to perfectly compliment the wine. In time, and as the wine took further effect, Michael playfully picked up a raspberry saying "do you remember the time we went berry hunting and got all cut up in the briars, your mom was so mad at me." She laughed, saying "it was worth it to have you feed me berries" and with that he reached across with the berry in his fingers and she leaned in to envelope it softly and seductively, so laden with juice that it dissolved as it touched her lips, her eyes folding into his as they had that day, a sultry kiss to his fingertips as she parted savoring its fruitfulness. Michael's heart stopped!

After a few more moments the waitress returned carrying two plates with the main entrée topped with a buttery, tarragon and sage infused sauce, accompanied by a mélange of wilted radicchio, leeks and tiny bite-size new potatoes dripped with a creamy white sauce, fresh baked poppy-seeded dinner rolls and butter, greeted with an oh and an ah. The waitress topped off their wine glasses before leaving them to enjoy. And enjoy they did. Michael buttered half a roll, passing it to her for a bite, which she gladly accepted, the sweet butter just starting to melt and leaving a glistening sheen on her lips. He gazed approvingly toward her, garnished with the intoxication from the tart red and the candlelight reflecting in her eyes. They finished their dinner as the crowded restaurant began to slowly empty. Finally Sean reappeared saying it had been a while since he tried this, prepping a fiery cherries jubilee for desert before them, joking he hoped he didn't catch the place on fire as flames shot up into the air. The meal, the wine, the desert were fabulous, but each other's company was even better.

Thanking Sean profusely after they finished, Erin casually locking her arm in his as they strolled uncaringly toward the Belle for an after dinner nightcap. The cool, crisp spring evening air gently blew on their face as they merrily made there way up Main. Michael wanted to see if Trish and Kevin were still around, and able to stand, and when they weren't, that was just fine with him too.

They listened to the piano player for a set, had a cup of coffee and then Michael walked Erin to her car. She looked ravishing in the moonlight, an enchantress under a heavenly sky. He thanked her for the nicest evening he'd had in the longest time.

"Yes, it has been nice" she replied, continuing "I've missed your smile, horrible jokes and conversation terribly through the years Michael" bringing a smile to his face.

"I've been silly for not staying in touch Erin, I had forgotten how much fun it was to be with you, it was my mistake." He leaned over and pulled her toward him softly by her tiny waist, wrapping his other arm around her to hold her in a tight hug. He kissed her softly again on her cheek before she pulled her head back, looking intently into his eyes before ever so slowly drifting her lips to his. For what seemed like an eternity, the troubles of these two people were instantly a million miles away. They held each other closely, knowing the moment would become a memory that would bring smiles to their faces many miles and years down life's highway. After several seconds they parted, each not truly wanting to, but knowing it to be necessary.

"I'm sorry Michael, I probably shouldn't have done that" she slightly winced.

"I didn't mind."

"I know, but still" and she giggled like the young school girl he remembered. He nodded, saying "I know" because he too had many things to think about that the intoxicating wine could not instantly solve. "I'll be in the office early in the morning, call me if you still want me to go…"

"I think it would be nice" he said sweetly. "Or if you decide you want to go, come meet me at the Spruce in the morning and we can figure it out over breakfast. I'm in Room 2 and I'll promise an adventure."

"It sounds like fun and I'd like to spend some more time with you but I really need to think about it. It's been too long since I spent time with someone I actually liked" and they both flashed a knowing smile to the other. He watched as she drove away slowly with a wave. Michael was in a daze and stood quietly for several moments for the third time in several wonderful hours.

The drive back to the motel passed slowly as his mind concentrated on the evening's events, conflicting with the thoughts of Lori. Was he betraying her? Of course not, she wouldn't think that way, she would want him to enjoy life. And he had had a wonderful time and felt good for the first time in a long, long time. As he pulled his vehicle into a space at the motel he was still a bit excited, his breath coming in short gasps, thinking of the tension the two women presented in his mind. He ambled toward his room, fumbling with his keys in a newfound anxiety. All the memories of boyhood angst and "does she like me" feelings welled up inside him, pushed hard against his memories of Lori and that nagging voice saying "too soon, too soon." As he reached the door he paused vowing that he wouldn't worry about it any more tonight and just see where things led. Maybe she'd join him in going to Kayenta, maybe not, but at least he had something to look forward to tomorrow, well perhaps. Inserting the key in his door he reasoned that even if she joined him he wasn't betraying Lori's memory, she would want him to move on even though it still hurt. He felt good with that thought as he entered and pushed the door closed behind him, relishing in the moment and wondering what the future may bring as he reached for the light switch.

A sudden thud crushed against the back of Michael's skull. Sharp pain shot through his muscles as he collapsed helplessly to his knees and the floor. He could see two pairs of shoes shuffling near his nose and he desperately tried to clear his head and regain his balance. A forceful pull of his hair yanked him back on his knees. Seconds later he felt the knife blade at the base of his throat.

"What do you want?" he pleaded, now truly powerless.

Gravelly words echoed from behind his right ear. "We don't like you defending that gut-eatin' Navajo. If you know what's good for ya, you'll back off. A person could get hurt. We don't like outsiders sticking their noses in where they don't belong. Understand?"

When he didn't answer quickly enough, a knee to his ribs made him flinch forward and he felt the knife scratch against his throat. The sharp edge of the steel blade made him pull back despite the knee protruding into his side.

"You understand me, boy?"

"Yes . . . yes," he gasped.

"Now you get outta this town like the good little city boy you are. If we have to come back then maybe we'll just bring that cute little filly in the black skirt you were with tonight to play with. Maybe we'll have a real party then. You understand me, boy?"

"Leave her out of this. She doesn't have anything to do with this."

The response brought another knee edging Michael's throat back against the blade again.

"I asked you if you understood me, boy. I don't think you pay good enough attention."

"OK, OK. I understand. I'm outta here."

"Good. Don't forget it. We won't be so nice next time. I promise."

The man withdrew the steel slowly across Michael's tightened skin, making sure it drew a small amount of blood as it etched its way in retreat. Another thud to the back of his head sent his head reeling back toward the floor and into confused darkness for a second time.

He heard the door slam and pulled his way over to the corner of the window to see a silver Ford with antennas pull into the street before he crumpled back to the floor, pain fading to darkness.

DAY SEVEN

Trouble Afoot

The persistent knocking at the door finally brought him out of his daze. With the cracking open of his eyelids he established that it was light out, but he was sure of little else. The pounding on the inside of his head made sure of that. He pulled himself up, far enough to turn the door handle, letting it slide open a few inches.

A female voice called uncertainly. "Michael???"

With no answer forthcoming, Erin slid the door open slowly, finally noticing his figure lying on the carpeted floor. "Michael! Oh my God . . . are you all right?" She quickly knelt and offered a gentle caress to his back.

"Yeah, yeah, I'm fine. Just peachy," he mumbled.

"What happened?"

"Nothing to worry about. I'm just clumsy and stupid. Help me to the couch, please."

Erin pulled him up with her and eased him onto the couch.

"What happened to you?"

"Seriously, just clumsy. I fell. Could you give me some water? Got any aspirin by chance?" he glanced at her with crooked smile.

She went to the sink and ran a cold glass of water. Reaching into her purse, she pulled out an aspirin bottle and extracted two pills and returned to him with the water.

"Here, take these. They'll help." She handed him the pills and water.

Michael obeyed her command, tossing the aspirin into his mouth and washing it down with a gulp. He leaned his head back against the top of the couch.

"Michael, your throat!"

He reached up to feel, remembering the blade that had come far too

189

close.

"Just a scratch. I'll be all right." He leaned his chin forward to hide the wound. She sat next to him, taking his hand in hers.

"What is going on?"

"Well, I guess not everybody in town likes me. Let me get a shower and I'll tell you about it over some breakfast, if you like. But it's nothing. . . . really." He tried to sound assuring.

"Well, I certainly want to hear the story, so I guess I'll wait."

"Thanks. I like cooperation." Michael faded, heading for the bedroom.

"Oh, I can be very cooperative . . . if I want, but you'd better tell me what happened." She watched as he wobbled into the bathroom, pausing to nod his head as he shut the door.

He emerged after several minutes to find her seated in a chair.

She looked up and smiled as he came out of the bedroom, clearly looking much better. He'd been right, the cut on the neck didn't look nearly as bad as she'd feared. But how did it get there? "Feeling better?"

"I'm feeling a whole lot better, thanks to you. How about some coffee?"

"Nice try. You want to tell me what happened?" she persisted.

"It's really nothing." He tried to keep his voice light as he downplayed the whole business. "Seems like a couple of redneck cowboys don't like me defending Benjamin Yazzie."

"What?"

"Coupla good old boys smacked me upside the head when I got back here last night."

"Good God, Michael, are there still people like that here?"

"Afraid so. Guess they've progressed from rolling Indians to rolling their lawyers. Ah, I'll get a bodyguard some day," he snickered.

"Sounds like you need one. I hadn't really decided on joining you but maybe I need to make sure you stay out of trouble for a few days," she said playfully.

"Well can't imagine I'd get into too much trouble in Kayenta, but I'd feel much more secure knowing that I have a bodyguard" he smiled.

"I think you do need someone to keep an eye on you after this."

"Promise?" Michael returning his own playful grin, but Erin didn't look exactly happy.

He was hoping she'd decide to join him and he certainly didn't want to alarm her with all that had happened. But there'd be no place safer for her than the middle of the Navajo reservation if these guys really meant her harm, at least until he could find out who these guys were. Unknowingly he'd now gotten her into this and his guilt rose to a different level. Changing the subject, he turned to the task at hand. "Are you ready?"

"Sure, but lets skip the breakfast. If we're going to go let's get out of here before these guys come back. All I've got to do is stop by the house, grab a few things and drop my car."

"What about Frank and your job?"

"I already talked to him, told him I was going with you to Kayenta before I came here" she winked, turning out the door.

"Well then, let me throw a few things together and we're out of here."

She took a couple of steps toward him and lightly hugged him, withdrawing after a short moment and looking again at his throat. "Why don't you meet me at my house when you're ready?"

"Gladly," he whispered, his heart beating quickly.

"OK, but be careful since I won't be around to guard your body. Oh, 297 Riverview. Think you can find me?"

"Ohhh yeah, as quick as I can . . . ."

"I like cooperation too." She smiled coyly as she turned back out the door.

He watched from the window as she left. Then he scanned the lot for Kevin's Jeep, which wasn't parked in its normal place. When he couldn't find it, he thought for a second, then the obvious came to mind. "Trish!"

He stepped back from the window, still steadying his aching head, and dialed her room.

"Stratler Hotel. How may I direct your call?"

"Patricia Cochrine's room."

"Thank you. I'll connect you."

"Hello."

"Trish, what have you done with my friend?"

"Relax, I didn't break him. I was just having him for breakfast. I mean over for breakfast. You know what I mean."

"Very funny. I know exactly what you mean. Can you and Kevin meet me at the New York Bakery in twenty minutes? It's just across the street. Kevin knows where it is. That OK?"

"Sure."

"See you then."

He hung up and quickly gathered his belongings from the room, consciously making a spectacle of his sudden departure. He returned several times to the room, grabbing things and haphazardly throwing them into the Explorer. In less than five minutes he had packed and was ready to roll. If they were watching, and he figured they would be, he needed to make sure they thought they'd scared the living hell out of him.

He took a circuitous route to the bakery, going up the back way to Fort Lewis and then doubling back to downtown. No way they could follow him through the switchbacks down the front side without being seen. He kept one eye on the mirror, assuring himself he wasn't being followed. They'd probably had the motel's phones tapped by now, and maybe even his cell, but just in case they hadn't been listening, he'd at least try to throw them off for a little while. He parked in the alley behind the restaurant and went in the back door. He stopped at the waitress station to talk to one of the servers, before finding Kevin and Trish were seated in a booth.

"You look like hell, boss," Trish greeted him. "What happened to you?"

"It's been a rough several hours."

"I can see that," she agreed.

He explained to them what had transpired, this time including the threat to Erin, and when he'd finished, both of their mouths stood wide open. Finally, he stated the obvious. "It looks like this is getting very serious. If either of you wants to back off, I'll understand, but I'm going to nail these pricks." His voice rose, his anger now clearly evident.

"Michael, whatever we're in the middle of, I'm already involved," Kevin said matter-of-factly.

"Trish, maybe you should sit this one out. It isn't your fight and it could get dangerous."

She reflected for a moment before distantly retorting, "Nahhhh, boss. You've never known me to shy away from a battle. I think I'll stick around and see what happens."

"All right, all right." Michael relinquished his opposition. "Maybe it's better we stick together anyway."

Both Trish and Kevin nodded their agreement and Michael continued, rubbing his forehead. "We've got to throw them off our trail somehow." They thought for a moment before Kevin blurted out, "Well, you still fly, don't you?"

"I suppose. I mean, not in a while. What, you still got that plane?"

"Sure. It's out at the airport. I've kept it up over the years. Had a total rebuild done on the engine last year."

"Really. Well, that gives me a pretty good idea." He paused for a couple of moments before continuing. "OK, here's what I have in mind. First of all, Kevin, any luck finding Nick Hinkley?"

"I called and took another ride up there yesterday, but no."

"We've got to find him."

Trish interrupted. "What do you want us to do?"

"Just lay low, mainly. See if you can find Nick and see if Luigi and him had talked about anything lately. In the meantime, I'm going to make them think they've scared me off. Trish, I need for you to file a substitution of attorney motion or a motion to withdraw. It doesn't matter which. You got anything on that laptop?"

"Of course. You're gonna quit?"

"Of course not. You know me better than that. They've just pissed me off now! These sons o' bitches need to go down, whoever they are. Besides, my plan is to get their ass before they get mine. I'm not sure I have much other choice."

"I've got faith in ya, boss. So just who do you want me to sub you out for?"

"The client."

"The client? Just how do you think I'm going to get him to sign it? They won't let me in to get the signature."

"Actually, they would, but I don't want his signature on there anyway."

"But without a signature it's defective on its face. They'll kick it."

"Of course. But you make sure you get it stamped and lodged and then fax a copy up to that AUSA in Denver for service. It'll find its way to the proper ears. That should make them think I'm running. Don't bother sending one over to the PD or DA's office, but put them on the proof of service anyway. Get it done ASAP. Sign it; you do a better job with my signature, anyway. Got it?"

"Got it."

"Kevin?"

"Yeah?"

"I think I need to borrow the plane."

"No problem. And I'll do you one better and have it warmed up and checked out by the time you get there."

"Great. Tell your service guy a friend is borrowing it to fly up to Denver, but no flight plan. Can you also call Joseph and ask him to pick me up at the Kayenta airport around noon? That should give him plenty of time to get there from Window Rock. He was planning on being there today anyway, at least when you talked to him last, wasn't he?"

"That's what he said, early afternoon. But Denver?"

"Well I certainly don't want anyone knowing where I'm really going."

His friend nodded. "OK, I will, but you're going to be sitting there a while even if I get him to meet at noon, it's a short flight."

"Yea, but that's ok, we won't be waiting long. I'm going to take my time. I'm going to fly Erin up north, over Engineer and Red Mountain. They'll think I'm headed for Junction or Denver. Then I'll fly low over the Colorado River, Moab and then sweep down toward Kayenta over the Mokidugway. If nothing else, it'll be a beautiful flight."

"I want to go . . ."

"Later, Trish. You've got things to do."

"All right. Doesn't seem fair, though."

"No, but then again I am trying to keep us all from getting in a pinch and solve a murder at the same time."

They both nodded again, in full agreement. The waitress arrived, handing a large to-go sack and a bill to Michael. He glanced at the bill, pulled money from his pocket and left it on the table.

"I've got to get going, but Kevin, you do whatever you'd normally do, as if nothing is going on. If anyone asks where I've gone, tell them Hawaii with Erin. Cover that one for me, too, Trish. In fact, maybe call the airlines and book a flight from Denver to Honolulu for her and I, that's a good cover story. I don't care with whom, but make it look real. Obviously, I won't be picking up the ticket anyway. I need you guys to call me together tonight around eight. Kevin, be very careful what you say over the phone at the motel. I've got a feeling it's probably tapped by now based on what they were saying last night. It would be a good idea for you to keep in mind, too, Trish. One last thing, Kevin. Where's your jeep? I need it to get to the airport and I know they've been watching mine."

"It's parked behind the Stratler. Here's the keys." He slid them across the table.

"Mine's in the back. Stash it somewhere good," he replied, sliding him back his own. "They might think I took off in it if they don't catch me going to the airport. Trish, rent a four-wheel drive for yourself today. We'll need it eventually. And get a new cell phone somewhere and use it for anything on the case."

"Sure."

"I'll talk to you both later. Remember: careful with phones; and we're in Hawaii. Call me on Joseph's cell phone tonight at 8 on the new phone. And if you find Nick or anyone else who knew Luigi, ask them about this Cody guy."

Michael was up and out the front door in a heartbeat, zigzagging across Main Street. He felt sure no one was following him, but just to make sure he cut through the Diamond Belle, across the lobby and out the rear door. He found Kevin's Jeep parked out back. He drove around several blocks before stopping by the Explorer to grab his stuff. He was quickly on his way again, off to pick up Erin.

In a few short minutes and two quick stops, Michael pulled into the driveway, and hurried onto the porch, still trying to assure himself no one was following. After a couple of seconds, he rang the doorbell. Erin opened the door dressed nicely in tight-fitting jeans, a light sweater and hiking boots.

"My, don't you look good."

"Thanks, compliments get you points," she said with a brimming smile.

"Great!" He smiled back, stepping through the door. Once through the door she embraced him, pulling him tight to her, hugging him. "I was so worried about you earlier. Are you sure everything is ok?" He pulled back and tried to assure her it was nothing, before moving both hands to hold her head and landing a slight kiss to her forehead before gazing back to her awaiting eyes.

"It will be ok, I promise" he said, pausing for a moment before the reality of the situation forced him to conclude, "but you should get your things before we get side-tracked. I've got a special surprise for you."

"You do? Like what?"

"You'll see when we get there," he called as she disappeared around the corner and down the hall.

Michael's mind again anxiously returned to the situation. They needed to go before anyone might decide to check Erin's place. Almost on cue, she reappeared toting a purse and an overnight bag. Michael took the bag and followed her to the door. She locked it behind them.

Michael deposited the bag in the back of the Jeep and opened the passenger door to let her in.

"Aren't you the gentleman."

"My Lady, your carriage awaits." He waved his hand toward the opened door.

Hurrying around to the driver's seat, he jumped in and in a few more seconds, they were on their way.

At the river crossing, they turned east onto 160.

"Michael, I thought we were going to Monument Valley."

"We are."

"Well, I may not have been the best student in geography class, but I always thought it was west of here. Aren't you going the wrong way?"

"Sort of. You trust me, don't you?"

"Of course."

"Well, dear, then you'll just have to wait and see."

She leaned back in her seat and surrendered. In another ten miles, a magical smile lit her face as the Jeep's blinker went on and a sign appeared, predicting the right turn to the airport.

"A little surprise, huh?" Her eyes sparkled. "I didn't know there were flights out there."

"There are and there aren't." He smiled back.

He pulled up to the charter office.

"Let me find out what the deal is."

He reappeared in a few seconds to say everything was set and they grabbed their bags. He led Erin around the building, through a gate in the fence. There, parked behind the office, was the single-prop, four-passenger Cessna 172 he remembered. Michael's pre-flight check confirmed that Kevin had taken good care of her over the years. He stowed their bags in the back of the passenger compartment.

"Jump on in and make yourself comfortable. I'll be right back. I need to drop Kevin's keys." Michael turned, noticing a car just pulling in next to the Jeep. He quickened his pace into the building's back door.

"Hey" he called to the man across the empty room at the counter, "here's Kevin's keys. He said he'd be by to pick them up later."

"No problem," the man replied, reaching into the air to snag the keys from Michael's quick flip.

"You file a flight plan?"

"Nah. Just gonna fly up to Denver by way of Junction. Then a week in Hawaii with the little number."

"Gotcha. I'm sure you'll have a good time."

Michael just winked and smiled widely. "Yeah, should be a good time." He added, "Maybe even stay a while longer. Never know!"

The service manager nodded as Michael hustled back out with a wave. From the plane he noticed two men starting to emerge from the car. He slid into the pilot's seat and cranked the engine over. The propeller caught quickly and soon a high-pitched hum surrounded the cabin.

He idled up the Cessna's throttle and circled the plane back toward the two men now approaching the fence. As he rounded for the taxiway he took a good look at the two men before increasing engine speed as the little Cessna turned past them, any race now lost. He looked back with a slightly satisfied look as the plane swung around quickly, watching as their hair ruffled and their ties disheveled from the prop wash hitting them squarely in the face and forcing them to step back. He glided quickly down the taxiway, checking the flaps, rudder, instruments and his other pre-flight as he went. The checkout complete, he cleared the tower and rounded off the taxiway onto the main runway, pressing the throttle to full. The small plane jolted forward, speeding toward its eventual lift into the crisp blue Colorado sky.

The plane left the asphalted ground rapidly behind. After twenty seconds he rolled left and noticed the airport reappear as he concluded the hundred-eighty-degree bank. The silver Ford remained parked next to the Jeep. The two men were standing next to their car, looking up as the plane passed over them. He thought he'd been more careful than that. How in the hell could they have followed me? They must have seen him grab the bags from his truck. As he lost sight of them, he could only conclude that they were either very professional or very lucky. Which one didn't really matter. They didn't have a plane!

He banked left again and pointed the plane's nose toward Missionary Ridge and Denver. He'd flown the route many times before, scouting for the hunters who made their yearly migration from elkless states in the hopes of bagging an eight-point bull.

After a few minutes of a steady climb, Durango and the Animas Valley appeared before them. Michael angled to his right before placing Missionary Ridge beneath him. In a few more minutes his eyes subconsciously picked up the small brown dots on a rolling green meadow in the foothills a few miles ahead. He eased the plane's heading a few degrees west to bring the dots in a line toward the right wing. Slowly, he began to descend.

"Something wrong, Michael?" Erin asked nervously.

"Nothing at all. Look over there; I've got something to show you." He pointed in the general direction of the meadow.

He leveled off about five hundred feet above the pines, as the herd came slowly into focus.

"Michael, they're beautiful," she said, as the fifty or so elk passed under her view.

Michael nudged the plane back into a gentle climb. Below, the Animas Valley retreated past the plane's tail. The glacial valley was now replaced by rolling foothills, building upon themselves, forming a giant crescendo that became the peaks of the San Juan range ahead of them.

Michael pointed out Purgatory Ski Area to the west and Twilight Peak rising to meet them in the northeast. Below passed the canyon that provided the river's egress into the awaiting Animas valley, now twenty miles behind.

Emerald Lake, Colorado's largest natural lake appeared serenely before them. The shiny green water reflecting the three thirteen-thousand-foot peaks that nestled it into the cradle of their arms. Coal Bank and Molas now shot up beneath the western wing. Their northern slopes finally gave way to the valley that held the sleepy mining town of Silverton, ten miles or so ahead in the distance.

Michael began a slow bank to the north and west, keeping the bald head of Engineer Mountain well to his left. Ahead, Red Mountain now began poking its own rust-covered head from behind an imposing ridge directly in front of them. Michael crept low over the ridge, keeping a short but safe distance above the treetops and peaks. If anyone was bothering to watch their path, they would register as just another tourist flying a little too low for safety. It was the perfect distance for up-close sight-seeing, something the local FAA officials had all too often seen and complained to pilots about as dangerous and as messing with their radar blips.

Red Mountain came into full view now, its peak arrayed with brilliant reds and yellows leaching from the minerals that built the mountain's foundation. Green pine trees dotting the mountain added contrast to the color cascading down the slope. At her base, the Idarado mine's weather-beaten old buildings provided a striking brown parallel to the mountain's colors. Gliding through her valley, they came over the box canyon walls that surrounded the tiny town of Ouray, named for the Mountain Ute tribal leader who'd spun the treaty that still affected the entire area. Ahead of the town lay the canyon's glaciated emergence, opening to the rich farming lands of Delta and Montrose.

Michael reached over and gently began caressing and rubbing the back of Erin's neck. She reached for his hand, pulling it to her check and then kissing its back.

"I've been through these mountains a hundred times, but I've never seen them like that. That was absolutely beautiful. Any more wonderful surprises?"

"Ya know, ya just never know."

As they emerged from the box canyon walls Michael banked due west, setting the course headings for Moab from memory. It had been a long time since he'd last flown this direction, but the flight path was well etched in his memory.

"How about some brunch" he asked, and transferred control to the autopilot.

"Indeed, you have thought of everything."

Michael unbuckled and reached behind him for the sack he'd brought and handed it to Erin. "Let's see what you can find in there." She pulled out two sub sandwiches, a container of pasta salad, some drinks and paper plates. She arranged food on the plates, while the plane's engines continued their humdrum duty. From the bag emerged forks and napkins and she passed him a plate, leaving her own in her lap. She poured some tea into plastic glasses, handing one to the pilot.

"You are surprising, Mr. Kincaid."

"Thank you. To you," he said, raising his glass. "Thanks for coming with me."

"And to you, kind sir. Thanks for bringing me."

The plastic glasses touched each other with a dull thud.

"Sorry, next time I'll bring the crystal" she said.

"Just as long as there is a next time."

They both smiled, each betraying their hope they would have many more opportunities if wishes were indeed sometimes granted, the unpleasant memories from their pasts slipping away as quickly as the fruit trees of the Grand Valley passed below them.

The couple ate their sandwiches and pasta, talking and laughing their way to Moab, which crept into view after about an hour. Beyond it lay The Dollhouse and The Maze of Canyonlands National Park. In the distant southwest desert, the confluence of the Green and Colorado Rivers ebbed peacefully toward Lake Powell, majestic red bluffs dotting the carpet of coarse brown sand surrounding them.

Wresting the reins from the autopilot, Michael descended, his mission a closer look at The Maze. He followed the pathway of the Colorado for half an hour before banking slightly northward near the confluence. After the plane leveled, he slowly lowered to five hundred feet above ground level as the canyons gave way to the Colorado Plateau with its thick blanket of pine trees just below.

"How about a little flying fun?" he suggested.

She replied, "Sure."

They glided softly above the trees in a slow, semi-circular arc. Suddenly, and without notice, the trees abruptly stopped as they exited at the half-arc's southern end. The boundary-line of evergreen immediately gave way to the now fully exposed floor of Monument Valley and Valley of the Gods below. The Goosenecks of the San Juan passed below the nose. The San Francisco Peaks loomed large in the distance to the south. Michael swooped down over the Mokidugway toward the desert floor two thousand feet below and leveled again at five hundred feet as Erin let out a "weeeeee" followed by a warm smile.

He looped around several of the monuments that jutted from the valley floor, much to Erin's glee. Reluctantly he contacted the Kayenta Tower and set up on approach, the monuments passing to their sides. They glided to a soft landing moments later, then taxied to the south hangers before stopping and shutting down the engines.

Erin leapt from her seat, throwing her arms around him and planting a wet kiss on his mouth.

"God, do you know how to show a girl a good time or what?"

"I've only just started."

"Keep going. I'm loving every minute."

She kissed him again, deeply, caressing his shoulders and chest. She leaned back, starring into his eyes, on her face the mesmerized look of a schoolgirl.

They exited the plane and Michael grabbed the bags. They walked into the charter service and Michael made the arrangements to leave the plane, not taking the time now to have it re-fueled.

Joseph was waiting outside in his old pick-up truck. Michael put the bags in the bed and opened the truck's door to let her in.

"Erin, I'd like you to meet my friend Joseph."

"Nice to meet you."

"Nice, uh, to uh, meet you too" Joseph stammered with a quizzical look.

"It's OK, Joseph. I did the same thing many years ago when I first saw her."

"Yeah, I'll bet. Where did you find her? Simply amazing!"

"Long story," was Michael's curt reply.

Erin hopped up into the cab and slid in next to Joseph. Michael joined her, placing his arm around her shoulder along the seatback as Joseph edged the truck forward.

Conversation quickly erupted as Erin re-traced the journey that had just ended. Then Michael and Erin, at Joseph's insistence, filled the time passing on their trip to the Begay home by explaining their re-encountering each other. Joseph was truly pleased and happy for the both of them, but not half as happy as the smiles on the couple's faces indicated.

The truck wiggled its way onto the dirt side-road for the final stretch and Erin noted the monuments around which they'd just flown. The dogs surrounded the vehicle with their customary greeting as it pulled to a halt in a dusty cloud.

They were soon in Ellen Begay's kitchen going again through introductions and explanations. Mama Begay was ecstatic and even stopped her work in the kitchen to get the full story. After they completed their tale of twenty or so years, Mama Begay smiled and nodded at Michael, saying, "I wondered when she would come."

Michael and Erin exchanged glances, neither knowing quite what she was talking about. Joseph just smiled and nodded.

After a bit, Mama Begay went back to work preparing dinner for the newly arrived guests, along with the others who would shortly follow. A full table was always the fare when guests came to the Begay home. Erin eagerly dived in at her side, saying she'd always wanted to know how to make the delicious Navajo dishes she'd eaten many times before. The two men quietly talked at the kitchen table, Michael explaining the past few days' events , saving the knife point threat for a more opportune time. The women toiled silently in their preparations, listening to the details of Michael's unfathomable story.

"But," Michael continued, "I just don't understand what Luigi meant by 'Yeh Tay' and who this Zell person is. Do you know anyone by that name, Joseph?"

"No, not that I can think of. I've been wracking my brain trying to think of anyone even close. 'Yeh Tay'. Cody Zell. 'Yeh Tay'. Hmmm. Just don't know."

Mama Begay turned and brought some pepper and salt to the table. She smiled, and then paused, apparently not wishing to interrupt the two men, before returning silently to her counter.

"I know the feeling." Michael said dispiritedly. "I searched the name but really didn't find anything close in the Four Corners. I even had a friend over at the telephone company check the name through the information computer. The only two hits were for a Charlie Zell in Chinle and a C. Zell in Pagosa Springs. That turned out to be a Christy Zell, but neither knew anyone named Cody or Luigi. Other than that, nothing in the entire Four Corners area."

"Sounds like a dead end."

"No, I don't think so, Joseph. Besides, it's our only clue to the truth;

it's got to lead somewhere. I've just got to figure out where. I need a break."

"I'm afraid I can't be much help."

Mama Begay returned to the table, setting a Navajo taco before each of them, smiled and nodded as she received their thanks.

"Mom, do you know a person by that name?"

"No, I don't, son," she politely replied. Joseph and Michael sat silently, lost in thought, while Mama Begay smiled as if waiting for them, before returning to her spot by the stove next to Erin. The boys quickly gobbled down the food. Michael had always loved Mama Begay's tacos and had missed them for years.

"What do you make of 'Yeh Tay,' Joseph?"

"It's obviously bad Navajo, that's for sure. Our people don't bastardize the traditional greeting like that."

Ellen Begay's head turned slowly, looking at her son with piercing eyes.

"Sorry, mom." Joseph continued, "but 'Yeh Tay' has no meaning to me other than that."

The two friends continued to ponder the problem while they finished their last bites. Just as they finished, Ellen Begay was back to the table to pick up the empty plates, now politely intervening.

"You might ask grandfather," she said, drawing the boys' attention away from their thoughts.

"Thanks, mom, but he never leaves Fourth Mesa. And I know there's no one around here named Cody."

The boys chuckled, perhaps a little impolitely, drawing another stern look. Her smile slowly returned before she turned, concluding as she neared her cutting board, "No, son, that might not be true. For example, your grandfather had an old dog named Yeh Tay and he knows nearly everyone around here. Perhaps he knows more people than you do."

It took a few moments for the words to pass through their snickers and apparently wax-filled ears. After a few more moments it registered in their brains. "Mom, does grandfather knows Luigi?"

"I am unsure. Your grandfather is more well-traveled than you might think, but I think it is for him to speak to you of this. I have heard him mention the name Luigi before, but I have never met this man. I think it might be worth your time to ride up to the mesa and speak with him of this, but this can wait until tomorrow. Tonight we have guests. These questions for your grandfather can wait until the morning."

Mama Begay returned to her place at the kitchen counter, with a smile toward Erin, who replied with an approving smile. The older woman never missed a beat, despite the conversation, and was soon back immersed in the preparations. Erin looked over her shoulder, giving Michael and Joseph a "so you think you're so smart" look. She smiled again, then turned back to join the elder woman, leaving the men with their dumbfounded looks and thoughts.

After several moments they had resumed their discussion. This time they spoke a little louder, to ensure the matriarch could hear every word and comment as needed.

"But how could my grandfather know Luigi? I don't think he's ever been here and I've never talked to him about the students over there." Both men immediately turned to Mama Begay, who remained immersed in her work.

"Grandfather only rarely went to Durango. There must be another connection." Joseph, like his friend, was searching for logical answers.

"There just might be" Michael pondered this. "Luigi and your grandfather both fought in World War II. Who knows? Maybe they somehow met there. Or maybe they met through the VFW or something. I don't know, but there may be something there. Joseph, do you know anything about your grandfather's service?"

"Not really, only rumors. He'd never really talk about it himself. Mother?" They both turned to her with questioning eyes. She finished what she was doing before addressing their question.

"He spoke in detail of it only once, before they honored him in Kayenta, before you were very old, Joseph. Several years after the war was ended, our people honored the dead, as well as the living Code Talkers. Your grandfather was one of them. He spent three years in the islands in the Pacific, even won some medal for something, I think. It has been a very long time. I'm not sure for what. They say he saved many men's lives. The rest you would have to ask of him."

She stopped and looked out the window as an old green pick-up drove into the yard. The driver shut off the engine and waited until Ellen Begay went outside to formally invite the guests into her home.

The driver, a heavy Navajo woman, exited the vehicle, and was soon joined by a younger woman with black raven hair rounding out of the passenger side. She was pretty, approximately seventeen and probably Benjamin's sister, the girl Mary he'd seen before, if Michael had it figured right.

Mrs. Begay introduced the two Bear Clan Yazzie women to Erin and Michael. Mary nodded politely to Michael again and gave him another kind, reserved smile. They all sat down at the kitchen table while Ellen Begay hurriedly brought more food and plates to the table, with Erin's assistance. Michael and Joseph accepted more tacos and the women then joined them.

The six dined slowly as tradition demanded. They spoke of the general goings on in the Nation, but Mrs. Yazzie barely spoke, instead allowing her daughter to speak for her. Erin could read the sadness in her weathered face and drooping swollen eyes. She could only sympathize with her and the thought of knowing her son lay in jail accused of a terrible crime. She watched the woman carefully, her cheerless and forlorn look, slouched meekly into her chair, worry weighing heavily on her mind but a willingness to fight for her child to whatever end in her eyes. With their plates empty, Erin got up and began clearing the table, hoping that Michael and Joseph could help ease her misery, as Mrs. Begay simultaneously moved to her place in the kitchen leaving Mrs. Yazzie and her daughter, Joseph and Michael alone.

Joseph gently initiated the conversation, which had been the reason for the gathering. He started with the general background of the Bear Clan family, explaining to Michael that Benjamin's father Sam and his mother had a small sheep ranch over by Cameron out by the Grand Falls of the Little Colorado. With a son in college, they'd started selling jewelry sometimes to the tourists visiting the Park to make ends meet. Mary had come to live with her sister, who Michael had met before, her freshman year so she could go to Shiprock High rather than having to be bused from Cameron all the way back to Tuba City. Mrs. Yazzie interrupted to say something to Joseph in Navajo to which he told Michael that she said she was very concerned about her son and hoped that perhaps he might help her.

The lead-in was plenty sufficient and Michael picked up the conversation, his voice steady, measured and thoughtfully reassuring. "Mrs. Yazzie, I'm sure you would like to know, your son is fine. I met with him yesterday and he said to tell you he was doing very well. He looked good Mrs. Yazzie." Erin looked over at Michael from across the kitchen, watching as his eyes clearly connecting with the mother and daughter as he began to explain her son's difficult situation. His steady paced voice exuding the confidence of a seasoned trial veteran that settled the room quickly. It was a side of Michael she'd never seen before in him, completely reassuring and in full control of the situation, his voice full of certainty.

Mrs. Yazzie eased in her chair, as Joseph translated into Navajo, a somewhat smile slowly growing on her face. While it seemed clear to Erin that she understood English, it was clearer still that it was much easier for her to fully comprehend in her native language.

Michael continued that Benjamin was being treated well, seemed ok under the circumstances. He told her that his friend was the jailor, who promised to watch over him, and had allowed Michael to take Benjamin his prayer sticks in order that it might bring him some peace and Erin thought she noticed a wave of comfort wash over her face. He told her that he did not believe her son had killed anyone, explaining a few of his reasons through Joseph, much to the woman's further relief. He also explained that the legal work had already begun and what he planned for the future, in the event a trial was necessary. Through it all, the woman listened attentively to both Michael and Joseph, asking no questions, as was the Navajo Way.

Erin listened intently too. She smiled proudly, listening to him, his words evidently soothing the worried Navajo woman's face and reaffirming the good man she knew he was.

When he concluded, the woman smiled and spoke to Joseph in the old Navajo tongue. In turn Joseph spoke to Michael. "She says she is happy with what you tell her and that she has confidence and belief in what you say. She does not have much money, but has brought you three hundred dollars and will pay you whatever you need, if you can give her some time to sell her sheep."

Michael smiled politely, replying, "Tell her I thank her for her kind offer, but I do not wish her money or her sheep. The man that was killed was a friend of my family's and I owe it to him to find out who did this. Slaughter a lamb when your son returns and we will join you for the feast and dancing, if you will have us."

The woman smiled again, long before Joseph had finished translating, a tear clearly welling in her eye, and then spoke again without her translator as Mama Begay strode from the kitchen joining her cousin and placing her hands on her shoulder in support.

"My Corn Clan cousin and sister were right when they spoke of the goodness of your heart." She spoke slowly, choppy, patting Mama Begay's hand on her shoulder. "My daughter has also told me that she has met you before, here, that perhaps you have been sent to us by the Yei to help. She told me that she sees you are a good man and of a good heart. She says she sees much white light in you and she is gifted in these things. You have given our family hope. We will look forward to you visiting our home soon, with your friend." She smiled politely toward Erin, who nodded, her own eyes now holding back tears, before the older woman again turned to Michael saying "I thank you for my family," reaching her hands across the table.

"You are very kind and very welcome," Michael answered earnestly. Michael rose, extending his slightly cupped hand to the Bear Clan woman. She clasped it with both of hers and squeezed. "I will leave you to talk with your cousins, if you have no other questions for me. I will need to talk to Joseph a little more. Thank you again for coming to meet me. I promise I will do my best for your son and as soon as I know anything, I will get word to you." Her round face nodded thankfully as Michael stepped away from the table. He walked easily, but with added weight, outside into the cool breezes of the fast approaching evening. Erin joined him shortly and entwining her arm around his, leaning her head on his shoulder and taking a newly accustomed place beside him. They watched silently as the sun's leading edge dipped below Fourth Mesa and its light began to wane.

"I am so proud to know you right now Michael Kincaid," she whispered in his ear, then further in to him to place a kiss on his warm check.

"What was that for?" he asked a bit baffled.

She offered no reply, only a slight smile of approval, allowing herself to pull closer to him.

They stood motionless, watching the colors change in the clouds over Fourth Mesa, where they would soon find Hosteen Begay. Joseph joined them a few moments later, suggesting to Michael that they speak in the sweat lodge. Joseph left to build the fire and Michael pulled Erin tightly. "You are a good woman Erin. Thanks for coming and your support. It is always so hard for me, talking to the families. I'm sorry, but it doesn't look like we'll make it back tonight."

"Its ok, there's no other place I'd rather be right now" and she nuzzled her check on his shoulder.

After they had held each other tightly for a few more moments, Erin broke from him with a quick smile, saying she'd check to see if the women needed help finishing the cleaning. "Besides, you two boys need to talk. You need to help Benjamin. I'll see you soon baby!" She whirled with her smile and was on her way.

When she reached the door, she turned her head with a sultry look and a wink, entering the house, leaving a somewhat confused looking man behind. It had been a long time since she'd called him baby. He eventually turned and joined Joseph, who was already seated in the now steamy sweat lodge.

"She's a good woman, Michael. I wouldn't let her get away," his friend greeted him as he joined him in the circular den.

"My old friend, I'm a little confused, but I don't think I'll make that mistake again."

"Talk to me my friend." He offered as the fire crackled between them.

* * *

Tielson sat alone in his bedimmed cave. The little light that existed came from the desk lamp perched over the phone. It had been several hours since the two operatives had last reported and the little man's nervousness showed. He apprehensively noted the passage of time with each tap of his pencil. His mind resided somewhere else.

The sudden and insistent knock at the door barely startled him. His cold contorted face glanced up as he loudly invited the intruder in.

"I trust you have something to report," he said slowly.

"Yes, sir. Tompkins is on the secure line."

Anderson watched as the wrinkled hand blurred as it swiftly grasped the receiver from beneath the lamp. He noted that the troll looked smaller than usual in the dim light, red eyes protruding from the seemingly sunken sockets in his head. The grotesque little figure looked more menacing today than Anderson could ever remember.

"Report!" he demanded rudely into the phone.

The voice shook nervously on the other end. "Everything went according to plan, but we've lost him."

"You what?" the crackling voice rose in anger.

"He flew off in a private plane. We had no idea he could fly. It took us totally by surprise."

"You two are paid to expect the unexpected, so don't give me your lame bullshit."

"Yes, sir. I merely meant that his quick departure took us by surprise."

"No matter, as long as he's out of the picture."

"That appears to be the case. Our warning paid off. He ran . . ."

"Your warning? He ran?" The inflection in his voice changed to suspicion as he cut off the other man. "Now what are you talking about?" His voice ascended and pressed on the last word. Anderson studied the troll, wondering what was next, wondering what the other end of the call was saying. He desperately wanted to go back to his desk and eavesdrop on the call.

"Well, sir, he was pretty confused and dazed last night. The fear was obvious when I threatened him and this girl he's been hanging out with. I think . . ."

Tielson curtly cut him off. "You did what? You didn't. You didn't tell me that. You know what? You're not a fool, you're a fucking moron!" his voice now rose again with intensity. "You were told to follow my orders explicitly?"

"And we did." Tompkins exclaimed defensively, wondering to himself what game the man was playing.

"Then why did you threaten the girl? I didn't tell you to involve others."

"Well, as you suggested, we waited for the right opportunity to put a little fear into him and it just developed that way. Sir, it was the perfect way to bring it home. We know what we're doing and these tactics have worked well in the past, as you are well aware. We figured he'd run from the threat and that's exactly what he's done."

The little man finally backed off with an "OK, OK. I understand. What's done is done," perhaps not wishing to push it further. He finally placed his stubby fingers over the mouthpiece, confiding to the junior man, "You know, Anderson, these two are really fucking cretins."

The man on the other end was continuing, now saying, "Sir, you're not out here and my read is that he's on the run."

"No, Tompkins, I'm not out there," he stated more softly, "and unfortunately I must depend on your eyes." He paused. "But you damn well better be right."

"Look, he took the girl and ran, I'm sure of it. He won't be back for a while." His own irritation was now waning toward the little man on the other end.

"Tompkins, if you're so sure, then how do I know that he's not just manipulating you to think that way?"

"We've confirmed some things this morning which have been sent on. We had a talk with the court's clerk. She was more than happy to have us interview her for an article in 'The Denver Post.' This guy Kincaid signed on to the case yesterday, and then abruptly filed a substitute of attorney motion this morning. He even served a copy on the US Attorney's office in Denver from what we now know. I'm sure you have ways of checking it out if you like. After he took off with the girl, we spoke to the charter agent at the field where the plane was kept. Turns out it was the motel owner Daniels' plane. The agent said our man was flying to Denver and then on to Hawaii. He didn't know either of them, just wished it was him who was going. Their intentions seemed pretty sure to him. We also confirmed two reservations on the afternoon flight to Hawaii. I'm telling you, sir, he's long gone. I'm sure of it."

"You'd better be right, Tompkins. You'd better be right. If you're not, we're all screwed. You two keep close tabs on that motel owner. Keep listening in and report anything new, immediately! Do I make myself clear? Immediately!" Tielson didn't wait for the other man's response, mulling over the possibilities. If he's associated with the motel owner then I'll bet he's not out of it just yet. This guy's up to something and I can feel it. Then he spoke to the man at the other end: "You two fuck up again and you'll have plenty of time to think about this. Understand?"

"Yes, sir. Perhaps he's in need of a nap if he should return. We don't like this any more then you do."

"Damn it, Tompkins, I just told you to follow my orders specifically. We'll discuss further options at another point. You observe, listen and report back. That's it. Do you understand?"

"Yes, sir. Observe, listen and report."

The conversation abruptly ended as Tielson slammed down the phone.

"Is there something to worry about, sir?"

"I don't know." He was short and curt again with the junior man. "There's far too much at stake here, Anderson, those two are making me very nervous. If this falls, it all falls . . . and your men aren't following orders."

The lieutenant commander was not humored by his superior's patronizing tone. He watched the troll's beady eyes constrict, brain toiling anonymously on some vague detail. Distorted stubs massaged its upper lip. "There'll be some information coming. We need to get some other intel on these other players. See what you can find out from Justice and our other sources, then get back to me ASAP. I'm going to work on another angle."

"Yes Sir."

"And get our other man in place in case anything else goes wrong and we need to act fast."

"Yes, sir." The junior man withdrew as quickly as possible from the troll's den. Going down the hallway, his stomach tightened to a knot. He had to distance himself from the troll, but how?

* * *

In a rocking chair next to Joseph on the Begay front porch, Michael was drifting in and out of a dreamy state upon their return from the sweat lodge. They had talked a little about the case and spoken to Kevin and Trish at 8:00 as planned. Everything seemed quiet in Durango but Kevin had no luck yet finding Nick and nobody had ever heard of anyone named Cody Zell. He'd talked to a couple of people who knew both Nick and Luigi, but nobody had seen Nick in several days, which was a little, but not completely, odd. Everyone seemed to agree it was likely he was on a bender somewhere. One of the guys he ran into at the El Rancho on Main lived up on the mountain and said he'd keep an eye out for him. If he saw him he'd give him a message to call Kevin on the number for the new burner cell. He had a couple of other ideas, another guy told him Nick sometimes went up to old Coach Cullen's cabin at Vallecito to fish, so Kevin and Trish were going to take a ride up there tomorrow. When Michael said they would be staying the night and likely the next, they decided that they'd call again tomorrow at 8 with any news, but Joseph warned that they were taking a ride somewhere and might not have service. He knew of a spot near where they were going that usually had service, but it was sometimes a bit dicey as was service anywhere on the northern part of the reservation and southern Utah. He'd be there at 8 but if he couldn't reach him, trying texting him or try them around 10 a.m. the next morning when they should be back in the Valley and in range.

After the call, Joseph and Michael had talked a little about Lori's death and a lot about his newfound friend before Joseph left him alone to go back into the house. He now rocked quietly alone, ignoring the sounds coming from inside the screen door. He had long since stopped thinking about the case, his mind now focused solely on the conflict and contradiction inside him. The pain of losing Lori had totally overwhelmed his being in the months before he'd finally surrendered to it and left LA a week before. So much so that he'd had to run from the insanity it had produced. Just like a little boy chased by the local gang of bullies, he'd rushed to the one place he knew he'd find salvation: home. Had his flight garnered him freedom? Or was this just another cruel event in a chain that had started three years ago? An argument began inside him.

He thought of how wonderful a woman she had been and the thought warmed him on the chilling night. Long walks along the beach in Laguna, gazing across to her over a candlelight dinner, her warm breath tickling his neck as she lay tucked in next to him after a night of lovemaking. A tear slowly dripped from the corner of his eye as he thought of that Christmas morning she'd found the ring in her stocking and said yes, an enchanting smile coming across her face. She had always been so vivacious in her pursuit of life and her spirit had always drawn him to her, and somehow, that spirit now gave him comfort and acceptance that he did not have a week ago. He knew she wouldn't want him to dwell on the past. He knew she wouldn't want him to go through life alone. He knew she'd want him to go on, remembering her, but advancing until they could see each other again. He relaxed into the rocking chair a bit more, not noticing the disappearance of the anger he'd consistently felt the past year whenever his thoughts turned to the loss. His subconscious mind had seemingly come to something like peace or acceptance of the loss over the past few days and somewhere he could hear her voice saying "go on my love."

He wiped the tear from his eye with his knuckle, his thoughts turning to the last couple of days he'd spent with Erin. He could sense himself opening to the thought of feelings again, which he'd consciously suppressed for a very long time. Their reencountering had been nothing short of a blessing. Thoughts of Erin soothed him now. Perhaps due to familiarity, maybe a past better aged with time and memory, or perhaps it was just nice to be around a good woman again. It had been so long since he'd even thought about another woman, he wasn't even sure how to react to the emotions welling inside him, but maybe it was time he did something said.

He closed his eyes harder as the other nagging voice argued that maybe it was too soon to care about another. His protective barriers screamed What if it doesn't work? Or worse, what if something happened to her? If he followed the road of these feelings, his protectionist subconscious reasoned, it would surely devastate him. Can you take the risk?

But what if you don't? His heart now countered. Are you really prepared to be alone for the rest of your life when a wonderful woman stands before you?

The thoughts raced through his mind as his methodical rocking continued. Was he being unfair to her memory? Or was he being selfish and unfair to himself? "Go on my love" he heard her say again loudly beneath the shadows of his closed lids, shutting out the sound of the screen door opening, then quietly shutting.

Startled by the first touch to his shoulder, he let the wide rocker come to a slow stop. He was pleasantly surprised to find her when he opened his eyes, glancing back to her soft caress. She slid in next to him, smiling sweetly. "It's a beautiful night," bending into his body.

"Indeed a beautiful night Erin," he answered, sliding his hand around her shoulder. "A bit chilly," she said, producing a reddish woolen blanket, flipping it open and covering them both. She began to slowly rock in harmony with him, swaying back and forth peacefully with her leg as they lightly moved together. They gazed out toward the millions of twinkling lights that dotted the night sky. As a shooting star arced across the heavens, each made an unsaid wish before their eyes returned to each other with quiet smiles.

Edward Donovan

DAY EIGHT

Enlightenment

He was watching her as she disappeared over the dune with a wave, Coyote trailing behind mischievously. Michael startled a bit when the screen door creaked open. He registered a shadowy silhouetted figure emerging, the morning's first light rudely intruding upon his slowly opening eyes. He lifted his head with a yawning groan, his eyes probing for focus, careful not to disturb Erin's head still resting on his shoulder, his arm still draped around her.

"Ah . . . there you two are," came a teasing voice. "This is your morning wake-up call. Mother's getting breakfast ready."

Erin's mind and eyes now struggled to awaken; reflexively, she pulled the blanket up to the nape of her neck and leaned closer to Michael.

"If you two have thoughts of taking a shower before we take off, I suggest you take the opportunity now."

"Sounds like a pretty good idea," Michael said, slowly rising and stretching.

Erin pulled the blanket around her as she followed suit, turning slowly to Michael, regaining her sea legs and resting her head lightly on his shoulder. He placed his arm around her waist, giving her a little tug to pull her hips in next to his.

"There's towels for both of you in the shower and the coffee's on whenever you're ready. Sun's already up and we've got a long ride so we should get going as soon as we can." Joseph retreated back into the house.

"Long ride . . ." and her questioning voice trailed off.

"Yeah, three or four hours up to see Joseph's grandfather. Would you like to ride along or would you rather stay here?

"Horses?" she perked up. "I love horses. Sure; I'll go as long as I can have the shower first." She poked him in the ribs, giving him a quick peck before rising and heading inside, Michael in tow.

* * *

Tielson had been shut up in his office for hours. He'd contacted the one person he could count on to tidy up any additional problems, who was on his way. He'd phoned his connection at Justice and confirmed the substitution Tompkins had reported, but was surprised to learn who he was dealing with. For the past hour he'd been re-reviewing the dossier Anderson had provided him and the other information Tompkins had sent. He'd sensed that he knew this Kincaid from somewhere. His contact at Justice certainly knew of him; he'd been a thorn in their side for years. If need be, he now thought, he could work this to his advantage. The others involved were barely worth a look, particularly with the lawyer now apparently out of the picture. He paused, focusing upon the information he'd carelessly missed the first time. He smiled when he realized where he remembered the name from. He now felt confident the group wouldn't provide such a great obstacle. And if they did, that's what the cleaner was for. After all, who'd miss one dead criminal lawyer? Tielson leaned back in his chair, warm with the thoughts that he finally had the operation back under control.

* * *

"Good morning," Momma Begay called as Erin and Michael entered the kitchen.

"Good morning," they cheerfully chimed in unison.

"Michael, you know where the coffee is. Help Erin with some if she'd like. Then take a seat; breakfast is almost ready.

"Can I help you with anything, Mrs. Begay," Erin volunteered.

"No, but thank you dear, but call me Mama, you're part of us now" she graciously answered. "Get showers if you like and then have a seat.

Breakfast will be ready in a few minutes and you must be hungry and you have a long day ahead of you. I should have woken you both up and brought you in last night, but you were both sleeping so peaceful and happy together I didn't want to disturb you" she beamed with motherly approval which they both noticed.

They both hurriedly took a shower and when they returned the table was set and once again laden with food. The three gathered around the table, eagerly dug in to their breakfast and discussed the trip up Fourth Mesa. When they were finished with breakfast Mama Begay hurried them off, saying she'd take care of the dishes and for them to get going. She retrieved two bags from the refrigerator containing the sandwiches and drinks she'd already put together. She also withdrew a bag of ice from the freezer and handed it all to Joseph. "Here's some lunch and drinks for each of you. Ice them down in your saddlebags. Some for grandfather and Jaxson, too. You should get going. I'll expect you back tonight or in the morning." She shuffled them from her kitchen.

The three gathered the other necessities they'd need for their adventure and were quickly out the door and around the corner to their already saddled mounts. Michael helped Erin adjust her stirrups and get settled in her saddle before adjusting his own gear. The three rode out of the small corral, following Joseph at a slow trot northward toward the mesa.

When they'd been on the trail nearly two hours, the three came abreast as they neared the edge of the mesa. Joseph began explaining the area to Erin and pointing out the various sights. To the northeast lay the Valley of the Gods, the San Juan River goose-necking through the foreground. He pointed to a slight indentation in the mesa's wall, telling her that was where the road up the Mokidugway climbed out of the valley to the Colorado Plateau. He explained that in a few more minutes they would begin their own climb out of the valley, up Fourth Mesa, to the summer camp where his grandfather and his brother Jaxson would be attending to the sheep.

She gazed upward at the massive wall of rock and boulders. "We're riding up that???"

"Sure. It's really not that bad . . . if you know where you're going."

"I'll bet. Joseph, you said your brother was up here. Is that your only sibling?"

"I also have two sisters, Kacie and Kathy, and another brother, Johnson Jr., after my father ."

"I meant to ask about your brother J.J. Where is he? Your mom didn't even talk about him," Michael asked, jumping into the conversation.

"She doesn't talk much about him anymore. I don't blame her; he hasn't even really called or written or anything since he got his new assignment down in Grants. I think Jaxson's the only one who's talked to him at all."

"You're kidding?!?" The amazement was evident across Michael's face. Navajo families, and the Begays in particular, were pretty tight.

"No, unfortunately, I'm not. When I get a hold of him I'm going to give him some grief. Ever since he went into this work, he's been different. I haven't talked to him much; he's been at various places since he started."

"What does he do?"

"I'm not really sure; I don't think much of anything. From what I hear, he guards or watches some old abandoned installation out on one of the mesas north of Grants. It's been out there for as long as anyone remembers. Nothing ever goes on out there. My cousin in Chinle told me that they have a few Navajo guards and I guess he's one of them."

"So what's his problem?"

"I don't know; he's just been weird since he joined the Marines. I guess he became all gung ho or something. Nobody hears from him. Can you imagine? You haven't seen him in a long time, Michael. He was still a little kid when you went to LA and I went to Baltimore. He was always getting in fights, raised hell with Mom, all kinds of problems. Everybody thought it was the best thing for him when he went into the Marines. Might straighten him out. Maybe it did; I don't really know."

"Yeah, real straight, doesn't even call his family," Michael snapped.

"Well, anyway, Erin, that's my brothers and sisters."

It was a few more minutes before they began their slow progress up Fourth Mesa. The track switch-backed for an hour before pointing the horses and riders toward the grove of pine trees that announced the rim's edge, now a mere quarter mile away. Joseph, or perhaps his horse, led the way. Erin came next, playfully glancing back at Michael every so often when the terrain permitted. Bringing up the rear, Michael sat in the saddle, ever mindful of the danger that might yet be at their back door. But nobody could follow them by plane, vehicle and then up this trail without him seeing them. His mind eased as the increasing elevation gave them the strategic advantage of sight.

In the distance he could barely make out the Begay hogan and the road that led in. The monuments were silhouetted against a hazy blue southeastern sky. He could easily see a hundred miles out into the remoteness.

A wide spot in the path gave the three a chance to come alongside each other, the horses happy for the blow after the long climb up. They dismounted, giving Joseph the opportunity to point out the various sights to Erin before they reached tree line above. Michael scoured the landscape below, not finding any plumes of dust escaping a vehicle's undercarriage or anything else that might indicate someone had somehow found them. Erin came over and put her arm around him.

"First a Jeep, then a plane, now a horse. Any other means of transportation you have in mind, Mr. Kincaid?"

"Never can tell."

"You've taken me to the moon. So inventive, aren't you!"

"I try." He smiled.

They remounted and in a half hour reached the summit. Their heads slowly popped over the last rise to see the lineshack nestled on a sloping incline among the first line of lodgepole pines, the azure sky backdropping the long spindly brown trunks reaching up toward their emerald-green boughs. To its left was a small hut made of mud and aspen poles with a smokestack poking from the roof. A relaxed breeze softly rolled from the knoll to greet them. Sheep grazed lazily on the grassy glade to the northwest of the lineshack. A smallish black and white border collie lay among them. The dog wearily rolled his head, eyeing the approaching pack. He raised his snout to the sky and yelped once, rolling his head back to the ground, never moving his torso. He stretched out his white legs, yawned, then closed his eyes, returning to lazy dog-daydreams, his job done, his keep protected.

The signal drew a cock of the head and an eye toward the riders from the young man nestled into the small hillside at the edge of the flock, cooling in the shade of the gently swaying pines. He reached his hand to his hat-brim, glancing first at the riders approaching and then pulling it closer to his nose, stopping when his thumb touched. He returned his careless gaze toward the underside of the hat's brim, slowly closing his eyes.

As the group neared the lineshack, a second, medium-sized older black dog ambled from the doorway. He gazed toward the trio arriving before taking up a seated position between two wooden rocking chairs on the front porch. Moments later, as they dismounted and tied their horses to trees, Hosteen Begay emerged. The old man took the first chair, to the right of his guard.

"Hello, Grandfather," Joseph called as he approached the first of the two steps to the porch.

"Hello, Joseph. I see you have brought me visitors."

"Yes, Grandfather, I have. This is a friend of Michael's, Erin."

"I am very pleased to meet you." A warm smile creased his weather-beaten face.

She amiably received his welcome, saying, "I've heard much about you."

This brought a nod from his flowing, silvery mane.

"Please join me." He motioned toward the available chairs to his left and right.

Joseph pulled a chair to the right of his grandfather. Erin, followed by Michael, stepped up to the porch, taking the double rocker to the right, politely leaving open the seat next to the wizardly figure. As Michael her, the black dog lay down, gently resting his muzzle on his crossed tan front paws.

Erin gazed out from the high perch toward the monuments standing sentinel in the valley floor stretching southward in front of her. To the southwest the Superstitions jetted upward from Flag and to the east lay the Ute, napping quietly in the distance, billowy white clouds aimlessly dancing around his folded arms.

"What brings you to the top of Fourth Mesa?" the old man began.

"I've come to speak to you of old friends."

"I see. And who might this be?" the shaman calmly inquired.

"Of Luigi, Benjamin, a man named Cody Zell, and Yeh Tay, your dog."

The black dog lying between them raised his head a bit, opening his lids with a questioning stare toward the newly arrived guest. With a rub to his head from his master, he laid his head back on his paws, returning to his previous state.

"I see. Two of them I understand, but of the other two, I see no relation," he said. He leaned forward with a quizzical look, his chair closely in tow. "Speak to me of what you have learned since we last spoke."

Michael told him everything, leaving nothing out. He knew the shaman would need all the information to truly help. Erin squirmed a bit when she heard the full account of two nights ago and finally understood the peril Michael felt he had unwittingly exposed her to. He concluded with Luigi's dying greeting. When he finished, Hosteen Begay leaned back quietly in his chair before slowly speaking.

"Luigi Morrealli was not just a friend to me, he was more. We were comrades. We fought together in World War II."

"So do you also know this Cody Zell person?" the lawyer's mind instinctively and impatiently queried him.

"Yes, I know of what he spoke. First, you must understand other things before you learn of what you ask." Hosteen Begay paused in reflection before he spoke again. "We were based at Pearl Harbor when we met. My friend Luigi was with special operations and I with communications."

"Then you were a Code Talker, Grandfather." Joseph's face lit up and he leaned in closer.

"Yes, I spoke the code, Joseph, it is not something I talk of often, but you get ahead of me. The army came from the base over by Flagstaff to our schools here after the war began. They had heard that the Navajo were good runners over long distances. They were looking for runners to carry messages between battle groups. Communications were not very good back then. Our Corn Clan ancestors had carried the messages to the Peoples for centuries. So we volunteered to serve, believing it was the right thing to do. We were Americans despite our troubled past with the government. Some of our brothers went directly to units. The best runners of us were sent to San Diego. There were twelve of us at first."

He paused before continuing. "We trained hard for many weeks, running in the sands at Coronado. One day a colonel came to our training. He heard us talking in the old tongue and asked if we were Navajo. I told him we were. He knew of our language and ways, he said. We later found out he had been raised as the son of a missionary over near Crown Point." He paused again and the trio edged farther forward in their seats.

"After two weeks the colonel came back. He said that our enemies were breaking the white codes and asked if we could help. He said that our ancient language was not known by many and that if we coded it we could save many lives."

"So Luigi was the colonel?" Michael interjected again.

"No, my young friend. Be patient and you shall learn."

He paused a few more moments in what seemed further reflection upon his friend.

"We helped the colonel and when they learned that their own people could not break our code talk, they sent us to Hawaii to train our other brothers in the code talk. I had been training in the code talk for four months when the general came to see me. He had heard of the success of our code talk. He also heard I was good at running. He asked me to volunteer for a very important mission. One that would take me behind Japanese lines. I agreed and they took me from my group."

"They trained me with two others, Luigi and Mack. They wanted us to scout an island for an operation they had in mind. They were looking for a base to launch bomber runs against Thailand, the Philippines and to push back the Japanese. They hoped to cut our enemies' supply lines in half before they could take Luzon and the other islands."

"For many weeks we practiced landings using a seaplane and raft. We were finally assigned the Palau Islands, part of what they later called the Caroline Islands."

"Palau? Luigi spoke of these islands to me once."

"They were nothing more than rocks, but our enemies had built a runway on one, Peleliu." The name hung heavy on the old man's breath and his face subconsciously tensed. "The Japanese had taken the islands from the Germans during World War I and built bases throughout the Palaus, but The Point, as they called it, had the runway. Luigi and I were flown in to find a landing zone, map the island and troops, then get out." His voice slowly trailed off before finally concluding. "The operation was called Code Easel."

The old man sat quietly, waiting for Michael to respond. It took time for it to hit him, but when it did, it hit like Babe Ruth. Cody Zell. Code E. Zell. Code Easel.

"That's why he left the clue to your dog."

"Not quite. I am Yeh Tay. It is what he used to call me when we trained on the boats. Yeh Tay, short for Yeh Tay Hey, hello in Navajo of course. The dog was given to me by him many years later. He gave him that name and it took. But the message is to me."

"Did anything happen on Peleliu that would give someone reason to kill him?"

"No. We went in off a submarine drop, set up Easel, spent a couple of days in the jungle mapping it and got out. Mack picked us up in a seaplane and took us back to Ulithi Atoll. The whole plan was about getting the intelligence so we could quickly take the landing strip and to use it to bring in troops and supplies after the Marines landed at Beach Orange 3. After the invasion we ended up on Peleliu for a couple of months I think."

"Who's Mack?" Joseph inquired as Michael had with Luigi days ago.

"Howard McRae. You might know of him grandson."

"You mean the Howard McRae. The guy who's probably the next president?"

"Yes, Joseph."

"I thought Luigi said he fought off a carrier group in the Palaus or something." Michael now interjected.

"He did, before and after our mission. I was sent back to the Code Talkers and eventually to the Philippines, but Luigi and Mack ended up back on Peleliu together after the Marine landing when Mack was assigned air defense duty at the new base. After Mack flew against that cruiser, they pulled him back to Pearl to get his medal and tour the US. I spent the rest of the war with different units and occasionally saw Luigi on various assignments, but never Mack again. We were quite valuable to the government then as our code talk was never broken and it helped us to defeat our enemies. Over the years Luigi and I stayed in touch." The old man leaned back in his chair and began a slow rock.

Michael reflected on the story, not quite knowing what to make of it. He knew it had importance, but what? He soon came to the conclusion that needed to be reached. "I don't wish to alarm you, my old friend, but if someone killed Luigi for something he knew about Code Easel, you and Senator McRae might be in trouble too. You might want to stay on Fourth Mesa until I can get this sorted out."

"They would not wish to hunt an old man like me. And they could not even find me anyway, but I must now ask you again for another favor and send my warning to McRae. They might try and hurt him too."

"I will, I promise." Great, Michael thought, now I've got a goddamned senator to worry about too.

"Did you speak to Luigi or do you have any idea what he was doing in, say, the last month?"

"Yes, I would speak with him every few weeks when I would come down from here. He'd call sometimes when I would be home for Saturday dinner. I spoke to him twice in the last few weeks. One Saturday, two or three weeks ago, he told me he was going to Los Angeles on business. Then about a week ago he said he was coming to the area and would try and stop by. He said he wanted to talk to me about something, but he never came by."

"Do you know what it was about?"

"No, but you might ask his friend Nick. He spoke with him more than I."

"I've been trying to."

* * *

He listened as the phone rang in his ear, finally answered with "Si. Buenos Dias, Señor," he called loudly.

"Buenos Dias, Amigo," came the immediate response.

"I understood you were working at home today. I hope I am not interrupting anything."

"No, of course not. Just doing some paperwork. What can I do for you?"

"I just wanted to let you know that we have selected someone to head up our US operations."

"That's excellent news. I trust then that we will be on line again shortly."

"We certainly hope so, provided everything is handled on your end."

"It is my understanding that everything is fine here, but we were concerned that there might be some form of security problem at your end."

"What do you mean?"

"Well, from what I understand, your man has checked in and asked for some assistance with cleaning up a small issue. I was wondering if this is somehow related."

"Not to my knowledge. I've been assured everything is fine."

"It might be in your best interests to personally look into this and assure yourself that indeed it is. This seems an odd request if everything is proceeding smoothly."

"Perhaps. I'll need to look into it further. This is the first I've heard of this request. I'll speak to my people as soon as possible."

"What do wish for me to do with this in the meantime?"

"Proceed with the request. It may be unrelated to this matter."

"We'll trust your best judgment in the handling of this."

"Thank you. I'll be in touch, otherwise let's continue forward."

The phone clicked and the Old Man placed his head in his hands, wondering what this was about and what Tielson had been up to. He quietly rued the day he'd brought the hideous little man on board.

* * *

Joseph and Michael had gathered the saddlebags that held the provisions from Momma Begay. With Erin's assistance, sandwiches, chips and cold drinks were laid out on a small table on the front porch. With a call and a wave from his brother, Jaxson was invited to join them. Joseph disappeared into the small lineshack, returning in a few moments with an extra chair for his brother who was slowly approaching. "Erin, this is my brother Jaxson." She smiled at him softly, saying, "Nice to meet you." Jaxson shyly smiled at her and nodded without reply, taking the seat his brother offered. Joseph handed his grandfather a sandwich and an Orange Crush, then served Erin, Michael and Jaxson, before taking his own and his seat.

"Ah, a cold drink. It is one of the things I truly miss when I'm on Fourth Mesa," the old shaman commented, taking a long cold sip off the can. They otherwise ate in silence, enjoying the early afternoon break.

After several minutes the silence was broken by the sentry guarding the flock. Just a mild, quick bark, letting Jaxson know that something was around. "Probably a bird," he grunted, rising to his feet. "Thank you, Joseph."

"Sure" came the answer.

Jaxson made his way back to the flock, taking up his position on the knoll. Joseph cleaned up the remnants of the meal and took them into the lineshack with Erin in tow, leaving Hosteen Begay and Michael rocking in tandem.

Finally Michael's thoughts took over, remarking how this all didn't make sense.

"It is quite confusing, my young friend."

"Tell me more about the operation. Were there any troubles?"

"Not to speak of. We mapped the area and got out. In a few months, the Marines launched their offensive and took the island. They established the air base and I think they flew a few missions, but they were basically to stock the island for other operations according to the plan."

"I don't understand. What do you mean 'according to the plan'"?

"I don't know exactly what went on there; I only know what my friend told me later. He said the original plan was to establish a base and make strikes to take back the Dutch East Indies oil fields, a vital resource for Japan and Royal Dutch Shell. Luigi said that they brought several planes of supplies and stocked the island, but never started their bombing. A few months later the war moved north and away to the Philippines and soon after came Hiroshima."

"It still doesn't make sense. It doesn't have a connection to us here, can't be oil."

"The only connection that I could think of would be to the depots."

"The depots?"

"Sure. Most of the major supply warehouses were in the West. We were at war. During those years they stocked munitions, tanks, Jeeps, everything for the war at depots all around here. Arizona, New Mexico, Nevada and Utah. It was from the main depot down around Gallup that they flew supplies in to Peleliu after we took the island. They'd refuel in Hawaii, fly it in to Ulithi Atoll where they had the big secret base and on up to us on the front lines. These depots were very remote, removed from everywhere, just in case our enemies had ideas of sabotage."

"Didn't you say that Luigi was planning on coming out here a few days ago?"

"Yes, but I never did speak with him and I don't know if he did."

"Do you know if any of those depots were around here?"

"Yes, there are many. There are some near Grants, most were closed many years ago. The main depot near Gallup has a few people still around, it is where the colonel came from that visited us for our help with the war. And there is also one over by Chinle, I think it is where my grandson works."

"J.J.?"

"Yes. I think he is stationed there. But you would have to ask Jaxson for sure. He is who his brother speaks to most."

"Perhaps I should. This has taken an unusual twist."

The two were interrupted as Erin and Joseph emerged from the line-shack. Erin was laughing at something Joseph was telling her. She took one look at Michael, then stepped backwards, pulling her hands to her face to suppress her giggle. Michael glanced up at Joseph, showing a sheepish grin. Obviously his friend had been sharing something Michael was sure he'd wished he hadn't. "Having fun at my expense?" Erin burst with laughter and stepped off the porch. Michael turned to Joseph with a look and "What have you been telling her?" before following behind her and catching her with his arm and saying "don't listen to him, probably untrue" with a wink and an exaggerated smile.

He playfully pulled her with him in the general direction of the sheep and Jaxson, telling her that he needed to speak to him for a few minutes. As they approached Jaxson, Erin parted from him, turning her attention to the flock. Michael sat on the ground next to Joseph's youngest brother and talked to him a few minutes about J.J. and what he'd been doing. Jaxson didn't really know a lot, but he knew that his brother had been transferred from Gallup to someplace up around Chinle. He didn't hear from him much anymore and when he did, he didn't say much other than that he was staying in quarters on the base full time.

They talked about a few other things before pausing to lean back against the knoll. The sun was drawing low in the western sky. Michael gazed down the meadow watching this beautiful woman sway among the sheep, drawing them to her path as she went, reminiscent of some fairy tale of youth.

"Is she the one Kokopelli played for?"

Michael looked strangely toward Jaxson. "What do you mean?"

"Perhaps she is the one Kokopelli played for. She is the spirit who came to visit you in the sweat lodge. Grandfather and Joseph spoke to me of her after your sweat with Joseph down below. You should take a sweat with him and ask him if you do not understand."

Michael nodded silently. "I think I understand, but I believe I will talk to him."

Jaxson rose as he noticed a couple sheep slowly heading up a draw where they didn't belong. He ambled off quietly leaving Michael in thought, watching Erin amidst the sheep continuing to gathering around her.

What were these dreams he was having? Everything was spinning in his mind now, but he no longer cared. He gazed across to the woman now approaching him and pulled her close as she sat next to him.

"Thank you so much for bringing me Michael, it has been a wonderful" and she leaned over, stroking his face softly before leaning in to kiss him. Their lips met cautiously at first, pecking lightly has he pulled her near. After several seconds they released, gazing back in each other's eyes before Erin pushed Michael back to the ground and lay her head on his pounding chest, draping her arm across him. They watched as the clouds slowly drifted past, the sheep baaing as Jaxson chased the stragglers back toward the pack, the two resting peacefully.

* * *

"Good evening, Lieutenant Commander."

"Well, good evening, sir. This is a surprise."

"Yes, I suppose. I need to speak with you about some things."

"Of course, sir. Any time."

"How about 6:30 tomorrow morning by the pool. Could you make it then?"

"Of course, sir. I'll be there."

"See you in the morning. And thank you."

He set the receiver down with a final "Yes, sir." What in the hell was going on that he should need to meet with the Old Man? He didn't like this at all.

* * *

The southern constellations had begun to take shape as the group of five sat upon the lineshack porch. Smoke communicating Jaxson's fire efforts billowed from the stack atop the smallish mud sweat lodge, wafting slowly toward the sheep in the northern pasture with the gentle springtime breeze. They listened to Hosteen Begay as he began to explain the star patterns' significance to The People. He pointed out and above the San Francisco Peaks where Monster Slayer lived, the protector, high in the sky. He stood watch over the home of the gods and the Peoples. They listened quietly, nibbling on Navajo tacos and frybread, enjoying the warm early evening air. He continued with the other con-stellations, each having its own connection to the Diné.

After several minutes, the elderly shaman suggested that they take a sweat to help clear their minds so they might focus upon the task at hand. The family patriarch politely invited Erin, but she declined, say-ing she would take care of the cleanup and then probably call it an early night, the ride having taken it out of her. The four men stepped from the porch and rounded the dwelling toward the sweat lodge, Michael glanc-ing back to give Erin a warm smile.

The four disrobed outside, Michael took a plain, white, woven blanket hanging from knobs buried into the adobe that made up the sweat lodge's circular walls, draping it around his waist. Hosteen Begay opened the door and as they stepped through, a blast of hot air hit their faces. By the light of the fire, they each found seats on benches against the walls. Jaxson and his grandfather sat on the far side of the fire, while Joseph and Michael took seats near the door, the soft mixture of sand and straw from the floor squeezing in his toes. Jaxson poured a little water from a pitcher on a small table onto the rocks in the pit next to the base of the fire. As steam poured through the room, beads of perspira-tion formed on their faces.

After several minutes, the four began speaking of the task at hand. They could come to only one conclusion: Luigi's death was somehow tied to Code Easel and perhaps had something to do with the abandoned base near Chinle. It was the likely reason for Luigi's sudden trip to the reservation, as Kevin had related to him before, but likely having noth-ing to do with the student excuse he'd given or the visiting of other friends Luigi had across the Nation. Jaxson suggested that perhaps J.J. could help, since he was supposedly assigned to that area. Michael and Joseph agreed that they would try to talk to J.J. as soon as they returned.

The elderly shaman concluded the conversation, saying, "My old friend Luigi was a careful man. He had to be. He dealt with many prob-lems and fought many battles. I tell you this for a reason. You have missed an answer somewhere. If my friend knew of these things you speak of, he would have been careful. When we were together on Peleliu it was Luigi who was sent to protect me. He always had a second, a third and even a fourth option. Our trainers taught us to do this. When a life is in danger, one must do this in order to ensure the mission is completed. My old friend Luigi knew he could not complete his mission when he called to me with his words. He was trying to point me toward what he had learned. That is the meaning behind his last words. But I am an old man who sits upon a mountain. I am not able to carry this burden. If you wish to carry it, then you must understand Luigi. You must, as I've told you many times before, look for that which is out of place. From that which is out of place will stem both danger and salvation. You must heed these two things, for your sake and those that surround you. I tell you this because if Luigi was killed for something he knew, his call to me means he would have left something to show me of what he had learned. Look for something close to him that is out of place. There is where you will find the answers you seek."

The two friends nodded their heads, the cleansing sweat dripping from their bodies.

"To find these people you must remember to become the blackened hunter. You must walk silently, always in the shadows of the trees, ever vigilant of the mischief-maker Coyote. He is always lurking in dangerous times. Listen for him and know he can take human form, yet the bushy hair above, and sometimes below his nose always gives him away. Never break from the cover you now have or you will again become the hunted. You must go in the morning and work quickly, before your prey knows that you stalk it. In the morning, I will give to Joseph the medicine pouch and blackening powder that will help you in your journey." His voice trailed off as he finished.

After several minutes of silence, Jaxson excused himself to check on the sheep and make sure they were bedded down. Joseph left, saying it was getting close to 8 and he needed to hike out to the outcrop to see if Kevin would call, leaving Michael alone with Hosteen Begay. It was a few more minutes before the old shaman spoke again.

"Tell me of your dreams. Have they continued?"

"Yes, they have."

"Tell me again of what you have seen, from the beginning, and with as many details you can."

Michael again began telling him everything that had haunted him for months, this time leaving out no detail, and now the various versions of the dreams he'd had since the sweat lodge days ago. Hosteen Begay listened intently, taking in every detail. When he'd finished, the old shaman leaned back and sat silently for several minutes before concluding, "I will need to speak again with the dreamwalker. I am not gifted in this way, but to me it seems the dream is now being fulfilled."

"What are you talking about? Dreamwalker? Who?"

"One who is very gifted in walking with the dreams. I have spoken of this to him before and I believe the Yei are trying to show you not only your past, but also your possible future, both good and bad. I will need to call him through Joseph, but from your description I believe the Yei chiefs that have visited you are the twins of Changing Woman, Monster Slayer and Born for Water. They are the protectors of the Diné, the slayers of the demons that haunt us each, and the givers of prosperity and peace. They began by bringing the man forward and dancing with the woman lost, your Lori, showing her the way to her journey home, to peace. Kokopelli plays her sad song, guiding her way. They have taken her home over the sandy hills. Big Fly is their gift to you, to guide you and to keep the trickster Coyote and his constant danger away. He is also there to show you the other gift the Yei have provided for you as Kokopelli returns to play and to welcome this Ku?itu masked figure in to your life."

"And who is this?"

"That I cannot tell you, and that is why you cannot see the faces, at least for now. It is many people; it is your own confusion. It is the monster come to be slain by the Yei chiefs with their weapons and to bring you peace through their fire offerings. When it is time for you to let go of your monsters, your vision will clear. When it is time."

"I am ready for them to be gone."

"Then sit by the fire and warm yourself; let your monsters leave with the smoke billowing into the air. Look deep inside yourself, forgive and allow the Blessing Way, the cycle of life, to move forward."

"Yes, I understand, but it is difficult."

"Yes . . ." the old man paused reflectively, his carriage changing from wise shaman to caring grandfather, before continuing and placing a hand on Michael's neck, pulling him closer. "Yes, it is. Life is often difficult, but I have learned it is much easier if you share the burdens and joys with another. I have watched the two of you. I think you both need each other and I believe the Yei will show you the way if you allow them. If she is the one the Yei have brought you..." Hosteen Begay paused, his eyes subconsciously and subtly diverting toward the entrance and house beyond... "you must protect and cherish her, for she has been harmed by this life as well. The Yei have granted you a great gift of healing. I know your heart lies heavy over your loss, but you must not mourn forever, my young friend. That is what the Yei are telling you, what your dreams in the sweat lodge tell you. Perhaps now is the time to let another near you."

"And the other Kachinas?"

"You will speak soon to the dreamwalker of all this, for the Yei have shown me many things in the sweat lodge that may lie in the future. But you must understand going forward from here: Coyote always waits and you must protect her, yourself and the others from him. There is danger in your dreams with that trickster lurking."

"I understand what you say. You are a very wise man and have always led me to the right way, as if you were my own grandfather. Yes, I believe that the Yei have granted me a great gift, bringing me here to you and also to her. I will try to hold her close and protect her, as you suggest."

"It is good that we have had this talk. I will leave you to your thoughts, as I am an old man and in need of rest." He slowly stood, using Michael's shoulder and his old walking stick, shuffling across the sandy floor and out of the steamy lodge.

* * *

Tielson had received his evening reports and was quite pleased by the news. There was still no sign of Kincaid or the girl. Perhaps they really were gone. The motel owner and Kincaid's secretary had been spending some time together with the others gone. He wasn't clear why she'd still be there, but it didn't worry him much. He'd know soon enough. Still, though, he was edgy.

The cleaner had called and was in place. Tielson had given him some additional instructions, informing him of the good fortune unwittingly bestowed on them. The cleaner agreed that he would make the contact as instructed and report back. Easel's security had been upped; things should be at ease in a short time.

Tielson stared blindly across the room, his mind reassuring him that this would all be over in a matter of days. He'd soon be able to get back fully to the business at hand.

* * *

The fire and steam continued to deliver their warm breath upon Michael as he leaned reflectively into the heat, his elbows on his knees, his faced cupped in his hands. Sweat dripped down his chest, absorbing slowly into the towel draped across his lap. After the others had left, he had moved next to the fire and closed his eyes, drifting off to thoughts about the woman who now graced his life and the one he'd lost. Conflict and contradiction continued to permeate his thoughts but he now knew he could accept and move forward from her death. Her voice a reminder to move on. Perhaps this was a gift, as the old shaman had said. A chance at rebirth. He hadn't looked for this, but now that it was here he wasn't prepared to let it disappear as it had too many years ago.

Some minutes passed before he heard the door to the sweat lodge open and shut. He stayed with his thoughts instead of opening his eyes, just assuming Joseph had returned to report any news from Kevin or Trish. He continued to absorb the fire and heat as quiet footsteps neared him. He was a bit startled at the first touch to his shoulder but was pleasantly surprised to find Erin as he slowly turned his eyes to her. She was shrouded from the shoulders in a reddish, woven blanket, her beautiful silhouette lit by the flames flickering from the other side of the room, standing at shadows edge. In her right hand she held a bottle of wine and two cups, her left clutching the blanket at the nape of her neck. She was barefoot, the edges of the blanket parting just above her tanned knees. The seductive open space revealed her long silky legs, which disappeared beneath the reddish curtain near the top of her thighs.

Michael gazed upward as she bent nearer to him.

"Care for a glass of wine? I happened to have brought this with me from home, hoping there might be a nice time for it," she whispered, extending a cup toward him.

"That was some fine foresight by you," he said, taking a cup from her slender fingers.

She poured some wine into each cup. Sitting down next to him, she set the bottle on the small table, next to the water pitcher.

"To a wonderful woman" and he hoisted his cup.

"Thank you, Michael, but not this time. This time I want to drink to us, you and me. I think I'm falling for you all over again."

"And I you, Erin. But maybe it's too soon. My heart is such a mess right now and I haven't been with a woman other than Lori in so many years. I might not be the best companion for you and I wouldn't want to disappoint you."

"It's OK. You won't, Michael, I know you," she said, looking earnestly into his eyes. "I've had my own share of heartache as well and I want to be here for you and you for me if you'd consider that. To help each other through these troubles and toward what lies ahead. I want to give my love again; to wherever it leads. It has been a very long time since I've been happy being with a man. The little time we've spent together has reminded me of how happy I felt when I was with you. I've realized those feelings never really went away and I feel I want to nurture them, not cast them aside. Maybe it's a quick and foolhardy decision, but I'm willing to take the risk to see if those feelings are real, if you're willing to take the risk with me."

He gazed toward the fire across the room, his heart flickering in beat with its flames licking the air. His eyes returned to her, his subconscious melting the few remaining barriers that had gone up when he'd first felt love again in his heart. He smiled gently at her and raised his glass towards her. "Then to us it is."

"Yes, to us" and they tipped their cups against each other and sipped, the fine malbec leaving a tingle in their mouths. Their eyes locked for several seconds, a moment revealing their souls through respective emerald and blue windows. The heat of the room grew more intense as perspiration began to form at the opening of the blanket, near the base of Erin's neck. Michael was already soaked from the near hour he'd already spent inside the hot room.

She finished her wine, finally eyeing what she searched for. She stood up, the blanket still wrapped in her hand. He watched as she retrieved a plastic pitcher from the table. Slowly and elegantly she pirouetted, the blanket briefly revealing both legs to the thigh as it spun open. She walked seductively back to him and deftly poured a small trickle of water down his muscular torso, sending a shuddering sensation through his every corpuscle.

"You look very hot," she toyed with him.

"I am," he replied breathlessly.

"So am I." Dropping her grasp, she allowing the blanket to spill to the floor, revealing her naked beauty.

Michael stood up, allowing his towel to drop and kicking it away from the fire. He reached for the plastic pitcher, taking it from her hand as he drew her near.

They met. Their sweaty bodies slid against each other's. Their mouths entangled in an impassioned kiss. Michael pulled her tight with one hand, lifting the pitcher up and slowly pouring it's contents over their heads. The cool water tantalized them and he discarded the container with a flick.

Erin wrapped her arms around his waist and pulled him forward with her, nearer the fire, never once letting her lips leave his, moving him slowly with her. She broke the embrace, for just an instant, toppling the table and spreading out the blanket on the soft sand and straw, then took his hand and pulled him down to where she now lay.

Michael began at the nape of her neck with gentle kisses. He slowly journeyed to her protruding nipples, rubbing their hardness with his lips' soft caresses. She gasped with excitement as his tongue traced the bounds of her breasts. His hand moved slowly to explore the confluence of her legs. She simultaneously began to softly caress his thighs.

"Make love to me, Michael. I need you now."

He raised himself above her, while she guided him into her. A quarter of a century of want exploded into rhythmic passion. The shadows from the firelight told of entwined bodies filled with desire. Her body pulsated around him. They began slowly with a coordinated serpentine motion; their hands and legs groped and explored the other's rigid body. The sounds of their bodies meeting resonated from the walls, rising above the crackle of the fire. Their love and desire pulled them deeper, their pace quickening, thrusting themselves into their eagerly awaiting passion. They burst simultaneously into a chasm of ecstasy and with a singular, total collapse, their bodies fell into each other's. Only the heaving of their lungs and pounding hearts now provided movement.

Michael finally lifted his dizzied head and kissed her gently, before his drenched body slid from hers. He wrapped her waist with his leg and pulled her nearer his heart.

"Oooh, Erin. Indeed, here's to us." He retrieved a glass of wine for each of them, until she burst into joyous laughter, soon joined by Michael's, celebrating what they had wanted to share, oh these many years.

After a half hour of caressing and an emptied bottle, they drifted off to sleep, entwined and becoming one to the other's soul.

DAY NINE

A Change in Plans

Anderson found a parking spot a short distance from the edge of the Tidal Basin. Emerging from his car he wondered again why he'd been summoned so secretly before the Old Man. He collated his thoughts on the operation as he walked the approximate half-mile around the monument, making his way through the wooden channel necessitated by the restoration project and the hordes of governmental safety engineers.

When he emerged from the tunnel at water's edge, he noticed the cherry blossoms dancing as the morning breeze waded through them. The Tidal Basin reflected his quick movement down the pathway toward the awaiting man.

"Thank you for coming so early, Lieutenant Commander. Please sit down."

His greeting seemed warm, but Anderson remained wary just the same. "Thank you, sir."

"Lieutenant Commander, some disturbing news has come to my attention. It seems there have been problems created with our operation as a result of some of your superior's actions. I am sure you are aware of the ongoing recovery efforts," he said, receiving an affirmative nod. "Last evening I spoke with some friends who imparted some disturbing insights into the handling of this Los Angeles matter. I was led to believe by your superior that everything was being handled quietly and efficiently. Now I've learned that this is not the case and that I have been misled for several days." The Old Man's voice rose in pure anger before he took a few moments to compose himself. "You have always served your country well, Lieutenant Commander, and I hope you will continue to do so. I am particularly interested in what insights you might have as to what's really gone on here. Speak straight with me. The survival of our mutual cause may depend upon your frankness."

"Well, sir, all I can tell you is what I know."

His mind raced. How much did the Old Man know? And what had the troll told him? Did he have any idea just how far Tielson had gone? Did he know the destruction their operatives had caused? What had he found out on his own? Anderson quickly reasoned that the Old Man must not be blaming him or otherwise he wouldn't have met with him at all. Maybe this was his chance, his chance to free himself from this entire sordid affair. If he played this right, he might just get out of this after all.

"Well, sir, as I understand it, the operation may have been compromised due to something falling into unsecured hands. I believe it is some form of memorandum."

The Old Man nodded with a wince.

"I was only made aware of a general problem by Tielson when he asked me to secure two independent assets to handle what he termed a surveillance matter. At the time I was unaware of the true nature of the problem. He handled the final briefing with the assets himself. I was not a party to that briefing, therefore I cannot tell you what it entailed. Over the past few days I have discovered several disturbing things, not the least of which has been the unnecessary and unfortunate involvement of others. I believe Tielson has greatly overstepped his bounds in the matter, as I now see it, and has seriously jeopardized the operation. Unfortunately, sir, matters have been set in motion which, if allowed to continue, could have severe and even terminal consequences to the operation. Sir . . . you should also be aware that this has resulted in the elimination of at least two already."

The Old Man shook his head and sank back against the bench in what Anderson perceived to be disbelief.

"I also have grave concerns that these events will eventually lead back to him—and I fear back to us."

"I see," the Old Man said after a moment. "This greatly disturbs me and is indeed as unacceptable as my friends made it out to be. Our cause was not intended to rise on the backs of the dead." He cursed himself inwardly for being so stupid as to leave operational affairs such as this in the hands of a thug like Tielson. He had no finesse, no couth. None of this should have ever happened. There was simply no reason for it. This stooge was out of control and would probably cost him everything. He'd have to clean this up himself, with finality and some help, if he had any hopes of surviving. "Lieutenant Commander, this has become a very delicate matter. Apparently, based upon what I have learned, he has indeed overstepped his bounds and I too am concerned for the entire project. I need addition information. I need to know exactly what this is about, what needs to be done to solve the problem and who is aware of it. I also need someone I can trust. Do you have any suggestions, Lieutenant Commander?"

"Not at this moment, sir. I will need to look into this further and find out the details before I have anything to add. With your permission, sir?"

"Granted. It'll need your immediate attention."

"Of course, sir."

"Keep me informed and telephone me immediately once you have your information and an idea on how to proceed."

"Yes, sir. I'll phone you as soon as I have something concrete to report."

The Old Man reached into his jacket pocket and pulled out peanuts for his friends, quacking and congregating about ten feet from the bench. He passed a handful to Anderson, saying, "I have the utmost faith in you, Lieutenant Commander." With a smile, the junior man tossed the nuts to the anxiously awaiting mallards. He rose with "Thank you for your trust, sir" before turning and tossing the remaining feed toward an old mallard that had arrived late. Empty-handed, he headed back up the pathway.

* * *

It was early when they rose to head back down Fourth Mesa, the light just leaking out from the distant Sleeping Ute and Star Mountain over in Colorado. Joseph stepped onto the front porch to find Erin and Michael rocking slowly in the chairs, their hands entwined and wide awake, covered in blankets, sipping coffee. "Good morning, you two."

"A wonderful morning to you, too, Joseph." Michael smiled pleasantly.

"Yes, a very wonderful morning," Erin said, pulling Michael's hand to her lips and kissing it lightly.

"I see . . . hmmmm," Joseph answered, before ambling off the porch and looking back at them before continuing. "I looked for you both last night after I came back. Saw that the fire was still burning in the sweat lodge, you two have a nice warm night ? I assume you didn't sleep out here." He smiled a wicked little smile.

"Yes it was quite nice." Erin volunteered, pulling up closer to Michael with a grin. "We had some wine, I guess it made us tired and we eventually fell asleep in there" which brought a bit of a smirk for Michael, and Joseph.

"Anyway you two, I got a text from Kevin and tried to call him back but it wouldn't connect."

"Well…what did it say" Michael exclaimed!

"'Found him. We need to talk'."

"Found who, I wonder. Well I guess we better get going." Erin added.

By 7:30 Joseph and Jaxson had caught the horses grazing alongside the sheep, and had them reined and saddled. Erin had joined them and was rubbing her horse's nose and quietly talking to him as she offered an apple she'd brought from home. The grandfatherly shaman had joined Michael on the porch for a few more words before they left. He told him that he would return to the valley in the next day or two and promised to talk to Joseph or Michael upon his return. They mounted their horses, and with a wave, set out down Fourth Mesa to the uncertain fate that awaited them below.

* * *

Tielson had received his morning reports. All was still quiet on all fronts. His man had also telephoned and reported that contact had been made and he had been assured of full cooperation. This had been the most uplifting news he'd received in days. Now he had his mole and he'd soon have the intel he needed.

* * *

When they arrived on flat ground again Michael rode up to Joseph who was on his phone probably talking with Kevin, though the connection was not very good based on all the 'what did you says' going on. Cell phones, ethernet and GPS may have been all the rage in Los Angeles, but on the reservation they were aggravating at best. Erin lagged behind them a bit, admiring the barren beauty. After a few minutes Joseph hung up telling Michael that they'd found Nick up at Vallecito and had a long interesting talk with him. Said, like we've learned, Cody Zell wasn't a person but Code Easel and Nick apparently had some additional things to say but he didn't really want to talk about it over the phone. He said it may be his imagination, but he thinks he and Trish are being followed and he seems very nervous about the entire thing. I told him you'd be back today and you two could talk but he didn't want to wait. Said he was driving over but would make sure he lost anyone along the way. Michael reflected on this for a while before he spoke.

"Joseph," Michael spoke softly, "I need a favor from you."

"Sure. Whatever you need," he answered.

"Shhh. I don't want Erin to hear. I need you to get your mom to let

Erin stay there for a couple of days. This might get too dangerous for her!"

"Michael!" her voice called out sharply from behind as she trotted up, closing the several feet between them. "Don't think for one second that you're going to leave me anywhere. I'm a big girl; I can take care of myself."

"Erin, it's getting too damn dangerous right now. It's not safe for you to be with me. Grandfather Begay even said so himself."

"Michael, and with all due respect for your grandfather, Joseph, it's not real safe for you to be without me. Need I remind you that the only time I've let you out of my sight in the last few days, you managed to get beat up. I'm not going to let that happen again. Besides, I just might be of some help."

"She's got you there, Michael. But Erin, really, Grandfather is right."

"I don't care if he is. I'm going with you and that's it."

"It's too dangerous, Erin!"

"I know it's dangerous, but I'll take my chances with you and that's exactly what I'm going to do. Nobody associated with this knows me and that might be of some help. Now that's settled."

They continued on in silence for a while, before taking up other subjects. When they finally reached the Begay home, the sun had reached high overhead. They had agreed on the trail that a few things needed to be done quickly upon arrival. After unsaddling the horses and giving them their much deserved grain and water, Michael called Trish at the Stratler. He updated her that all was well in Hawaii and that he'd be in touch again tomorrow. Joseph talked to his mother to find out if she knew anything else about where J.J. was stationed. She told him what little she knew. She suggested talking to a couple of his friends he occasionally saw in Kayenta.

An hour later they were dressed and on their way to town. Their first stop was the public library so Joseph could try to find out any information about the base near Chinle from the old tribal maps of the area.

While there, Erin took up a little research on Peleliu, as Michael looked through some information on Southeast Asian imports and exports. By the time they had finished, they'd reached several conclusions.

Peleliu was part of the Palau Islands, located in the Western Pacific about six hundred miles due east of Mindanao in the Philippines. They had been visited by Spanish navigators in the early Sixteenth Century, but not colonized by the Spanish until the late Nineteenth Century. Spain sold them to Germany in 1899, and in 1914, under the fortunes of World War I, the islands along with many others came under Japanese rule via the Treaty of Versailles and the League of Nations South Pacific Mandate. The irony was obvious. The Allies had just handed their future enemy the very bases Imperial Japanese forces would use to as outer defenses and help in their rule of the Pacific.

In the '30s, the Japanese indeed established a major base on Peleliu. In the '40s, they added a landing strip from which they launched hundreds of sorties. Recapture finally came in 1944 at the hands of the Old Breed Marine regiment after ten weeks of the purest hell the South Pacific had ever seen, just as Luigi had told Michael.

When the war ended, it became part of the Caroline Island Group under US administration, and then in '79 Palau became independent. While generally thought to be part of what is now commonly called Micronesia, in 1986 Palau concluded a Compact of Free Association with the US, similar to that of the Marshall Islands and the Federated States of Micronesia, relying on the US for defense and security in exchange for a 50 year agreement to allow US military access to the islands. The US Navy still held a presence in the islands at US Camp Katuu, primarily through Civilian Action Teams that assisted in local infrastructure projects and maintaining the base. It was primarily an agricultural and fishing economy, with some mining of phosphates and bauxite thrown in. Assuming Erin's fingers were right and the scale was close, it would be less than a thousand miles from the heart of Southeast Asia, Indonesia or Sumatra and, as it turned out, the old East Indies oil fields. A nice short hop to any of the "friendly" nations that made up the region now.

Michael's research returned the obvious: the plan, whatever it was, likely involved bringing something through the area, certainly not oil but maybe drugs or something. Joseph's research returned fruitless, not even a telephone prefix for the area, no maps, nothing. His friend the librarian only knew that there were bases out there, but not much else. Leaving the library, they knew what they had to do.

"You got cell phone service Joseph?" Michael asked staring down at his roaming phone.

"Of course. Here in town its not too bad if you've got the right service. I've got a special tribal phone that works better than most out here."

"Could you see if you can get a hold of Kevin and get him to meet us over at your mom's tonight. We're going to need some help. Call him on that new phone, but be careful what you say, someone could be listening I suppose."

Joseph nodded and started around the corner, leaving Erin and Michael outside the door. He glanced at her with a smile, saying, "I need to make a quick phone call." He found a pay phone next to the entrance, deposited some change and dialed directory assistance. "Yes, Washington D.C., please. The number for Senator McRae's office, please."

"Thank you." He hung up, dialing the number using his credit card even though his cell phone finally had service.

"Senator McRae's Office. May I help you?"

"Yes, attorney Michael Kincaid for the senator. Is he in?"

"I'll see if he is available for the call, sir. May I tell him what this regards?"

"Yes. Luigi Morrealli and Hosteen Begay."

"Pardon me?"

Michael repeated his request and waited through an interminable silence. Finally, another voice came on the line.

"Mr. Kincaid?" the voice echoed.

"Yes."

"Please hold for the senator."

"Thank you." Michael was surprised that he could actually complete his promise to Hosteen Begay on the first try. Amazing, really.

"Mr. Kincaid, this is Howard McRae. What can I do for you?"

"Thank you for taking the call Senator. How are you?"

"Just fine, sir. Working a little too hard, but I guess that's why they sent me here. Haven't we met before?"

"You have an excellent memory, sir. One time in California, at a fund-raiser in Century City." Upon later reflection, it probably was just the standard line, in case he'd met the caller before. After all, never upset a constituent.

"Well, thank you. I only have a few minutes before another committee meeting; is there something I can help you with?"

"Forgive me sir, I don't mean to take up your time needlessly."

"You spoke of Morrealli and Begay. You obviously know my old friends."

"Yes, sir, I do. I regret to inform you that Luigi has been killed."

"Oh, no! I can't believe that." The senator seemed genuinely shaken by the news.

"It's true, senator. He was murdered last week."

"Murdered." Outrage rose in his voice. "What happened?"

"I'm unsure sir, but I have my ideas."

"I just spoke to him last week. A good friend. He called up complaining about governmental improprieties, as he always did. He was that way, you know."

"Yes, sir, I know."

"I can't believe he's dead. I wish I'd have spent more time with him instead of pushing him off because I was too busy for an old friend. This is terrible news. He was a good man," he said reflectively. After a few seconds pause, he continued. "What can I do to help find the people that did this to him?"

"Not much, really. They have a man in custody, but I don't believe he did it. I've got some leads, though, and if there is something you can do, and there well may be, I'll let you know. However, sir, I must tell you that I have reason to believe your own life may be in danger."

"Excuse me?"

"Sir, this has something to do with your old Code Easel mission."

"Code Easel?" The senator exhaled audibly. "That was a very, very long time ago."

"Yes, sir. But Luigi's final words were, 'Yeh Tay Code Easel.'"

Michael listened to several seconds of silence before the senator spoke. "I see."

"I believe this was a warning to Mr. Begay."

"And you believe if he warned Begay, I should also be warned."

"Actually, sir, Hosteen Begay believes you should be warned."

"Ah, I see. He is a good friend, also. Where is he, you say? I trust he is safe and well."

"Yes sir, he's fine. I do agree that you should alert your protective staff, though, just to be on the safe side."

"I shall. And thank you for the information. If there is anything, anything at all that you need, don't hesitate to call. And please, stay in touch and keep me informed. Is there a way I can get in touch with you if I need to?"

"At this time there isn't, but I will try to keep you informed. Thank you for taking the call. I know you're very busy."

"Never too busy for an old friend. Please call again soon. Good-bye."

The senator hung up the phone in disbelief and sat motionlessly in his seat. How could this have happened?

Michael returned to Erin and put his arm around her. He kissed her sweetly on the cheek and whispered in her ear, "When this is all over with, I'm going to take us away where we can be alone." Erin smiled, turning her head to give him a kiss and cooed, "I'll look forward to it."

Michael grabbed her hand and the two strolled silently toward Joseph's truck, finding him leaning against it.

"Did you get a hold of Kevin? Where are he and Trish."

"Yeah, he said he'd meet us at Mom's as soon as he could get out here, maybe around dinner. It was pretty short and sweet."

"Good. Where to?"

"I wanted to stop by and talk to a couple of friends of J.J.'s. Then I figured we'd take a little drive and I'd show you guys some interesting places out here. That is, if nobody has any objections."

"Not from us." Erin smiled.

They spent an hour inquiring about J.J.. Nobody really knew much about his whereabouts or the old abandoned base. His friend Billy had been down there to see him, but it was all locked up and there was no guard. Big fences were all Billy could see. The trio decided it was time for an afternoon drive.

The time passed quickly on their way to Chinle. It was a pleasant drive through the red-rock terrain. Curious sandstone sculptures lined the roadway. They followed the road through Chinle and found the off-shoot that would take them to White Horse Ruins. In a few moments they were back in the middle of nowhere headed southwest toward First Mesa.

Michael had gotten out the map and was trying to pinpoint with some certainty their eventual destination, while Erin sat in the rear watching the scenery go by.

"That won't help much," Joseph remarked as the truck hummed down Navajo Nation Road 4.

"Probably not, out here" came Michael's answer. Joseph's lifelong knowledge of the Nation's almost indistinguishable buttes and mesas let him know exactly where they were. Besides, as Michael knew, these maps wouldn't show abandoned military installations or the rutted dirt roads that led to them.

In about a half hour Michael noticed a sign indicating jewelry for sale one mile ahead. "We must be close," he said matter-of-factly to his friend.

"Yeah, wonder if we're lucky enough to find them open?"

From the back Erin asked, "What are you two talking about?"

"You'll see in just a minute." Michael turned and smiled back at her. "There's a jewelry stand up here. Maybe they're open."

"Oh! . . . You going to buy me some jewelry, Mr. Kincaid?" She laughed, smiling back at him, then leaning forward to give him a quick kiss.

"Well, that too."

The pickup slowed a few moments later as they came upon White Horse Ruins. A graveled road angled off to the west and with the paved road formed the intersection and parking area for the walk up to the ruins to the southeast. At the edge of the parking area stood a lone tarped booth, a red, white & blue banner flapping in the wind above it, a lone vehicle sitting in front. "There really can't be anyone out here, can there?" Erin remarked from the rear.

"Never can tell," Joseph answered.

Laid along a table in the booth were several velvet showcases featuring traditional Navajo silver and turquoise jewelry. A few pots and bowls lined the table's inside edge. In the corner, sat an old Navajo woman working on a silvery piece with plump, weather-beaten hands. To her left sat a teenaged boy, smiling toward their new customers. "Hello," he called to the trio, rising to greet them. "Hello," Joseph called back as Michael and Erin began their inspection of the wares.

Joseph walked over and started a conversation with the boy, and eventually with the old woman, in Navajo. By the time Joseph had finish talking to the woman and her grandson, Erin and Michael had found a couple of pairs of earrings and a necklace she liked. Michael gave the grandson the twenty dollars called for without negotiation and the three returned to the truck.

As Erin admired her new charms, Joseph told Michael what he'd learned from the old woman and the boy, taking note of the pickup's odometer as they left. She said there was not much traffic on the road. Occasionally military vehicles with soldiers came along, but not very often. Maybe once a week big airplanes would glide low over Second Mesa. Sometimes other cars went up the road, generally returning a few hours later, occasionally a large truck. There wasn't anything up the road, just the old military base that, until about a year ago, no one ever went near. The road ended, the boy had told him, at the foot of Second Mesa. Mostly though, it was just the tourists passing through here on their way to pick up I-40 fifty miles south.

Other than the initial ruts close to the highway, for the most part the road was well taken care of. It was nicely graveled after the first five hundred feet. They made good time going up and down the small hills that defined the region's contour. In about twenty minutes they made out the silhouette of two larger buildings slowly coming into view. Joseph eased off on the gas, approaching the complex with caution. The road leveled out for about a quarter of a mile and then after two small hills, gave them a solid look at a massive fence. Joseph stopped the truck at the top of the second hill and they observed the complex from a distance.

The dirt airfield was immediately obvious, and a big one at that. Certainly capable of landing the large cargo planes of which the old Navajo woman had spoken. A large building at the runway's edge, along with some smaller buildings probably used as barracks, completed the installation. For the most part the place looked abandoned, but for the lone uniformed man watching from near one of the barracks. Noticing this, Joseph pulled forward and continued along the fence as Michael and Erin took a closer look into the compound. At the end of the fencing, Michael told Joseph to turn around and head back. They'd seen what they'd come for. Their future had now been dictated.

* * *

Tielson listened quietly, slumped back in his oversize chair, while Tompkins updated him on their surveillance. The motel owner was largely remaining quiet and at home. He'd spent most of the morning in his house and later worked in his shed. He'd taken a mid-afternoon call from someone named Joseph asking for his help and had left soon thereafter. They'd continued their surveillance of the motel as instructed, but had seen nothing out of the ordinary.

"Report back when he returns."

"Yes, sir, we're already doing that."

Tielson hung up the phone, uncomfortable with the way these two were operating. He needed additional information. He searched quickly through the notes strewn across his desk, finding the phone number he needed.

"Stratler Hotel, how may I direct your call?"

"Room 346," he demanded sternly.

"Thank you, I'll forward your call."

The call was picked up on the first ring and Tielson came right to the point. "Where did the motel owner go?"

"Apparently to meet someone named Joseph and perhaps others. Somewhere over on the Navajo reservation."

"You're staying close?"

"Extremely close."

"I'll be back in touch soon." Tielson hung up the phone. So perhaps Kincaid and the girl weren't in Hawaii, he speculated. Meeting on the reservation in Arizona. What are they up to? Could he afford to wait for their return to find out what the group knew? Any closer and he'd have to act, he concluded. He picked up the phone and called AZ directly.

* * *

It was late in the afternoon by the time they returned to the Begay home. They found Kevin and Trish seated at the table having a talk with Joseph's mom. The three guys immediately disappeared to talk.

Kevin told them that Nick was pretty freaked out by Luigi's death and had disappeared up to Vallecito because he really wasn't sure what was going on. Said Luigi had been raving about some plot involving drugs coming to the US and government involvement down in Arizona on the reservation someplace. Said Luigi had seen and gotten a copy of some memo or something when he was out in LA doing some work that outlined what it was all about and he was going to do something about it. Said he thought that's why Luigi went over to the reservation the week before he died, but wasn't exactly sure where but said something about White Horse Ruins. Joseph nodded to Michael. There were a few other things they'd learned, but that was the nutshell of it. This confirmed to Michael that this memo was surely what they were looking for at Luigi's and likely what they found in the drawers in their second search. But Hosteen Begay also said Luigi would always have a back-up plan and in that he could hope, but that would be for another day.

They talked about the whole affair for a while longer and made a plan, crazy as it was, based on what they knew and what they could surmise. At about seven they ate a nice leisurely dinner. After dinner, Joseph made up the excuse that he needed to go to the hospital in Kayenta so he could check in on a patient he hadn't been able to see because of all that was going on today. Kevin and Michael quickly volunteered to ride in with him under the guise that when he'd finished they could go out and have some fun, just like in college.

None of the three women bought the story for an instant, but they didn't protest. Whatever the men were up to had—hopefully—been well thought out and needed to be done. They left, saying they'd be back late and not to wait up. After they had disappeared into the darkness, the three women went into the kitchen, made coffee and started what would likely be an all-night vigil.

* * *

It was around ten when they finally slipped back into the Kayenta airport. The plane had been refueled earlier at Dr. Begay's request and was ready to go when they arrived. They waited and talked through their plan for a while, wasting time until it grew later and they loaded up and were airborne several minutes later. They were in no real hurry. The later their arrival, the better. Kevin flew at a leisurely pace, further extending the trip, flying southeasterly towards Grants, before turning due west and into the heart of the Navajo and Hopi nations.

Their plan was simple. Fly in low, from the east over Canyon de Chelly, as if they were landing in Chinle. They'd cross the road south-west of town and head straight for First Mesa at low altitude. They'd fly parallel and level to First Mesa then come in low over the top, cutting the engine just over the other side. With a little luck they could find the flat part of the road and land. Then they'd just slip through the fence, into a guarded U.S military installation. Find the warehouse. Find out what's in the warehouse. Slip out undetected. Take off and return. Simple. Sure, their collective thoughts sighed.

In the distance, the lights of Chinle became visible off the right of the plane's nose. Kevin banked the little plane slowly to the west. Though it was clear out and the moon shone bright, once they passed Chinle, they'd be at the full mercy of the night and their memories for navigation. The success of the plan lay squarely in their ability to get in undetected. No doubt they'd need some luck and they knew it. As if on cue, Joseph pulled the blackening powder from the backpack at his feet. "We must be blackened. Grandfather said to hold it for the right time," he said, passing it between the seats to his comrade.

"I can't think of a better time. We can certainly use all the help we can get." Michael glanced back to his friend with a devilish grin and continued, "And just for the record, you know this is crazy, don't you?"

"Absolutely." Joseph nodded his head in full agreement.

He dipped his first three fingers in the soot, blended with the ashes of various plants, and passed it up to Michael. It was the ancient rite of anteec, used by the Navajos for centuries, prior to battle. It had long been associated by the Peoples as the earthly equivalent of the armor of Monster Slayer. The old shaman had given the powder to Joseph to protect them against any evil they might encounter. It worked equally well as camouflage. Michael wiped it all over his face and hands.

"Think of it this way, boys," Kevin now chimed in. "They'll never be expecting a doctor and a lawyer."

"There you go," Michael's answer rose mockingly. "We have the element of surprise!"

"We'll see," Joseph countered, spreading the soot over his face. "Coyote is always out there."

As they passed over the southern edge of Chinle, Kevin descended lower, as if on approach, heading straight toward a beacon south of town. They caught a break when Joseph spotted a truck on the road toward White Horse Ruins giving them a general bearing on their next goal, the foot of First Mesa. They cut south of the airport and the plane drew a line toward the north edge of First Mesa, now about 15 miles out. Closing in on the gigantic wall, Kevin slowly climbed to an altitude approximate the top of the approaching cliffs before leveling off. On their return from the earlier excursion, they had clocked the westerly distance to the base at about 14 and a half miles. Kevin figured he'd start over the mesa at about 11 miles and noted his watch and air speed as he banked right, coming parallel to the mesa. In five minutes he shut down the plane's running lights. Joseph pulled binoculars from the backpack. In two more, Kevin banked the plane to the south with Joseph's agreement, climbing slightly as they came flush over the plateau. Joseph looked hopelessly through the field glasses into the moonlit darkness, trying to find a reference point. Scouring the valley floor, he finally picked up what he believed to be lights from the base. He backtracked, finding the road headed due west toward the target. "Out there," he said, pointing to the small twinkling light. The tension rose with each passing second until Kevin caught sight of the light about three miles ahead.

"The road should be just over there," Joseph said, pointing ahead through the cockpit's left windscreen.

"OK, Joseph, I'll trust your memory. We'll come over the side and try and put this baby right on this flat spot you tell me exists."

The little plane banked slowly south, about four hundred feet above First Mesa. They sat silently for a moment and then, with a quick flip of a toggle switch, the propeller ground to a stop and the plane went into a silent glide. It edged slowly downward off the mesa, making a controlled fall to earth. In a couple minutes they'd have to make the decision to restart or continue on and be forced to land, whether they were in the right place or not.

Michael wasn't worried about the glide or the landing. He'd been through this with Kevin many times before and with a 9 to 1 glide ratio at 65 knots they should have plenty of time, he hoped. When they first started going up to spot for elk for the upcoming hunting season, Kevin would create some scenario about the engine cutting out and into a glide they'd go. He'd almost pissed his pants the first few times it happened, but he gradually caught on. After a while it had become a game, seeing how long they could go or bouncing touch and goes off remote forest roads out in the county. Kevin was far more daring than Michael and he swore they'd almost burned in a couple of times, but Kevin always seemed in control. He'd grown up in the thing and learned from the best, his father, a former bush pilot for years in Alaska. Now here they were again, playing the same game they'd played nearly two decades before. This time though, a mistake would undoubtedly be more costly.

The plane continued its silent glide, slowly down, maintaining reasonable speed as they searched for a glimpse of the roadway, a light wind whistling past the otherwise silent propeller. Joseph estimated they were about a mile out now from the lights that they hoped would lend them some answers. Still plenty of time he hoped as the seconds passed by.

Michael finally caught sight of the road about 500 yards out as they were about to cross it. He pointed it out to the pilot, who quickly banked the plane to the right, placing their impromptu landing strip directly below them. Kevin adjusted the flaps a bit, readying the plane for what promised to be a bumpy landing. He searched the ground before them hoping to catch a glimpse of the flat spot, but knew they'd reached their fail-safe point and he was going to land her no matter what.

Joseph finally picked up the hill that topped at the spot where he'd hoped to land. Kevin figured he had plenty of height and nosed the plane forward toward the highest point. They swooped low over the top of the hill, touching down softly a hundred feet on the other side. The little plane bounced only once before settling quietly on the wide gravel road. The plane's speed waned as Kevin applied the brakes and Michael finally let go of the breath he'd been holding for what seemed like an eternity. As the plane neared the next hill, Kevin edged the plane as far as he could to the right before circling it around, its momentum finally spent, now resting quiet to the side of the road.

"Nice landing," Michael whispered, as if someone might hear.

"Thanks. I'll claim that one."

They quietly opened the doors and scrambled out of the plane, Joseph pulling the backpack with him and Michael just behind. Joseph quickly rechecked his gear: binoculars, wire-cutters, a flashlight, a camera, a gun with extra rounds, cell phone - check. He pulled the straps over his arms and huddled with his friends.

From their vantage point, no fence was in sight and all lights had disappeared. Michael placed his hand on his friend's shoulder. "Joseph?" A tinge of skepticism rose in his voice.

Reassuringly he replied "it's here, over the hill. C'mon, we're wasting time."

"All right, oh great scout Tonto, take me to the fort," Michael grumbled sarcastically in Kevin's general direction, a questioning grin on his face.

"Yes, Kemosabe," Joseph grunted, passing next to Kevin with a "You do know that means 'Great White Asshole' in Navajo" just loud enough for Michael to hear as he disappeared up the road into the darkness.

Sure enough, as they approached the top of the rise, Michael could make out the fence line and the turnoff road leading to the gate. The three knelt near the top of the hill and watched for any movement for a full fifteen minutes. Kevin kept his eyes scanning back to the east, the lonely road meandering toward the main highway many miles in the distance, searching for any approaching headlight. Joseph scanned the terrain forward toward the base with the binoculars, watching intently through eyes trained by endless hours of surgery. The moonlight was both kind and cruel at the same time. It gave them enough light to see, but also to be seen.

In the distance they heard the yips and howls of a coyote baying at the moon, his voice echoing in the still night air. Joseph glanced at Michael and murmured, "Coyote is aware. Trouble may lie ahead in this."

Michael simply nodded.

Satisfied that they could detect no movement, Michael and Joseph headed out at a forty-five-degree angle toward the fence across the sand and sagebrush leaving Kevin to guard the rear and their escape from the highpoint. Kevin watched as his friends stayed as low as possible, reaching the fence in short order. They examined the rusty chain-link, topped with concertina wire, thankful to find that at least it didn't seem electrified. They could now make out the outlines of two buildings and for the first time noticed a very long dirt runway stretching out in to the dark. Lights appeared to be on in the far building, twinkling through a large cottonwood. They continued down the fence line until the other building blocked the lights from sight. They cut a small hole through the bottom of the fence and slithered through to the other side. They paused to survey the angle from the building, knowing they'd need their bearings to get back to this exact spot and make a quick get-away.

They rushed across the open space, stopping every so often to check for movement.

They reached their target seemingly unnoticed, a mere few feet from the entry to the warehouse. The building itself was old corrugated steel, vintage World War II. They found a rear entrance, but it was locked, so they cautiously moved along the side to the front of the building. Michael peered around the front corner, noticing a short stairway leading up to a concrete ramp, faint light spilling to the ramp from a bay door slightly ajar. In the courtyard, between the two buildings, a lone sentry walked past two Humvees parked in front of the barracks, before disappearing around the corner and out of sight. Michael tapped Joseph, motioning for him to follow. Quickly, but quietly, they slid in the door, moved off into the left corner and found cover behind a forklift from the dimmed lights running down the center of the warehouse ceiling.

From their vantage point they could see along the far wall a collection of various old military equipment, with a transport truck and two old Jeeps, likely of the same vintage as the building itself. Michael wondered what old surplus Jeeps were doing here, replaced years ago by Humvees throughout the military. To their side, lay six pallets, loosely covered with tarps. They quietly headed down the near wall towards the first pallet, taking cover away from the warehouse door behind the pallet. Michael gently pulled back the tarp, finding shrink-wrapped pallets of two-foot square boxes. He pulled out his pocketknife, slicing through the shrink-wrap before carefully removing a box from the top of the stack, setting it and the knife on the floor. Joseph took off his backpack and pulled out a small flashlight, which let them clearly see the labeling: "MRE/Contaminated – Not fit for Human Consumption" stamped in red across the top of the box.

Joseph whispered, "What's an MRE?"

"Meals, Ready to Eat. C-Rations, my dad used to call them. We'd use them backpacking."

"Great, but I've already had dinner."

"I expect these contain more than the usual GI battlefield meal."

They impatiently yanked open the box, the ripping the cardboard echoing a little too loudly off the corrugated wall behind them and they winced. Inside, they found stacked layers of drab brown plastic pouches similar to those Michael had seen before. Joseph retrieved one and inspected the simple stenciled label that defined its contents. "Care for some beef ravioli, buddy?" he whispered. Michael picked up a pouch too, carefully feeling the contents, kneading it between his fingers, considering what they had found.

"Freeze!" A voice from behind them demanded as a strong beam from a flashlight lit them up. As Michael's heart sank deep in his chest, he instinctively groped for the knife.

* * *

Anderson rose from his bed. Outside his window not even the birds had started their morning ritual. He showered quickly before returning to pack. He took only what he'd need for three days. That which remained, along with his former life, would have to stay behind. He grabbed what personal effects he had, including a picture of him receiving his diploma from the commandant at Annapolis. He returned to the chest of drawers and pulled his 9mm Glock from its resting place. He carefully examined the chamber and gun, placing it inside its case with the accessories he had earlier pulled from storage. The entire case went into the satchel he rarely carried.

The sun was rising as he stepped from the brownstone for probably the last time. It had been his home since he'd come to Washington and he hoped he'd see it again sometime, but he doubted it. It was likely that no matter what happened from here on out, today would be the close of this life.

* * *

Michael looked over toward Joseph as he finally caught the knife in his hand. He slid his hand over the knife, grapping firmly around the grip, not sure what he was going to do.

"Stand up and turn around," the voice demanded. They rose slowly, Joseph turning slowly into the bright light, Michael keeping a tight grip on the knife and hesitating.

After a short, uneasy pause, the voice from behind called, "Joseph? What are you doing here? And why are you blackened?"

"J.J.?" Joseph exhaled, turning fully to the light as Michael froze.

"Yeah, big brother. What the hell are you doing?"

"Could you turn off that light?"

The spot went out as Joseph instinctively rubbed his eyes and Michael released his grip on the knife letting it slid from his hand back to the floor.

J.J. holstered his pistol as he stepped closer. "What I want to know is what are you doing here? And who's he?"

"That's Michael, he's my friend. You probably don't remember him."

"The lawyer guy from LA? So what's he doing here? What are both of you doing here" he demanded.

"Trying to solve a couple of murders and maybe stop a couple more," Michael answered, his eyes still a bit dazzled by white light, trying to focus back to the ambient light.

"On a military base? Yeah, sure. Like who?"

"Like Luigi Morrealli."

"Benjamin's case? I heard the story about it, but I couldn't believe my ears. There's no way Benjamin would kill anyone, I've known him for years. But that still doesn't tell me what you two are doing trespassing on a military base."

"Well, J.J." his brother softly answered, "it might have something to do with these boxes right here."

"Sure, Joseph. And I'm Kokopelli. Give me a break. You two are in deep trouble if they find you in here."

"Forget that right now," Joseph said. "Why the hell don't you call or write Mom? You get some big-shot job and you forget your family!"

"Bullshit, Joseph. I write all the time. I haven't heard back from any of you."

"I hate to break up old home week guys" Michael interrupted "but I think J.J. your brother is right and the answer to that murder is right here" holding up a pouch.

"In expired C-Rations. Certainly a national security problem, Michael. Probably a damn government conspiracy too, right? You two have been watching too much television."

"First of all, it is a government conspiracy. But since you know so much, tell me why an abandoned military installation has a warehouse full of heavily guarded C-Rations?"

"Well, Michael, that happens when they become contaminated. These have been contaminated with low-grade bacterial agents or something."

"Bacterial agents?" Joseph interrupted. "Are you serious? You mean like salmonella or something? Come on, J.J., you can't be that dumb and my brother at the same time."

"Hey, they pay me good money to keep an eye on a bunch of boxes they drop in here by transport plane every few days. It's junk and what the hell do I care what's in them, I'm not eating it and it gets destroyed by some company down in Phoenix, that's all I know. It's great duty and I answer to one guy, who knows what the brass thinks or does anyway."

"And who's that?" Michael inquired.

"My boss. Pentagon brass. Lieutenant Commander Anderson. A real straight-up guy."

"Anderson, huh? Anybody else?" the lawyer continued.

"Not that it's any of your damn business, but occasionally I make reports to another guy over at NSA. Guy by the name of Tielson."

"Ever hear of something called Code Easel?"

"How do you know that name?"

"Jackpot!" Joseph exclaimed.

"Jackpot what, Joseph?"

"Look, J.J., your brother and I are telling you the truth. These aren't rations. There's something in there, and it sure as hell ain't beef ravioli by the way it feels. We don't have a lot of time to explain so let me just show you."

"Michael, if you open that, you expose us all! That's what they tell us."

"BS! It couldn't hurt you unless you ate it" Michael countered before glancing back to the doc with a "right?" look. With a nod and a "probably" he ripped the top off the pouch, spilling some of its contents into his hand.

The three looked at the contents queerly for a couple of seconds before Benjamin said, "Pills? What are those, aspirin, vitamins or something?

"Now that is indeed very strange" the doctor said. "It's certainly not what I was expecting. Let me see those, Michael" reaching to grab a few of the pills. He looked at them carefully, shining them in the light of his brother's flashlight, studying them. He finally looked back to Michael with a questioned look, shaking his head. "Looks like maybe Klonopin. But something's not right with them."

"Huh?" Michael replied.

"What's going on here, Joseph?" his brother quietly inquired.

"I really wish I knew, little brother, but I do know now's not the time to figure this out. Your bosses aren't exactly going to be happy if they find us here. Right now we've got to get out of here, and fast."

"How did you guys get in here anyway?"

"Cut the fence and ran across," Michael interjected.

"There's sensors all over this place! I can't believe you didn't trip one or get caught on video. You're lucky, we've been having problems with the system."

"Well J.J., how do we get out of here without anyone noticing?" the older brother asked.

"Forget it. You've been amazingly lucky to get this far. You go out there again and they'll shoot you on sight. This entire place is on alert. Has been for almost two weeks now. Shoot first, ask questions later. We've had reports that some radical leftist group is supposed to try and seize this stuff in the next day or so. Orders from above."

"You don't believe that, do you?" Michael interjected.

"I'll admit I'm had a few problems with it, but I'm not your problem, anyway."

"And just who is?"

"That company of Marines stationed out there right now. Came in last week. Real gung-ho types, so everyone's real tense. Not your typical security guys and they aren't going to care whether you're my brother or not. And they do a check around the perimeter and the road every two hours. They'll fire up that Humvee out there any minute."

"J.J., we've got to get out of here with some of this evidence. Otherwise we'll never get to the bottom of this. Can you help Michael and me?"

"I don't know what to do. They might even shoot me if I got caught out there, which is why I stay in here in the office mostly. Besides, you're asking me to betray my duty."

"Duty? Screw your duty!" Joseph exclaimed. "You're working for some very bad guys. They're only interested in power and control. They'd have you shot in the back as soon as look at you little brother. Michael and I think they've already killed somebody. They don't give a damn about anyone but themselves. Duty my ass! Your duty is to your country and your family. These people are not your country or you family. Now can you help us get out of here?"

"All right, all right. Settle down, big brother. How'd you get all the way out here in the first place? You got a car out there or what?"

"Flew in. The plane's on the road. Kevin's out there waiting for us right now."

"A plane?!? Kevin? Are you nuts?"

"Probably so, but we still need to get out of here."

"Why don't you just surrender to me? I'll put you in my custody and get the Tribal Police out here and turn you over for trespassing. I'll say I found you out by the fence. That you're my brother and you were just looking for me."

"No way, little brother. If these people find us here they're going to know we're on to them. We think they already do and they'll want us dead, not in custody. Michael is Benjamin's lawyer; it's all tied together somehow."

"Well, you'll never get out of here walking, that's for sure. You might have a chance if you take one of those Jeeps," he said, motioning across the warehouse. "They'll be on you though, in a hot flash, the second they hear that thing start. There are sentries all over this place and, like I said, they're pretty edgy and pulling patrols every other hour."

"And what are you doing with those Jeeps? There're like fifty years old!" Michael demanded.

"Don't ask me. All they send us is crap, old surplus stuff. The Marines brought in the Humvees out there. Its almost like they don't want to spend any money on this operation or they don't want anyone to know about us. Weirdest operation I've ever been involved in."

"Interesting . . . . Fine, an old Jeep it is," Michael concluded. "First, though, get some boxes from each of those other stacks and into the Jeep. We need evidence."

They pulled a box from each of the other five piles and followed J.J. to one of the Jeeps near the bay doors.

"Look, I'll give you as much time as I can, but don't hope for much," J.J. said.

"J.J., you better come with us," his brother replied.

"Are you kidding? I'll be a hell of a lot safer here! Besides, someone's got to give you a little time. Those Marines won't be on you as quick if I stay behind. They won't be suspecting me. I'll be fine."

"Help will be on the way fast, I promise, little brother."

"Well if you have plans on stopping this stuff, it better be quick or it won't be here."

"What? Why?" Michael asked.

"They're due in the next day or so and we're not supposed to getting anything else in for a few weeks. Everyone from here is supposed to go on furlough next week."

"Who?"

"Some company out of Phoenix called AzMediCo. They supposedly take it out and destroy it and they notified us today to have all this ready for transport."

"Sounds like we might be making them nervous Joseph" Michael smiled.

"Yeah, maybe, but right now I'm nervous about getting out of here, I'll drive" hopping up into the driver's seat and finding the key in the ignition as Michael and J.J. loaded the last boxes in the back. Pulling the camera out of the backpack, Michael quickly snapped several pictures without the flash and climbed in next to his friend.

"When they figure out you're on the loose, I'll fire a couple of shots over your heads and you'll know they're on you. Let me take a look outside."

J.J. peered out, gingerly sliding the warehouse door open. There was no movement outside as of yet. He stepped back to the Jeep.

"It's all clear out there now. OK, Michael, hit me."

"What?"

"Hit me, damn it, or they'll be asking me too many questions. Now hit me."

"OK." Michael walloped him across his chin, sending J.J. into a slight stagger backwards. "Hope that didn't hurt too bad," he said sheepishly.

"I've had girls hit me harder Michael. Stick to lawyering. Good luck."

"Thanks for your help, little brother."

"We'll see how much help I've been. This will probably be your funeral."

"Not a chance, J.J., we're blackened with Monster Slayer's armor."

"Yea, and the Marines have big guns. I'd stay low and pray, all the same."

"Regardless, be careful and get out of here and up to Mom's as soon as you can. I've got the feeling all hell is about to break loose."

"I'll be OK" the little brother concluded, rubbing his chin a bit.

"Joseph, let me snap off some pictures, then let's bolt." His friend nodded and Michael flipped on the flash, waiting the couple of seconds for the red light to give its approval. He fired off pictures as quickly as he could, the flash lighting the warehouse for an instant each time. Joseph started the engine; Michael was still turned backwards shooting pictures of the far pallets when it lurched forward.

Attracted by the flashes of light, the sentry in the courtyard was headed for the warehouse as the old Jeep burst from the bay door. The guard backpedaled and fell, rolling over and instinctively taking aim with his M-16 toward the intruders. J.J. reached him just as he leveled the rifle, pushing it aside. "Stop, you fool! They'll want them alive. Get the others!"

The guard immediately recognized J.J. and bolted off, screaming, "Intruders!"

J.J. pulled his pistol from its holster and leveled it above the Jeep. He was squeezing off two rounds as the Marines came scurrying into the courtyard responding to the commotion.

"Over here!" he called, turning and running for the warehouse and the other Jeep. By the time the first Marine rounded the corner, J.J. was cranking over the engine, somehow never quite catching, buying invaluable seconds. "C'mon, C'mon!" he shouted out the still open door.

A sergeant rounded the corner seconds later as the engine finally caught and J.J. popped the clutch, causing the vehicle to lurch forward and die. The Sergeant yelled toward J.J. "What the hell is going on?"

"Some idiots with a camera were just in here. They hit me and took off in one of the Jeeps," he responded, still cranking on the engine.

"Forget that piece of junk. Get the Humvees. Let's go, Marine."

With that the sergeant and the other Marine were out the door. J.J. started the engine with no problem, rolling out onto the ramp just as the first Humvee lurched from its parking place, right towards J.J. He screeched to a halt, forcing the Humvee to slow and go around the Jeep. He sat motionlessly as the Humvee screamed around him, kicking up dust as a second Humvee started up to his left, joining late in the chase for their prey. "I hope that was enough time, big brother," he muttered, getting out of the Jeep and watching down the road. "I hope it was enough time." I placed the Jeep in gear and rolled off slowly following the chase.

Michael saw the lights from the first Humvee as it rounded from the cover of the warehouse to fall in behind them as they bounded down the road toward the entrance gate. "Faster, Joseph, faster! They're on us now!" The Jeep bounced through some washboards in the gravel, twisting sideways but quickly closing on the gate. In the moonlight, Michael could see Joseph's eyes grow wide.

"Ram it, Joseph. Don't even think of stopping!" Michael screamed, eyeing the approaching fence as fully automatic weapon fire whizzed above their heads from the pursuing vehicle. They hit the gate at fifty, sending metal fencing flying in every direction.

Kevin could hear the commotion and gunfire. He quickly started the plane and rolled up the road readying himself take-off and, he hoped, giving his friends enough room to see him as they popped over the hill, edging it as far off the left side of the roadway's center as he could. The engine roared as he gave it a little more throttle, silence no longer at issue. He glanced back, noticing the lights turning toward the main road and bouncing off the little hill behind him. This had better be them. This had to be them. He flicked on the plane's landing and running lights and tossed open the right side passenger door.

Joseph raced down the road, the vehicle kicking gravel and dust behind them. Michael monitored the Marines' progress as they sped after them. The first Humvee's headlights bounced as they sprang over the first hill behind them, the second bounding down the entrance road. "Slow down, Joseph," Michael hollered. "Kevin should be on the other side of this hill." Over the edge of the second rise they flew, instantly picking up the Cessna's running lights and the engine's hum a mere couple of hundred feet in front of them. Joseph hit the brakes, fishtailing in the gravel and sliding to a sideways stop a few yards from the plane's tail.

"Howdy, boys!" Kevin yelled out the door. Over the rise a second set of lights now swept across the horizon, turning onto the main road. "C'mon boys, they're not far behind you."

"Take these!" Joseph handed the boxes to Kevin, who slid them onto the seat behind him. Michael rounded the jeep's hood, gun in hand, leveling it toward the danger. The evidence loaded, Joseph scrambled into the back with the boxes.

"Let's go, Michael," Kevin shouted, revving the engine as the first Humvee bounded down the flat, only the hill now separating them, the second several hundred yards behind.

Michael flung himself through the door, grabbing at the seat frame and trying to pull himself in, yelling, "Go, Go, Go." The plane jolted forward as Kevin let off the brake and powered up to full as Michael's legs drug down the gravel road. He switched off his lights just as headlights began cresting the hill, almost upon him. The Cessna was finally gaining good speed as the Jeep leapt over the hill, closing quickly.

Michael scrambled to pull his legs into the cabin, as Joseph grabbed him by his clothes and pulled. Behind them Kevin could see the flashes from the muzzles pursuing them.

The headlights of the first Humvee suddenly darted left, the driver braking and swerving in a spray of gravel to miss the discarded jeep sitting astraddle the road. It swung wide, bouncing into the ditch, losing nearly all momentum before lurching back toward the roadway. It was a fair race again, with the Marines had the clear firepower edge. The plane 's pace continued to quicken as the Humvee's driver battled to regain control, finally pulling back into a straight line and down the road in chase, as the second fishtailed to a halt. A rattle of slugs pinged against the exo-structure, more muzzle flashes in the growing distance behind them.

"Get in, damn it!" Kevin screamed. Joseph clawed at Michael's waistband, finally yanking him through the door as the plane glided off the hill at the end of their makeshift runway. The door slammed behind him. The little plane gained altitude, banking left, only a flicker of muzzle flashes showing where the M-16s were firing, the little plane now too high and out of range for any further damage. Michael struggled to gain his balance and get into the seat, noticing the shadow that was First Mesa growing in the windshield.

"Hold on, boys," Kevin shouted, pulling the yoke deep into his lap. The little plane whined as its nose shot drastically upward, the momentum slamming all three into their seats. The mesa's shadow slowly gave way to a backdrop of stars, the cliffs finally passing a few scant feet below them. Kevin leveled off over the plateau and then shot down the other side in a direct line for Kayenta, finally bringing the plane to a comfortable altitude above the arroyos.

Joseph leaned forward in his seat and let out a deep whoosh. "Everybody all right?"

"I think I'm all right. Maybe a few scratches. Kev's good. Man, that was crazy! Probably about time for a swig off that bottle you've always got stashed back there, Kevin. It would do my nerves some good."

"Up under your seat there, Joseph."

"How you doing up there, Kevin?"

"Fine so far, but I think I might need a sip to steady my own nerves. All of those bullets couldn't have missed everything." He accepted the bottle of Jack Daniels from Michael. Below them the twinkling lights of Chinle passed far to their right. "Ah, just what I needed" taking a healthy swig.

"Well, how we doing, captain?" Michael asked, taking a second sip of the brown whiskey and passing the bottle back to Joseph.

"OK, I guess. We've got about an hour of flying time to Kayenta and I'm not a hundred percent my little bird's going to make it that far."

"Oh, here we go again, Doc," Michael mocked him, rolling his eyes.

Kevin backed off the engine slightly. "I'm serious this time."

"Something wrong?" Joseph called, leaning forward again.

"Probably not, just being safe, but we seem to be using a lot of fuel. Either we spent more than I expected getting out of there or . . ."

"What exactly do you mean, 'using a lot of fuel'?" Joseph nervously questioned.

"Don't be bullshitting. You do this every time," Michael loudly scolded the pilot.

"Well, I'm not this time. That fuel gauge doesn't lie," Kevin insisted, pointing to the instrument panel. "Believe what you want, but we might want to start thinking of a place to set her back down."

Joseph turned to Michael. "Great. After all of this, he's going to kill us on the way back. Let me see that map, Michael. Kevin, give me some cabin lights."

Joseph and Michael pulled their heads together, trying to get their bearings. Chinle had passed about ten minutes before. If they continued on their present north-northeast course, they'd intersect Arizona highway 192 somewhere between Rough Rock and the Chilchinbito Trading Post. "We'll have to make it at least that far. There's nothing between here and there but mesas and arroyos," Joseph concluded. "We should start seeing some lights to the left and right out there about thirty miles ahead. The road should be between them . . . I hope."

"We should be all right on fuel as long as it doesn't get any worse."

"Well, you've pretty much just jinxed that into happening," Michael groaned.

"Probably so," Kevin said. "But with a little luck, we might even make it to Kayenta. It can't be more than another ninety miles."

"Maybe, but there's not a whole lot between Chilchinbito and Kayenta. If there's any question I'd rather call a taxi than take an unnecessary chance. Landing in that area would be impossible."

"Maybe so, Joseph, but I'm imagine it's a little tough finding a taxi out here. Let's see if I can get this on the road first."

"How much further before we clear this stuff, Doc?"

"Shouldn't be much longer, Michael, but I'm not sure. I don't spend much time down here."

"It better be quick," Kevin chimed in. "This gauge is going down quicker than I'd like!"

Michael saw the lights in the distance first. "Over there," he said.

"Yeah, I got em," Kevin noted after a few moments.

The plane sputtered a bit as the arroyos and mesas gave way to a flatter desert floor. To the right in the distance they could see the lights of the tiny enclave of Rough Rock. To the left, the lights of the trading post beckoned, fewer lights for landing but much closer. Kevin cut a beeline for the left edge of Chilchinbito and the plane sputtered along. "Just a few more minutes, baby," the pilot pleaded.

Ahead, about two miles, Kevin began to make out the roadway, thankfully empty of vehicles at this late hour. The plane sputtered several more times as their landing strip drew closer. "Hold on, baby, hold on," Kevin pleaded, banking slowly to the left and lining up the road beneath them. The anxious moments of set-up passed as the engine kept sputtering. The plane lightly touched down at the edge of Chilchinbito, taxiing to a slow halt and swiveling into the trading post parking lot. "That's my baby!" Kevin smiled, mercifully shutting down his coughing engine.

"Told you he was bullshitting, Doc."

"I don't care," Joseph retorted. "Just let me off this damn thing. I'm gonna pee my pants."

* * *

Nodding in his oversized chair, Tielson was summoned awake by the phone ringing on the Easel line. He bent forward and shot his stubby little hands toward the receiver. "Yes, what is it?"

"Sir, AZ has been breached."

"What!" The little man sat straight up in his chair, fully awake.

"Yes, sir, and it appears that the contaminated shipment has been compromised. Our men found them in the warehouse."

"What?!?" Tielson was incredulous. He demanded answers, but the Marine on the other end didn't have many. The intruders had not been captured and no one got a good look at them. It was a professional job, though, the men escaping by plane. They were currently inventorying in an effort to determine what was missing. He'd report again as soon as he knew something.

Tielson hung up the phone in utter disbelief. How could they possibly have figured out the connection with AZ? Even if they had a copy of the memo, they couldn't know about AZ. Tielson was completely bewildered. He rose from his chair and began to pace back and forth, his eerie shadow following the wall again. He knew what he had to do now.

* * *

The threesome had regained their land legs and were gathered near the engine as Kevin assessed the damage. Joseph had emerged from the plane after inspecting their treasure. What they'd found actually proved very interesting and quite unexpected. The six stacks of pallets contained six separate drugs. Joseph seemed sure they were quality counterfeits, as opposed to fakes, and maybe a few expired ones with older markings. Joseph explained that what they had was a standard drug regime prescribed for psychiatric disorders for people having problems following a traumatic event. When Kevin asked what that meant in laymen's terms, Joseph responded with the simple acronym "PTSD." Joseph explained that he had seen the cocktail many times before, particularly with Navajo kids returning from the Middle East wars. The cocktail typically consisted of a sleeping pill, an anti-anxiety, an anti-depressant, and an anti-psychotic. Sometimes they'd even add a stimulant like Ritalin or Adderall or maybe even a painkiller.

"So let me guess," Michael interrupted, "that's exactly what we have in these six boxes."

"You're a genius, Mr. Holmes," he cracked, eyes rolling to the heavens. "So the box we opened is full of Klonopin. It's an anti-anxiety and there's a lot of them. Two of the boxes have Adderall and Norco, which you probably know better as Oxycontin. Another has Paxil, an anti-depressant. Then we've got Ambien for sleep and finally Seroquel, the VA's favorite antipsychotic. But they're all counterfeit, I suspect. the markings just don't seem right. I'd have to look in a PDR to be sure, but something's off base with these."

"Well, isn't that interesting," the attorney said. "Perhaps we need to think about this a little different now in light of what we've found." The three talked for a bit about the possibilities before eventually turning to the issues with the plane.

That was the simpler issue and quickly evident to the pilot: a cracked fuel line was leaking. Probably more the result of their hasty, bumpy takeoff rather than gunfire, which had left only a hole or two near the rear of the fuselage. Other than that, she'd taken little damage. Kevin said he could fly her out if he could get more fuel and a new line.

"I can probably get that handled," Joseph volunteered. "Just tell me exactly what it is you need."

Kevin nodded, pulling a pad from the plane and starting to make a list.

"We need to get mobile real fast," Michael said, mostly to himself before turning to Joseph. "If you've got service on your phone, Joseph, let's get somebody on their way. I need to get back to Durango and see if I can put the pieces of this puzzle together and I need to do some research and make some calls to do it."

"All right, I've got service" Joseph said. "I'll get Erin on the phone and you can talk to her. And then I want to check out our little packages back there some more. Something quite strange is going on here and I have a couple of ideas what it is."

DAY TEN

One Last Adventure

S tratler Hotel, how may I direct your call?"

"Room 342," the caller demanded sternly.

"Thank you, I'll forward your call."

Tompkins picked the phone up on the second ring, but before he could answer, the troll was barking his orders.

"I have a report that suggests the subjects may be returning. Monitor accordingly. I want to know the second you've re-established contact."

"Yes, sir."

"And Tompkins, begin looking for an opportunity to resolve the matter fully. When you get your chance, act on your latest instructions. The sooner the better. I don't want that damned lawyer sniffing around any more! Do whatever it takes!"

"I understand." The man set the receiver back in the cradle. "Let's get the equipment going. He thinks we may be having company."

"I'll be right there," came the call from the bathroom.

* * *

It was about nine in the morning when Erin and Michael arrived back in Durango. They'd left the others behind, but in control of the situation. Erin had driven Joseph's truck and Trish had brought the rental. They'd stopped in Kayenta on their way to pick up some canisters of aviation fuel and the part Kevin needed from Joseph's friend at the airport. They'd arrived just after sunrise and Kevin had the fuel line in place in a matter of minutes. The men poured the fuel into the plane and Kevin quickly had it cranked up and purring.

Kevin had joined the others near Joseph's truck, pronouncing the aircraft sound and good to go. He would fly it back to Kayenta if the others could get him a safe take-off. They agreed to use the trucks to stop any traffic until he could get airborne and then Trish and Joseph would drive up to meet him at the airport. In the time it would take them to get there, he'd have the time to reassess any problems with the airport mechanic and get refueled. Joseph would then drop Trish at the airport with Kevin and, assuming the plane was sound, they would fly back to Durango as soon as possible. They'd meet Michael and Erin at the motel around four, giving Michael the time he needed to clear up loose ends in town. With plan in hand, they blocked the road, made sure Kevin got in the air and then went their separate ways.

It was a little before noon when Michael pulled the rental car into Erin's garage next to her car. Michael surveyed the block, not finding anything out of place, before shutting the garage door. He came around to help Erin with the bags. She put her arms around his neck and hugged him, whispering in his ear, "I could really use a long hot shower and a nap. Wanna join me?"

He grinned, giving her a long wet kiss. "Can't think of anything I'd rather do."

Around two Michael woke from a little sleep to the beautiful woman nestled up against his back, her leg draped over his thigh and her arm around his waist. He gently caressed her hand, circling her fingertips with the pad of his index finger. She stirred a bit, tracing her foot down his leg to his ankle. He raised her hand to his mouth and gently kissed it, turning around to face her.

"It's about time we got going, babe. I need to make a stop before we meet them at the motel."

"OK, I'll get dressed," she said softly, slowly lifting herself from his side. He watched as she floated across the room to the dresser. She gazed back at him through the mirror, smiling innocently. "Come on, get dressed. We've got to meet them at the motel."

He smiled back at her reflected face. "Only if you insist, but I'd rather watch you."

* * *

Benson's ears perked up instantly. "They're back," he coldly informed his associate.

His partner glanced back for confirmation.

"Kincaid and the girl are back," he affirmed, taking the earpiece out. "They're meeting the other two at the motel."

Tompkins smiled and quickly dialed Tielson on the cell phone, made his report and received his instructions. "Are you sure, sir?" After a moment, he nodded. "Yes sir, I understand. First available chance."

* * *

Erin drove to Mercy Hospital as Michael requested, albeit a little confused as to what they were doing there. He jumped from the car with "I'll be right back, just have to pick something up," slamming the door and disappearing inside. Erin listened to the radio and before she knew it, he was back in the car, carrying a small envelope.

"Let's get out of here."

"Where to?"

"I'm not sure. I guess the motel, but we might still need to waste some time before Kevin gets back."

"Sounds good," she said, and put the car in gear. Michael leafed quickly through the reports as they drove. The GC analysis indicated the presence of a complex hydrocarbon, but the retention time didn't seem to match something simple. The quantity was in the parts per million range. The chemist noted on the report that it had probably been broken down somewhat between the time it was introduced to his system and the time he died, a period of about an hour. While the results were inconclusive, something certainly was present in the deceased's blood that shouldn't have been. Michael would have to wait for the mass spec results from his friend up at the Fort for the qualitative information, but no matter what it was it was something that shouldn't be there.

"What is it?" Erin inquired when Michael looked up from the papers.

"The first hard chink in their armor. This pretty much confirms that Luigi was injected with something before he died."

"Injected? For what?"

"Interrogation, I imagine."

They slipped into the motel's lot through the back alley and Erin made a wide rounding turn into the first stall next to the living quarters' back door. After making sure no one was watching them, they sneaked in, undetected as far as they could tell.

Thankfully, Trish and Kevin were already awaiting for them inside.

"Hi, Trish. Did you ever get the results on the blood split?" Urgency tinged Michael's voice.

"No. I called, but they said it would be a couple of more hours."

"Well, call them back and tell them I needed it yesterday."

"All right, but I left the numbers back at the hotel. I'll take the rental back to the hotel and take care of it and be back in a bit."

Michael nodded, collecting his thoughts.

"Hey, I thought you always had everything with you?" But she was already out the door.

"Did you find something, Michael?"

"Maybe, Kevin. Not really sure. Hopefully some irrefutable evidence for Bontani and Benjamin. If nothing else, it's another confirming clue for us. I'm pretty sure now that they used a drug on Luigi, but we'll find out for sure when I hear back from Les or that other lab report comes back. Dr. Bustee's report shows there was some type of hydrocarbon in Luigi's system that shouldn't have been there. It had started metabolizing, so it had been there at least an hour. It makes me think they must have been interrogating him about something. That's still a missing piece, though. Once we have that and hopefully the memo, then we'll also have them. I take it you haven't found anything new?" He acknowledged the anticipated shake of Kevin's head before he continued. "We've got to keep looking, then. It's here; I can feel it."

"I'd just started the shed yesterday when Joseph called; looked throughout Luigi's things in the morning. Turned this place upside down. The shed should be easy. Not really much space to put a safe."

"Remember . . . ."

"Yeah, I know. Something out of place."

Kevin disappeared out the back door and once again Michael and Erin began looking through Luigi's former home.

* * *

Tompkins and Benson had split up when they left the hotel. They'd agreed on the positions they'd take up in order to cover the entire grounds. When they were in place, they confirmed their position to each other via radio.

* * *

Kevin had returned and the three sat at Luigi's kitchen table, discussing their failed search attempts.

"Kevin, I just have to believe we've missed it a hundred times. Hosteen Begay seemed so sure that whatever Luigi might have hidden would still be around here, but I sure don't know where. Maybe it's somewhere else. Hell, maybe it doesn't even exist. I'm out of ideas. Anybody else in need of coffee?"

"I'll make some, honey. Sit still."

"It's up in front, Erin." Kevin pointed toward the office.

She gave a rub to the back of Michael's head as she passed and disappeared into the front office.

The two men mulled their own thoughts, looking for something the dead man could have hidden something in. Erin poked her head through the door.

"Can you help me?"

Michael looked up with a "Happy to" look. "Yes?"

"Where's the coffee?"

"In the front, next to the water cooler," Kevin volunteered.

"A water cooler?" she asked. "You know, that's something that's always amazed me. The coldest, purest water I've ever tasted, and yet some people around here will actually buy water. You'd never see that in a local's home."

Michael and Kevin nodded their perfect agreement as Erin turned back to her duty. In another half second, a crooked smile began to rise across Michael's face as he realized the import of her observation.

"Water?" he queried. He paused before gleefully concluding, "Of course. Tó! Bottled water. Uh, Erin, dear, come on back here for a second. I need to kiss you!" Upon her return he grabbed her hand, pulled her toward him and pecked her quickly. "Not only are you beautiful, you're brilliant too. You were right yesterday. You are a great help. I think you just found Luigi's safe. Hey, Kevin, come on back here. And bring something to dump some water in."

Kevin grabbed a plastic trashcan. "What's up?"

"Tó Kevin Tó! Why do you have a bottled water cooler?"

He looked oddly at his friend. "Um, for the guests?" He paused before he continued with a shoulder shrug. "Luigi got it, it was a big joke with him. Filled it with tap water. Why?"

"Bring me that empty trash can."

"What did you find?" He handed it over.

"I'm not sure. Something Benjamin told me that I didn't even really think about until now. I didn't think it was that important at the time. Benjamin told me that just before Luigi died, he asked for water. What if he wasn't asking for a drink but was telling Yeh Tay where to look? In the water."

Trashcan in hand, Michael glanced out the office windows, surveying any danger that might exist. He nonchalantly set the can down next to the water cooler. Unconcerned about the splashing water, he ripped the jug from the dispenser and poured out what remained. He flipped the dispenser onto its side, trying to divert the remaining water into the can. He looked underneath, but found nothing. Tipping the cooler back, he let his hand scurry round the ceramic cistern inside.

In a moment, he smiled back at them and produced what they'd searched for, a sealed plastic sheath containing a document. He needed only to see the introduction on the first page to know he'd found what Luigi had been killed for. With a wave of his hand, he flashed the document saying Tó before turning back for a better study. Erin looked questioningly back towards Kevin before taking one step toward Michael.

Kevin's attention to his friends was snapped by the sound of the exploding glass. In a millisecond, a silent missile hit its intended mark, bringing its victim crashing to the floor.

* * *

Anxious moments passed as he gauged the situation. "Benson! Confirm!" The radio squawked back. The silence was maddening. "Damn it, Benson, confirm!"

Another shot rang out, followed by the earpiece squawking "Yeah. One down for sure. I think the second shot took the other target down. Two marks, two down."

"OK, OK. Get out of there. Now! Report to my position. I'll survey for movement. We need to get in there fast and get that letter he had."

Benson opened the case next to him and removed the cloth from inside. He unscrewed the barrel and placed it in its holder, wiping the metal clean as he went. He coolly pulled the sight and found its proper storage place with the ease that comes with the confidence of repetition. Throughout his packing, he kept a watchful eye on the surrounding terrain. Nothing moved. The stock eased into the case next. In moments the weapon had become a small cased musical instrument, one that he played quite well. He pulled off his gloves and retreated from the knoll toward his car, instrument in hand.

* * *

After the sound of the breaking glass, Kevin dove to the floor in the living quarters. He'd just landed when he heard the whistle of the second shot. He lay motionless for what seemed an eternity before he heard a low groan from the other room.

"Michael! Erin! Are you OK?"

"I'm hit, Joseph" his friend's strained voice finally answered, "but I'll live, damn it! Erin, crawl over to the other room and keep your head down."

Into the living quarters Erin slid on knees and elbows below the half-wall and through the glass. A few moments later Michael, still clutching the papers he'd found, rounded the corner to relative safety. Kevin immediately noticed the crimson stain on his left shoulder and the pained look in his eyes.

"Kevin. Call 911!" Erin yelled.

"Is he hurt badly?"

"I don't know. Just get some sirens coming. Maybe it'll scare them off."

Kevin reached for the phone as Erin examined Michael. "Shit, they've cut the line" grabbing the cell phone and dialing 911.

"They'll be on us in a few minutes, then," Michael said. "They've got us bottled up." He was growing in alertness, but he was still dazed, holding the papers in a vise-like grip, a grimace locked on his face.

Erin ripped the bottom of her shirt after taking a close look at Michael's wound. She stuffed the material into the hole, bringing a loud moan from the patient.

"Jeeeeez, Erin, that hurts."

"Sorry, baby, but we've got to get that bleeding stopped," she commanded, without even a whisper of hysteria.

"I know, just trying to retain my delightful sense of humor in the face of danger." His face grew urgent. "I gotta get out of here and draw them to me. We're all three sitting ducks right now."

"Michael, you can't go out there. They'll kill you for sure."

"That might be true, but they're after this right here." He held the paper up in his hand. "They're not going to wait. They're coming in here to get it and get rid of anyone around. The only chance is for me to draw them away. They're watching us right now. Gotta make a move. Gotta shake 'em up a bit." His breathing was labored. "How in the hell do they know our every move?" he said to himself and no one.

With the aid of the desk, Michael pulled himself to his feet. From his waistband, he withdrew the .38 Joseph had loaned him earlier in the day. He was a bit wobbly, but stood firm. "I'm headed for the car" and he staggered toward the side door. "Give me a few minutes to get out of the parking lot, then you two head out the front door and up the street. I'll draw them to me and you get this someplace safe." He extended the paper to Kevin, who took it and shoved it into the back pocket of his jeans. "Give me your keys, Kevin."

"Michael, you're crazy. Please don't do this," Erin pleaded.

"I have to. That document has to survive. If we don't split up right now, that's not going to happen." He glanced out the side window. "Fortunately, Kevin's Jeep is in the first stall and a van's pulled in on the other side of it. As long as they're not on the roof, I should have cover. Now give me your keys!" he demanded.

"Michael!" she said, exasperated, "You can't drive. You've got a bullet in your shoulder. For Christ's sake, you'll pass out before you get two blocks."

"That's fine. That's all you two will need. By the time they catch me, you'll be long gone."

"I'll go with you, then," she stated matter-of-factly.

"The hell you will! Kevin, give me your fucking keys! Erin, I'm serious. You stay here, wait a few seconds from when you hear me leave the parking lot and then you and Kevin go out that back window over the sink. Get the hell out of here over to KFC and wait for the cops. These guys want me, not you, and somebody needs to tell this story quick or we'll all be dead." Reluctantly, she nodded.

* * *

Tompkins heard the footsteps behind him. He turned to acknowledge Benson, who asked, "Any movement?"

"No, nothing. Looks like good shooting."

"Good. Then it's time to get in there."

The pair slid across the alleyway from their position, to the cover of the shed.

* * *

"Michael," Kevin interceded, "you'll never make it. You'll pass out in ten minutes and probably take out somebody with you when you do. You and I'll go."

Michael knew his friend was probably right and he relented. "Erin, honey, you stay here until we leave and then out the back window. Get somewhere safe and call Joseph. Kevin, give her Trish and Joseph's cell numbers." Kevin jotted the numbers on a piece of paper he found on the desk and handed it to her. "Tell him there's been a change in plans and to meet us at the airport in Aneth. Tell him what happened and to get his sewing kit ready. We'll be there in an hour."

"Michael, you'll bleed to death in that time! Your first stop should be Mercy," Kevin countered.

"Don't you think they'll have the same thought, Kev? Look, I'll be fine. The bleeding's almost stopped, its really not that bad. Damn it, don't argue with me. If you're coming, then we've got to get out of here, now! These guys are pros and they're coming in here. We're wasting time. Please, Kev, do what I ask or otherwise go with her, it's the only way." His intent was evident: he was going with or without him. "Erin, get a hold of Trish and the two of you meet us as soon as you can over in Aneth. We'll call you later and tell you where we are. All right, then, buddy. Time for you to get us to the airport."

Erin turned to the two of them with a look of combined disbelief and amazement.

"Well, if you're so damn set on getting the both of us killed," Kevin declared, "I guess it's time to go!"

He bolted from the side door, running toward his Jeep. He opened the passenger door and slid across to the driver's set. With one continuous motion, the keys were in the ignition and the engine started.

"Keep your damn head down," Kevin yelled as Michael joined him, plunking into the front seat with a moan. Michael pulled the door shut as Kevin slammed it into gear and the Jeep roared backward.

* * *

Benson and Tompkins had just made it to the corner of the shed as the Jeep ejected from its parking space. It was still moving backwards when the transmission rammed into first, making a mechanical wail answered instantly by squealing tires. The Jeep angled directly toward the men's path, cutting the corner as it swung left into the alley. Tompkins dived backwards, the vehicle barely missing him. Benson twirled, leveling his handgun too late as the Jeep vanished behind the shed in a cloud of dust. He fired off three rounds toward the Jeep as it passed from behind the shed, but by then the vehicle was already turning onto the paved street just a couple hundred yards away. Benson squeezed off another two inaudible rounds. One of them shattered the Jeep's back window, but it kept going, out of sight behind a house. In the distance, a siren plaintively wailed its approach.

"Shit! Let's go," Benson called to Tompkins, who was scrambling back onto his feet.

* * *

Erin could clearly hear the sirens approaching. They weren't far away. She punched out the screen, wriggled through the back window and quickly slid around the corner of the motel's back fence. In a few more seconds, she'd made it to the relative safety of KFC, pulled out her phone and began making her calls.

* * *

The two men ran down the alley and jumped into the silver Ford, Tompkins behind the wheel. The car made an abrupt U-turn and hurried onto Main as they searched the street for any sign of their intended prey.

"Nice shooting, you idiot" he yelled at Benson. "Can't even confirm one. Hell, you probably only nicked him. Step on it! They're probably halfway to the damned airport by now." Thompkins pounded his fist against the dashboard.

Benson grabbed the phone from the seat, dialing frantically, I'll do it. "Sir, we cannot, repeat, cannot confirm he's down, but from what we could hear we know we hit him. We think they're running for the airport. We need further instructions." Tompkins sped the car along as the voice screamed from the earpiece.

"Yes, sir. . . . I see . . . Uh, yes, sir. I understand. We're headed there now and we know where they're going. We'll finish the job there. We think he's found the papers you wanted . . ." Benson's voice trailed off. Tompkins glanced at him as Benson paused, listening to the yelling even his partner could hear coming from the earpiece.

"Yes, sir. As I said, they're headed for the airport and we're in pursuit. The job will be finished, I assure you." He paused again, listening to the yelling begin to subside.

"Yes. sir, we'll let you know."

* * *

Tielson hung up the phone, his fury clearly visible to Anderson.
"These guys are complete screw-ups."

"Yes, sir," Anderson said quietly, working hard to dodge the cold eyes and bushy eyebrows.

"This is your fault, Anderson. They're your people. Now I've got to fix your problems."

Anderson glared at the despicable figure. He couldn't take much more from this ogre. In a flash, Tielson was back on the phone.

"Stratler Hotel, how may I direct your call?"

"Room 346."

"Thank you, I'll forward your call."

The phone rang once before the Spanish-inflected voice answered curtly. "Yes."

"This is Tielson. Have you been monitoring the situation?"

"I have, with the assistance of your operatives' equipment. They appear to be on their way to the airport."

"You have your orders. He's already taken one; he should be easy. I don't want any trace left. And while you're at it, take out whoever's with him, along with those two idiots that started this mess. Anyone else who shows up, too. We know there'll be at least one other, maybe more. Clean it all up."

The second Tielson hung up the phone, Anderson demanded, "What are you doing?"

"Look, Anderson" the little man began, condescension writhing in his voice, "you may not have the guts to do what it takes, but I do. Now get out of my face. You're just like the rest of these fools. No brains, no guts."

Anderson was happy for the dismissal. He'd wanted to choke the living shit out of the little bastard. Right then and there. But more important things were at hand and that had likely saved the troll's life, for the time being, anyway. He turned and exited, taking a direct route toward his office. His decision and his plan were now set. He was definitely getting out, one way or the other, and he needed to talk quickly to the Old Man and let him know what the troll was pulling.

* * *

Kevin was bouncing down side streets and alleyways. Every so often the hitting of a pothole would bring a pained sigh from Michael, who clutched the gun he'd pulled from his waistband. Down Second Avenue the Jeep now roared, veering right on the road that led down the riverbank. Kevin barely slowed for the left onto 160, bending right onto the bypass around the train station and downtown. After four miles he cut off the main highway to Old La Posta Road and sped toward the entrance to the secondary airport.

He thanked God that most of the visitors to their small town knew nothing of this out-of-the-way little strip. It was used almost exclusively by locals, for non-commercial flights. He pulled the car up almost next to the plane on the ungated strip.

"Stick around, buddy. I'll get the plane open and be back for you," he told Michael.

"I'll be just fine. Get that damn thing started."

Kevin had just cranked over the engine as Michael staggered up. Jumping down, Kevin steadied his friend, helping him up into his seat.

"I'll get rid of the car. Be right back."

Michael buckled himself in, keeping a watchful eye and placing the gun into the hold between the seats. His right shoulder ached from the bullet wound, but using his left arm he flicked a series of switches and began the pre-flight. Kevin returned to the pilot seat and pulled the door closed. "Everything's a go," his co-pilot announced. Kevin retracted the brakes and the plane lurched forward. They rounded on to the straightway and Kevin revved the engine to full throttle. Kevin used practically the entire runway before the Cessna finally glided off the ground, barely clearing the rim of treetops at the runway's end.

"Nice takeoff, buddy. Out of practice?"

"I'm just fine. My nerves are a little frayed right now. Sit back, shut up and relax," Kevin replied. The plane steadily rose above the mesa's plate. He pulled back on the controls and lofted past Perrin's Peak in a bank to the west.

The ridges of the mountain range passed easily below them and Kevin set a due-west heading. He engaged the autopilot with a slight climb before turning toward his companion. Michael's eyes seemed dimmed, but alert. The blood seemed to have drained from his sallow face en route to the seeping wound on his shoulder.

"Let's get another bandage on that. How you feeling?"

"I think I'm about a quart low, but I'll survive."

"Yeah, you'll be fine." Kevin's voice sank as he looked at the wound.

"Sure. I'll be all right. It's really not that bad, but it is zapping my strength. Just get us on the ground and to Joseph," he gasped, managing a grin. "A couple of pain-killers, a quick sew job and I'll be back in the game . . . Six inches to the right, though, and it's a different story. They missed anything vital, just clipped me under my shoulder. Clean through, maybe, but it hurts all the same."

"You've lost some blood, though, buddy. Let's land in Cortez and we'll take care of it."

"Just go to Aneth, its another 20 minutes. We've got a doctor waiting. It looks worse than it really is. I'll be fine; they can't get rid of me that easily."

"Let me see if I can find something back there for a better dressing." Kevin started reaching into the cabin's rear half. "That bottle's still back here. You need a stiff drink. For medicinal purposes, of course."

He returned moments later with a white T-shirt and the bottle of whiskey. Michael took the bottle and downed three big swigs before pouring some on the wound with a yelp, took another sip, and then handed it back to Kevin, whereupon he took a couple for himself.

He ripped a strip from the shirt and stuffed it inside the bullet hole. "I'm going to be pissed if you get blood all over my plane." With the remaining piece, he looped it around Michael's shoulder, tying it off at the top.

The bandaging finished, Michael reached over and took the bottle from its resting place between the seats and had another drink. He slumped quietly in his seat while Kevin returned to the controls. The plane crossed the La Platas and Kevin corrected the course, heading straight toward the folded arms of the Ute. They both sat motionless, save for an occasional drink, until the plane crossed over the Sleeping Ute and a series of red-rock mesas.

"Hang in there buddy, we're about ten minutes out. I'll have you on the ground shortly."

He eased the plane into a gradual descent, gliding easily over the first line of mesas that straddled the state line and following McElmo Canyon toward Aneth. He set up in the middle of the valley. In the distance the two friends could see the little airport's welcoming beacon, flashing green and white, and Kevin corrected his glide path. The runway enlarged with each passing moment. The plane edged down slowly and Kevin adjusted the flaps and airspeed as necessary. The strip was now just five hundred feet in front of them. The plane jumped a bit as it caught a warm air pocket wafting from the desert floor below.

"Nice flying, bud!"

"Shut up and bleed or I'll kick you off the flight."

Just over the end of the runway, Kevin began slowly cutting back on the throttle and nosed the little Cessna down. It bounced a bit on initial contact, jostling the pilot, who struggled with the stick as the plane bounced back, finally settling softly onto the pavement. He cut back on the engine and slowed to a nice taxi speed.

"Nice flying, buddy boy. You sure can't drink and fly."

"We're on the ground and you're still alive aren't we?"

"I suppose."

"Well, that just proves it," Kevin proclaimed. "Any landing you can walk away from is a good landing."

"Now that's original. Think I've heard that before."

The plane pulled to the left toward an open gate by which Joseph stood.

As Kevin locked on the brakes, shut down the engine and unbuckled himself, Joseph ran to the plane, finding Michael taking a big swig off the whiskey bottle. "Well, I guess you're not in that bad of shape."

"Ah, hell no, Doc. Just patch me up, give me some painkillers and I'll be on my way," his friend slurred.

The Navajo retorted, "Yeah, let's get the poor little cowboy all fixed up. Can you walk, Wyatt?"

"I'll be just fine. Have the valet there collect my things," Michael said with a flick of his chin toward his pilot.

Michael gingerly extricated himself from the seat and wobbled out of the plane, his balance bolstered by his friend. "Hey, and you might want to get that gun," he yelled back. "The rest of that bottle wouldn't be a bad idea, either."

"You've had quite enough, I think," his doctor advised him.

In a few minutes, they had arrived at the Navajo Regional Hospital. Joseph angled his pickup through the parking lot to the emergency entrance. He jumped out, returning in moments with two nurses and a gurney. Kevin watched as they wheeled Michael through a set of shiny metal doors. A nurse led him to a seat where he plopped down to wait.

* * *

Anderson had been sitting in his office contemplating how to resolve this mess. He'd pretty much decided on the major details when the private line rang. He answered, expecting someone else.

"Yes!"

"Anderson?"

He immediately recognized the voice and changed his tone. "Oh, ah, excuse me, sir."

"Quite all right. I got your message and I think we need to meet again. Things have taken unnecessary turns and I'd like to discuss matters with you further."

"Yes, sir, I agree."

"Eight o'clock?"

"Yes, of course, sir."

* * *

He had read the memo, his astonishment growing as the matter unfolded before his eyes. When he'd finished, he sat for a long time in stunned silence. No wonder they'd killed without regard or remorse. Pulling himself together, he went to the desk where a Navajo nurse was seated.

"Yes, sir?" she inquired.

"I have a rather unusual request."

"Oh, anything sir."

"Do you have a copy machine?"

The nurse looked at him quizzically at first, but her expression quickly changed to acceptance. "Sure we do. It's down the hall here." She led the way and in twenty minutes he returned and took his seat again, this time with several copies in hand.

Dr. Joseph Begay rounded the corner after another twenty minutes, wearing a white smock and a wide grin. "The guy's a cat with nine lives."

"I take it he'll be all right?"

"Yeah. The three of us had worse scraps than that in college. You did a great job of stopping the bleeding. He'll be fine in a few days. You want to tell me what happened?"

"We found out what's going on. You'd better take a look at this. Here's a copy."

Joseph sat to read, spellbound. When he had finished, he sat in the same stunned silence his friend had experienced. Finally, he asked, "Could they really do this?"

"I don't know, but Michael was right. These guys are serious."

"Damn serious."

* * *

"Sir, this is Tompkins."

"Have you located them?"

"Not yet sir, but we believe we're right behind the two women. We should be pulling into the hospital in Aneth in about five minutes and we'll see if the information you have is correct."

"Very good. Check it out; they're there and they can't stay at the hospital forever. They won't be able to do anything about this from there, so they'll have to go elsewhere. Follow them. When you get them away from people, finish the job. Take all involved. Get back to me immediately."

"Yes, sir."

* * *

Trish and Erin leapt from the car and ran into the emergency room. They didn't notice the silver Ford pulling in at the other end of the sparsely used lot.

Erin came around the corner first and turned toward Kevin and Joseph, seated in the waiting room. Her eyes were red and puffy. They could tell she'd been crying. Trish was right behind her.

"Is he?" The nervousness was evident in Erin's voice.

"He's fine, Erin," Joseph answered. "He's lost some fluids, but we're replenishing them now." A wave of relief crossed the women's faces.

Trish said, "I'm sorry I look so disheveled; I thought he might be hurt worse."

"He'll be fine. Lost a little blood but no worse for the wear," Joseph assured her. "I'm going to check on him again and should have him ready to go in about thirty minutes. You can both see for yourselves then." He retreated toward the emergency room, motioning for Kevin to join him. "I'm not sure it's very safe here for any of us. They seem to know our every move. They are good at what they do and if what's in that document is true, then we're all in a lot of trouble. I'll get Michael dressed and ready. Then we'd better get out of here before someone else shows up. We can sort this all out later."

"I'd certainly feel much safer away from here, that's for damned sure."

Joseph left him and Kevin rejoined the two women, taking a seat next to Trish.

"What's this all about, Kevin?" she asked.

"Well . . ." and he began explaining the contents of the memo and what it meant to them both. When he'd finished, Trish abruptly stood up, saying she needed something from the car. She hurriedly bounded out the emergency room door. Kevin sat silently with Erin, going over the ramifications in his mind, until Joseph interrupted his concentration and pulled him aside.

"Michael's getting dressed now, so we can head on back. We really should get out of here. Where's Trish?"

"I don't know. She left about ten minutes ago. She said she had to get something from the car."

"Find her," he said with urgency, "then come back to the examining room. The nurse will show you back. Be quick."

Kevin raced out to the car, but found no sign of Trish. Returning to the waiting room, he found her hanging up the pay phone.

"Come on," he told her. "We're going back to see Michael."

The two strode briskly down the wide hallway to the nurse's station. They were promptly escorted through the shiny double doors to the room where Michael, Erin and Joseph sat.

"You're looking better than the last time I saw you."

"Thanks, Kevin. I feel a little better, too."

Michael was seated on a gurney, his arm in a sling, shirtless, his color returning. His eyes moved slowly to Trish. "You want to tell me what the hell is going on?"

"Well, boss, it's like this. Your hunch was right. I talked to the lab. They discovered trace amounts of sodium pentothal in the sample. No doubt they interrogated him, as you figured. They're re-confirming it right now with the mass spec."

"That's as expected. What else?"

"Leonardo's people confirmed that the silver Ford is a government car. He said he had to dig through several layers at DMV. It was a real pain, but he got it. Could be one of a number of agencies; FBI, NSC or some other alphabet soup. And you were right about the other, too."

Michael nodded knowingly.

"You want to let the rest of us in on this?" Joseph said, now somewhat perturbed.

"Go ahead, Trish. We're all in this together."

"As you suspected, they've been very close to us for the last few days. Yesterday one of Leonardo's investigators swept the motel, Erin's house and my room in the hotel. Bugs everywhere. The guys who did it knew their business well, according to him."

"Go on."

"They've got the room next to me at the Stratler. The investigator found some pretty sophisticated listening and taping devices. Military class stuff. Strictly governmental issue. I called the hotel just now and they haven't checked out."

"So they're still there?" Erin asked.

"I don't think so." Trish continued. "I noticed a silver Ford sitting in the far corner of the lot when I was out there earlier. There's one guy in it and I'm pretty sure it's one of the same guys I saw coming out of the room next to mine two nights ago."

"Any others with him, Trish?"

"Not that I've seen, but that means nothing. I've got the feeling there's at least one more out there somewhere."

"Any word on which agency these guys are with?"

"As I said, Leonardo's boys tracked the registration back to several agencies, but I would bet they're probably with NSA."

"Sounds like their style, sneaky," Michael said. "But this feels more like an independent operation."

"That's about it."

"Good work, Trish. Thanks."

"Sure, boss."

"Well, boys and girls, looks like we need a plan. Any ideas?"

The five of them began to share ideas, all equal conspirators. The first thing to do was obvious. They needed to get away from their pursuers, however many there were, after which they'd need the protection afforded by media attention to a story. They'd divide between the two vehicles. Kevin and Michael would take the rented Explorer and Joseph would take Trish and Erin with him in his pickup. Since Michael and Kevin seemed to be the primary targets, they'd be first priority in the silvery menace's mind. They would take back roads and a northern route back towards Bluff and Mexican Hat. The other three would take the southern cutoff. Their shadows would be forced to make a decision. Michael felt sure that the pursuers would follow him and Kevin. He was even surer they could lose them. If there was more than one tail, as Trish had suggested, both groups would have to lose their tails of their own accord. Regardless, they'd both be on their own from the cutoff on out. Provided they lost their tails, they'd meet up at the Begay house. They could hide there without anyone noticing, until they could get to someone who could help, but their first priority had to be to get away.

"Trish, where's that extra cell phone?"

"Right here, boss," she said, reaching into her front pocket.

"Give it to Kevin, and the keys to your rental. Joseph, keep your phone on until we see you again. I'll call you if we can after the split. We should get going; it's getting dark out and the sun's on our side now."

Kevin took the keys and phone from Trish. Michael pulled her over to the corner to have a quick chat with her; they talked quietly for a couple of minutes, eventually resulting in some clear agitation from Michael, before he calmed down a few seconds later. When they were finished, they found Joseph, Erin and Kevin waiting just outside the door of the room. They walked down the hall toward the side lot to where the pickup had been moved.

"Something up?" Joseph asked as he neared.

"Later Doc. You still got that gun Kevin?" Michael asked.

"I've got it," he answered. "Expecting some serious trouble?"

"I suppose. I can't see them changing horses in midstream."

"Probably not." And the two friends waited near the hospital's entrance door.

Trish and Erin were already in when Joseph plopped down behind the truck's steering wheel. He pulled out of the side lot and continued through the main parking lot, hesitating near the exit. In the rear seat, Erin had already dialed the number and it was ringing.

"Yep," Kevin answered.

"We're ready."

"So are we." He pulled the door open for Michael. "If they shoot me, I'll never forgive you."

"If they shoot us," Michael retorted, "it won't matter whether you do or not! Let's get this over with."

Michael and Kevin walked quickly, but steadily, to the rental car, trying hard to look as if they hadn't a care in the world. Tompkins spied them immediately and struggled to catch a better view through the scope sight he'd pulled from its case. "They're leaving in two vehicles" he called over the walkie-talkie. "You lead out and I'll follow in behind."

Kevin revved up the engine as Michael settled into the passenger seat. Joseph was pulling from the exit way as the Explorer rolled out of its space.

As Kevin pulled from the parking lot, Michael watched as the silver Ford hesitated behind them, a passenger jumping from the vehicle and running across the lot. The sedan finally pulled out, reassuring Michael that nothing was likely to happen before their planned split. Regardless, his eyes remained glued to the rear and the trailing silver sedan, wondering when the second guy would join.

The defining moment of truth came in a short few miles. Kevin pulled up to Aneth's lone stoplight in the right lane, Joseph to his left. The silver Ford pulled to a halt a few cars behind them in the right lane. When the light turned green, Kevin made his right turn and Joseph pulled forward through the light and into a gas station on the intersection's far side, slightly diverging from the plan. Joseph watched as the silvery menace hesitated for a moment, its driver talking to someone as he turned right to follow the Explorer. Joseph paused for the light to change twice before slowly proceeding south as planned. Erin maintained her vigil on the intersection until she saw what Trish had reasoned.

A champagne colored Buick sedan pulled into the gas aisle across from them.

"That's the other guy right there," Trish said, motioning toward the sedan. Its driver keeping his head turned slightly from view.

"Are you sure?" Joseph quizzed her.

"Positive. Would know that man anywhere."

Erin broke in suddenly. "Hey, look at that," pointing back toward the intersection. Trish and Joseph watched as another silver sedan drove through the light and followed along Michael and Kevin's route.

"So?" Joseph asked again.

"They're following them, too," Erin said as the big car rounded the corner.

"Maybe, maybe not," Trish said. "It could be coincidence, but then again I can't imagine why a town this small would need an undercover car. Better tell the boss, just in case."

"Hold off 'til I get rolling. We can make sure this other guy is on us."

They pulled out of the station and Trish took the phone from Joseph. She dialed the number and Michael quickly answered.

"Yeah."

"I think you've got two on you, boss. The two I saw in the Stratler have split up and are in separate cars. One on us, one on you in the first silver car."

"First silver car?"

"Yeah, they're very unoriginal. I could only make out one for sure in the second car, but it could just be coincidence and have nothing to do with us. I can't be sure. You should be looking for them, though. It could be back-up or it could be nothing."

"OK. That helps. I'll keep an eye out."

"You'd better ride fast. The second is probably only a mile behind you."

"You get your copy of that memo from Kevin?"

"Got it."

"If we don't get through, you know what to do."

"I do, but you will. You've been in tight jams before."

"Yeah, let's hope so. Call me in forty-five minutes. That'll tell us."

"Good luck, boss and remember these guys always have another." She hung up and handed the phone back to Joseph.

"Now, what are we going to do about our friend behind us?" Trish asked.

"I think I've got a plan that might work," Joseph said calmly, putting the phone on speaker and dialing.

"Navajo Tribal Police."

"Chief Yazzie, please."

"May I say who's calling?"

"Dr. Joseph Begay."

"One moment, please."

"He's Bear Clan. A distant cousin of Benjamin. I fixed his kid's broken leg a couple of weeks ago. Said if I ever needed anything, just call. This seems like an appropriate time."

"Can't think of a better time," Trish said, relief apparent in her voice.

The phone crackled. "Dr. Begay, what a pleasant surprise. What can I do for you?"

"I have a little favor to ask."

"Anything, Doc."

"I'm just outside Aneth, on my way down 191. I've got a Buick tailgating me and I don't think they're just trying to get to know me better."

"Yeah, we've had some problems with some cowboys up there. Drove my son off the road and banged him up, but you know that."

"Yes I do. Maybe the same guys, so I'm a little nervous." Joseph turned and winked in Trish and Erin's general direction. "Do you think you could get one of your boys to intercept them? I've got a surgery patient waiting for me in Kayenta and I really don't have time for this nonsense right now."

"I've got someone up there now. Checking speed just over the reservation boundary. I'll give him a yell with the proper solution. Give me a call back if you have any other problems. Are you in your truck?"

"Yes, I am. And thanks, Chief."

"We'll handle it."

Joseph hung up and set the phone down on the console. "That should take care of our problem in about ten minutes."

In less time than expected, they were crossing into the Navajo Nation. A beat-up old black and white Chevy Blazer with the nation's insignia sat ahead and perpendicular to them. Joseph waved to the tribal cop as he passed and the Blazer pulled out, placing himself between the two vehicles.

Joseph accelerated, noticing in his rear-view mirror the Buick slowing behind the Blazer. The Buick's driver clearly didn't quite know what to do now that he was trapped behind the tribal vehicle. Joseph began putting distance between him and the sedan until finally the Buick burst from behind the Blazer and began to pass, the driver's hand clearly forced by the danger of completely losing his target. The tribal officer hit his lights and siren before the car had even pulled in ahead of him, but the Buick continued on, now obviously in pursuit at high speed. The old Blazer fell back in the distance, lights still flashing. Joseph stepped hard onto the accelerator, keeping his distance from the pursuit.

In another ten minutes Joseph slowed as he crested a long hill, the trailing vehicle now a mere half-mile behind. He turned right at the unannounced intersection and onto U.S. 160, through a gantlet of Tribal Police vehicles. As soon as Joseph eased around the corner, the road was completely plugged by the vehicles.

When the pursuing sedan crested the hill itself, its brakes squealed and it veered to the right shoulder. Dodging around the line of cruisers, its driver tried desperately to round the corner. The bumps and sand along the shoulder did nothing for steering and the sedan danced over the asphalt of 160, across its southern side, before becoming airborne for a few seconds and crashing back to the ground in a cloud of dust.

The tribal cops instantly surrounded the dust-covered sedan and Joseph sped away with a chuckle. Trish grabbed the phone from the console and dialed.

"Yeah," the transmission crackled.

"We got rid of ours. We're safely out."

"Turn left here, Kevin" and a loud rumbling came from the other end. Trish tensed.

"Michael?"

"Yeah. Yeah. We're still here. Man, can this boy drive!" Laughter cackled through the receiver. "We're having a little trouble with ours. Gotta go. We'll call you later. Hopefully." The phone went dead.

"Turn left here." The Explorer fled down another unpaved road, sliding to find its course. The rear vehicle erred slightly and slid off the side of the road, the silver sedan swerving dramatically, but the driver finally regained control, after being forced to an almost full stop. The menace got back onto the roadway, but had lost valuable time in its pursuit, now nearly a mile behind. As it regained speed, Michael made out the second car's lights easing around the corner, not making the same mistake. The second car was obviously not in the same hurry.

"Kevin, you know where we are?"

"Somewhat."

"Well, here in about two miles you're going to make a left back onto the paved highway. We've got plenty of time to get around the corner, so don't miss it."

"OK."

"Once we get on pavement you need to start getting a good lead on 'em."

"What do you have in mind?"

"A little surprise if we do it right. After you get on the pavement, punch it to eighty-five and hit the cruise control. The road's perfectly straight."

"Then what?"

"You'll see. Just trust me, OK?"

"Okay, but that's a dangerous thought."

"Fair enough. The turn is just up here; slow down!"

Kevin hit the brakes in time to make a controlled turn and then accelerated quickly.

"By the way, how's your night vision."

"Not bad. Why?"

"Well, I've got a plan. In a second we're going to turn off the headlights and give 'em something to think about."

"My night vision isn't that good. I won't be able to see a damn thing."

"Only for just a few seconds. It's almost a full moon. There'll be plenty of light after our eyes adjust. Whadda ya say?"

"I say you're insane."

"Just a bit, but they don't know that. They're on our turf now and they'll never know what hit 'em. You just strap in. We're going to take them for the ride of their life. When we get stopped up here, get away from the car as fast as you can. Keep that gun with you and be ready. Don't worry about me, just get away. Remember, there might be a second car."

"I got it, but I don't like this."

"Neither do I, but we don't have much choice in the matter. Try and think of it as excitement in your life. Once you crest this hill and they're out of sight, kill the lights."

"You mean kill us." Kevin shut off the lights on cue, sending them into total blackness for a few anxious seconds. Their eyes slowly adjusted and everything started lighting up. Michael looked back and watched as the two sets of lights reappeared. The first trailing driver flashed his brights on and off in a desperate attempt to find the Explorer.

Michael turned back to his friend. "Here's what I've got in mind . . ."

* * *

"What the hell are they doing?" Tompkins asked himself out loud. His military GPS didn't have any thing on its maps but a straight line. He hadn't heard from Benson in a while despite squawking him several times on the radio and he was beginning to wonder what was going on with his end. His eyes strained hard through the darkness, catching an occasional brake tap in the distance from his prey. Probably just trying to fake me out, he thought. Probably try to turn off and ditch me, but I'll be watching. Again the vehicle in front of him hit his brakes. He can't see a thing. The road's perfectly straight and he's braking, trying to find a way out. He's trapped and he knows it. The little mouse. Now I'll fix that bastard. He accelerated to catch the fleeing vehicle.

* * *

"Anyway, Kev, you got the idea?"

"I guess."

"Come on, boys, don't let up now!" Michael exclaimed back toward their pursuers.

"You really have lost your mind."

"Just keep tapping your brakes every so often."

Kevin kept the speed up and, at random intervals, he touched the brakes once or twice as if he were slowing. Michael could just hear what they must be thinking. "What is this guy, stupid? Doesn't know where he is?" Just keep coming, he thought, chuckling aloud.

Kevin looked at him queerly. "I hope you know what you're doing."

"I do too, but we'll know soon enough. There'll be some signs up here on the right. You need to take them out."

"Gotcha. I'm getting the plan."

"Good. You ever been this way?"

"No, only from the other side with you and Joseph, but I've got a pretty good idea what to do when I get there."

"Good. Slow down a bit and let him catch up a little."

Kevin eased up on the gas. He spied the diagonal yellow sign ahead in the distance. He slid to the right a few feet, onto the shoulder, clipping the post with the right front bumper as they flashed past.

Michael did some quick math in his head. "There should be a couple more signs, Kev. When I tell you, start counting seconds with me."

"Why?"

"Timing, buddy . . . timing. When we get to that last sign, we should have about a half mile left. Keep us around fifty for fifteen seconds and then slow her down as fast as you can without hitting the brakes. Let's try not to let him know what's up."

"I've got the idea." He swung the Explorer to the right again as a second diagonal yellow sign appeared in the distance. Michael noted the mileage on the odometer as Kevin moved further to the right and clipped the sign from its base.

"Nice shot."

"Thanks but the rental guys aren't going to be happy." The explorer continued its flow along the asphalt course, over the small waves of rises and valleys.

"There should be another sign in about fifteen seconds. Nail it and then back off the accelerator, get to the middle of the road and roll the windows down so we can hear."

Kevin began counting fifteen seconds to himself, staying on the right shoulder. The truck glided down the small hill and he slid his foot to the brake giving it one hard press. He angled toward the last sign, smashing it down with the bumper. Just then the pavement ran out, and the left tires hit gravel. Simultaneously Michael began the count, yelling, "One! Two!" Kevin started his own count, rechecking the odometer as the truck rolled up another hill. The Explorer slowed to forty, then thirty-five, speed continuing to drop as they cresting the hill. The sedan gained momentum and crested the rises a half mile behind them, quickly closing the gap.

"Fourteen! Fifteen!" Kevin slid the transmission into second as he started down the ridge into another dip. The Explorer's chassis lurched forward as the wheels dropped to the lower gear and the engine let out a loud wail. The vehicle slowed quickly and Kevin pulled the arm down into first, sending it into a slight skid as it reached the crest of a final ridge. He stayed off the brakes, slowing to twenty, fifteen. The seconds passed like an eternity and Kevin corrected course to the middle of the road, the chase car bounding over the last rise behind them and closing fast.

Kevin moved his foot nearer the brake and glanced at the odometer, watching for some point in the distance and slightly downward. The tail car dropped from immediate sight behind the last low rise, now only a few hundred feet behind them.

* * *

I've got 'em now, Tompkins told himself. They won't get away this time. Hold her steady. Just a couple more seconds.

* * *

313

Kevin finally caught Michael's point of reference.

"Hold on, buddy," he hollered, yanking the parking brake and turning the wheel hard to the left. His right hand dived to the gearshift, slamming it up to neutral as the rear slithered around behind them, bouncing off washboards, seemingly out of control. Kevin pounced on the brakes and let go of the wheel, the truck completing a one-eighty, bouncing to its left into the side ditch, bumping up against a small furrowed berm just outside Michael's door and slamming him into the passenger door, pain shooting through his shoulder. The rotation had brought the pursuing car into full view. "Hit the lights!" Michael screamed and Kevin instantly pulled the switch.

* * *

When he crested the hill, he was instantly blinded. "What the fuck!" and he instinctively hit his brakes, but it was far too late. He'd been had.

The silver car passed the Explorer at high speed and leapt headlong into the roadless separation of the Mokidugway, headed in freefall to the valley two thousand feet below.

* * *

"Get out!" Michael screamed breathlessly, grimacing from the pain in his shoulder, trying to open the door but only pounding into the side of the berm.

Kevin scrambled from the truck, instinctively slamming the door behind him, heading for the rear and watching as the silver menace's headlights bent down in its death charge toward the valley floor. He was rounding the back of the Explorer as the second set of lights crested the hill in front of him. He stepped back behind the vehicle.

The car closed cautiously on the gravel road. The Explorer's broken grille squarely fixed in its lights as it approached. It pulled to a stop in front of the Explorer blinding Michael in its bright lights. He tried frantically to open his door banging it into the bank. He could see the man get out of his car and start toward the Explorer. Michael tried to scramble over the seat toward the back but his shoulder wouldn't permit it. The man advanced and in a moment was at the driver's side door.

He smiled coldly, stroking his bushy mustache between his forefinger and thumb. "You've been very troubling, Mr. Kincaid," he said as he reached inside his jacket pocket, pulling a 9mm from its shoulder holster. He raised the gun toward Michael's head.

"Time to go to bed, Mr. Kincaid."

An explosion shattered the still night air causing the man to step back for a moment, surveying the fiery scene far below them to his right. "I see you've been very clever Mr. Kincaid. Thank you for making my job easier." The cleaner leveled the gun back into position as Michael pushed with all his might against the door, it finally slowly pushing open. A deafening gunshot rang out, the projectile landing with a deep thud, penetrating its mark. A moment later a second shot lit the sky for another millisecond. The berm finally relented and the door slid open, spilling a limp Michael to the ground with a thump. His body released a loud sound of air escaping from the force of the landing. "Uhhhf!"

"Michael!" Kevin called as a lone coyote's sullen wail began to rise over the Mokidugway.

* * *

"Good evening, sir," Anderson said when he reached the bench at the base of the Tidal Basin.

"I'm not sure about that, son. I've learned some distressing things about our operation in the past several hours. It is my understanding that our mutual associate has significantly overstepped his bounds on this assignment. It appears you were right. I want this shut down and stopped, right now. This was never supposed to end up like this. Do you have a plan for this?"

"Well, sir, I do. Unfortunately, though, from what I've learned, we're going to have to let some of this play itself out. But I must also tell you that it seems to me, if a wolf is creating troubles in your chicken-house, then you'd better do something to get that wolf out of there."

"This wolf is certainly creating problems. Do we have a possible solution as to this wolf problem, Lieutenant Commander?"

"Possibly, sir, and perhaps remove myself from further involvement in order that the operation may continue at some future date. We must assume that my position has been permanently compromised with the agency by these affairs, too."

"For that you have my apologies, Lieutenant Commander. As I've said before, you've always served our cause well and someday I hope you are aptly rewarded. If you have a plan that will end this, I would long be grateful."

"I'll spare you the exact details, sir, but I do believe that with your help this will solve the problem."

"I will trust your judgment here. It seems you are our last hope of salvation. Please let me know what you need."

"Yes, sir. First, I'll need full access to our resources in the Caribbean."

"That will be no problem. When will you need it?"

"By tomorrow."

"I'll have it done immediately. I assume while you are there you should eliminate the financial strings that may become problematic. Move things somewhere that no one can find it after you obtain what you'll need. Once you wrap this up, perhaps you should take yourself a long vacation. I'll have someone arrange your emergency deactivation for health reasons. Do you have any idea when this will be finished?"

"Tonight or tomorrow, sir."

"Upon completion, perhaps you'll allow our Caribbean friends to accommodate your extended holiday. I'm sure they would be happy to entertain you for a while. You deserve it. I'll get in touch with you through friends after you're well rested. Bigger and better days are ahead for you, son."

"Thank you, sir." He knew he'd never see these people again if all worked out. One last thing, sir. . . ." and Anderson leaned in to the Old Man's ear.

After a few minutes and a couple of nods by both men, Anderson rose from the bench and began to walk back down the pathway leading to the wooden tunnel and the parking lot, leaving the Old Man behind. He glanced over his shoulder when he was halfway back to his car. The dark figure continued to sit by water's edge, feeding the ducks gathered at the pool's edge with peanuts he was extracting from his jacket pocket. He seemed a paradoxical figure compared to the massive nearby cast of the man who had been so instrumental in this entire affair. From his hand had come the creation of the monetary and power systems that had become the mistresses of the Old Man and EZL, and now their likely doom. He was enraged to think that the Old Man and their cause would take the hits for the troll's blunders. But with the proper execution of his plan, maybe, just maybe, he could get them both out of this with their skins intact.

* * *

The seconds passed like hours as he scrambled over the berm to reach his motionless friend.

"Michael! Michael! Talk to me, buddy!"

"Calm down," came a groan from the still figure. "I'm all right." In a few moments he lifted his head to look at Kevin, saying, "Well, I guess I'm not dead, so I take it you're a pretty good shot."

"I do all right in a pinch. But I gotta tell you, old buddy, that's twice today I've thought you were dead. Don't do that anymore."

"I'll see what I can do."

He rolled over to a sitting position, glancing under the vehicle to see the dead cleaner only a few feet from him on the other side. Kevin helped Michael up and they walked around to the back of the vehicle and took a seat on the top of the berm.

"Ahhh, I always loved the Mokidugway, Kevin. The prettiest spot on the planet."

"For most, anyway," casting a finger toward the sprawled man, now oozing crimson into the desert sand. "You ok Michael?"

"I'll manage. It seems we've got some clean-up to do just in case there's a third group."

"Don't even think it."

"You think you can get that thing out of there?" he asked, pointing to the tilted Explorer.

"I don't know. I did a pretty bad parking job. We'll see."

"I think we should grab his gun too. Don't touch it, maybe there's a rag or something in the vehicle."

Kevin stood from the berm and walked back up to the vehicle, assessing its stability. He dragged the mustachioed man's lifeless body toward where he had parked his car, just minutes before, in his previous life.

He returned to the Explorer, retrieved a t-shirt he found in the back, got the gun, got in and started it, dropped it into four-wheel low, and on the second try, it came out easily. He pointed it down the graveled mountain roadway and shut off the engine and lights before rejoining Michael. He was pulling the sling from his neck and stuffing it into his back pocket.

"Lets get that nice little fellow up in his car."

"Let's also try not to touch anything on the car, just in case," Michael warned.

Kevin opened the passenger side door with his shirttail, and they pushed the body in. Michael pulled his arm from under the corpse and kicked the door shut. He flexed his left arm slightly before going around to the driver's side.

"I'll pull the car over here to that hidden spot in the trees," Michael explained, pointing up the road. "We'll have Joseph call it in—later—to his friend the chief. Then we'd better get out of here and get this thing exposed before we join him."

Kevin was nodding as Michael got in and backed the sedan up to the top of the knoll. He was careful not to touch anything except with the hand now encased in the removed sling. Someone would eventually need to look through this for evidence and he didn't really want to add any of his own. He put the car into drive and eased forward into the deep pullout surrounded by piñon and cedar trees. He put the car into park and turned the engine off, pulling the keys and slid them under the seat. As he got out, he pulled the dead man flat into the seat with his good arm. Perhaps he would remain unnoticed by any passerby until the tribal police got here. Kicking the door shut, he turned to head back to the Explorer. "Do you still have the gun, just in case?" he called.

"Of course."

"Good, grab the phone and then come join me for a little chat. Let's see if we have service and maybe we can figure this shit out." Michael walked over near the edge of the Mokidugway, taking a seat on the red rock that formed the top of the massive cliff. Kevin joined him in a few minutes and took a seat on the monolith that had saved their lives, two old friends enjoying the moonlit view. They both gazed over the edge to the burning wreck far below them. "You sure we shouldn't go, Michael? What if someone sees that burning car?"

"Right now I'm not sure about anything, but don't worry. There isn't anyone around here for forty miles. Nobody would find it for ages if we didn't call it in. There's not even a road out there. Just sand. The fire will be out in a bit and nobody will notice until we tell them."

The phone rang in Kevin's hand, the shrill ring piercing the still air. He handed it to Michael "I'm sure it's for you."

"Gee, thanks," he said, taking the phone. "Heaven, how may I direct your call?"

There was a slight pause.

"I guess you must still be alive. Where in heaven are you going to find a lawyer?"

"Very funny, Erin, but I've heard that one before."

"Everything okay?"

"Just peachy. We lost our friend, so we should be there in an hour or so."

"Great. See you then."

"Bye."

He hung up and turned back to Kevin. "Well, what do ya think, buddy?"

"I think this is a big mess!"

"That's for damn sure."

"What's this all about, Michael?"

"Money and political power, I suppose."

"Yeah . . . but I still don't understand," Kevin said.

"I'll agree that it's pretty tough to figure, but you read the memo, didn't you?"

"Sure, and I get the general idea, but it does leave some gaps."

"Well, you have most of the information, but let me fill in a few of the details you might not have and then I think you'll get the bigger picture. It's really pretty simple, but very sad."

"All right, we'll see."

"Seems it all starts many years ago. Two guys were sent in to scout a Japanese-held island; a third was used to pick them up at the end of their mission."

"Peleliu, I suppose?"

"Seems that way. Anyway, the mission was named 'Code Easel.' The idea was to go in and sketch the area so the Marines could take it and, most importantly, its airfield. It was the first part of Luigi's dying message, 'Cody Zell.' Same thing as in that memo, except they called it 'Code EZL' but if you sound it out . . . The second part of the message was to alert Joseph's grandfather. Luigi had nicknamed him 'Yeh Tay' during their training in the war."

"So Luigi was trying to warn Joseph's grandfather?"

"Kind of, I think, but not really. I think he was just trying to let him know some form of the operation was active again and he was dying because of it. A clue to his death, really, as opposed to a warning."

"But how in the hell did Luigi get hold of the memo?"

"I'm not perfectly sure about that, but it really doesn't matter. I'm sure we'll find out pretty quick. All we know for sure is that Luigi flew off somewhere last week. A few days later he ends up dead, leaving behind that little gem we found stashed in the water cooler. Next thing we know we've got people shooting at us. The only thing I can guess is that wherever he went, probably LA, he went there on business. Maybe in the process of opening a safe he saw the memo. Operation EZL/Peleliu showed up pretty easily in the title so I think maybe he snatched it."

"But wouldn't they have seen him take it?"

"Well, I don't know. Based upon what Luigi told me, maybe not."

"Whaddya mean?"

"Well, we had a pretty long talk the day before he died. One of the things he told me was that he was routinely alone when he opened safes for people like the DEA. Apparently the DEA made it a practice of clearing the room when he'd open a drug dealer's safe just in case it was booby-trapped. He told me that left him alone and in peace to do his work so he never dissuaded them from their assumption. Besides, it gave him a chance to browse around inside the safe before they got their grubby little hands in there."

"You know, Michael, I seem to remember reading about some large-scale DEA bust in Los Angeles last week. Now that I think about it, probably about the same time as when Luigi left, and certainly within his turf out there. The newspaper said that when the agents got inside, they found the guy dead on the floor. Did you hear anything about that?"

"Yeah, now that you mention it, I believe I did. Something on the radio when I was leaving LA. Wasn't the guy some sort of big cheese for one of the cartels or something like that?"

"Maybe, I mean I think that's what they thought at first, but I also read somewhere he had ties to some pharmaceutical company in Arizona."

"I remember thinking that it sure seemed odd that the guy would be dead before they raided the place. Very strange. I wonder if it fits in this."

"But how did a drug dealer get a document like this in the first place?"

"Well, that is the sixty-four-thousand dollar question, now, isn't it? Who knows? But if we're right, he got it somehow and it really doesn't matter how. I'd bet, though," Michael paused before continuing, "that he was the conduit."

"Conduit? What are you talking about?"

"Bear with me a sec; trying to sort it out myself. I really only got a cursory read of that memo, so correct me if I'm wrong here, but it talks about using EZL to covertly fund what it calls 'capital improvements.' Luigi probably would have never have even noticed the memo if they hadn't been so stupid as to put EZL on the subject line. So . . . I guess the last piece of the puzzle is what are these 'capital improvements' and where they're being done. Then maybe we can get to the ultimate answers."

"Seems a reasonable approach to me," Joseph said. "Got any ideas?"

"Some guesses, that's about it."

"Well, let's hear 'em."

"Well, people like this don't do something unless it benefits them substantially. That being a given and the elaborate nature of this entire thing, what if this was to in some way benefit a US 'capital improvement'? Let's say what we're dealing with here is really a reversed Code Easel and the target is the US."

"Oh, yeah, right. Japan's going to bomb us with our government's help. Get real!"

"No, no, no. Hear me out. What if the ultimate objective was to make something happen here to benefit whoever's behind this? Luigi told me that one of Code Easel's primary objectives was to have a base for protecting McArthur's backside and possibly targeting Thailand. Let's assume this Code EZL had Thailand sitting as the source rather than the target. They send those cases of MREs filed with counterfeit pills from Thailand to Peleliu somehow. Then they pack them up into a big C-130 or whatever and drop them off out there," Michael said, pointing out from the Mokidugway across Monument Valley toward White Horse Ruins. "Now if you're going to go to that much of an effort to set up a clandestine operation like this, there's got to be a damn good reason . . . and I don't think it's just the money."

"Probably," Kevin interjected. "It's a logical conclusion. That memo's certainly about generating big bucks for something."

"So I would guess the idea was to ship large quantities of these knockoff prescription drugs via Peleliu to White Horse Ruins and then through that AzMediCo company to the world's largest prescription drug-consuming nation, the U.S. Simple economics, supply and demand, and maybe even backed by one of the cartels."

"Wouldn't the Peleliu people find the drugs?"

"Under normal circumstances, maybe, but these aren't normal circumstances. First, we have drugs marked as MREs, purposely mislabeled likely under the guise of not letting the average soldier know these were prescription drugs and risk theft along the way, at least according to that memo. Then AzMediCo picks them up to be destroyed, which really is not the case. So as a result, we've got a dead drug dealer with the memo, who may have ties to an Arizona pharma company, and I doubt that's a coincidence." He glanced to his friend with a wry grin. "We have to be dealing with some pretty high-ups in the US government, higher than this Tielson or Anderson. Look at who's been chasing us. The use of the US Attorneys office, the missing body and the military eavesdropping equipment Leonardo's people found. Even somehow using US military planes to bring it in. So since Peleliu was a former US trust territory after the war, there'd be no problem getting drugs in and out under these circumstances. US military planes have been landing there for years."

"So the U.S. government is dealing drugs? Come on, Michael, I can't believe that."

"Believe it, buddy, because it is true. Maybe not the entire U.S. government per se, but certainly some of its ranks. That memo also mentions 'other foreign contacts'. As deep as this goes, that also means some pretty heavyweight people like Thai or Central American cartels or both."

"All for money?"

"Probably not just for money, but then again, why not? Capitalism at its best. Which brings us back to the conduit. I'd bet that dead drug dealer and his people were in it for the money for sure. Let's just say he's the conduit for this entire operation, the dispenser of the drugs and the collector of the money. He gets his cut and EZL gets its, so we need to find out who this AzMediCo sells to. They in turn probably pass the profits through some cartel run, no-questions-asked offshore bank, funnel it back to whomever to be used to serve their purposes. It's these other purposes that make this so interesting."

"Other purposes?"

"Sure. The best part. The other part, I gotta believe, is that other great seducer of men. Power."

"Power?"

"Power. Which brings us to the author and the addressee of the memorandum."

"Mr. Tielson and Mr. Mak?" Kevin suggested.

"Yep," he returned.

"Who are they?"

"I think you know Mr. Mak."

"I do?"

"Sure. My bet is it's the Right Honorable Senator McRae from California."

"Not Howard McRae," Kevin protested. "Not the guy running for president. Not Luigi's friend."

"The very same one."

"What makes you think Mak is McRae? Mak could be Asian, too."

"Yeah, but there's only one Mak involved with Easel. Couple that with the fact that Luigi called him only days before he died and its way too many coincidences."

"But why? What would make him want to kill him?"

"I don't know. Maybe he didn't have much of a choice; maybe he doesn't even know. There may even be some form of political blackmail going on here. For years, politicians have had a habit of taking contributions from some pretty nefarious fellows. And the election laws let them."

Kevin sat quietly now, taking it all in.

"They all do it and we allow it. It takes millions to win a Senate seat and millions more to become president. You can't do that on a Congressional salary. You might be able to do it on old money and clout like Kennedy or Bush, but McRae's not old money. With each step up the ladder of power, there'd be new fundraising and new alliances. What if his hunger for power became so great that he didn't care if he allied himself with a cartel to form EZL? And what better way to keep Justice out of their business then to have their own man at the top? I don't know. We'll probably never really know, but I'll bet these 'capital improvements' were meant for Washington. 'Capital improvement' with its reward of the highest kind of power. They must have thought they could buy a presidential election with all the money they'd be generating. Probably could have from his position. Look at what money did for Perot and he didn't have half the standing of a McRae."

"You mean they were funding his presidential campaign with counterfeit pharmaceutical money?"

"Certainly looks that way. If I'm right, that would certainly be a good enough motive to kill. I've seen people killed for a hell of a lot less reason."

"I guess so." But Kevin couldn't really understand or believe this. He was still puzzled. "But getting those pills in without any inspection? How can you just land a plane from overseas, drop off a bunch of pills and nobody notice?"

"All good questions. All easily solved by the ranking member of the Armed Services Committee."

"McRae?"

"McRae. Oh, and this Tielson too. That's where he comes in."

"Yeah, him. Who's he?"

"I have absolutely no idea, but I've got a guess based upon what Joseph's brother said." He paused a little too long.

"C'mon, Michael, quit playing your jury games."

"OK. OK. You deserve not to be held in suspense, but it's only speculation. Tielson brings us back to Code EZL. He's got to be someone McRae could trust, probably a former aide or something. Tielson actually is probably the main guy. The facilitator, the one making it happen on a daily basis."

"But they still had to get the drugs here from Peleliu and sell them to get money."

"Well, let's say McRae was seduced by power. He knew the tactical significance of Peleliu and Code Easel. After all, he was the third man on the original mission and, more importantly, he was the pilot. He could have laid the route right out for them, then easily sold the operation to the military or to the Armed Services Committee as clandestine and without much detail or simply say they were rotating old MREs or expired pharmaceuticals, doesn't matter. I can think of couple of ways they could have sold it, as in the memo." Kevin nodded his understanding.

"Joseph told us the military hands out prescription drugs like candy. The government buys them in large quantities from the big pharmaceutical companies for the military, the VA and other projects. But prescription drugs expire. When they expire they can't be given and have to be destroyed. What if McRae somehow got control over both the VA's med acquisition and destruction operations. He could get the old drugs and probably repackage the stuff if he got it all back to one spot in the U.S., then sell it to someone else with a remarked expiration date. He could gather all the old stuff from all the bases in the Far East, bring it into Peleliu, then add in some extra counterfeits brought in from Thailand to build out the full load. They'd have secure supply lines from all over Southeast Asia into Peleliu and eventually then on to the Arizona desert. All through the military and through whatever excuse they dreamed up to sell it. I assume everything gets gathered on Peleliu where there's minimal activity these days, and then launch the planes from there back to the United States dropping their cargo out there near White House Ruins. The counterfeits come in from Thailand, South Korea, Vietnam or China, take your pick, all have counterfeit drug manufacturing issues. It's a reverse Code Easel with the supplies coming out of instead of in to Peleliu. Add in some in-air refueling and they wouldn't even have to land. All they needed was someone to run it once set up."

"Tielson?"

"I guess. McRae certainly has the power to appoint a special position or a National Security Advisor from the committee. No one in the military would ever question anything Tielson did; he was the chairman's boy. They'd give him whatever he wanted. After all, why take a chance pissing off the guy who's got the most control and influence over military budgeting? 'You want a C-130 and crew, Mr. Tielson? Sure, no problem. You want special military clearance and refueling on some far-off western Pacific island, Mr. Tielson? Sure, no problem.' No matter what he asked for, he'd have gotten, no questions asked."

"But that still doesn't answer how they could bring the drugs in."

"The same way the Colombians and Mexicans do. Fly it into that remote dirt strip out there; the military guys can land on anything. Hell, they could swoop in low on so-called training missions and make pinpoint drops by parachute, with their ground people standing by to pick it up. Then the plane just flies on to wherever it's supposed to go, no questions asked, or something to that effect."

"But if they land or swooped down for the drop, wouldn't somebody ask questions? I mean, those are pretty big planes."

"That's just the pilot and the FAA in you saying that, Kevin. Generally you'd be right, but for the fact of where we're talking about. There's nothing out there but a few hogans. And as I said, they'd just make the drops part of the maneuver; stops and drops happen every night out in that area. There's so many."

"And obviously they're dropping the packages at that base where Joseph's at?"

"Exactly. That's more or less what the Mexicans do, on smaller scale of course. Just watch the horizon out there. If you watch carefully you see planes dip down out of sight, then a few minutes later they rise up again, in basically the same spot. According to people I know, FBI and others, it's a pretty common practice. That's just the various drug shipments coming in from Mexico. When I was younger and more naive I used to come up here and think they were planes landing in Phoenix. I came to learn it was just the multi-million dollar business of drugs. Their runners pick it up and a few minutes later it's headed in several different directions to various distributors all over the country. People make a big deal about cocaine or heroin coming in on boats to South Florida but that's a drop in the bucket compared to what's dropped out here and driven across the Arizona border."

"How do you know this for sure?"

"Let's just say I had a client I defended a couple of years ago who taught me more about the drug trade than I ever wanted to know. The feds made him out to be the largest supplier in the entire western United States. I guess to get me to understand that he wasn't, he explained all this. I confirmed most of it with my buddy at the FBI. What's interesting, though, was that he was always saying someone, and I didn't ask whom, made him look small time. He said they wouldn't just bring in average quantities, but very, very large amounts of whatever they wanted to."

"And you think that could be McRae."

"You mean McRae and his associates? You bet I do; just not how I originally envisioned it."

"This is crazy, Michael."

"That's for sure, but what's really crazy is it's obviously possible and no one will ever believe us unless we tie it all together in a nice neat package and get it to the proper people. Only then will we be safe. They'll be out of business then."

"Have you got any ideas?"

"One."

They sat motionless for several minutes watching the stars, lights and planes. Kevin finally made a snort of disgust. "Let's go, bud. Let's finish this. I keep watching all those planes out there and thinking of all the damage they're doing. Now you tell me the guy who might be our next president is involved in this and I just don't know what to think."

"Try not to; it'll just drive you crazy. We'll get to Joseph's and I'll start making some calls. I've got to figure out how AzMediCo fits in all this. We've got these bastards now, though. You can count on that. And they're not getting away."

"I hope not."

Slowly, Michael stood up, the stiffness of the last twenty-four hours having set in. They got in the vehicle and Kevin drove them down the mesa's steep, narrow exit. As they neared the bottom, they noted the plume from the now smoldering car, the flames long since gone. By morning it would appear from the distance as merely an old, abandoned burn-out, exactly what it was.

They were back to Joseph's in a short thirty minutes. Michael had sat quiet in thought for most of the way and Kevin was on the verge of sleep by the time the dogs greeted them. Erin, Trish, and Joseph were out the door with the first bark.

"You look like hell," Joseph observed.

"Fresh as a daisy," Kevin volunteered.

"You two OK?" Trish asked.

"Fine," Michael answered as Erin came to his side with a hug.

"You'd better let me take a look at that shoulder there, cowboy" the doctor ordered. "Then you're off to bed for some rest."

"You're the doc." Michael headed for the porch with Erin under his arm, his physician in tow.

In about twenty minutes Joseph returned, saying his patient would be fine and that Erin and Michael had retired. He stepped outside for a few minutes, returning with a twelve-pack of beer, offering one to his remaining guests. They drank slowly, sipping the cold brew until Kevin asked Joseph, "What happened to your guy?"

"Not sure, really. Last time we saw him, my friends from the tribal police had him surrounded like a covered wagon."

"Now that's some ironic frontier justice" and Kevin went back to his beer.

DAY ELEVEN

Questions Answered

Anderson had emerged from the bank by 9:15, a large smile barely suppressed on his face. In fifteen short minutes he'd managed to pick up enough traveling money to keep him going for a while and transferred the remaining several-odd million to a recently established Argentinean account. The bank was only too happy to immediately process their regular customer's request, having received prior notice and approval.

"Where to, mon?" the driver called as Anderson reached his ride.

"Back to the airport." The driver swiftly complied.

In another ten short minutes the car was parked in front of the terminal.

"I'll need you to pick me up again tonight or tomorrow. The pilot will call you with our ETA."

"Back so soon, mon?"

"Yes. I've been told I need a vacation after I've finished this trip. Thought I might do a little fishing. What do you think?"

"That's OK, mon. The fishin' is gooood now. I'll take you to a spot."

"Sounds good, Jim. I'll see you soon." He disappeared out the rear door.

The driver watched as the man hurried into the terminal. "Strange mon, that Anderson mon. But I guess he'll finally get to do some fishin'." Even so, Jim didn't really believe he'd show.

* * *

On the flight back, Anderson had gone over in his mind the escalating events of the last several hours. Tielson had called him about an hour out of Dulles with the news that one of their assets had been arrested by some Navajo cops. He'd had to arrange bail, which was plenty, and then re-arrange more bail after their first attempted to show Washington might brought more charges including flight, destruction of federal property and assault on a federal law enforcement officer for ramming through the roadblock. Apparently the Navajo Nation still didn't think too much of DC messing around in its native lands.

Tompkins and the cleaner hadn't been heard from at all. Tielson was clearly worried. Not for them personally, but for their links to the operation, to him, and what they could divulge. The base was on full alert with orders of "shoot to kill" and "ask questions later." And now the Old Man wanted a meeting with them both as soon as possible.

Anderson was still quiet and cool by the time they had hung up. He'd already confirmed with the Old Man that he now believed it was only a matter of time before this all unraveled. The Old Man had been very angry and it required little effort convincing him to end everything and finish tying up the loose ends. Overnight, the little troll had justifiably been given the blame for the entire mess and had lost all favor with the group.

He sat back in his seat, his eyes closed. The other shoe had now dropped, but he'd known it was coming. He'd do what was necessary and asked of him. He'd already helped clean up the mess with efforts already under way to disband the group, hopefully with no one the wiser. In twenty-four hours, there'd be no sign of Easel. Trucks were being dispatched to close out operations at the base. By evening it would be abandoned again. The appropriate people would issue a debriefing to the Committee announcing that the operation to destabilize a southeast Asian militant wing had been successful; that opposition forces had been supplied with the necessary equipment and arms to eliminate the threat and that the outlook for total success in the region was good. What the debriefing wouldn't tell the Committee was the dirty little secret and side deal that Tielson had made and that Anderson had discovered only over the last few days. There would be some severe heat, but in the end, the links would go unconnected and uncorroborated. Everything would settle down in time, all nice and neat.

Still, Anderson was deeply troubled. How had he gotten mixed up in this entire sordid weapons for drugs affair? He'd only learned the other half of the operation in the last week. How could he have been so stupid as not to have seen what was really going on? When he'd gotten the job with the Committee, all his Annapolis dreams had come true. The Committee had the power to make his career, so he followed each order to the letter, without question. When he'd been promoted to the position with the chairman, it seemed it would all be fulfilled.

All he'd wanted was to serve his country, proudly and professionally. By the time he'd realized the troll had a different agenda, it was too late and he was in too deep. Ironically, he thought, it was now this same sordid operation, and the funds it had generated, that might finally give him the chance to extricate himself. It would be a pleasure, finally, to clean up.

* * *

By the time they reached Keyenta, the Tribal Police offices were a hubbub of activity. Michael, Joseph and Kevin each grabbed two boxes and stepped through the front door. The friends were led back into a conference room where they were quickly joined by the chief and several other officers. "Dr. Begay, thank you for your call."

"Certainly, Chief."

"You've had a rather exciting twenty-four hours, it seems."

"Yes, we have. You need to have a look in these boxes, Chief, then I can explain some of this to you."

The chief and his officers gathered around the table, allowing a plain-clothes detective to inspect each box, and then its contents. Astonished gasps echoed through the room when the detective poured out several hundred pills of Oxycontin onto the table.

"Where did you get this, Dr. Begay?" the detective inquired.

"Over near White Horse Ruins. There's a whole warehouse full of it." He turned to the chief, adding, "This is my friend Michael Kincaid. He can explain the details a bit better."

Michael gave the chief and his officers a thumbnail sketch of the situation, from the murders and the evidence they'd found to the man dead up at the Mokidugway and his friend burned to a crisp on the valley floor. He finally suggested that they get a warrant for that base and seal it off as quickly as they could before things started disappearing. In the end he concluded saying what he really needed was access to a fax machine and a phone for a few minutes to tie up some of the leftover loose ends. Joseph and Kevin began filling in other details as one of the tribal officers led Michael to a desk and showed him the fax and phone. In a short fifteen minutes Michael had completed his research, updated the memo with some handwritten last details, and with the help of the officer sent faxes of the memo and a short handwritten note outlining the affair to the numbers he'd gotten from Trish that morning. The officer then led him back to the others as the chief was thanking them for their assistance. "Thank you too, Mr. Kincaid. We can handle it from here. We've already got men on the way to watch over the base and to secure the sites up at the Mokidugway."

"Thank you, Chief."

"Where can I reach you three if I need to?"

"Durango, Chief. You can get me on my cell phone. Seems the counselor's got a client to get out of jail," Joseph said proudly, drawing a smile from the room.

Outside, Michael stopped Joseph and Kevin near the car where Erin and Trish sat, saying, "It's the VA. That's the final piece. Leonardo somehow got their annual report and it shows AzMediCo's biggest purchaser is the VA."

Joseph shook his head, understanding the implications. Erin looked confused, asking, "Are they giving these to soldiers?"

"I'm afraid so, Erin," Joseph answered, "and very sick soldiers at that."

They split up into the two vehicles. Joseph needed to make some rounds at the hospital and would come over to Durango later. Erin and Michael would drop Kevin and Trish off at the airport as they passed through Aneth, then head straight to Judge Maas, armed with a motion to dismiss the charges against Benjamin. The hearing was already set for 3:30 and they'd barely have enough time to make it as it was. They'd all hook up at the Diamond Belle around five for what Michael promised to be a good time.

They pulled away from the tribal police station, waving good-bye to Joseph. Michael instinctively turned east on 160, this time with no hesitation about his direction home. Ahead, Church Rock announced the way. It had been one helluva ten-day adventure since he'd last passed this way. He turned to Erin with a smile, which she returned. In about forty-five minutes they'd dropped Kevin and Trish at the airport and headed up McElmo Canyon toward the Sleeping Ute.

* * *

Anderson had finally arrived back and was immediately summoned to the troll's den for an update. He gathered what he needed, then walked down the hallway, thinking of his career with the miserable troll. Now, thankfully, it was coming to an end. He knocked and walked in.

"You want to explain what the hell your people have been doing? You've created an awful mess this time and I've got some ideas on how to clean this up. But first we have a meeting." Tielson barely looked up as he gathered things, preparing to head out the door.

"There's been a bit of a change in plans," Anderson said. "We're to meet him near the Tidal Basin." Tielson just nodded, still not looking up, as they rounded out of the office and on their way.

* * *

They'd arrived back in Durango by 1:45. Michael spent the extra time rattling the cages of a couple of senators and congressmen he knew in Washington. He checked in with his old law school friend at the Justice Department and was quite pleased with what had progressed in the last few hours since he faxed him. An announcement would be forthcoming. By 3 they were headed to court.

Michael met Bret Bontani in the courtroom just before 3:30. In a matter of minutes, Benjamin had been brought out, the district attorney had joined them and Judge Maas was seated on the bench.

"I have a motion to dismiss in front of me, Mr. District Attorney. What is the People's position on this matter?"

"Your Honor," he said, rising to his feet from the counsel table. "Based upon the information we have received from the Justice Department, speaking with Detective Snow and the ballistics report from the Navajo Tribal Police/CBI, which I believe Your Honor has a copy of . . ." Maas nodded from his perch. "It appears that we have a match on the weapon and the likely motive. Therefore, in the interests of justice, the People of the State of Colorado concur and ask that charges be dropped at this time."

"Very well, then. The Court orders that the charges against Mr. Benjamin Yazzie are hereby dismissed. You are free to go Mr. Yazzie. We apologize for your inconvenience."

"Thank you, Your Honor." The young man smiled.

"The Court will be in recess, then." The judge tapped his gavel lightly on the bench.

"Thank you, Mr. Kincaid" the young man beamed.

"It's Michael, Benjamin. How many times do I have to tell you?" He smiled. "Come on, there's some people waiting to see you."

They turned, accompanied by Bontani, and strolled freely past the gallery rail. Erin joined them at Michael's side and the four walked victoriously from the courtroom. They waited for a few minutes to confirm with Sgt. Jess that the guys in the room next to Trish's had been visited and he was happy to report that hotel management had confirmed they had left rather abruptly. As they rounded past the Elks and towards Main, Michael asked Erin if she could walk with Bret and Benjamin down to the Belle, where Trish and Kevin would be waiting and he'd join them in a few minutes. He had one last errand to run to close the case, parting with a quick kiss to Erin.

* * *

Tielson and Anderson walked slowly, Anderson's pace constrained by the little man's short legs, toward the isolated bench near the Tidal Basin. The afternoon sun was slowly edging down the sky. Near a small stand of trees the two men paused. "Anderson, I think I have a way to get you out of this," the little, bent man said. "In fact, I'm sure of it." Anderson suppressed his disdain with a simple "Yes, sir" and "I'll wait for you here, sir." Tielson walked on toward the empty bench a hundred yards further down the path, mumbling to himself. Anderson watched him take a seat and then withdrew back up the path and into the stand of trees to better observe the two men's meeting.

From the bushes behind the bench Anderson noticed a man approach, quietly and with purpose. His hand slapped the back of Tielson's neck as he rounded the bench, Tielson's hand reaching up to rub the his neck before turning and getting a look at the man. The troll instinctively recoiled, astonishment in his eyes. The man sat down next to him and whispered into his ear. Tielson twisted a bit and clutched at his chest before his head slumped toward his shoulder. The man place two fingers to his carotid artery and in thirty seconds the man was gone, retracing his route back into the bushes. Anderson turned with one last glance back and he was gone too. Only a few ducks looking for food kept the stubby figure company.

* * *

It was about a half hour later when Michael arrived at the bar carrying a rectangular object covered in manila paper. He found Erin, Trish, Kevin, Bret and Benjamin around a table and joined them, leaning his package against a table leg.

The whole group talked, keeping some attention on the television, tuned to CNN just as Luigi would have liked it. After a while Trish made it around to Michael's side of the table and an empty chair next to him. "I've thought about this a lot and I want you to have this," he said, pulling up the wrapped rectangle. "You've done good work on this one. Think of it as a bonus; you've earned it."

"Whatcha got for me?" Trish leaned over to hug Michael, readily accepting his gift. She pulled off the paper to find the Youngblood painting she'd asked him about, shrieking with obvious glee as trumpets from the tube announced something out of the ordinary. They turned to see a "Breaking News" banner flash across the screen.

"We're still following these late-breaking details in the ongoing story out of the Justice Department," the announcer blared. "We're now going to go live to the Attorney General's press conference."

All were now fixated on the television. The cameras followed as a shorthaired woman stepped to the lectern. In the background, camera shutters clicked in a steady rattle.

"Good afternoon, ladies and gentlemen," the Attorney General began. "We have uncovered a large-scale counterfeit pharmaceutical operation, based out of Thailand, which involves several senior governmental officials dispensing counterfeit and expired pharmaceuticals to the Veteran's Administration in the U.S., among other customers. We have uncovered a coordinated money-laundering operation through offshore banks in Colombia linked to this activity. This investigation is continuing and we do not have all the details yet, but I can also tell you that at approximately one o'clock this afternoon, an arrest warrant was issued for National Security Advisor Donald Tielson on a variety of counterfeiting, drug-trafficking and money-laundering charges, along with two open counts of murder and conspiracy. Mr. Tielson is believed to be a principal in the operation. A material witness warrant was also issued at that time for Lieutenant Commander Ronald Anderson, Mr. Tielson's immediate subordinate. We are currently interviewing other persons of interest, including Senator Howard McRae." An audible gasp rose from the media crowd.

She paused for a moment before continuing. "Both Mr. Tielson and Lieutenant Commander Anderson were under the direct control of the Armed Services Committee, chaired by Senator McRae. Senator McRae has denied any knowledge of the scheme, through his attorneys. However, as I have said, our investigation is continuing. At around four o'clock this afternoon, District of Columbia Park Police found Mr. Tielson deceased on a park bench near the Tidal Basin, from what appears to be a heart attack, according to preliminarily investigation."

"I guess sometimes they do get what they deserve," Michael commented quietly to Trish and Erin. "But why don't I think it was that simple?" He snickered.

"We cannot divulge further details due to the ongoing nature of the investigation and its far-reaching implications. More details will be released in briefings later. I'll take questions," and a din of shouts erupted. "Yes." She pointed to a woman reporter in the crowd.

"How was the operation uncovered?" she yelped.

"It was a joint investigation of the FBI and the Navajo Tribal Police, along with a few interested civilians. Both agencies executed search warrants near White Horse Ruins, Arizona, and in the Phoenix area this morning, uncovering a large stockpile of what is believed to be counterfeit pharmaceuticals, imported from Southeast Asia, destined for distribution at VA medical facilities and to our veterans, along with thousands of what our investigators believe are expired drugs."

"You said that certain civilians were also involved. Can you give us additional information on this?"

"We cannot comment on that at this time." The questions continued rapid fire on the tube. Yes, they were on Anderson's track, believing he had fled to resources in the Caribbean. No, they had no idea how far the investigation might take them; no, they didn't know the extent of any damage to veterans or current military, but chemical analysis of the pharmaceuticals were being conducted and updates would be provided; yes, it was a very significant bust involving counterfeit pharma, and on and on it droned.

But Michael knew the real story. His friend at Justice had somehow found out that Luigi had apparently been hired by Tielson, under NSA guise, to crack the safe at Antonio Escobedo's home. Escobedo was believed to be the point man for a Thai-Colombian drug cartel but everyone at Justice had thought it dealt with heroin; nobody ever suspected that the cartel owned almost all of AzMediCo through what was essentially a very hostile takeover. Apparently, DEA agents had been anonymously tipped and arrived at Escobedo's home only to find him already dead. This was the likely result of a hit ordered by Tielson and carried out by one of his men. Justice hadn't really believed for a second that Anderson had fled to the sanctuary of friends in the Caribbean, but strongly suspected he was actually somewhere else. A large cash transfer had been transmitted from a Caribbean bank, believed to be holding the tainted assets, to a Brazilian bank, but the money had been transferred several more times in recent hours and was now missing. No telling where he and the money were by now. In addition, they'd already confirmed several large soft-money contributions funded by AzMediCo to both McRae and his party through various campaign finance loopholes. Code Easel was falling apart.

Joseph had now arrived from Keyenta. He politely said hello and then motioned for Benjamin to join him just outside the barroom doors. They spent several minutes talking before signaling through the window for Michael to join them outside. Michael got up and slid through the swinging doors, rounding the corner with "it's a happy day, boys," as he joined them.

"Yes, indeed," Joseph answered, with a slap to Benjamin's shoulder.

"Mr. Kincaid, I want to thank you again for your help. sir" he said reverently, extending his hand.

"I keep asking you to call me Michael. Mr. Kincaid was my father. And now 'sir'. Oh, my. But you are very welcome, Benjamin. I am just happy something so terrible turned out OK," he added, shaking his hand.

"It is only with respect that I refer to you as 'sir'. My mentors, Hosteen Begay, Joseph and others, have long taught me to respect and honor the elders that are here to teach us." Both slowly withdrew their hands.

"Elder? You're not doing so good here Benjamin" Michael widely smiled.

"Ah . . ." Joseph now chimed in. "You're getting older, my friend, and you're going to have to accept it."

"I agree, it does sound funny…um, Michael," Benjamin began with a calm and wisdom beyond his young age, "but the Blessing Way teaches us an elder has nothing to do with age. It is knowledge one seeks from an elder, as I have sought knowledge from Joseph, his grandfather, and now you. To help us walk in harmony with the Blessing Way."

"Yes, this is true, I suppose." Michael answered. "Hosteen Begay and Joseph have taught you well. You will make a great shaman for your people like Hosteen Begay."

"Perhaps, but perhaps not. Hosteen Begay believes my calling and that of my sister's are very different from his. My sister Mary is a seer, I understand you met her also, twice; she feels the white and black of a person's soul and she has spoken to me of you also. She found you very kind and knew you would take care of her brother as you possess the white light. My gift is as a dreamwalker, and in that perhaps I can help you."

"You're the dreamwalker?" Michael asked, surprised, despite Joseph's affirmative nod, instinctively sizing the young man up quite differently from when he first interviewed him and focusing on the uniqueness he'd felt from the kid that day, and now his sister.

"Yes, it is said I can walk in others' dreams, it is a gift I have been given at a very young age like my sister and her gift" Benjamin answered.

"Well, I guess it's good we got you out of jail, then," he said with a slightly crooked smile. "So what do you mean you can help me?"

"I too have seen your dreams. I have prayed with the prayer sticks you had returned and your visions have visited me several times over the last days. Hosteen Begay asked that I capture them and try to help you with them, as yours, mine and his have all been intertwined. I have talked with him a few times about this by phone." This met with another quizzical look from Michael, to which Benjamin responded, "Your friend Sgt. Jess was very kind to me and allowed me to have calls with my family and Joseph. He thinks quite highly of you and I am sure that is why he allowed it." He accepted a nod and a smile from Michael. "The first time I spoke with the shaman was the day following your first vision at the sweat lodge, and before this horrible thing with our friend Luigi happened. We spoke again a couple of days ago when Sgt. Jess allowed me to call, after Joseph sent word I should and one other time. I have just now again spoken with Joseph and he seems to believe the dreams have now resolved themselves."

"Perhaps they have, Benjamin. Haven't had the dreams in a couple of days now. I'm not sure I understand them completely, but I'm becoming at peace with them."

"I'm glad that they have now brought you such peace" the young man said, calmly, serenely. "I'm sure you have thought much about them."

"I have, but I would also be interested in what you might add, as some things are still rather confusing."

"We of course find our own meaning in the visions we see, but I too have seen the sadness of your dreams, the happiness of the Hopi jesters and the surprises they bring as Coyote lurks in the shadows" the young man continued evenly. "But in this I think is your gift from the Yei for your continued path down the Blessing Way."

Michael's mind raced through the details of the dreams as the dream-walker spoke. His eyes subconsciously diverting toward the woman who'd reawakened his heart sitting inside. "I am thankful for their gifts Benjamin, but I'm not sure I have really followed the Blessing Way" Michael concluded, as his eyes returned to the young man.

"Oh, but I think you have, and more important, it seems the spirits agree. Many of them came to visit you in your visions. They also brought you to help me in my own hour of need and with my own visions, in order that I may return to the Diné to complete my destiny. Our destinies together were linked through the Yei and Kachina, starting with your first vision in the sweat lodge."

"Linked, yes, through Hosteen Begay" Michael said, rocking and shifting his weight between his feet, his attention now fully gathered again.

"In some ways, but also between you and I so that I was able to walk in your dreams with you. Each time, the Yei are showing us a little more of your future, taking away a little more pain from your past." Benjamin now again began to explain what the old shaman had told him days earlier on the mountain. The Yei of his dreams symbolized the twins of Changing Woman. There first to help slay the demons carried in our hearts, but in time growing to give their songs and other gifts, prosperity and peace, fertility and love, symbolized by the throwing of pine boughs and yucca leaves into the fire.

"The dreams also symbolize the marrying of two cultures Michael" the young shaman continued. "Of two peoples into one heart. One of the Kachina - Tasap as we know him – he is the Hopi embodiment of the Navajo Yei, two peoples into one. He is the negotiator between our peoples and why he led the Kachinas to the Yei, to discuss this coming together of these two new people in your dreams. There was Mudhead with his drum and his friends Kwikwilyaka, two of the Sacred Clowns of our Hopi brothers. Always interacting with the peoples, dancing, mimicking and showing them their foolish ways. And during the Spring, they too are part of the Fertility Dances, helping to bring rains with their friend, the rainbow lute player and guide Kokopelli. Together, they eventually gathered to sing and dance for good fortune as your monsters were chased further away. Yet always lurked Coyote, the troublemaker, staying as a constant warning to you that danger lurked at a distance, wary of your friend and guardian of the Diné, Big Fly, sent to protect man through his journeys and whose goodness Coyote fears."

Joseph now interjected, "Many have taught us over the years that our dreams help us heal, Michael. In this case, to take you through the loss of Lori, who you could easily recognize, taken by Kokopelli over the sandy hills to the Fifth World. And it doesn't take Freud or a dreamwalker to know that your dreams spoke of the passing from unhappiness to a new time. The unrecognizable masked figure came into your life to bring you back to focus and the Blessing Way path from which your heart had drifted. You came to the sweat lodge in need of healing and the great spirits heard your cry."

Benjamin now added calmly, "The only mystery I suppose, was always when the masked figure would emerge. When she finally made herself known, then your visions changed. Coyote, the trickster, finally took her mask, revealing herself to you. And I believe you have now found her" he concluded, glancing in through the window and nodding his chin toward Erin.

"Yes, Benjamin, I believe I have."

"With the vision fulfilled, the dreams have subsided, their task completed as is mine, their gifts given . . ." The dreamwalker's voice trailed off and he nodded before returning to the bar leaving Michael with his old friend.

Michael smiled, saying softly, "yes, I understand" in parting, thinking silently, until after a few moments Joseph broke the silence.

"But there's still another issue, Michael."

"What's that?" his friend replied, focusing back into present time.

"Our spy. Someone knew what we were doing all along."

"Yes, indeed, someone did. Trish," Michael retorted, matter-of-fact-ly.

"Trish. Why would she do that?"

"It's a long story, but I've known about it for years. Ever since she got me to go to the good senator's meet and greet years ago. You know how suspicious I am." he smiled, to which Joseph nodded. "I found out her brother got in some trouble with drugs and then magically it disappeared before I could even offer to help. She never mentioned it but I knew strings were pulled. She came clean to Lori a couple of years ago when the government wanted to do some snooping on a case I was involved in. We've been playing them ever since. I didn't tell you, because you and Kevin are the worst actors in the world, so I couldn't take the chance until I knew for sure what they were up to and why. Trish is how we've known they were always behind us and not in front. Which is why I bought her that original Youngblood, 'Yei Dancer,' it's called." He pointed through the window at the painting. "I don't pay her enough for what she deals with. So? Any other loose ends we need to clear up?"

"I'm sure there are," Joseph replied, with a slightly astonished look and a laugh, "but I think it's time for a beer."

"Couldn't agree more, my friend. Time for you to buy, Doc!" and they laughed their way back into the Belle.

Michael slid into a seat next to Erin and kissed her gently on her cheek, saying, "I think I was always meant for you."

"And I for you," she replied.

In another fifteen minutes, they got up and politely excused themselves, saying they needed some rest. They walked, holding hands, toward the door.

"Ever been to Tennessee, Erin?"

Somewhere above, high in the sky, Big Fly circled, enjoying the gleeful music coming from Kokopelli's lute, their work now finished. He looked down, watching Erin smile and shake her head no, as the barroom doors to the Diamond Belle drew Open & Shut.

EPILOGUE

After two weeks in Hawaii, Michael and Erin had made it back to the mainland. Before they returned home, Michael insisted that he had a little surprise waiting for them in LA. They made their way downtown, parked and it wasn't long before Erin found herself in front of the federal courthouse on Spring Street. Michael just smiled, telling her to come along with him.

They quietly made their way to a seat in the back row of the majestic courtroom, which was unusually packed. He leaned his tattered satchel against the glossy mahogany railing, looking up past the counsel tables to the ornate bench, which was sitting unoccupied for the moment. He tried to push down the small dry lump in his throat that visited him every time he walked into this courtroom.

Michael glanced around the room, noting the finely tailored suits that were quickly packing the large space. He felt oddly out of place in his blue jeans and cotton shirt. He reached over and took Erin's hand in his own.

"All rise," a bailiff suddenly boomed. "The District Court of the United States of America, Central District of California, is now in session. The Honorable Daniel Deal, chief judge, presiding."

From a hidden door in the paneled wall behind the bench emerged a parade of law clerks, court clerks and bailiffs, followed by the black robed Judge Deal. The bailiff bellowed the first matter, The United States of America v. Howard L. McRae, et.al. With that, the opposing attorneys walked through the gate in the mahogany railing to their respective counsel tables. The courtroom quietly came to order as the senator emerged from the door hidden in the paneled wall escorted by two US marshals. With a smile, Michael gripped Erin's hand a little tighter.

Edward Donovan

Edward Donovan

Edward Donovan

www.ingramcontent.com/pod-product-compliance
Lightning Source LLC
Chambersburg PA
CBHW060932120726
47910CB00002B/297